D0630851

Headhunter

Uwe Timm

ALSO BY UWE TIMM

The Snake Tree

Headhunter

Uwe Timm

Translated from the German by Peter Tegel

A NEW DIRECTIONS BOOK

Manufactured in the United States of America
New Directions books are printed on acid-free paper
First published clothbound in 1994
Published simultaneously in Canada by Penguin Books Canada
Limited

Library of Congress Cataloging-in-Publication Data
Timm, Uwe, 1940–
    [Kopfjäger. English]
    Headhunter / Uwe Timm ; translated by Peter Tegel.
        p.   cm.
    "Published simultaneously in Canada by Penguin Books
    Canada Limited."
    ISBN 0–8112–1254–8 (acid-free paper)
    I. Title
PT2682.I39K6713   1994
833'.914—dc20   93–10382
                                                       CIP

New Directions Books are published for James Laughlin
by New Directions Publishing Corporation
80 Eighth Avenue, New York 10011

For Dagmar

Chapters

Headhunter

Uwe Timm

The call

I'll come straight out with it: they're looking for me. By rights I should be in Hamburg in prison. But I'm here, in the garden of my country house in Spain, in a green stillness only interrupted now and then by the snipping of garden shears. For six months I've been living here with my wife and daughter, here, where I'd actually not intended to move for another twenty years.

I had the house, built in the Andalusian style of the beginning of the century, renovated last year (it was registered under my sister-in-law's name), a place for holidays and, as I said, for our old age.

Here in quiet I wanted to write my book about Easter Island, for which in my extremely limited free time I'd been gathering material. I want to contribute—even though I'm only self-educated—to the significance of Easter Island culture, above all to the script which hasn't yet been completely deciphered.

Over the last weeks I've begun writing a little, or rather commenting on the quotes and notes stored in my laptop. I had the thing brought to me, after a complicated bureaucratic process, in prison where I was being held on remand. And after my escape Britt collected it from the court authorities—the formalities were endless—so I could continue the work begun while I was held for interrogation.

Yesterday I wrote about the settling of Easter Island more than 1500 years ago and the consequent diet: The pigs must have drowned during the landing. Only the chickens survived. Probably the outriders capsized in the high surf. The dogs and pigs on board went under in the breakers while the chickens flew and found refuge on the swimmers' heads, flew when a wave washed over the swimmers, then settled on their heads again—that way they reached the shore. For centuries the only meat on the island was fish and chicken. And only later in the 18th century with the first European ships came another source of meat—the house rat and the brown rat. The main item of the diet however was the sweet potato, that starchy tuber with its dull taste, which was washed ashore carefully packed on small wooden rafts. According to one of the islanders' sayings: "We come into the world—we eat sweet potato, then more sweet potato—and then we die."

With the monotony of the diet as a starting point, I

wanted to establish the connection between cannibalism, which there had been on Easter Island, and language, or rather poetry. Today almost all ethnologists dispute that cannibalism existed for reasons of taste. But to me it seems quite obvious that aversion as a consequence of a one-sided diet should bring about a taste for human flesh, just as poetry arises from monotony.

We know that in Easter Island script there are ideograms that depict figurative turns of speech. A glyph of Easter Island script shows a figure eating, which signifies "eating singer," but in a broader sense also means: the reciting of Rapa Nui texts.

Since last night I've not been able to work on my text, not since the figure, the unique irreplaceable figure fell from my desk, or rather I knocked it from the desk. I'm not superstitious but all the same this seems like an evil omen.

My mother phoned last night. We'd finished the evening meal, Britt, Lolo, and I, and I'd sat down again at my desk, when the phone rang. My mother is the only person in Germany to have found out my phone number here in Spain. For almost two months, when the phone rang it was only Dembrowski.

He lives just 14 kilometers from here and when he phoned it was to arrange some bridge, tennis, or swimming. But then, some four months ago, I suddenly heard my mother's voice on the phone. She wouldn't tell me from whom she'd gotten the number. Certainly not from Britt who for years already held the receiver at arm's length and passed it to me when it was my mother on the phone.

I suspect my mother got the number from Dembrowski, although he denies it. He'll have phoned her and asked a favor, for instance the address of his former wife who'd moved without giving him the new address. I know Dembrowski, who lives here with his much younger girl friend, secretly phones his wife, talks to her and to his sons. My mother will have gotten his wife's phone number for him and, I suspect, in exchange asked him for my number.

—It's raining in Hamburg, my mother said.

That's always the first thing my mother says. I have a suspicion my mother has it rain in Hamburg far more often than is the case.

—Sunny where you are, is it?

—Yes. Do you need money, I asked her.

—No, I don't want any of your money, you know that.

—Good, if you don't want, then you've already got. It goes without saying she didn't phone just to tell me it's raining in Hamburg. She nearly always has some news she knows, or should know, will irritate me. She—normally so stingy, this time not put off by the cost of a long distance call—now reads me newspaper articles about my former business activities, tells me what Pastor Werner, who confirmed me more than twenty years ago, thinks of me, or what former clients, who phone to swear at her because of her offspring, are saying about me, but whom she immediately interrupts. I say to them, she says to me, I broke with him a long time ago.

—Do you know who was here yesterday?

—No.

—Sonny.

—So?

4

My uncle, only four years older than me, I haven't seen him in over thirty years and—at least in the last few—have hardly given him a thought. Only occasionally when I read his name, or when my mother told me about him.

—What's he doing?

—He looked very well, suntanned, he was in Brazil, a reading tour. She said all this with a lot of emphasis, didn't swallow any syllables as she usually tends to do. Whenever she talks about my uncle she switches to an elevated tone. She probably thinks she owes it to him because he writes books of which however, of this I'm sure, she hasn't read a single one. But she hears about him now and then on the radio or television.

Ever since I can remember my mother has talked about my uncle in such a way that I'm obliged to ask myself why I'm not my uncle. In detail she'd tell how and when my uncle graduated (I left school early, or rather was dispatched from it), where and what he studied, when and with what grades he passed exams (he worked hard, you have to hand it to him), when he passed his orals (the way she said oraaals!), she talked about the lovely (naturally!) blonde woman he married, the lovely children, the lovely family he'd married into with its lovely six thousand cattle that bent their lovely horned heads over the lovely family-owned pampas: and my uncle, who as a child hadn't been given the nickname Sonny for nothing, was always somewhere in Paris, London, Rome, New York, or wherever, and with his stories earned his money, not a lot, but honestly. He cheats (you only need to look it up in Plato) and gets paid for it, and travels world-wide at the taxpayer's expense.

—He asked after you, my mother said. What you're doing? Where you were and all the rest.

—And what did you say?

—Me, nothing, I said you phone now and then, ha ha. I told him I hadn't seen you for three years. Only he wanted to know what work you did. All you'd been doing in the meantime. He knew you didn't graduate, also that you'd worked as a magazine salesman and that you sold life insurance. He had all the information, knew all about your attempts at being a broker. He'd read it all in the papers. And that you were sentenced. Even knew what the public prosecutor had said, your criminal energy and all that. To deceive you have to have the power of persuasion, Sonny said. —Yes, I said, to think as a child he didn't even want to talk, only then he made up for it and always the craziest stories. —You could never say Sunny, you always said Sonny. You started talking very late, but you started the fantasizing and the lying soon enough, I think the two went together, not saying anything and then a lot, even if nothing was true. You know, I think he wants to write about you.

—What?

—He wants to write about you. Hello, she said, what's the matter? Hello.

—Nothing, I said and hung up.

I went back to my desk. Once again my mother had succeeded in disturbing me, in effectively stopping me working. I sat down again at my desk, in front of me La Pérouse's account of his travels in 1797. In irritation, or rather in a rage I pushed it aside against another book, the movement continued in accordance with the law of kinetics to a writing pad which in turn passed it on to the wooden figure—and pushed it off the table.

It broke, no, shattered on the tiled floor into a thousand pieces. I hadn't realized wood could shatter like porcelain, even when it was as old and dried out as this piece. I crawled on the floor and I shrieked in dismay, shrieked in rage and disappointment, and picked up the larger wooden fragments and splinters. It had been a yellowish brown piece of wood, on a first glance resembling a root, driftwood, brittle, dried out, cracked, but priceless all the same, as precious to me as a figure by Riemenschneider, because if you looked closely you could see that wood had been worked: a man lying on his back who—the artist had cleverly exploited the natural torsion of the wood—raised the upper part of his body as if in torment, also his lower extremity, a bird's tail. This bird man came from Easter Island. I'd bought him not quite three years ago and since then taken him with me everywhere.

The wood, as I knew from a report I'd been commissioned to write, came from Alaska and was a branch of a sitka spruce that some four hundred years ago had fallen into a river. Rocks and waterfalls smashed the tree, this piece was carried to the Gulf of Alaska, got into the warm Alaskan current, was carried in a huge circle into the cool Californian current, went into the increasingly warmer north equatorial current, for years was carried in the Pacific until it reached the shore of Borneo, lay there forty, fifty years in the blazing sun, dried out, and was again pulled back into the ocean by a great wave of the receding surf, there siezed by the equatorial countercurrent and driven back in an easterly direction to the Galápagos Islands, entered the

Humboldt current, at that time not yet called the Humboldt current, that had always been cold until it was again carried into the warmer south equatorial current, turned in a circle of some hundreds of kilometers until finally after many decades inconceivable happenstance washed it ashore on Easter Island, solitary and lonely in the ocean. There, where there were no trees, only stunted shrubs, it was considered precious and transformed by an artist with an obsidian knife into this bird man (the penis is clearly emphasized), a human being halfway between heaven and earth. Now he lies on the ground, his hands held as if bound behind his back, and with all his strength seems to be lifting the upper part of his body and the lower part that ends in a bird's tail. But you can see he'll never quite be able to lift himself off the ground.

Cook's ship's doctor acquired the figure by trading and brought it to England. For over two hundred years it lay in the mahogany cupboard of a private collection, from which I bought it, legally (I could have bought it illegally too), and paid a small fortune for it—and so not quite three years ago the bird man came to my office onto my desk. Sometimes I even took him home on the weekends simply because I didn't want to miss him, I wanted him and with him his long journey in front of me. It was the only thing I'd asked Britt to bring to the prison where I was held on remand. And I'd also brought him here. No one, not even Britt, understood why I'd paid so much money for this piece of wood and what it was that I found so remarkable about it.

I carefully pushed the crumbling fragments onto a piece of paper, the word "glue" went through my mind. I couldn't help laughing, a despairing laugh, and I thought: It's grotesque really, this business of glueing, it's a pitiful attempt to undo something that's happened. Because even if you don't see the break—in this case inconceivable—what's been glued together will always be a deception.

Britt came in. She'd been sitting on the veranda.

—Was it you that shrieked? She saw the wooden bits on the paper. Oh no, she said, knelt beside me and picked up the little pieces still lying on the floor. It was so brittle, she said, it just crumbles, and she crumbled a piece between her fingers.

I could have yelled at her: hands off, but I said nothing.

—Who phoned?

—My mother.

—And?

—She says my uncle wants to write about me.

Britt couldn't understand why I found this so upsetting.

She didn't know my uncle, she'd only seen him once on television ten years ago when he gave an interview. (Why does he wave his hands around like that, she'd said at the time.) She started reading one of his books, a novel, but after forty pages she stopped. It didn't interest her.

—If he writes about me it'll be someone who isn't me: ridiculous, unscrupulous, avaricious, or sly. Most authors write about themselves or about people who never existed, invented imagined people, but my uncle writes about members of the family, he totally exploits them. You suddenly find yourself in a book and you're someone else. He'll go to clients, so-called victims, for-

9

mer colleagues, question friends who turned out to be enemies, read court files. He'll make my case his business. He'll literally bring everything out into the open. He'll expose me, because that's what it would be, an exposure. I'll appear in his book like in a mirror on Hamburg Cathedral, crudely distorted, fat, stupid, whatever occurs to him.

—Write it yourself, Britt said and got up. Come on, she held out her hand and pulled me up from the floor where I was still sitting.

I could load my computer and fire away. Why not? No ceremonial sheet of paper, so deterringly white and empty, simply begin with the phone call (now filed under that heading), with my mother who worked as a hairdresser until the age of 65 and has been a pensioner for two years.

She wasn't one of those artists who models hair styles according to faces, who first carefully studies faces, especially the asymmetry that determines the individual: eyes, nose, mouth, forehead, cheekbones, and chin—and how each of these parts relates to the other. A hairdresser should be amazed that so few parts permit an infinite variety (a problem, this, for the holders of the chaos theory). The artists among hairdressers work with this asymmetry by concealing what sticks out, bringing out what's too small, doing away with what conflicts, in other words harmonizing.

My mother—I'd feel better if I could put it differently—was a listless, lazy hairdresser who couldn't have cared less. And she was a bad hairdresser because she had a sharp eye for flaws. She couldn't bring out good features because she didn't even see them, she was so struck by the flaws. She never worked more than a year in any hairdresser's salon, even in the suburbs where it was mostly undemanding pensioners who had their hair done. After seven months at the most word got round that permanents set by her didn't hang limply just by chance or because of an Icelandic cyclone. Whatever she tinted was so harsh, so far removed from the desired color, that some of her employers voiced the suspicion that she was color-blind or had even been bribed by a competitor. She cut layers where hair was meant to fall smoothly, and what was meant to be straight came out slanted. She always had to correct what she'd done, there'd always be a longer strand of hair which she'd then cut and make a wedge. One woman who wore a pageboy sued the hairdresser after my mother had shortened her bangs by a good five centimeters and turned it into a kind of floppy Iroquois hair style.

You couldn't talk to my mother about this. She always insisted it was because of the head, because of the client who didn't keep still, or because the hair was too thin. For a time, and this was the longest period, she cut the hair of immigrant workers. Well-paid work done on the side. (My mother is so piously honest, she anonymously sent on her income tax to the tax department.) They must have been staunch men and they must have had considerable language problems because my mother maintains there were never any complaints. Even so, after two years no one would come to her anymore, which she put down to pay increases. People just want to spend more, she said, and sit in a proper hairdresser's salon.

Naturally I thought over whether to write about my mother, if already only for the reason that it might serve as a mitigating psychological testimonial on my behalf. Might it not be fairer simply to keep silent since such a complicated mother-son relationship can't be briefly described, but ought rather to be a subject on its own. But I can't avoid it, or my uncle will do it, something of which my mother in her unrestrained admiration of him certainly has no suspicion. Unfortunately there are several stories that require telling. All I want to do now is mention a few in order to establish copyright, as it were: Women with half-dyed red hair, a woman with a deep cut in her right earlobe, two or three women whose hair fell out after intensive bleaching, lilac hair in the days when the color was extremely unusual. A woman with green hair came to our flat to curse. She looked like a little gnome. And finally the woman who one day stood with her husband at our door, baldheaded, and threatened to bring a charge of assault, though as in other cases nothing came of this. After all, it was work done on the side.

You should say nothing bad about your parents, that's what I learned in my confirmation class—out on the street too: you should honor your mother and father, and if they beat you, you should defend yourself.

My uncle always wanted a different father, I always wanted a different mother and more fathers.

This is one of my first memories: We were in the Old Elbe Park that probably even then was full of shit, of knotted condoms in the bushes, a quickie behind a bush, the cheap beat was near here. On the hill a stony Bismarck, stiff as a post, gazed across the harbor to the west, eagles at his feet, that was how he stood on the little hill, gigantic, massive, granite somber. That's where she went with me—it was almost round the corner—on Sunday afternoons. Hagenbeck, Planten un Blomen, the Harburger-Berge were all too far for her, too exhausting. I'd been playing on the asphalted parkway and run to a gate and put my head through the ornate iron railings. When I wanted to pull it back I couldn't get it out of the iron bars, I was stuck. I screamed. In my iron collar I could see my mother. She was sitting on the park bench and with two, three quick draws she finished her cigarette (admittedly cigarettes were then still expensive), then she conscientiously put out the stub, and only then got up, came over to me and guided my head out of the iron bars, which turned out to be quite easy.

A certain movement, a slight turn of the head was necessary for this, but that went against the reflex of pulling the head back. Later my mother liked to tell this story to people, and then always with the comment about turkeys, so stupid that when they put their heads through wire netting, instead of pulling back they tried to escape by going forward through the netting.

Once, I must have been six or seven at the time, my mother found lice on my head. But she didn't want to cut my hair, didn't want to go to the barber's with me either, that was too embarrassing. So my grandmother took over and took me to the barber's.

—Can't see any, he said. He only reached for his scissors after my grandmother had given him more money. I was told to sit on the barber's chair, a revolving metal chair, armrests at the side as if you were meant to be strapped to them, a movable headrest screwed below to a metal rail. I'd watched once when the same barber had cropped the tail and the ears of a dog, a boxer. (My ears are quite big.) The barber pointed to the chair. I ran to the door, but the man grabbed me. I struggled, hit out, the man wrapped a cloth around the top half of me and knotted it—my arms were pressed against my body—tight. I saw myself in the mirror, my mouth open and screaming. With two, three swoops of the scissors the man cut off my hair, reached for chromed clippers—I screamed—and sheared the tufts of hair, a painful plucking with knives. It was only later I learned the name of this instrument: clippers. Skull bald, ears huge and red, the clippers at work on my head. (Keep still!) Then he washed my head with a strong smelling solution. He washed his hands, carefully scrubbing his nails.

Outside in the wind I could feel my head. And the sensation has stayed clearly in my memory: my head was suddenly smaller. It had shrunk. Then my grandmother took her scarf and bound it round my head.

Naturally my mother, the hairdresser, could herself have cut my hair. But she was repelled. The lice repelled her, that surely meant she was repelled by me because these were lice that had fed on my blood, therefore also on hers. She was also repelled by herself.

And it embarrassed her that I had so many lice before she noticed how often and how hard I scratched myself. My scalp was already covered in scabs. But she didn't get my lice. And she must often have held me.

Or perhaps she simply hadn't felt like going to the barber on that occasion. My mother was capable of just sitting for hours and smoking. Now and then she'd read some cheap novel, sometimes she leafed through magazines, but even that was too much of an effort. She just sat there—and I'm sure still sits—smoking: yellow teeth, yellow fingernails, and the tips of her right index and middle fingers are brownish yellow. I'd like to know what she's thinking.

Somehow if I needed her, she was never there, and if she was, then, as I've said, she sat and smoked.

When I was hungry or thirsty, when I had to do my homework, when I'd scraped my knees, when I got beaten up, when snot ran from my nose, when one of my fathers had again thrown me out of the apartment, then I went round the corner to the Grosse Trampgang, up the narrow stairs—the quick ticking of the light meter—and knocked on the door at the top, a special knock, a signal, b-bb-b--b-: and the door opened.

—Blow, she'd say, and hold her apron out to me, a good blow, and if I was sobbing my grandmother Hilde would say, —And now take a good deep breath. And she wiped away my tears. I can't remember my mother ever holding out her apron to me to wipe away my tears and my snot. If my memory's correct, she never wore one. So there's no need to say a great deal about my mother and I'm only doing it to complete the picture.

I know I was an accident, she told me so herself. Whether she tried to get rid of the accident I don't know. But—and she tells me this every time—when she was giving birth she felt as if she was being torn in two.

But she does have a special talent, something I don't always immediately remember because I don't attach much importance to it—she can lay cards. And many people say she really can read the future in the cards.

People came to have the cards read, relatives, people from the neighborhood, even strangers from far away recommended by acquaintances: Was the Jack of Hearts the man in the background, the one who'd joined the firm two months ago, the assistant manager? Was he the man for life? And the Queen of Spades? Could that mean something gained at home? Not money, but perhaps something to do with the plot? What? A garden? Yes, a garden. Hmm. That could be Aunt Gertrud's patch. Perhaps she doesn't want it anymore, she's slipped a disc.

With my mother's help people discovered their most secret desires. I don't believe in divination, nor in reading palms, nor in the stars, nor in laying cards, but I believe that my mother had the ability—especially with her eye for defects, mistakes, and weaknesses of all kinds—to point out to people events that she read in their uncertainty and fears. She saw what those who had come for advice wanted, what they were afraid of. (You can see I'm a self-made man, that's to say the opposite of a fatalist.)

She laid the cards. And people put the questions aloud that troubled them in secret: whether to betray a husband with the new assistant manager in the fabrics department or not, whether to give notice and take the new job or keep the old job after all, whether to go to the doctor because of the swollen lymph glands or wait, whether to have the uterus removed or not? One doctor says: yes. The other: no.

—Go, said my mother, who saw the dark side of everything, —have it removed, at once, before it turns black. So possibly she prevented misfortune. So she got a reputation for being able to read the future.

But my mother didn't have second sight. No one knows this better than I. The cards revealed nothing to her, or I wouldn't be what I am. They could have told her that night (I'm assuming I was conceived at night)

16

she shouldn't have slept with the Swede, or that he should have got out sooner or she should have had some protection, a cap or spermicidal jelly. Because one thing is clear, I shouldn't be what I am, you could say, and there lies a metaphysical dilemma. Her cards are silent. And the accident and the accident's victim had and have nothing to say to each other, nothing, absolutely nothing.

The stone dream

Perhaps he was already there yesterday, possibly even the day before, but I didn't spot him until this morning. The man sat in a Fiat parked at an angle opposite our garden gate. I only saw his outline through the dark reflecting windscreen. As every morning I'd woken Lolo, made her breakfast, and then taken her to the garden gate where the school bus collects her. She goes to the German School. Not only Arabs, English, and Latin Americans live here on the Marabella coast, but also quite a number of Germans, mostly sprightly pensioners who got out early, a few resigned economic refugees and numerous company representatives.

Cars are only rarely parked on the street. All the villas have their own drives. That's why I immediately noticed the car parked opposite our garden gate. A cheap Fiat, and grey green too, that practical color adapted to dirt. Probably one of those cheap rented cars that you get at the airport in Malaga.

As I went back to the house over the crunching

gravel meant for parking I said to myself, perhaps he's out there to watch the garden gate, the house, therefore us. Fortunately the house is set so deep in a garden, you could call it a park, full of cork oaks, that from the street you can only see the roof but not the veranda where I'd already laid out plates and cups for breakfast. (In the morning Lolo only has some health-food muesli into which she cuts an apple and a banana.) I turned on the espresso machine and went up to the second floor to wake Britt. She sleeps at least nine hours, an addiction to sleep incredible to me who can only sleep six. Sometimes in the morning when I wake and it's still dark I envy her for sleeping. She doesn't snore, she doesn't talk, she doesn't twitch in her sleep, she lies in bed as if pretending to be dead, like the Sleeping Beauty, never with her mouth open, mostly on her back and you can hardly hear her even breathing.

This morning she'd already got up and showered.

I looked out to the street. But from here, from the second floor the fieldstone garden wall with its rampant roses blocked a view of the street. I fetched binoculars from my room and went up to the attic, into the sticky heat that had built up for weeks. I could see the car from the skylight. I saw the man sitting behind the wheel, but couldn't make out his face, either a twig or white shrub roses kept getting in the way.

When I came down from the attic, my shirt soaked in sweat, Britt was already sitting at the garden table on the terrace, carefully made up, but with tangled wet hair that she always lets dry in the sun. Only then does she comb it and then she has the mane of a lioness. She'd made the espresso and prepared the two slices of toast that we ate in the morning with our homemade marmelade, the oranges grew in the garden. And the previous day's German papers were also on the table. I tore through them looking for the financial section, skimmed the interest rates, the international commodities prices, leafed back to "miscellaneous," then again to the financial section.

—What's the matter with you, Britt asked, you're like a tiger in a cage.

—Why?

—Perhaps, she said, the figure can be restored. I'll make enquiries. Perhaps there's somebody in Malaga or Madrid.

—We'll see.

—Anything the matter?

—No. That's to say there's a car outside the gate.

—Yes, well?

—There's a man in the car. It could be my uncle.

—Nonsense. You're seeing ghosts, Britt said. Why don't you go and look?

I didn't want to. Because if it really was him—and I could believe it of him—then it meant he knew we lived here.

—Screw your uncle, said Britt who has an admirable, but sometimes also brutally direct manner. She got up, went to the garden gate, opened it, and went out. A moment later she came back.

—Your uncle's hair, is it a reddish blonde?

—No.

—It's not him then, unless he's dyed his hair. The one outside's thirty, forty at most. Your uncle must be getting on for fifty.

Britt has put a vase with white roses on my desk where the figure used to stand, a loving, sympathetic gesture that only made the absence of the bird man more painful. It looked like a funeral wreath. The larger bits of wood and some splinters still lay on the desk, a little wooden greeting on a white sheet of paper.

You couldn't have guessed from any of the broken pieces, although some of them were quite big, that they once represented a bird man.

I fetched a black plastic bag from the kitchen and tipped the bits of wood into it. The bag looked like one of those plastic bags in New Zealand in which you can take home the ashes of the cremated person.

I'd firmly made up my mind to continue working on my book about Easter Island in the morning. I turned on the computer and in the data file looked up the first meeting of the islanders and the Europeans.

In 1722 the Dutch sailor von Bord of the "Arena" discovered the island. The ship dropped anchor. The natives crowded to the shore. One who was particularly brave swam to the ship and came on board. In the most natural manner and not at all intimidated he felt the ropes and sails, scratched the planks of the deck and the masts, then began to measure the ship with a small rope that he'd picked up. As the Dutchmen gazed at him in amazement he must have behaved on deck not like a savage, but like a self-confident technician. He only lost his nerve when he was shown a mirror and wanted to grab the person apparently opposite him.

Laden with presents he left the ship.

Other islanders now came trusting and inquisitive to the ship. It must have got very lively. Women and girls approached the sailors, the men offered the strangers the women. A loud merry commotion began, until some of the natives stole the sailors' hats and leaped with their booty into the water. The captain's tablecloth disappeared through the porthole. The islanders had an eye especially on the tablecloths and hats. The Dutchmen chased them from the ship.

In the afternoon the Dutchmen landed. Some islanders gave a friendly greeting, others bent down to pick up stones. This reaction of the islanders to the foreigners typified what was to come. The order to fire was suddenly given and a musket salvo followed. A sailor had been robbed. After the smoke had cleared several natives lay groaning on the ground, among them the brave fellow who had been the first to board the ship.

The other encounters with Europeans also went according to this pattern. For the first time, if only from a distance, the Dutchmen saw the massive statues, like giants sunk into the earth staring darkly ahead.

The island seemed like a stone dream.

In 1774 James Cook came to the island and his reception differed little from that which had awaited his predecessors. The islanders were lively and friendly, but at the same time showed a lot of nerve and had fun being deliberately dishonest. The baskets with the sweet potatoes that they offered in exchange were filled with stones at the bottom, and the goods that had almost been exchanged they stole so they could offer them again a second time. These little swindles were not always without danger: one provoked officer fired at a native who had stolen his purse. The apprehensive women bestowed their favors in exchange for paltry gifts "in the shadows cast by the giant statues."

It was this aspect of the discovery of Easter Island that especially troubled me: what does theft mean. Theft can, I believe, signify a kind of gift that binds the recipient and the giver, there is an obligation to exchange gifts. The stranger is free to take something himself. The Easter Islanders stole with a clear conscience, and with a clear conscience the Europeans fired back. The islanders took what they coveted and in exchange offered their women. But the sailors wanted them from the savages for free.

My uncle when he was a schoolboy won a reading competition. I sat in the front row and listened. He read without once looking up and without once making a mistake. He read the story from Thor Heyerdahl's *Kon-Tiki* when the parrot gets washed overboard. My uncle sat up there, calm, as I've said, even relaxed, but I knew him and could see that in his sandals his toes were tensed, as if they needed to hold tight like claws.

Since yesterday I've constantly tried thinking of something else, but since yesterday a humpbacked little man's here and he won't go away—my little uncle.

I went up to the attic again with binoculars.

The Fiat was now parked at another spot. The driver

had followed the shade as it moved. He'd rolled down all the windows. I focused until I was able to clearly see the previously milky blurred face. A young man with reddish blonde hair. The man was drinking Coke from a can. He was probably, after all, one of those tourists who get on a cheap flight in the morning, without a hotel reservation, who then hadn't found a room, and spent the night in a rented car. He was probably looking for accommodation. But it's strange, I thought on my way down, that he's looking for it of all places in this district.

▼

A year ago I was arrested in my office in Hamburg. For three years with Dembrowski I was director and owner of the brokerage firm Sekuritas. My uncle is sure to like the name. We ran the firm for two years, dear uncle, not three as it says in the papers. The press reports were sloppy, but the more sensational for it: Crooks get away with 26 million. Commodity futures trading, a giant fraud. What happened to the money for pigs and copper? Investors asked to pay up. Robin Hood in a shady investment business.

We had a large office in the best location with a view of the Alster. Thirty investment counselors sat at computers that showed the share prices in Tokyo, Chicago, New York, and London; the latest quotations on corn, live pigs, and soya wound from telex machines, thirty hands reached for the phone and dialed people who, it could be assumed, had money and wanted to invest it so it could multiply in marvelous fashion, so that the multiplied sum could then be multiplied further. And this from one day to the next, just as the investment counselors promised, and not through long investment, not through the slow rise and fall of shares that one had to follow for weeks, but money won (and naturally also lost) from one minute to the next like at roulette. But this was no simple game where only the roulette wheel turned, these stakes turned the world, made politicians tremble, oil sheiks increase production, owners of plantations burn their coffee crops. The phones rang, the counselors advised, the computers bleebed, the fax machines whirred. I was exhausted, overworked that day as I'd been for weeks, had gone to the office with great reluctance, had the urgent desire not to go, simply to turn back, to run away (like when I didn't go to school), but no sooner was I back among the ringing phones, the talk, the whirring machines than I was high again, admittedly lifted by two captagons and three cups of thick coffee. What, on a three-year investment only 4.5%, you're joking, look, we laugh at that here, if we place the money well, for instance yesterday in pigs which rose sharply today in London, in a quarter we can make 8.2%, that in a year makes exactly: 24.8%. You can see why your savings account makes us laugh, why don't we try, ok, let's say a trading order for 15,000, 25,000, maximum. Saldin, our star salesman over the phone, raised a thumb like a jet pilot. One more with a margin of 25,000 on board. I spoke to London where the price of cotton had again gone right through the floor although I'd put three hundred thousand on longs yesterday, spoke to Frankfurt with a broker who also talked about a drop in metals, especially silver, spoke to an investor who asked about his 50,000 that had disappeared without trace with the sinking price of cotton. Where had it gone? Oh, 'tis lucky not a soul doth know my name is Rumpelstiltskin ho ho ho! Then Gerda, my efficient and (as she proved later) faithful secretary showed the two men into my office. She must have thought they were investors. Not me. With the trained eye of a window dresser I could tell immediately what firm they were from in their short leather jackets and rinsed jeans. The cops are always a little behind the trend in their outfits. In '68 they sat in ties and collars among the demonstrating students, later when batik was the thing at peace rallies they wore parkas, and now when wide double-breasted suits are in they're still running around in jeans and leather jackets.

One of them, the blonde, showed me his badge, said, you're under arrest, and took the handcuffs out of his trouser pockets. I felt the steel on my wrists, it wasn't cold but warmed by a cop's thigh, a thought I found unpleasant.

—Call Dr. Blank please, I said on the way out to Gerda, who was standing there as if she wanted to pray.

We met a client on the stairs with whom I'd arranged a meeting. I said would he please come the following week. He gave an emphatically understanding smile. (He was still new, the smile hadn't been wiped off his face yet.) He was one of those open-minded doctors, if I remember correctly—a gynecologist with a thriving practice. He must have thought I was on my way, hand in hand, for a weekend with an athletic, suntanned friend.

I'd been afraid of this, I'd suspected it, I wasn't even surprised, I was even relieved when the two men in leather came.

The last few weeks before my arrest I'd only slept four, at the most five hours. I'd sit at my desk at night as the last reports from the Chicago Stock Exchange came in, saw the flames flare, threw back one or two captagons, in the morning I was the first in the office, the investment counselors' personal computers ticked, the telephones sat like great bullfrogs about to jump, the first ring of the phone always shattered me.

As I was being driven to police headquarters I thought, at last, and leaned back into the back seat in relief. And they let me smoke. I clearly remember how calmly, with what composure I lit my cigarette, a little awkward because my right hand was handcuffed, but the police officer readily raised his hand along with mine as I raised the lighter.

At police headquarters a superintendent was waiting, Section for Fraudulent Manipulation of Trade and Tax Laws, a polite man who wasn't surprised when I refused to make a statement.

—Yes, he said resignedly, let me first tell you what it's about: You are accused of having misappropriated 23 million marks in commodity futures trading, you and your colleague Dembrowski. Partly outright, partly through excessive commission charges.

We sat there for a moment in silence, smoking. I wondered who'd reported us.

It wasn't one of the investors who'd lost hundreds of thousands, not even the canned fish manufacturer who'd in the end staked 1,900,000, no, it was an investor who'd staked the pitiful sum of 30,000 marks, but the only one for a long time to make a good profit, 70,000, and now he wanted to take the money out.

Him, of all people. Only there wasn't any money. Ha, ha.

—Why are you laughing, the cop asked.

He pointed to a thick pile of computer statements.

—Nothing to do with that, I just am.

The superintendent didn't say what he could have: You soon won't feel like laughing. He was a tactful man who looked as if in his time off, to compensate for his inconsequential work, he played the cello.

—Yes, he said, the good old days when we dealt with well-kept accounts, with people who gave incorrect change or forged checks, who forged export licences, who wrote down kale and imported tobacco, now we sit with computer print-outs and check standing orders and transfers and backdating, and compare foreign rates of exchange.

—What do you do in your free time, I wanted to know.

—Sail, he said, I sail on the Alster every evening, rain or shine. After an hour I've forgotten all my problems, then I go home. Earlier when I used to go straight home from the office there was always a row with the wife and the kids. The wind carries away every problem.

—Yes, I said, I used to like sailing too.

Dr. Blank came in, put the hat he also wears in summer on a free chair. He talked to the superintendent. I've retained nothing of what the two of them said. I sat there and looked out of the window, to this day I don't know what the view from the window was. I was led away to prison for interrogation.

I was relieved, for a moment even thought Dr. Blank had got me out and I'd be going back to the office.

As I was being led away Dr. Blank, my lawyer, said,
—We'll sort this out.

But he sorted out nothing.

The Grosse Trampgang

The cell: narrow, whitewashed, a plank bed, a shelf,
a toilet. I lay down on the bed without undressing. The
blanket smelled of a disinfectant similar to the one the
barber had rubbed on the child's head. I soon fell
asleep.

It wasn't until the next day I found myself in an unbearable stillness that almost tore me apart, a sudden
incredible abysmal stillness against which I clenched
my fists.

I paced the cell, I looked at the door, at the peephole
that had opened and shut. I heard a shrill sound in my
head, my blood, I heard myself think, I heard myself
talk even though I wasn't moving my lips.

Or was I moving them?

I sat down at the table, the top was covered in for-
mica into which a pin had scratched a heart, a name,
and with great love for detail, male and female genitals.

I opened the Bible that some religious association
distributes everywhere, in hotel rooms as well as pris-
ons.

I hadn't picked up a Bible since confirmation classes.
The verses, the stories as I remembered them had absolutely nothing to do with me.

Here however I began to read: Abraham and his

sons, Lot and his daughters, the tale of the prodigal son.

As I read a sweetish thick smell filled my nostrils, the smell of semen. It was as if the smell came from these stories that were always about fathering and reproduction, as if origins always had to be established.

But the smell probably came from a flowering shrub outside the prison wall.

> *What can the false tongue do,*
> *and what can it tell you?*
> *It is like the sharp arrows of the strong,*
> *like fire in a juniper bush.*

I heard the wind outside rustling through the treetops and I smelled (it was a west wind) the Elbe, the smell of brackish water, oil, and darkness.

I could see nothing, nothing but a wall with barred windows. I couldn't see the trees in the yard, not even if I stood on a chair and pressed my face to the window, but I heard the wind in the trees and, if the sun ever came out, saw their moving shadows on the asphalt of the prison yard.

The prison where interrogations took place on Sievekingplatz was less than five minutes from Kohlhöfen where we, my mother and I and my new father at the time had lived, right round the corner from my grandmother in the Grosse Trampgang.

They locked me in a cupboard once.

I'd gone out of the door one morning with my satchel and instead of going to school had run down to the harbor, sat by the landing stage, and ate my packed lunch, throwing some bread now and then to the gulls swooping overhead, one beat of the wings, sometimes only a turn of the head, and they'd caught it.

When a tug or a ferry passed a little later the pontoon gently rocked. From the Stülknewerft came the boom of rivetting hammers. A freighter was slowly entering the harbor. One tug was in front, next to the ship, the other was being towed. The hawser was still in the water, then it vibrated spraying water as it tautened. On one of these ships was my father whom I had never seen, a Swede, tall as an elk, bender of silver five-mark coins, helmsman on a tramp ship and for years already traveler over the world's seven seas. In the evenings when I heard the hooting on the Elbe, mostly in November when there was fog on the river, I'd think: Perhaps right now his ship's being towed into the harbor, a packet freighter that had rusted on its long voyages.

At my mother's instigation, as I'd cut school for four whole days, my father (one of my fathers) first hit me—which I let wash over me in silence—and then locked me in a small cupboard off the hall (my other fathers locked me out). The smell of old shoes, of cardboard and shoe polish, of clothes (that reeked of cigarette smoke)—a small cupboard that, after my father (one of my fathers) had unscrewed the light bulb and locked the door, seemed infinite. If I remember correctly, I wasn't afraid of being locked in but of getting lost in the dark, and so I began to whistle, first quietly and then louder and louder, it's me here, and whistling I discovered that even in the deepest darkness slowly, very gently, the outlines of things emerged: the shelf, the ironing board, a large wardrobe trunk.

Outside my father (one of my fathers) hammered on

the door, but I whistled until he dragged me out, laid into me, pushed me out of the apartment, slammed the door behind me.

I went down the stairs still whistling, went to the Grosse Trampgang, in the hall Mrs. Eisenhart asked me, —Why are you crying?

It wasn't until then that the whistling turned to sobbing.

▼

Britt came and wanted to know if I really was writing about myself; she wanted to read something.

I pointed to the laptop that lay small, flat, and humming on the table, but on the screen there was only the directory tree.

—But leave my family out of it! Promise?

—Yes.

Britt didn't know the software. Those must have been strange times when one had to write on sheets of paper and any inquisitive person could read what you'd written.

Probably she'd call what I'd written about my mother unfair, too one-sided, and this though she can't stand my mother.

She saw the binoculars on the desk and asked if I'd been on the lookout for my uncle again.

—Yes.

—And?

—No, it's not him.

Britt wanted to drive to the beach, wanted to swim, then go for a light meal at the Barca. She picked up three or four rose leaves from my desk. How quickly wild roses lose their leaves. —Come with me, the wind's good and there are big breakers. Come on!

I think she wanted to spare me the sight of the bird man whose fragments lay in a little plastic bag on the desk. But I stayed behind, I still wanted to write something first. I saw her go to the garage and drive out through the garden gate. Outside she got out and locked it, as she did so looking across at the other side of the street where the Fiat was obviously parked. She dropped the key and leaned down slowly as though she were looking for something. But it was the car she was looking at.

I knotted the plastic bag and put it where it was clearly visible in the bookcase next to the early accounts of Easter Island, acquired over the years at antiquarian book dealers. I looked among the coffee-table books and the art books we'd brought with us for the photo album, the only one that Britt had brought from our flat in Hamburg. A well-worn album that my step-grandfather Heinz had compiled more than sixty years ago. Neatly stuck down mounts hold the photos, in white ink on the black cardboard sides are inscriptions: Peter with Aunt Martha; shawm band; 1932; in the countryside; a little lazybones; fish stew and coral. The photo shows my step-grandfather with his pompous chef's cap against the railing of a steamer, in the background a sandy beach and palm trees. *The Morning Cloud* at Boa Boa. What a name for this rusty old steamer, shown in one of the photographs. After my step-grandfather's death my mother just put the photos between the album's blank pages: me with a child's rattle in my hand, a crocheted cap on my head (the big ears already clearly visible), with the scooter, my

32

grandmother arm in arm with my step-grandfather, my grandmother with a white strand in her thick dark hair, at the time—so I think—still a beautiful woman as she stands there in front of the Affenfelsen at Hagenbeck, one hand holding the late arrival, only four years older than me, my little uncle, smartly dressed, dark short trousers, white shirt, neatly parted hair, the other hand, the left, holds me, quite a bit smaller, staring timidly, hair tousled, and if you look closely you can see my suspenders are askew. A button is missing. My mother had forgotten to sew it on. My memory of that day is that my grandmother had to fasten one suspender to the opposite button. A color photo: my mother in a chair I don't recognize with a big flower pattern, those famous bright blue shining eyes laughing. My uncle, Sonny, about thirteen, on a small wooden sailing boat that he's borrowed. I'm sitting in the boat and I'm allowed to hold a rope, that's all.

There's no picture in my head where my uncle first appears. He was simply always there. Not regularly, but like someone who has to run a long way to visit you, because his parents lived in Eppendorf.

For a time he came often, sat in the kitchen as in one of the photos next to Mrs. Brücker and Step-grand-father Heinz, on the Grosse Trampgang. He'd come running over from the other district, the Eppendorfer-weg, a street lined on both sides with chestnut and lime trees. There were no trees on the Grosse Trampgang, nor in Brüderstrasse. The houses, built in Gängerviertel 150 years ago, were very modern for their time, with toilets in the apartments and running water, façades as if of building blocks, columns, cornices, ashlars. The street had miraculously remained standing in the nights of the bombs. The rooms were dark and small, the ceilings low, the floorboards warped. Worn white kitchen chairs, a display cabinet with glasses. My uncle came from another domestic landscape, heavy oak, bull's-eye window panes, wide carpets, the ceilings high, an undisturbed stillness that, when he took me home, reduced me to intimidated silence.

My uncle was forbidden to go to the Trampgang and also, I think, to play with me. His father, my grand-mother's brother, threatened to lock him in (my uncle had to stay at home, I was turned out on to the street, the different fathers sometimes wanted to be alone with my mother during the day). But my uncle did come, but secretly. In one photo he's sitting between my step-grandfather Heinz and Mrs. Brücker who lived in the house, right at the top under the roof, Mrs. Eisenhart is staring into the camera with a distorted right eye. Mrs. Eisenhart lived on the right downstairs on the dark corridor. When you pressed the light switch an electric timer began to tick loudly in the stairwell and as long as it was going the light stayed on, a rhythm with which the house manager forced people to run quickly up the stairs, but before anyone had got beyond the second floor the stairwell was pitch dark and Mrs. Brücker who lived at the top on the third floor then had to carefully grope her way to the door to her flat, and feel for the keyhole.

On the ground floor lived Eisenhart, watchmaker, then already retired but still sitting at the window with a magnifying glass in his eye, fiddling with alarm clocks people in the neighborhood had brought him. It was better not to give him wristwatches, his sight was too poor and his hands too shaky.

In earlier days he'd taken part in cycling tournaments, once in Belgium in 1905, on his wall hung three dusty grey withered wreaths of oak leaves with dull gold and silver sashes, next to them photos: Eisenhart (my uncle always made stupid schoolboy jokes about the name, hard as iron) in short trousers, socks, a leather cycling cap on his head, his oversized feet in cloth shoes. Sometimes in summer he'd take his racing bike which stood in the hall onto the street and wobbling a little ride a lap, pathetically long-limbed and old and thin and hunched on his bike, while his wife stood in the entrance hall and waited, a nervous twitch under her right eye, a bottom like a barrel, arms heavy as thighs in the short tight sleeves of a pale blue flowered overall.

She's got the evil eye, said my mother, who should know.

In the afternoon Mrs. Eisenhart often sat in my grandmother's kitchen, she lived one floor up, the men hadn't come back yet from their shift, the housework finished, the shopping done, the neighbors would meet here. And my uncle, who made out he wanted to play with me, sat with them in the kitchen which was so dark even on sunny days the light was on, a light with a yellow glass shade, under it the table, a wax tablecloth with sometimes lozenge patterns, sometimes flowers, and sometimes with squiggles if there were too many cuts in the cloth, a skirting board painted shining ivory, a gas cooker, black spots on the enamel from all the chipped places. The sink, rough stone, dark, on the shelf white tin cans: semolina, sago, saffron. Saffron makes the cake yellow. They drank coffee and they smoked. (There were always cigarettes and coffee here even in the so-called bad times when my uncle's father in his good district had to smoke weed he'd grown on his garden lot. Here we were near the free port.) When I think of the kitchen I think of blue steam and stories.

Mrs. Eisenhart was always talking about her time in Mecklenburg on an estate where she'd worked as a maid, a small white starched apron, red hands washed with carbolic soap before serving, fingernails scrubbed then inspected by a supervisor, only after that was she allowed to carry the soup into the dining room. But just before going through the double doors she'd spit hard into the aristocrats' soup, six whole years she did it, and her right eye winked, an excited twitch that ran through her face and pulled shakily at the right corner of her mouth.

She had met her husband on a Whitsunday. He was cycling in a street race from Stettin through Western Pomerania and Mecklenburg. The course went past the estate. He appeared in a cloud of dust behind the fore-runners, braked and asked her standing by the fence for a glass of water. But she handed him a jug of cold milk, thinking it would strengthen him, which he gulped down without thinking. He wiped the sweat from his eyes, smiled at her, gave her back the jug, thanked her, got back onto his racing bike, put his feet hard on the pedals, bent low over the handlebars and was off, but he hadn't gone twenty meters when he stopped, got off, simply let the bike fall, slowly sank to his knees, held his stomach, rolled about on the dusty street, bellowed like a bull: she ran to him. He groaned, he moaned, he screamed, it was as if he wanted to give birth—to a green cheesy mass that he finally threw up.

In the kitchen the glasses in the cupboard suddenly began to clink and the glass lampshade quietly rocked. Everybody looked up at the ceiling and then at each other. My uncle's nose began to bleed. He had to have a wet dishcloth on the back of his neck.

Above my grandmother Hilde's kitchen lived Mrs. Claussen.

—Got a customer again, said Mrs. Brücker.

—Yes, said my grandmother, the Claussens have bought themselves some furniture, real birch, really nice.

Eisenhart had to give up the race. That night he lay groaning in the servants' quarters. She heard his moans. The poor man. During the day he lay shivering on the straw bed. His teeth chattered. He was just like a woodpecker. That's why on the second night she took this weakened man who was so thin, who was so terribly cold into her bed. Opened her thighs and first warmed his ice cold, oversized pedal feet, and then him.

That's how they'd got to know each other.

—But I couldn't get kids, she said, and a twitch flared across her face.

—That has its advantages, Mrs. Brücker tried to console her, having herself brought two children up on her own after showing her husband the door. Mrs. Brücker lived, as I've already said, on the top floor which she could never reach before the light went out, which was what eventually contributed to the invention of the curried sausage, because she, Mrs. Brücker, is the inventor of the curried sausage. (I know the uncle's after this story, but after Mrs. Brücker's death the only one who knows it is me.) Mrs. Brücker had a hot-dog stand on the Grosse Scharmarkt, it also fed both her children as she'd turned her husband out of the apartment when he came back one morning after another night with another woman and demanded a beer. —Have a look, she said, is that the postman outside or what. And while he was groping his way down the stairs in the dark she shut the door to the apartment and locked it. For a while he rampaged, tried to break down the door, yelled through the mailbox and threatened to beat his wife to a pulp, but then Claussen who drove an excavator came up from the third floor: —We'll have some quiet now, damn it, or I'll flatten you. Mr. Brücker left and was never heard from again.

That's what we heard, my uncle and I, I who was considered too small to understand what was being said and they forgot about my uncle because he sat in a corner of the kitchen as if he wasn't there, he'd vanished listening.

There was a knock at the front door and in came Mrs. Claussen, from above. Just a quick visit. Mrs. Claussen looked rosy, a healthy skin like red-haired people often have who come from the Blomschen Wildnis near Glückstadt, porcelain color, but that glowed a deep rose inside when she sweated.

Her husband removed war rubble with an excavator. Claussen didn't do badly but she still had to go on the game, two children, another on the way, and then all the new acquisitions; sets of chairs, a radio, recently a BMW (doesn't go in snow), secondhand, that expensive it's a crime. That's why she turned tricks, stood with her shopping bag on the Grosse Trampgang in the afternoon when the farmers and the provincials who'd done their shopping in the inner city wandered through the harbor district, curious and hungry for experience.

Excavator driver Claussen knew nothing about this, but could have known if he'd ever added up the installments and compared them with his pay slip. But he didn't want to know where the money came from for which his wife stood in the afternoon on the Trampgang, the amateur trick by which housewives and professional schoolgirls earn a little extra.

Mrs. Claussen sat down but first she had to tell, to pour her heart out. Had a cup of coffee put in front of her by my grandmother Hilde, smoked a cigarette.

—What they want from you, she said, it's unbelievable. Now I think it was just because of her that my uncle came running from Eppendorf to the Trampgang, to this dark kitchen with its little window onto the Grosse Trampgang that was so narrow, if my grandmother was ever out of salt it could be passed to her wrapped in paper on a broomstick from the opposite house. Mrs. Claussen drank her coffee and told about the men, held her stomach, she was in her sixth month, —You wouldn't believe it, he just went on and on, ramming away, I thought: Get on with it, squirt it out, then he goes and lies on my stomach, I couldn't breathe, watch it, I said, then he gets even wilder. I was really done in after that. And then yesterday the one from Segeberg, looked like a teacher, I was getting undressed, no, he says, just loosen your clothes at the top. For dirty stuff, I said, you pay more. So he paid, and I had to take off my blouse, bra, then put them on the sofa, skirt up, like this, and she showed the brown tops of her stockings and the suspenders, that's all, just lie still, then he went out and stares through the keyhole and masturbates. Easy money.

39

She laughed and with her little finger gracefully raised sipped her coffee. —They're the best, the ones that do it themselves, as long as they don't want to beat you, because those are the worst, the ones that want to beat, they don't come out with it either until they're on top of you, or that want to tie you up, you don't know if it's fun they want or something serious, like the one the other day that got done in, and she drew her hand across her throat.

My uncle sat there quietly, they called him the little prince because he sat so straight, because his hair was parted, because he kept his arms to his sides, because he listened, sat listening carefully and took it all in, the louse, even then I knew he was here because he collected stories, I'd hear him repeating the stories and being brilliant.

I'd hear him playing story ball. He used to play a lot with girls at that time, he was ten or twelve. He'd stand with the girls in the dark gateway, on Eppendorferweg, in the back yard of the battery factory HaBaFa (Hamburg Battery Factory: Now you see the light).

You throw the ball against the wall, catch it, throw it over your left shoulder, then your right, hit it with the flat of your hand, then again with your fist against the wall, and all the time you're playing ball you tell a story. If the ball drops it's the next person's turn to tell a story. He told the best and he knew stories nice girls couldn't compete with, so they arranged it that when he dropped the ball he quickly got his turn back so he could continue the story.

He got his stories from us in Granny Hilde's kitchen.

Because what you could hear at his place wasn't worth two cents, even when they were talking about the war. In front of the dark oak cupboard with the cut glass goblets inside, the battles of the Second World War were still being won, decisive tactical and strategic mistakes retrospectively corrected, Dunkirk was taken, the Barbarossa project postponed to spring 1942, the building of fighter planes intensified, treason prevented, the front line straightened in time. While in Grandmother Hilde's kitchen Mrs. Brücker from the third floor told about the late-returner from Russia— this was 1952—who came back unexpectedly to the Steinweg right round the corner from Brüderstrasse, a former tobacco merchant by the name of Brunkhorst, after almost eight years there he was at last ringing his own doorbell. His wife opened, it was about noon and a Saturday, there she stood in the silk pale blue dressing gown he'd brought her from Paris in the second year of the war and stared at him, speechless, as if he were a ghost. He looked ghostly too, scrawny because of his stomach ulcers, in an outsize padded jacket, on his head a quilted cap with the ear flaps tied at the top, so there he stood, the ghost, when a man's voice came from the back, from the bedroom, from his marriage bed, painted white, and the voice called: —Martha, who is it?

She said nothing, but pulled her dressing gown round her in front because she wasn't wearing anything underneath, and the ghost said nothing either, walked past her into the kitchen, took off his quilted cap, went to the bread bin that was still where it had stood eight years before, took the bread, took a bread knife from the drawer, the same bread knife that was still in the same drawer in the same place where it had been eight years ago, and cut himself a slice of bread. The nights in

Vorkuta, 40 degrees below zero, the toes on his left foot frozen off, cabbage soup and only one piece of bread half the size of your hand, the wooden bunks, the stove in the middle of the barracks, the snoring, the farting, the sobbing, the frozen water black as diamonds in a coal seam, the breath outside, tiny ice crystals—if you spat it made a tinkling sound on the floor.

—Martha, the voice called from the bedroom, who is it?

And then the man who's already been sleeping in the ghost's bed for three years gets up because after the door bell had rung, after the footsteps in the hall he's heard nothing, not a sound, and goes into the kitchen—and finds his wife lying on the floor, her dressing gown completely red, she's lying writhing on the floor, but silent, so silent the veins and tendons in her neck stick out. At the table sits a ghost and chews bread, dry bread, and sobs but without shedding a tear, without making a sound. Only then, only when the man cries "Martha!" is the scream set free in the woman's throat.

Such were the stories my uncle told at the dark gate at the entrance and for these he was allowed to touch the small breasts of the girls. (I was there too. I wasn't allowed to.) And I'm certain my uncle has all these stories in his head, sooner or later he's going to put them on the market.

But I'll say: I was there too.

I know him. I know how he operates. I've watched him. I'm the one who also knows. I've forgotten nothing. Because he'd tell me the stories I'd heard with him, repeating them as an exercise. I was present when he told the stories again and I heard the alterations that

42

took place between my uncle's hearing and my uncle's telling, for example the story of the worker who had fallen into a silo while repairing a conveyor belt.

In the third version that my uncle, who must have been thirteen at the time, told the amazed adolescents on the occasion of the confirmation of a distant cousin with dark brown curls, the conveyor belt took on a new significance. When we first heard it—I was there too in the kitchen—from the mouth of a docker this conveyor belt only played a small part. It had to be switched off while the man was dragged out of the silo. Only now my little uncle, the louse, put the man on the switched-off conveyor belt that carried the grain into the silo. The man was changing ebonite sheeting when suddenly (a favorite word of my uncle's) down below some idiot turned the conveyor belt back on, a very long belt that ended ten meters above the silo which was already half-full of wheat (my uncle added things like this in the telling). So the belt suddenly begins to move, the man leaps up and starts running against the direction the belt is going, he screams, they look up from the quay below, there's someone running up there on the con-veyor belt which has accelerated, now it's going at tre-mendous speed, the man up there's running for his life, according to later calculations up there at twenty me-ters above sea level he set a German 200-meter record. Down below someone races to turn off the belt, but up there you can see the man is getting closer and closer to the silo although he's running, running, running. Per-haps he could have done it, could have stayed at the same spot up there on the belt, if at that moment the first lot of grain hadn't appeared on the belt. It ap-proaches him, there's no getting out of the way, he's still running but now he's on the wheat, it's like running on sand, he's getting slower, staggering, and suddenly he's dragged in, tipped over at the end of the conveyor belt, plunges into the silo at the very moment the belt slows down and still tipping grain finally comes to a standstill. Workmen immediately throw ropes into the silo, but when none of the ropes stir a man in a breathing mask is let down into the silo. He finds the workman unconscious.

Being unconscious saved him, if he'd screamed, if he'd struggled he would have suffocated in the grain slipping over him.

So the man got out, all he'd lost was the pipe out of his trouser pocket. He's waiting for the silo to get cleaned, which only happens once in a blue moon, then he wants to get his pipe back as a momento for his children and grandchildren.

No wonder the girls crowded round my uncle who otherwise would have gone unnoticed except for his big nose; he didn't dive from the ten-meter board, played neither hockey nor the clarinet, didn't head for Paris or Rome, his happiest time he told me when I last saw him were the three months when he'd spend eight hours a day in a room in an office block sorting out Persian rugs and daydreaming. He must have been there alone with a view onto all the office windows lit early in winter, behind them the secretaries phoning, writing, taking shorthand, and, when it was nearly time to stop work, starting to put on their make-up, lifting their skirts high and checking the garters on their silk stockings. All those desires, fears, dreams just before the office lights went out that he'd now take with him into the evening and the night.

And he'd come to the dancing class, not exactly someone whose looks attracted attention, begin telling his second and third-hand stories and the girls sat still and listened. So now—I was certain of this—he'd have no scruples about telling the story of his aunt Hilde, my grandmother—and she used to say at the time: —That boy tells entire novels. He's sure to write books. She was convinced of it, even though he'd got the bottom grade again in German and his father considered him a failure.

But the stories from the Grosse Trampgang are my stories, and what belongs to me even more is my own story which he's now after like the devil after someone's soul.

Ascension Day

In the afternoon Lolo came, slammed her bag down on the floor, her face registering some math homework she'd lost, an endless double period of German, the second thermodynamic law, and a red sweaty glow after two hot hours on the bus. The bus had been held up in a traffic jam. She went into the kitchen and fished a sour gherkin out of the jar. Then she drank the lemon tea Britt had left in the fridge for her.

Had she seen the Fiat when she got off the bus, grey green, on the other side of the street?

No, she hadn't, but then she hadn't looked.

I went to the garden gate. The car had disappeared. Then it was a tourist, I thought. I persuaded Lolo, who would have preferred to swim in the pool, to come to the beach with me.

She agreed, but only on condition we didn't go by car. So we went on our bikes, past the parks and gardens in which the houses and villas lay mostly out of sight. And again I was overcome by the desire to throw a hand grenade into this cultivated stillness. I can't bear these white-clothed dozing suntanned sacks. Most of them and their red-clawed wives have come by their money in the stupidest way—by inheritance. All you can do is fleece them but otherwise keep out of their way.

There were only a few women on the beach. And they sat in their beach chairs sheltered from the wind. It's a private beach, not to be compared to the beach a few kilometers further east where German tourists lie in naked stupor, where hosts brown as roast chickens, heavy laborers in the entertainment business, set the singles loose on each other and help them pass the time with music and stupid games.

Here you have your own area and a private cabin to change in. You can only go in the restaurant and the bar with a club card. Britt, the lifeguard informed me, had gone shopping.

Lolo didn't want to go into the water right away, but have an ice first in the beach restaurant. The Spaniards, of whom there aren't many here, turned to look as she walked across the sand in her bathing suit which was cut high at the sides, she's five foot ten.

I hope we can stay here near the German School until she graduates, another year and a half.

The waves were running high because of the south wind, there were breakers sending up spray along the beach, which was rare. Pale sand, a strip of reddish-brown finely-ground shells, then ribbed sand in the shallow swirling water that surged to the beach from the retreating breakers that you had to dive through at the right moment and quite deeply. From far out drifting in the even swell I saw the coast, the palm trees, the whitewashed houses. A picture I'd often visualized during my time in the cell. Little clouds drifted in the sky, torn from the thick blanket of cloud that hung far out over the sea. Now and then the water darkened, grew gentle as if at the touch of a hand.

At dinner Britt said nothing about the tourist who'd stood outside our garden gate. But she gave me a smile. I know her, I knew what she was thinking, you see, it was nothing, you see, it was your imagination. It wasn't a know-all smile, only a calmly calming one. After the meal Lolo sat on the terrace and did her yoga exercises in the dark. She sat there long-limbed, slim, lost in her thoughts.

Lolo has already had two offers from two well-known fashion photographers who live here. The best age for a model, sixteen, seventeen, one of the photographers said. But she showed no interest and I wouldn't have allowed it. For two weeks she's been preparing a history project that she has to present in two days: the history of the Hanseatic city of Hamburg. A north German subject she herself suggested and that reveals some of her homesickness. She doesn't complain, and I'm grateful for it, that it's because of me she had to so suddenly leave Hamburg and her friend.

Britt wanted to watch a documentary about breeding Lipizaner horses on television.

—What about you?

I sat down at my computer.

The crime committed on Easter Island in the year 1808 was an advance announcement of the terrible fate that awaited the rest of the population half a century later. After a bloody battle the "Nancy," a North American ship, abducted twelve men and ten women from the island. The wretched natives were taken to the bilge and put in chains. The ship-owner's intention was to put them ashore on the island of Masafuera, where he hoped to be able to use them as slaves for hunting seals. Once the ship was three days' sailing distance from Easter Island he let his prisoners come on deck and had their chains removed. No sooner were the islanders freed of their chains than they leaped, the men and the women, into the sea and began to swim with desperate strength. The captain thought the waves would sweep them back on board: he heaved to and from a distance watched the dispute that arose among the swimmers about the direction they should take. As they were unable to agree some turned in the direction of Easter Island, while others turned north. Boats were now lowered to pick up the swimmers. But the natives would not get into the boats. Every time they were about to be seized they dived. Finally the sailors tired of the hunt and the natives were left to their fate.

The telephone rang. My mother's voice. —Yes, the weather's terrible, another of these Icelandic depressions.

As she stressed all the syllables I thought my uncle must have paid her another visit. —Have you seen my uncle?

—No. What makes you think that?

She'd forgotten to tell me something yesterday, what's more, my uncle had also been to see somebody else, he'd told her about it, a manufacturer of canned food.

—Canned food?

—Yes, or something like that.

—Canned fish products?

—Yes, he got that about your criminal energy from him. He told him the public prosecutor said you had criminal energy.

—You'd told the man, said my mother, some story about a house that sank into the earth on Ascension Day.

—Yes, I said.

She was just making a quick call. —Can't afford long distance calls.

She must have hoped I'd say I'd call back. But I never phone back. Not even on other occasions, not at Christmas, not at Easter, and definitely not on Mother's Day. Only on her birthday, then I send her a massive bunch of flowers through Euroflor and on the card that comes with it in the handwriting of some florist: Happy Birthday, your son Peter.

I'd no sooner hung up than Lolo was in the room, wanting to know who had called.

Every time the phone rings, which it does very rarely, she hopes it's her friend calling from Hamburg, a slender gentle boy who wants to be an actor, and apart from that devotes his attention to his blondish hair. I consider him a wimp, which naturally I only mention to Britt. Naturally this wimp hasn't got hold of our number here in Spain—unlike my mother and perhaps now—soon—my uncle. Lolo never phoned Harald, that's the wimp's name, from here. We made her promise not to phone him, to break off all contact, at least for a time. And if Lolo makes a promise she keeps it. She has willpower. Unlike the wimp she's strong. Once, this is ten years ago, she was seven at the time, we were at the Kaifu open-air pool sitting on the lawn there that smells of chlorine, suddenly she stood up and said: — I'm jumping from the ten-meter board. We laughed, thought she was joking, then we saw her go to the tower and climb the ladder, we thought she wanted to give us a fright. She climbed past the three-meter board.

—Surely she's not going to climb higher, Britt said, and her face took on a severe look. Lolo then climbed past the five-meter board, slowly and without once hesitating.

—Look at that, said a woman next to us, that little creature up there.

I leaped up and ran to the ten-meter tower. I'd just put my foot on the first rung of the ladder when Lolo stepped out on to the narrow diving board, looked down—and only someone who's stood up there knows how unbelievably deep the pool can suddenly be. I called, no, shouted —Lolo! And to Britt's shriek of horror she leaped feet first and arms waving into the water.

—Who phoned, Lolo asked.

—Grannie. (Grannie sounds strange. The word grannie and my mother don't go together. And nor did she on any of her calls ask after Lolo.)

—What did she want?

—Nothing.

—She must have wanted something.

—Nothing, for god's sake, nothing definite, she said it was raining in Hamburg.

—And that's why she phoned?

—Yes, that's why. And now I'd like to work.

▼

So I was right to be alarmed. My uncle had already snooped at my mother's, he'd also already been to see one of the victims. In fact the main victim, as he's described, the man had invested a total of 1,900,000 in our company. He got back a bare 25,000 after our bankruptcy, which the public prosecutor had initiated. Naturally he feels bitter. He was one of our first and our best clients. As soon as Dembrowski and I had made ourselves independent with our company Sekuritas I'd gone to him and succeeded in persuading him to invest 50,000 marks. His fish products were in demand at the time. This was before the worm scandal that paralyzed almost the entire fish industry because everywhere you read that there were worms in the fish that buried themselves in the linings of your intestines, then made their way to the liver and people died.

I succeeded in convincing him and his wife about commodity futures trading. I didn't talk him into it, that would have been wrong and would have failed with most of our clients. I'd simply shortened one of those deadly boring Sunday afternoons for him. That was my criminal energy.

I'd visited Fishy Fred, that was our name for him, in his weekend house on the Baltic. The weekend house, a bungalow, covered an area on which other people build a house and comfortably add a garden. Through a ten-meter window of non-reflective glass he looked out over the steep bank of Pelzerhagen onto the Baltic. A pane of non-reflective glass of this size is the most expensive thing you can get in glass. He didn't want to draw attention to himself with the house, he said, because naturally such a wide glass frontage onto the sea would have been like a gigantic mirror in the setting sun. That could have caused confusion to some sailor or other, because he'd quite simply be dazzled. Dazzling too was the interior decoration, by Count Pilati, his wife later managed to drop the name into the conversation: a lot of shining brass, any amount of marble, antique baroque mirrors, black and white vases, a column with a Corinthian capital planted in the center of the living area by the megalomaniac interior decorator.

Fishy Fred had occurred to me because I liked eating his products. My secretary Gerda, the loyal one, gave my name. She always did this very cleverly, phoned, asked to be put through by the secretary to the owner.

—Investment company Sekuritas. We'd like to make an appointment, in an advisory capacity. One of our two partners would be pleased to call on you. Naturally there would be no obligation.

Actually Fishy Fred didn't want to, and then he did, but only a meeting without any obligation, and then it would also have to be on a Sunday afternoon. So I drove up in my cream Jaguar. Admired the view onto the Baltic and the base of a genuine Greek column, also the ancient Roman swimming pool with its gold mosaic grotto and Fishy Fred's ornate initials H&K on the bottom of the pool.

A dainty man, lightly greying, with strikingly delicate ears, a delicately molded nose. His wife, a blonde with sorrowful wide-open eyes and the transparent slimness of the spouse-for-life fulfilling her social obligations in middle age, carefully evacuates all her waste matter, keeps her circulation in good order by a daily morning game of tennis, the suntan from Gstaad and the Bermudas kept going in a solarium, a few painful little lines around the mouth. She complained of migraine, at first wanted to leave us to ourselves, but then stayed with us as she was responsible for real-estate investments and at weekends looked in the papers for apartments and houses. She had, she said, a good nose for the right kind of thing, they'd snapped up a few already.

I talked about models of further investment.

There was no need to explain commodity futures trading to either of them, in contrast to many small investors. With them, the best way to get an investment was to quote the Bible: Book 1, Genesis, chapter 41, verse 14: Pharoah had a dream, and in the dream there appeared to him the seven fat and the seven lean cows, seven lean and seven fat ears of corn. Joseph explained the dream to Pharoah thus, that in Egypt there would be seven fat and seven lean years. Invested with high office and title by Pharoah, in the seven fat years Joseph bought grain and in the seven lean years sold it at enormous profit. For the leaner the years, the dearer the grain. Joseph was the first authentic speculator.

One has a value X, divides it by the time factor and gets a new value XZ. Z can be higher, but also lower. Because prices can also fall. The more exactly one forecasts Z the greater the profit, immaterial whether value X has risen or fallen. Ahha, said most potential investors at this point, having understood nothing.

The difference between speculation in biblical times and today lies in that we no longer need to wait for dreams and no longer need interpreters of dreams. Because we, Sekuritas, have a computer program, WWX, that stands for worldwide change, a program developed by renowned economists and stock-market experts that stores thousands of components of various stock exchanges, prices, rates, demand over the last few years. With the help of this system we can calculate various models for you, so that we can get an exact reading of the trends: are prices rising or falling?

Fishy Fred nodded, he'd never speculated before.

—A dangerous business, he said, you can lose a lot of money.

—Yes, but one can also make a lot. It simply depends on the knowledge you bring to it, you need a feeling for it. Commodity futures trading cannot be and never should be the sole means of earning money. One certainly mustn't be dependent on it. It's something for the future. But if one has some spare money it's frankly an easy way of quickly making more. It's exciting, you compare the rates day by day, you make a decision, buy or sell, sometimes it's a matter of hours.

—On the other hand there's the security of money safely invested.

—Fine, but even there you don't know, who am I telling, whether interest will rise or fall, devaluation, etc.

—Shares?

—Shares are always good if they're sound. There are examples of good profits, but also of steep losses. Here you don't even have to be thinking of Black November.

Naturally, said his migrained wife, she considered real estate the safest.

—By and large that's true, but even there the most unbelievable things happen, expensively bought land as a result of development suddenly borders a motorway, villas, country houses and then isn't worth more than a garden shed, because there'll be a garbage dump in the immediate vicinity. Who wants that rotting smell in their garden when the wind's from the west and there are swarms of shrieking gulls over the house.

Fishy Fritz's wife laughed, the migraine had vanished, and because it was the maid's day off she made the coffee herself and Fishy Fritz poured a scotch and we drank a toast.

—Or, I said, when his wife had joined us again, or you for example, you're also living here on a bluff with a wonderful view over the sea. My uncle would have appreciated it too, forgive me, I know uncle sounds terrible in German, but this is my real uncle, more precisely: great uncle. One fine day my uncle Hugo took over his father's little shipyard. Founded by his grandfather, one of those minor inventors of whom there were so many at the turn of the century. He had been a diver, had worked for years in the China Sea for an English company, then developed a sealant out of bamboo shoots, bran, and rubber, a mixture that held underwater and sealed leaks, a kind of tofu that turned stone-hard.

Tofu, it made them both laugh, it's what she ate at midday, and with her red javelin nails she scratched at the silver studs on her denim jacket, they spelled *love* twice. And with those transparent blue eyes opened wide in astonished suffering or suffering astonishment she looked at her smooth-shaven husband at whose side she had now already slept for twenty years (later they showed me their bedroom), and perhaps she thought, as she looked at him from the side: if only he'd at least grow a beard, hanging side-whiskers, a moustache carefully twisted into two volutes like Admiral Tegetoff, if then instead of playing tennis he were to wrestle in the Greco-Roman style in the Kiel alumnae team, flyweight, then, then she wouldn't have to take medication for migraines, wouldn't have to get rid of every gram of fat from her body with a low-calorie diet, wouldn't have to display every little bone, wouldn't need to go to the masseur, to the acupuncturist, to the homeopath, then, then at last something outrageous would happen. She would take the large pointed scissors and one night, with a snip, she would cut off his Tegetoff beard.

—This little Hamburg shipyard specialized in cleaning tankers and sealing the tanks. I have to say *specialized*, unfortunately, because under my uncle's direction the company went bankrupt.

—And why? Fishy Fritz's wife wanted to know.

—Because of inadequate reserves of capital—he never speculated, and because he withdrew too much money from the company for his personal use. I only visited him now and then, there were certain tensions in our family. A bungalow in Wellingsbüttel with a panoramic window, a swimming pool with an automatic roof, a hydraulically-sunken bar, an atomic bunker (the first in Hamburg) converted into space for parties with cream silk wallpaper, a red Maserati that he left at a parking lot at the entrance of the Elbe tunnel to get into a respectable dark blue Mercedes to drive to the shipyard. Add to this three women to pay off, several children and last but not least a house on Fuerteventura, built right on a cliff, that had a wonderful view, similar to this, over the sea. Beautifully furnished, exquisite antiques that were also meant to be a dead-certain investment.

Now they were listening, Fishy Fritz and wife, they were paying attention and they were curious. She filled the glasses again, hers and her husband's when I'd put my hand over mine, I still had to drive.

—Yes, Uncle Hugo often flew out for a long weekend, mostly accompanied by a woman or good friends. And that's why he died on Ascension Day in 1978. Instead of a business trip to Döhle he wanted to spend three days lying in the sun with two friends, bathing and playing skat, because this uncle of mine was an enthusiastic skat player. So here the three of them were in a pleasant 76 degree climate in the large living area, the panoramic window lowered, playing cards. One of them, the lonely bald one, a building contractor, had just played his queen when he said, there's rumbling. What? Rumbling. The other, Kleinschmidt, an electrical wholesaler parries and doubles. It's rumbling, Kähler repeats, listen! They listen. Rubbish, says my uncle, that's from below, it's the surf. Kleinschmidt inadvertently plays his ace. Can't you hear, listen . . . A crack appears, with a creak and a rumble the whole side wall of the living area splits, the valuable paintings fall, the ceiling creaks, a corner of the room moves, the floor laid out in marble slowly sinks, the table, the chairs start to slide, the three of them fall forward—and become witnesses to a unique natural spectacle: the house disappears into a cavern, totally buried by the shifting mass of sliding earth, and trickling down on top of it all the garden soil that had been brought here for the flowers, and the ornamental gravel. Where the house had been, in which the three men still are in shirt and trousers, barefoot, the skat cards in their hands, there's now nothing to be seen but a deep cavity, nothing, no stone, no iron girder, nothing to indicate that a beautiful white house once stood here, built with tax relief because at that time shipyards were heavily subsidized, tastefully roofed and tiled, the most modern kitchen, the beautiful bathroom (lime green), the genuine antique furniture, the expensive carpets, the valuable paintings, all of it—I swear to God—swallowed up from the face of the earth on Ascension Day.

—Incredible, said both as if with one mouth, looked at each other and laughed. We'll stay together a year, she said and crossed her fingers.

—Good, he said to me, speculate with 50,000, to see. We can always add more later.

On running across ice

In the morning I accompanied Lolo to the door. She waved when the bus came. There was no car in sight. The street was quiet and empty.

I went into the garden and asked the gardener not to mow the grass in front of my window today. There's no noise I hate as much as the clatter of lawn mowers. The gardner works freelance and comes to us once a week.

He has an ancient diesel mower that should have been in a German museum long ago. Frankly the really loud humming of my computer disturbs me equally, and I always have to make myself turn it on. But the clatter of the mower, the stink of diesel make it impossible to think.

Add to this my writing uncle, now breathing down my neck.

In the six months I spent in remand in Hamburg I only thought of my uncle once, at any rate I only remember this one time.

▼

I'd been woken in the morning by the shrill sound of the bell, gone to the cell window and opened it. From the outside came the smell of freshly fallen snow.

For four days it had been icy outside. During the morning walk in the yard one of the prisoners, an elderly man, had suddenly lain down in the snow. A guard came running and yelled: —Keep moving, get up, move! The man got up quite calmly and joined the line in front of me on the path already trodden to sludge.

In the afternoon Britt visited me in prison where I was being held awaiting trial. We were in the visitors' room and she unpacked the books borrowed from the State Library, among them at last the German lieutenant-commander Geiseler's travel report *Easter Island* from 1883.

I leafed avidly through the book while Britt explained that the bailiff had shown up again. But the flat was empty. Britt now wanted to buy furniture through a friend and then, so to speak, rent the furniture. Awful how it echoes, she said, now I understand Kubin sitting there in his empty six-room apartment. All our paintings, our expensive ones, the chairs covered in white antelope skin, the black sideboard covered in black granite, the two old Tibetan carpets in a soft blue grey, all had been seized on a distraint order and later auctioned. The bailiff found the captain's thatched house in Blankenese empty but for a table, two chairs, an armchair, a mattress. The public prosecutor naturally suspected we'd emptied the house in time, moving out the furniture, the antiques. He didn't want to believe me when I said that apart from the few necessary objects the house had stood empty for almost two years. And the owner of the house? My sister-in-law.

Lolo had brought her skates. It had snowed.

—Yes, I said, I've been in the yard.

Lolo told me about a biology paper she'd written about starfish. She'd gotten an A. Lolo already knew exactly what she wanted to study: marine biology. I've no doubt that she will. Her dream is to go to the Antarctic on the research vessel *Polar Star* and to winter at one of the stations there. For me, always drawn to warm regions, a hideous thought. Lolo told about a party at a friend's: totally great, totally hot, totally garish, totally stupid. "Totally" struck me, it was new.

Lolo held up her skates by the laces and let them swing backwards and forwards.

—If you want to go, I said, although they could have stayed almost another half hour, that's all right, go.

Lolo immediately leapt up. Britt got up too. She could have remained seated for at least another moment, a tiny moment, to relieve me a little of the seemingly endless time I spent alone. But probably no one who was never forced to be alone knows what time is.

—You see, Britt said apologetically, the Alster and the city canals are frozen over. Lolo's been looking forward to skating since last night. Harald's coming too. It's supposed to thaw again tomorrow.

—That's all right, I said, I understand. I quickly got up to hide my shame because they'd noticed my disappointment, no, it was envy, envy of everyone, even of my wife and daughter, who could simply go out into the freshly fallen snow, into the sun.

In the cell I leafed through the books Britt had brought me. One book about the bird man cult. The figure, whose fragments are now in the little plastic bag on the shelf, at that time stood on the small white table next to the plank bed. That way, when I sat reading at the table (I have to sit up when I read, if I lie down my thoughts immediately wander) it was in front of me. I looked at the wooden bird man, thought of Lolo who was now skating, and at that moment remembered my uncle.

In winter when the first thin ice had formed on the Isebek Canal, dark and transparent, not scratched by skates, not thawed grey and then frozen over again, when it was still thin and transparent my uncle and I went tilting, that's what we called it when we took a sliding step from the canal bank onto the sheet of ice and then without hesitating started running, taking slow swaying steps over the ice that yielded gently under our feet. It was like running on water. Christ must have felt this when he walked over the Lake of Gennesairet. Only you couldn't stop, you couldn't look down, you couldn't hesitate or you plunged into the icy depths. Then you have to hold your breath and crawl onto the ice, very quickly, my uncle said.

I heaved myself onto the ice which immediately broke away, but always got a little further along like a swimmer doing the butterfly stroke, until I reached the bank.

My uncle, who backed out of most tests of courage, never went through the ice and was the first to run across the canals that had just frozen over. It was then I heard from him for the first time that he wanted to write books. It wasn't a modest ambition considering his low marks in German. Everybody laughed. I believed him—and that's why for a while he took me everywhere with him. He needed someone who believed in him. He claimed he knew a magic spell from Easter Island that stopped him breaking through. He even made bets with other boys. Because they were all waiting to laugh as he ran across, followed by a crackling wave in the ice.

I fell through several times. Then sat shivering at his mother's, in the kitchen. Each time we told her I'd slipped on the bank and fallen into the water.

Once a boy went through in the middle of the canal. From the Osterstrasse Bridge we saw him come up again, but then he slipped under the unbroken sheet of ice. He couldn't break through from underneath, swam under the transparent ice, his hands groping, his face white—suddenly his mouth opened, bubbles of air poured out that slowly, silently made their way to the open spot, rose there and burst as the body disappeared, came up again, for an instant you could see the face, the eyes wide open, the hands under the ice, then he disappeared into the dark.

In the first days simply to prevent my head from bursting I clenched my fists against the silence in the cell, the physically painful standstill, symptoms of an abrupt onset of violent withdrawal. Only slowly after two or three days did I become aware of individual sounds. Voices, footsteps in the corridors, a laugh, aggressive hooting in the distance. So I learned to hear again. I'd actually got used to the silence in prison. If I wasn't reading—I'd turned down the offer of a television set in the cell—I lay on the plank bed and listened to the quiet whistling sound in my head, or I gave myself up to my thoughts. The cell on the left was quiet until one day I heard a thundering fart that lasted long enough to intone melodies. The court official told me it was a jeweller, but he didn't have his food brought from a restaurant, which can be done when being held on remand, but ate the prison fare, probably to demonstrate that he was modest in his expectations. Prison fare lies heavy on the stomach of someone accustomed to eating well. Now and then I let them bring me a curry sausage from one of the nearby hot-dog stands.

From the other cell I could hear constant mumbling. There two drug dealers were awaiting trial. The jailer told me they were learning Chinese. Far-sighted people, for if the Iron Curtain ever falls in China, because of the enormous discrepancy between desire and reality there's an inexhaustible market in the country for hard drugs. (After all, there's a long tradition.) I'd read in the paper that a bottle of Coca-Cola costs ten times more than here. And demand is a hundred times greater than production. China had never interested me, nor Japan, nor India. Sitting in the cell in a state of inner unrest, of stifling monotony that was hard to bear I regretted never having learned autogenic training or meditation because then I'd perhaps have found some peace from the thoughts leaping about in my head, the reflections on what I'd done wrong, what mistakes I might have avoided. I think I really moved my lips during those inner monologues with all the clients and investment counselors.

I only grew calmer after I began working on the history of Easter Island. (Occupying myself with this godforsaken island, my loneliness and isolation became more bearable.) Here's something I wrote in my portable computer at the time:

> *Probably the island, named by Roggeveen after the day on which he discovered it, never had a name. Each of its bays and every cliff had its own name, but the island as such had none. The island's inhabitants lived on it in isolation as if they were alone in the world and had probably never felt the need for a name to distinguish their home territory from others, of which in any case they had no knowledge.*

It makes a difference though whether you see the stars in the sky as signs of God or as other worlds.

Dr. Blank also brought me books and, throwing his hat down on to the table in the consulting room, asked me how the islanders were getting on. He thought my work was a bluff to impress the court, him and everyone else, and show that my interests were intellectual, and not driven by the low instinct to take money out of other people's pockets.

I didn't even try to persuade him to the contrary.

Apart from my academic research on Easter Island and the still undeciphered script, in the cell I also prepared my defense.

The ridiculous thing was that, of all people, it was a completely unimportant client who started the avalanche. A retired secondary school teacher put us inside. He'd invested 30,000 marks, expressly insisted: soya beans. After five weeks, as a result of an unprecedented surge in soya bean trading he'd got 70,000, a profit of the kind we always promise our clients, fast big money. *Invest and see your account soar.* The man phoned and wanted his money instantly. At first the counselor who was dealing with him tried to persuade him to reinvest the money, to go into silver, it was sure to rise, then he could easily turn his seventy thousand into a hundred thousand.

But the man didn't want to. Dembrowski, who'd already taken himself off to the Costa del Sol, spoke to him on the phone, to no effect. Finally I tried to persuade him to leave the money, to reinvest it. I talked about the fantastic terms on the international spot markets in oil. He could easily double his investment in a month if we now went into oil. No, he didn't want to. No, all he needed was 75,000 marks. That's why he'd speculated. He didn't want more. Why not, for god's sake? He could pay off his mortgage. I warned him not to run straight to our bank to clear his account. But he did and he was able to get just 400 marks. That's all there was left.

Dr. Blank didn't even ask: where's the money gone?

But the public prosecutor did. The criminal police went looking. It had vanished, totally vanished. Oh 'tis lucky not a soul doth know my name is Rumpelstilskin ho ho ho!

—And with what did you buy the house, the public prosecutor asked. The wonderful captain's house on the Süllberg in Blankenese that stood empty. —That belongs to my sister-in-law. You don't have to show where you got the money, not in Germany. And nobody knows about this house on the Costa del Sol—I hope.

23 million, gentlemen thieves, the press wrote. Into their pockets. And a left-wing leaflet wrote: Robin Hood in the dirty money investment business.

—23 million, good heavens, that's not peanuts, said Dr. Blank and laughed.

—It didn't exactly hit the poorest.

—Better not say anything like that in court.

—Still, it's something to think about, it's an important aspect. We didn't plunder pensioners' accounts, these were people who had money, admittedly sometimes saved over a long period, but who wanted more money, who were set on money, who were greedy for money, addicted. Who were drawn into dealing on the stock exchange, and it's no accident that it's called speculation. We never guaranteed anyone a profit.

—No, said Dr. Blank, no, you don't need to convince me. It's the court, the jury you have to convince. They'll ask you where the money's gone.

—It's disappeared where a hundred million disappears daily, it's gone in the crazy, unpredictable incomparable maelstrom of the flow of capital, it's become a part of the chaos, so to speak, disappeared into the black holes of the capital market, and yet, in accordance with the law of energy, the money isn't lost.

—No, said Dr. Blank, who happens to be an excellent lawyer, no, that won't get us anywhere. That's too vague, too picturesque, too alchemical, it's for poetically inclined observers, not for judges sharpened and honed by fraudulent manipulation, and it's certainly not for the public prosecutor. He'd only laugh. They want to know where the dough is (in his numerous financial cases Dr. Blank had got used to a fairly lax tone), was it a deliberately planned deception, or has this, shall we say, massive misappropriation come about because of the nature, that's to say the dynamic inherent in such financial transactions, you see, he said, that's the line I shall take in my defense, and looked at his gold watch that also showed a blue sapphire half-moon, which he wore on his wrist on a strap of some species of lizard about to become extinct.

—Grew up in the Grosse Trampgang. That's where we have to start, said Dr. Blank, that has to be our main line of approach. He read the life story I'd written for him aloud: fatherless, a latchkey kid, brought up by an honest, hard working grandmother, then various occupations, sales promotion for periodicals, insurance salesman, then into the stock market with the best firm of brokers in Hamburg, then set up on his own and then made the losses, not deliberately, but losses accrued in the course of events. Secondary school, didn't finish. Junior high, didn't finish. Commercial college, didn't finish. Trained as a decorator, didn't finish. There's a little too much here that isn't finished.

—Yes, but if you're not interested in it, then you don't want to study electricity, learn glucose formulas by heart, solve endless barren algebraic problems, unless you repress yourself like my little uncle who does literally anything and everything necessary to get ahead. You listen to it once, but then you do what you really want: Languages, history, geography, and German.

I said at the time to Dr. Blank: —I'm a school dropout. As for not continuing my training as a decorator, that's another story.

—Yes, all right, said Dr. Blank. Tell me about it some other time. We'll first lay down our main line of defense. Where we can score points: no previous convictions. Very important. In fact, the most important thing of all. Although there were any number of temptations, especially in sales promotion and selling life insurance. Always honest, always hard working, always trying to get ahead, eager for education, well, he said, one can see that from the rate you get through books. Very important, a straight path from the bottom to the top, that's what I want to say, until it comes to strictly financial matters.

—But the one thing has nothing to do with the other. My origins have nothing to do with what I'm to be charged with.

That's what you say, said Dr. Blank, but here the greatest allowances are made for people with social handicaps. That's the bad conscience of society, which has any number of grey zones. A person sometimes stumbles.

—Make notes on your biography, Dr. Blank said and reached for his hat that had a tiny blue feather on its band. You'll see, that's our lever, if not for an acquittal then for three or four years, that makes, subtract detention while awaiting trial plus probation, one year. That's almost nothing.

The spirits on parade

I'm flicking through the album, well-worn cardboard pages with frayed edges laid out, as I've said, by my grandfather. Here they are, now well nourished, then emaciated, in short skirts, in long, and suddenly in uniform. My mother in a low-cut summer dress, shoes with wedge soles. Her dark hair permed, she's beautiful, no other way to put it, a beautiful woman. The pale blue eyes of my grandmother, the thick dark hair (which fortunately she couldn't do herself). The dress is short and shows her long legs to above the knees. Probably the photo was taken just after the war, material was in short supply then. Those must have been dissolute times. Other photos show some of my fathers, some big, some small, I still know the names of a few, they were mostly the ones that stayed a little longer, they thought they had to reform me (there was one who was in the police force and always thundered at me: — Hold yourself straight), others I only remember as shadowy figures, they stayed a month or two, then came Herbert. Here he is in a suit, pin-striped, that's not how I remember him, I know him in a blue jacket, a yachting cap on his head. When I last saw him, over two years ago, he was sitting in the living room, crooked, could hardly get out of the chair. Slipped disc, comes from lifting.

—Yes, he said, there was a time when I could carry a

Steinway up three floors, two men on one side, me on the other, now I can hardly lift my backside.

One fine day Herbert showed up, one of my many fathers, but who then turned out to be the last. Not very big, stocky, compressed to a width that filled a doorway. Came home in the afternoons, had a long careful wash under the tap in the kitchen, put on a clean shirt ironed by my grandmother (not my mother), got himself a bottle of beer from the wooden box with the little knight on it, sat down in the kitchen in the chair standing there for him, snapped open the top, sat quietly while my mother smoked, my grandmother too, inhaling deeply, coughing, sometimes spitting into the sink, lung juice, and then Herbert let them tell him all that was going on and what the gossip had been in the kitchen and at some stage his head sank on his chest, he'd sleep with his chin hanging, in his hand the empty bottle, but which never—I was always waiting for it—fell from his hand.

And then they said he'd become a bargeman. Bargeman, I thought, that's someone who steers barges with a pole with a hook through the canals. At least they're something that floats, even if they're small, even if they don't have a sail or a motor, anyway, I thought, no comparison with my real father who travelled across all the seven seas of the world, four piston rings on his sleeve.

—What do you want to be? Herbert asked.

—A bargeman.

—Come and take a look, said Herbert and on school holidays took me with him to work. We cycled to the free port, to the East Asia Dock where he worked at that time. Herbert stood on the deck of a freighter. In the hold workmen sank their handpicks into sacks and dragged them on to a big net.

—I did that for twenty years, said Herbert.

Now he was up above at the loading hatch and waved up to the crane: Up and move it, with his thumb showing the direction in which the crane driver was to swivel. The crane operator sat in his little glass house at the top and drove the crane slowly on its rails along the jetty, swivelled the steel arm and the sacks in the net promptly soared to the accompanying sound of quiet buzzing. If only I'd been allowed to climb up into the little house on the crane. But that was forbidden. Even Herbert couldn't give permission. Once when the net got caught in the picks the crane driver opened a window in his little house and yelled: —Wake up, down there! And Herbert, my father, the bargeman stood there and said nothing. Later he slipped me two oranges from a crate that had broken.

Though he asked me, I never went there again. And I no longer wanted to be a bargeman and even less lift sacks down in the hold.

Herbert was the most silent of my fathers. Perhaps, I thought at the time, during the day he talks to sacks, crates, and tree trunks: —Come on, get up, get moving, damn you, shift. That's why he didn't feel like talking in the evening.

Unfortunately my mother won't let me talk to him. Earlier, when I still phoned her now and then—now she always beats me to it—at least I'd hear his voice when he answered, in his slow way he was just able to say —Hello, it's you ah . . . then it was my mother speaking. She'd taken the receiver out of his hand.

In one photo my grandmother is sitting next to my

71

uncle's father in a little car. My uncle's father wears a driver's cap, gloves, a big scarf round his neck. My grandmother is waving to the person taking the photo, probably my great-uncle's wife. There are only a few photographs of my uncle's parents. They didn't come to the Grosse Trampgang where my grandmother, then still a young woman, had moved. With her big transparent blue eyes and that dark hair she could have married anyone, according to my great-aunt, my uncle's mother, the only witness to that time still alive and who'd carefully observed everything and had an astonishing memory for the smallest, the most minute details.

Hilde first married a post-office official, twelve years older than her and a good match, at any rate entitled to a pension, and didn't beat wife or daughter. I never saw this man, my natural grandfather, he worked in the telegraph office, after working hours he'd be up in the attic, a modeller and radio enthusiast who fiddled with spools and tubes. In the evening, especially on Saturdays and Sundays he'd sit in the living room that Hilde—as one photograph shows—had done up in light colors, no dark plush furniture, but white art nouveau that pressed into your back, and wherever he sat, a large stately man, time seemed to grow heavy. A boredom that spread like the smoke from his cigarettes, dense, that slowly filled the room. In the sunlight that fell through the net curtains she could see the fine specks of dust in the blue haze.

If at least he'd felt satisfied in this paralyzing stillness, I thought, then perhaps he would have been bearable, but he must have sat there as if he were waiting for something to tear him out of this suffocating stagnation. In his vicinity, my great-aunt said, you felt quite heavy yourself. At the beginning it was always Hilde who kept talking, telling something or other, shuffling cards, who invited people at the weekends, who went for walks with him in the town, child in hand, looking at shop windows or going to the zoo, to Hagenbeck, polar bears stinking in the July sun, Planten un Blomen, baby carriages crunching over the gravel, Sunday afternoon concerts, The Blue Danube, the spirits on parade, two artiste divers in a meter-high aquarium swimming about like dying Pomeranian swans. Hilde laughed till she cried, but he just stood there, still, not grumbling, not complaining, but you could feel the weight of his boredom pressing him down, and with him others. He just didn't know what to do with himself, Hilde said later. She'd made an effort, a very considerable effort, and it had taken strength, six years of marriage, until one Tuesday afternoon she met someone at a counter in a savings bank. He was standing in front of her in line and wanted to deposit his wages. Three years in the South Seas, no white yacht, *Island of the Winds* or whatever, but a rusted shitty steamer. He'd gone as cook: three years Boa Boa, Society Island, taken copra on board, the heat outside and in the galley the heat, he'd been freezing ever since. And any amount of rust, rust had settled in his pores, eaten its way in, you could still see it in his nostrils, in the folds of his mouth. And on top of that they'd screwed him out of his pay, and how. The shipping company had deducted more than half for the cigarettes, brandy, and beer he'd bought on the journey, and then when he got back the money was only worth a quarter of what it had been.

73

—He should protest, said Hilde who stood behind him in line, he should see a lawyer.

But the man who would become my step-grand-father and was called Heinz just shook his head.

—They always screw you, nothing you can do about it, it only costs time and nerves, and in the end you still get conned.

—A dear funny man who takes things as they are and despite that feels satisfied, said Hilde. Two weeks later she left her post office official. I saw a photo of him, this post office official, he's tall and looks down at a little girl who one day would be my mother. When his wife told him she was leaving him for another man he didn't shout, he didn't hit out, but the ash dropped from his cigarette onto the carpet. Hilde moved from the large, bright apartment to the small, dark apartment on the Grosse Trampgang (a really dark district, her brother Hans said). It was only temporary until Heinz found other work, something better than what he was doing at the time: cleaning vegetables at the Hotel Atlantik.

He was never to find anything better, always only got minor jobs, cook's assistant, doorman, park attendant, office boy, even in the war (although he had six years to do it in) he didn't make it to sergeant, of which Hilde was proud. She told me and my little uncle, whose father had stomped around as a dove blue Luftwaffe captain, that Heinz was incapable of yelling. —That's the truth. Yes. He just couldn't yell, the sarge put him in front of the company and said: Come on! Give an order! And Uncle Heinz, your step-grandfather, said: Right turn, quick march! Off they went, ran across the parade ground, tramp tramp tramp! So then the sarge said, now call your men back! So Uncle Heinz called:

Company halt! But it was just a loud whisper, not a real shout, the men didn't hear it, they couldn't hear it, they just went on running. Yell, the sarge yelled, they're going to run until they fall over, your comrades! You'll lose your men!

—So Uncle Heinz opened his mouth, but what came out was just a forced croak, not a shout, it didn't reach the company, those marching boots had already nearly reached the poplars at the end of the square. You, the sarge yells, bring them back, they're your comrades, you slave driver! Then my step-grandfather, called Uncle Heinz by me, starts running after the company that's running from him, with the sarge and the other NCOs laughing at him. Uncle Heinz ran, the company was already nearly at the fence. What would they do? Get up on the fence? Climb over the fence? Go on running? Through the streets, through the town, tramp tramp tramp, out into the open country to the ends of the earth? Because that was the order: Quick march!

—But then a mighty voice reached Uncle Heinz, the sarge's voice, it boomed to the end of the parade ground, it reached the company racing ahead and it reached your uncle, who hadn't caught up with the running men: Company halt! And the voice had the company wheel round and march back in step, gasping like Uncle Heinz who had got in line, got in step, and marched back with the lowest rank. And that's what he stayed to the end of the war: a lance corporal.

Not like Uncle Hans, Hilde's brother, the father of my little uncle, strictly speaking my great-uncle, more closely related but more of a stranger to me than Uncle Heinz, my step-grandfather. Anyone who's studied ethnology knows the different forms family relationships take among different peoples, how rich and complex in other cultures, but pitifully poor with us, as the lack of words to differentiate degrees of kinship illustrates. For example the uncle, no matter whether on the mother's or the father's side, is always only the uncle, or the great-uncle, and there are no differentiating terms for the great-granduncles.

Great-uncle Hans was different from my step-grandfather Heinz, had a commando voice, always held himself well, chin down on his tie, always grey suits made by a tailor who made uniforms, liked to say, that's no good, would ask: Is that clear? Would size me up with his watery blue eyes and I know how he saw me: as a future failure, someone who'd never complete anything. Someone who always wants everything at once. Someone who quickly gets enthusiastic, but then quickly loses interest. That's how he saw all those who sat in his sister Hilde's kitchen: Failures, sluggards, loafers—and thieves.

Only once did he praise me, was even amazed. On a visit to him—I never went willingly—he'd watched me from the window fighting an older bigger boy on the street. The boy had given my little uncle, that big-mouth, a smack on the jaw. My little uncle immediately began shrieking, though he was already eleven. I leaped at the boy who was a head taller than me, a real oaf. He quickly threw me to the ground and sat on me. Slowly I wriggled from under him, got up, he threw me down, twisted my arm as I crawled forward, give up, says the oaf, give up, slowly and without saying a word I got free, and again he threw me down on the ground, pressed my face into the pavement, so I crawled with the oaf on my back to the curb, crawled over the pavement, my cheeks, forehead, temples scraped and bleeding, give up, the boy shouted and started yelling while I went on crawling, not saying a word but screaming from pain inside, crawled onto the street where there were cars, the tram bell rang shrilly, I'd laid myself on the rails with the oaf on my back, now the boy let go of me and at the same time my great-uncle came running to separate us.

—Hangs on like an eel, he said later, after he'd wiped the blood and dirt from my face with his handkerchief. No, he doesn't give up in a fight, that's what he told everyone now, and above all held up as an example to his son, that sissy had started crying instantly. Tough he called me, but apart from that . . . no real aims. They live from one day to the next, no thought to the future.

Like Step-grandfather Heinz who had spent three years' pay in three weeks. A trip with Hilde to Lake Garda, the honeymoon as it were, though they never married. And the money was gone. Step-grandfather was in the shawm band—what his sister had got herself involved in was beyond Great-uncle Hans's comprehension—of the German Communist Party. Uncle Heinz not only played the accordion, he also played the shawm, at the beginning of the thirties he marched down Altonerstrasse, across the Schulterblatt, then Eimsbüttlerstrasse, marched and blew the big shawm. German Communist Party? What's strange about that, we're the ones that get shat on. They deduct from your pay what you're forced to buy from the shipowner's shop on board: cigarettes, brandy, and beer, all costing four times more than it should. And on top of that inflation. Three years of heat, three years of coal, three years of the South Seas, the Fiji Islanders have barbs on their penises. Doesn't exactly make you feel at home. Then a trip to Italy, now that was something else. And didn't have to kill himself cooking. They didn't expect it, at any rate didn't ask what he cooked. Demands on board weren't high, and always the same, fish stew and hot pot. No, he said, they con you. Save money? How? You can consider yourself lucky to quit on a full stomach. Just compare yourself to old Mrs. Herbst, lives twenty years down four steps in a basement, ends up white-faced, bowlegged, crawls out of her hole sometimes, shuffles to the grocer's trailing her bandages, at the grocer's buys a little flour, some stale rolls, some bread hard as stone, mushy vegetables, at the butcher's sometimes some offal. Then one day she goes round changing all the marks she gets from welfare into groschen, everybody wonders what she needs all the coins for. To make a phone call? Who should she phone? The rich uncle in America. Ha, ha. Then, that afternoon, there's a loud bang. Everybody runs out onto the street. On the pavement there's glass, wood splinters.

Children had rung her bell, as they often did to annoy her. Firemen had to come and put out the fire. She'd put all the coins into the gas meter and then put her head in the oven.

When he was studying my little uncle, the wise fart, asked Step-grandfather Heinz: —Marx?

—No, never read him.

But Uncle Heinz could play the shawm and he played it cleanly, not ragged, at least that's what everyone said who'd ever heard him. He marched with the shawm section through the inner city and when the security police came they all ran off in different directions to meet again in half an hour at some other prearranged place. Then they started again. One, two, three, and they started to play, and that was fun. And then came 1933. Then the fun was over. The shawm was forbidden. True. The shawm section of the German Communist Party went over united to the Storm Troopers. They also wanted a night of the long knives. Let those on top get it in the neck, a community of the German Volk—not a bad idea, give us a slice of the cake too. So now they played the horn. A horn section for the Storm Troopers.

A shawm, you see, has got four tones, and you have to bring a lot to it, open a valve, shut a valve, it's like a small steam engine, you work with a lot of pressure and you have to operate the four valves right. It developed from the bugle among the tracklayers, it's a compressed sound, by comparison the horn is actually rather boring, it's nothing but puff, no valves, nothing, it'll blare as loud as a voice, you just need plenty of breath, like a loud voice, that's all.

They no longer had to run off in different directions, instead they now marched with the police in the lead, stood in a line on the Heiligensgeistfeld and blared when Gauleiter Kaufmann came accompanied by Hitler, Goering, or Ley.

Then one of them went missing. At the beginning of '34 Karl Jessen disappeared. Jessen played the horn atrociously. Hadn't been the best shawm player either, quite often played the wrong note. But had tremendous fun playing. When Jessen didn't show up at rehearsals they all thought the SA leader had forbidden him to go on playing the horn because he played so grotesquely.

On one occasion one of the Nazi big shots yelled, he decided someone was taking the piss, the way one of the horns suddenly stuck out, really shrill, while he was inspecting the Storm Troopers. You hear a wrong note with the horn instantly, it's quite different with the shawm, that drawn-out tone covers everything or makes a wrong note sound as if it were deliberate.

Jessen had disappeared. You didn't even run into him on the Brüderstrasse. As if the earth had swallowed him up. And that's why Heinz decided to pay him a visit and went to the landlady, an old woman, where Jessen had a room without a stove. In the winter he'd sit in the room wrapped in blankets and read, the water frozen in the bowl on the table beside him. Jessen read a great deal, also read Marx, the only one Heinz knew who did read Marx. Jessen was a riveter in the Stülken shipyard. When my step-grandfather Heinz rang the landlady's bell at first she didn't even want to speak to him from the other side of the door. But then she told him: two men in leather coats had taken Jessen away. Later they learned that he'd been held at Gestapo headquarters for two days, then he'd jumped from a window. It was said he'd headed a resistance group and jumped from the window during interrogation so as not to give anything away. They'd given him a going-over twice and he was afraid the third time he'd talk.

—Not everyone can take it, said Step-grandfather Heinz, and say nothing, stay strong when they push needles under your nails. I couldn't, he said, it's a shame. And again he fought back his tears.

—If you can't do that you have to make yourself small or you get mowed down, said Step-grandfather Heinz. Politics is shit.

But playing the horn was fun, not as good as playing the shawm, but not bad, until September '39. Then he had to go in the army. Went to the barracks in the Bundesstrasse, number 76. At the gate the two canons, muzzle-loaders, taken from the French before Orleans in 1870. Step-grandfather Heinz got a glimpse of Poland, then Denmark, Belgium, France, courtesy of the Reich's travel agency, then a long stay in Russia, then two wounds that sent him back home, one in the shoulder, one in the lower arm, three times leave, all this in six years.

Window display

Only someone craving activity like I do, who needs to run off inner tension like me, whose rage only dissolves on walks at night, can understand what it means to be locked in a three-by-four-meter cell.

Sometimes I wanted to leap and scream. I wanted to beat my head against the wall. What calmed me at such moments was the opportunity to write, to enter quotes into my laptop. For instance, about the power of magic on Easter Island:

> *You take a cockrel and bury it in a hole—head down. While you stamp the earth, beneath which the animal dies of suffocation, you recite according to a magic formula the names of those you want to harm. Success is guaranteed: the person targeted dies, unless some more powerful magician comes to his aid.*

Dr. Blank wanted to know why I'd been dismissed, why had I been sent away from the school for decorators. He wanted to be sure the public prosecutor wouldn't suddenly pull something out of a hat, a small, unreported embezzlement, a theft, some stupid young man's prank. —After all you were still very young, he said, wanting to build me a bridge.

But no bridge was necessary. —No, I said, there was nothing. I was dismissed because of a pornographic window display, that was the reason given by the personnel manager.

That was something new for Dr. Blank, who'd heard plenty.

—Yes, I said, the worthy staff member just said: Filth.

Dr. Blank, who'd only dropped in briefly as he was on his way to another client in custody sat down, took off his hat, glanced at his watch and said: —Interesting. Tell me about it.

Naturally my uncle, if he really is after my story, will be making enquiries here too. All he need do is ask my mother. She'd probably use much the same language as the staff member.

She understood nothing. She was always prudish (even down to her clothes!) Words such as sexual intercourse, laying, humping, screwing never passed her lips, let alone the word fuck. When the glasses in Grandmother Hilde's kitchen clinked, ah, she'd say, there's a visitor upstairs. That was it. The euphemism "to sleep" which has hardly anything to do with sweat, with groaning, with the squeaking of bedsprings, with trembling arms, with the creaking of the bed, with sticky mucus, with the smacking of lips, those words "to sleep" would have suited her, although today I can't be sure that even these passed her lips. In this respect my mother was untypical of the Grosse Trampgang, she could have come from my uncle's district, *Klosterstern, Jungfrauental, Nonnensteig.*

The attempt to show what before was literally kept under the blanket gets punished with particular aggression. Especially in the business world. I'm convinced that sexuality always underlies trading, something one can see in the behavior of the Easter Islanders.

There is no healthy sexuality. And a practise isn't normal because most people in the evangelical part of Central Europe have intercourse in the missionary position. Just as there's no healthy attitude to money. If by that one understands one shouldn't heed it, one shouldn't make a fuss about it, one shouldn't display it and so on, then my relationship to money is deviant. For me money always radiated something very enjoyable. It's a sinful act to count bank notes and with these notes, that can be folded so small, buy big things. It's this disproportion that I've always enjoyed, for example to go to a car dealer with a bundle of new notes and pick up a Jaguar. A hundred thousand marks is not as much as most people think who've never handled a hundred thousand marks in their lives. You think you need a bag, I used to think so too, but an envelope will do if they're thousand notes. You go in, put this bundle of notes on the table and you get a car you've wanted since you were a child. This completely disproportionate exchange is what's wonderful about money, you give almost nothing and you get an overwhelming amount in exchange. In trading, and I know this as a man with practical experience, there's always an erotic charge. Pay money and you're the one who gets something free, that's the true secret of commodity money.

▼

I spent two years as a window dresser for a large Hamburg store, nailed stands, laid out rust-free kitchen knives in rosettes on cutting boards, pulled tights over transparent plastic legs and around a plastic behind, known as the Lady without an Upper Torso, set up washing machines and refrigerators, unwound bolts of material, made material flow in waves in the display window, in their midst now a wooden rake, now a coach lantern, and always in the autumn dried, discolored chestnut leaves. I was given to Rita as an apprentice. Rita, dressed entirely in black leather, was studying sculpture and window dressing paid for her studies. She'd tried to decorate the display windows differently with topical details, for example twenty rubber truncheons tied together like a bunch of spring flowers, surrounded by jeans, or a barrier over which she draped sweatshirts. But her superior, the head decorator, a man who'd been in the profession so long his hair had turned grey, always had the display window cleared: —That's all we need. Politics in the window.

This was the time when outside on the Jungfernstieg demonstrators doubled past, among them, as my mother told me with some embarrassment, my uncle. So he also took part in the rampage. Students carried banners that waved back and forth in icy wet gusts of wind: Stamp on Springer's fingers. Power to the councils. Under the asphalt is sand.

That's what I got from the student movement while I

was bending those dummies into shape. And I want to say now (and I also stressed this in court)—unlike my uncle I was never much interested in politics. Still, Rita and I contributed our share to the changes of the times. Until '68 the dummies in the display windows stood stiff and rigid, clothes-stands with human heads. But I'll admit to a voyeuristic tendency that I share with my uncle.

So on an evening walk through the Grosse Bleichen I discovered a doll that had fallen over in the display window, there she lay, legs apart, skirt pulled up, her doll's hand between her legs as if she were feeling where she was joined as she walked.

Yes, I thought, the dolls have to display themselves to be able to properly display something, it makes what's being displayed clear.

—Good, said the head of the display department, do it, but please nothing political, no police helmets, no hooded faces, right.

Rita modelled naturalistic heads, dolls with kissing mouths, mouths rigid in a shriek of pleasure, lascivious bald heads, dreaming child women.

We dragged everything out of the display windows, threw all the display props in the storeroom, the wooden rakes, steering wheels, coach lanterns, butter churns, took the new ecstatically realistic dolls and arranged them in little dramatic scenes: a beauty with wild black hair in a red leather mini-skirt and blue lambswool sweater kicks a man in the backside with her red high-heeled shoe, a sharp kick that sends him into the open drum of a washing machine. All that's still visible is his behind and legs in fine corduroy trousers (150 Marks). Our display window created a sensation.

The papers carried photos: *Get on with it, sweetheart.*

Keep it up, said the delighted director. We decorated a window with toys: children fighting over a toy railway, hitting each other with spades, pulling each other's hair, throwing rails at each other. An acclaimed success, our windows were always besieged by people eager to see, we were asked to decorate a window with ladies underwear.

Until then underwear always lay around in the window as if it was somehow embarrassed, bras pulled over black velvet torsos, even when they were frilly and blue or red, looked like something in a special orthopedic shop. So we set up an exhibitionist, a baldy with his back to the window, who opens his Burberry coat with price tag attached, to display himself to three horrified dolls in garter belts and red, black, and green silk underwear, who back away.

We'd scarcely removed the curtains from the window and a crowd had already gathered that stretched into the road. The next day the store was charged with causing a public disturbance. In the night an army lieutenant in uniform had been seen jerking off in front of the window.

Three days later my contract as a trainee was cancelled though my exam was only six months away. The reason: causing a public disturbance and harming business.

The chairman of the committee refused to intervene under any circumstances: we don't get involved in filth.

I slapped my union book on the table and said:

—Good, go fuck yourselves. I'm my own man. Ha, ha.

I walked out and stood on the street.

The stoney stone

On this part of the Costa del Sol there aren't many mosquitos. I'm sitting outside on the veranda with my laptop, in front of me the blue light of the screen, above me a lamp, dull, but enough to see the keyboard. In the sky a heavy watery moon. On the radio the English station from Gibraltar. A rap group, one of those endless spoken songs that remind me of Rapa Nui. Poets, no, singers who recited the story of the sexes and of the land over and over, each time measuring the island anew, singing of boundary stones, boundary demarcations. The Rapa Nui reconstructed time and space, stepping back into the past to affirm the present. Research agrees on one point: the script, that mysterious Easter Island script is a kind of aid to memory for the singers and priests. A script now scattered on wooden slabs throughout the museums of the world and like on my bird man preserved on a few figures. (Anyone wanting to know more about the *Corpus Inscriptorum Paschalis Insulae* should consult Th. Barthel: *Grundlagen zur Entzifferung der Osterinselschrift*, Hamburg 1958.) A glyph, as I've said, is also carved on the back of the bird man, the sign of the eating singer.

Cook already knew about the script, missionaries later tried to decipher it. Because in the meantime the priests and singers had been murdered, carried off, or wiped out by smallpox.

The first attempt at deciphering was made by Pastor Zumbohm himself. He had native elders brought to him to question them about the mean-

ing of the symbols. As soon as they caught sight of the slabs they immediately began singing a hymn— to the point where they were interrupted by others who called out to them: "No—that's not it!" The lack of agreement among the Rongorongo was such that the missionary lost interest and no longer felt a desire to discuss the matter.

All further attempts also failed until in 1886 the American Thomson discovered an old man by the name of Ure Vaeiko, who had learned the signs in his youth and had been entrusted with the oral tradition of his ancestors, but in the meantime been converted to Catholicism.

Thomson had taken advantage of a stormy night to seek out Ure Vaeiko in the hut in which he'd taken refuge. Here he played on his vanity. He got him to tell old myths, helping him along with one glass after another. In this cheerful mood Ure Vaeiko wasn't worried about the beyond. It was no longer difficult getting him to "read": not that he read the slabs themselves, which would have been a great sin, but from photographs of the pieces that belonged to the good Bishop of Tahiti, Monsignore Jaussen. He had recognized them by certain markings and now, without the slightest hesitation, recited their contents from end to end. If one watched him however it was plain that he took no account at all of the number of symbols in each line. Even worse: Ure Vaieko didn't even notice when the photograph he thought he was reading was secretly taken away and replaced by another! Without fal-

tering he continued: he recited songs and myths until he was reproached in no uncertain terms with wicked deception. Completely thrown, he poured out explanations Thomson seems not to have understood.

This was one of the passages I was trying to interpret before my mother's phone call. Two completely different conceptions of reading and of memory collided here. It's as if someone were to ask about the symbols of a computer keyboard while the person asked was explaining the stored texts. The European's interest is always in the printed word, the book. Memory set in a lead mold like this only makes sense to someone who knows the aura of words, that thin skin of amniotic fluid of significance. Here another reservoir had suddenly been opened. Memory was structured, built on signs, because originally determined by objects; then, lifted from them, acquired a magic aura that made it possible to "psalmodize," to move away from what should perhaps only be read as a signpost, so that one could find one's own path. This then gives a deeper meaning to the fact that during their recitations the Rapa Nui held a dance paddle in their hands, a paddle with which they moved through the past. I wanted to establish that this script still combined two things: time and space, because space, this island, was so confined that it could still be indicated by signs. Memory and the script were still pictorial, in other words: mythical.

It's my opinion that remnants of a prehistoric culture are still with us, in fact in the pulp magazines. The various fates of individuals, and fates are always personal, enter the house as commonplace images. You're there when it happens, it's in front of your eyes: births, marriages, divorces, sickness, and death. The short captions to the pictures, the abbreviated sentences, are the work of the singers that count in the editorial office. The pulp magazine is the mythology of our day. I know, because for four years I sold magazine subscriptions door-to-door, never in a convoy, always a lone fighter.

They're the guerillas among salesmen, the head of sales, Berthold maintained (as he's still in business I only give his first name here).

Before that I'd been a cleaning contractor, that's when I met Britt. I was cleaning the glass frontage of an insurance company, standing on one of those little mobile platforms that are lowered like lifeboats on cables from the roof. You can pull yourself up or down by a rope. I passed a window where a girl (Britt had just turned nineteen) was working. She was sitting at a desk underlining a document with a ball-point. She was so engrossed in her work she didn't notice me at the window. Who expects anyone to be looking in from outside on the 14th floor, someone taking his time too: her nose tensed, her lips open a little, across her forehead the hint of a line that, I thought, would deepen later, dark lashes, now and then she twisted a strand of her dun-colored hair round her finger. She was lost in thought. After a while I knocked. She looked up startled, hesitated, then laughed and waved. I wrote with my finger on the dusty pane: Dammtor today at 4. She shook her head. I began cleaning the window and I cleaned like a painter works on a painting, bold sweeps, then dabbing away at tiny particles of dust with my finger tips. I leaned far back over the platform railing and she leaped up, frightened, and gesticulated. She sat down and I carefully surveyed my work that had spread round my message. I dabbed, wiped, polished. In the meantime more and more of the girls working in the office had noticed me. They stood there and laughed. And then this girl with the dark eyes that contrasted so conspicuously with her light colored hair lifted a piece of paper. And on the paper she'd written: O.K.!

I went to Dammtor station and I knew (my uncle will believe me): I wouldn't need to go on looking.

She said she hadn't at first been able to read what I'd written because from her side it was the wrong way round. That's why she'd shaken her head.

Ten months later we married, Britt by then was eight-months pregnant. We didn't go that late to the registry office because we were undecided (neither Britt nor I had the slightest doubt), but because it took so long to get all the documents together, especially proof of nationality (a disadvantage if one has many fathers).

In the *Hamburger Abendblatt* I saw an announcement: *Dream job. Quick money. Set your own working hours.* That sounded good. I'd already worked delivering drinks, as a pallbearer, and delivering cars. As Britt was in her last year of insurance traineeship, I wanted to be able to look after the child. You set the working hours, that was important.

I phoned. It was a magazine publisher, and Berthold was the head of sales. Berthold introduced me to magazine publishing. You have to lead the weak ones in convoys into the blocks of flats, he said, always have them under control, force them to sell, drive them into battle with a stick. Twenty men to storm a block.

Someone outside to drive the cowards back in and up the next stairwell, someone who can take the orders and see at once who's slack, who's weak. Everyone checking up on each other, pressure on latecomers, because everything is shared. Of course, this results in some false reports, cancellations as it were that can't be confirmed when people later write outraged letters that they never ordered the magazine, their signatures were forged.

On average the salesman who works in a convoy is never as good as the one who fights alone, who's tough, ingenious and ever like the gallant knight Ivanhoe.

Years ago Berthold had studied literature for several terms, worked as a printer on the side, and then got stuck in the business where he rose to head of sales.

—The eye in the door sees you, he said in his two-hour quick briefing, the nearer you stand to the door the more grotesquely distorted you'll look: a balloon head, eyes like Quasimodo, a cretinously twisted grin. An iron rule: don't stand close to the door, the further away the less distortion. Because part of the decision depends on what optical impression you make at first glance, the first assessment on which trust is built. Any hint of being a loser is to be avoided. Long unwashed hair, dirty fingernails, signet rings, crumpled old clothes stinking of beer and tobacco—that's the crackpot's image, someone whom you would under no circumstances invite in, whom you'd never trust with your signature on an order form.

—But you have to bring your own difficult situation into it. That's a contradiction, but an interesting one, and you resolve it like this: I need the premiums to stay honest, neat, and decent. Here everyone has his own life story. The social angle's best: concern for the child that came into the world too soon, for the medication, and/or the alcoholic mother, the father bedridden with multiple sclerosis. You have to make the stone stoney, Berthold said.

—Which stone, I asked. Berthold looked at me puzzled for a moment. When he wasn't talking his mouth took on a certain expression, blasé and derisive, which wasn't his fault as his lips were slightly pursed, it had a provocative effect on some people, especially if they were drunk. He was often physically threatened and he sometimes got a smack in the face just for standing there and looking around. He often came to the office with a black eye. For some strange reason he couldn't resist bars where the expression on his face was misunderstood and a blow of the fist counted for an answer.

—It's what's at the heart of the story, said Berthold. You have to tell it in such a way that it comes across, in other words exaggerate a little so it sounds credible.

I didn't need to exaggerate. We lived in a basement in Sillemstrasse. Lolo, just three months old, had whooping cough. At night I pushed the child struggling for breath in her carriage through the streets. Once I was stopped by a patrol car. The two policemen must have thought a child was being kidnapped. Here was someone racing through the streets with a carriage with a choking, coughing, shrieking child. After they'd seen the child they drove me to the hospital, the carriage folded up in the trunk. But the night nurse only said:

—Yes, yes, whooping cough, and so I had to race back from Eppendorf with the wheezing child. I cried— I don't normally cry. I ran through the streets and I cried because of the dark windows, because of the dead houses, because of the slushy leaves on the pavement, the empty cars in the street, the shrubbery with tattered plastic bags hanging from it, the monotonous yellow gaze of the street lamps, and because of him, my step-grandfather, whom I'd visited in hospital that morning. He was in an oxygen tent, struggling for breath and wanting to tell me something, but all I heard was a groan, no, a profoundly deep sigh. Yes, that night I wept for all those who slept, those who struggled because they had come into this life or were struggling to leave it, I heard Lolo wheezing in her carriage and finally I got home exhausted: I had to go down five steps. Outside the door paper and rubbish had accumulated, the wind always blew it there—my wish at that time was to live in a city where there was no wind, where no rain fell. I lifted the carriage down, the child had fallen asleep at last, her breathing rattled. It's not really the struggle for air, but the need to breathe out, the calming outbreath, the moment of rest, of letting go.

—Breathe out hard, my grandmother Hilde would say when I cried, a good puff.

The apartment, rented as a basement but actually a cellar, stank. Whenever it rained—and when didn't it rain in this city—it stank. A penetrating smell of ammonia. It came from a mold growing on the walls, greenish blue, that Britt insisted was a urine mold that formed in the brick work because the drainage pipes from the toilets weren't watertight, which gave the damp this ammonia smell.

I undressed, went quietly into the bedroom. There Britt lay asleep on her stomach, her head on her arm. Britt at that time worked during the day at an insurance company dealing with claims and then three evenings a week in a theater as a cloakroom attendant. In the mornings, if she wasn't ill, I'd take Lolo to a nursery, in the afternoon at half past three Britt collected her.

I carefully lay down beside her. She turned, mumbled something, and laid her hand on my chest, but went on sleeping.

Magazine salesmen do hard work. It's not just that you're forever running up and down stairs, it's the constant struggle with your own inertia, with embarrassment, with the temptation to give up right on the ground floor, after the first door that opened. And not giving up after the second door behind which, after you've rung, you hear shuffling and a question: Who is it? I'm from Readers' Subscriptions, then they shuffle away. You stand there and don't know if you should wait or not. But there's no more shuffling. Is it worth going up another flight? Isn't this the building where for months canvassers for subscriptions have had the door shut in their faces? Where the inhabitants react bluntly or aggressively when the doorbell rings? Tenants who'd been sold specialist magazines on numismatics, insects, or cauterization with an incredibly emotional sales pitch by quick-tongued salesmen? People driven by a desire for revenge who were only waiting for a magazine salesman to ring? Female pensioners who sat resigned on the sofa surrounded by glossy copies of *Vogue* and *Playboy*? This was the struggle you had with yourself if you wanted to go a floor higher, to ring at the next door that nevertheless always opened to the width of the safety chain: what do you want, a face squeezed in the gap asked. I'm from etc. The door slams shut. Next door. Ring. No answer though you hear the radio inside. Is that the floor creaking under prowling footsteps? At last. The next door opens the width of the safety chain. Readers' Subscriptions. The chain gets taken off, a young woman appears, her sweater stretches over two huge encased breasts. She lets you show her the various magazines, tells you the landlord has put up a notice down in the hall: hawking and begging forbidden. I'd not thought of myself like that before, hawking. She looks at me, curious whether I've seen the notice. No, I say, no. Well, she says, I'm of a different opinion to my landlord. She flicks through the Readers' catalogue, asks the prices, asks why, if she orders a magazine, there's no postage to pay. We deal with that, I say, because in retail there's also a margin of profit, and we pay the postage out of the margin of profit. What, it's that big, she says, takes a deep breath and forces me to look at her emerging breasts bursting out of her bra under her thin sweater. (Berthold's advice: always aim for eye contact.) She wants to know what I get per subscription. Oh, she says, that's quite good. Well, I say, with a wife and child. Yes, she says, but it really is good. I suppose so, I say, because I think it'll make it easier for her to take out a subscription if she believes what she contributes to me by doing it is good. She flicks through the sample copies again, concentrates on *Stern,* has me explain to her again the advantages to her of a regular subscription, no need to run downstairs to buy *Stern,* then they're sold out, especially the important, interesting issues. You get the magazines in the mail. She stands there, thinks about it. Make an effort, I tell myself. I take out the order form. Can she keep the magazine? Actually no, I say, it's my sample copy, but you can have it. Thank you, she says, and with her sweater pulls up the strap of her bra, then lets it snap back on her skin. What are you staring at?

—Me? I hold the ball-point pen in writing position.

—But, she says, if magazines come in the mail, you know, they always get folded.

—No, I say, we write: Do not fold.

—Yes, she says and smiles at me, but on the other hand it's nice to go out and buy your magazine weekly. You can chat a while to the man in the shop, she smiles. I've got to get a meal ready, the kids'll be back any minute. Good luck then, and thank you for the magazine. She shuts the door.

Bitch. Crass cow. Brainless fart. The next floor, that's the challenge, do you climb another flight or go straight to the next building (but it's no better than this one), or should you have another go higher up. Naturally the brainless fart is standing behind the door listening to what happens upstairs. The stairs creak. You ring, a face appears stony with mistrust, door shuts, ring opposite, the peephole darkens, the door doesn't open, keep going, ring, the door opens, no chain, no bolts, finally! —Do come in. One of those dust-free, highly polished living rooms in which the cushions lie on the sofas as if stupefied by a karate chop. —Do sit down—I was just making some coffee. That takes up your energy too, just sitting there listening (I've come to realize psychoanalysts must deserve plenty, at any rate when they're listening). The things people spew out, hesitating, stammering or it comes out in a flood, all the symptoms, eczema, noxious growths, gallstones, look at these, in a little tube two rattling little black stones (and I hadn't had breakfast yet), shifted anuses, roaming kidneys, petrified twins. One man showed me his little brother bottled in alchohol, he'd carried him around next to his chest till he was forty-three. Stories of doctors prescribing for a cold when it was lung cancer and he died, the wife sobs, and circulation problems where you see little stars, I didn't know this, they shine bright in the middle of the day while everything suddenly grows dark, attacks of giddiness, turning, swinging, whirling. And all the other commonplace occurrences, dogs that have run away, budgerigars that flew off, forgotten handbags, lost purses, muggings, suicides, incomprehensible ones, comprehensible ones, by hanging, leaping off the top floor, sticking a head in a gas oven, jumping in front of a subway train, and pills and always more pills.

Already in my first week in the magazine business I rang at the door of a basement apartment, similar to ours, in Torniquiststrasse. A woman opened the door, a stick in her right hand, in her left a bloodstained floorcloth, a terrifying avenging angel, her grey hair flying. The shock was so great I backed away up two or three steps. —Don't worry, she said, come in. I followed her cautiously into the living room, there she knelt down and wiped up a dried puddle of blood on the linoleum floor, wrung the cloth out in a bucket, the water was red, and wiped and scraped at the edges of the blood puddle. Yesterday she was sitting there, she pointed to the plush chair, watching television, a thriller, heard a noise, turned round, there was a man leaning over her, had crept in, she gave him one right away with her stick, right on his head, he fell over, lay there, she showed the stick, somebody had already broken in once, had taken her money, there hardly was any, just the rent, but the clock, the clock was from her husband forty years ago, a genuine Glashütte clock, and he'd taken the rings, both wedding rings off her, that was the reason for the stick, and she raised it, since that happened she always has it handy, at night she keeps it by her bed, here all you need do is push in the pane, down here. There he lay. She points to the floor with the stick. Then she rang people's bells in the house. The time it took before the police came. They took the man to Eppendorf into intensive care, his skull was fractured.

—I hope he'll be all right, she says, and wrings out the cloth, the red water runs over her hands. Are you from the police?

—No. I'm from Readers' Subscriptions. Would you like to take out a subscription for six months?

—Yes, she says, I will.

—Which?

—All of them.

—No, I say, and put the order forms away, I'll come again next week.

—The man was from next door, he moved in three weeks ago, always said hello, even in the evening. I hope he'll be all right. Or I'll have to go to prison.

—Shall I phone your family?

—No, my daughter's married in Morocco.

—I'll make some coffee, I say.

—Good, she says, and soaps her hands while from a shelf I take the bag of coffee held shut by a clothespin and in which there's only a little coffee left.

As a child she always had to fetch the milk in a tin jug. On one occasion she stumbled, fell, she'd tried to hold the jug up but she fell and the milk ran out, white as snow, over the pavement but got dirty, she said, turned grey. At some stage during her hectic story came a sob.

When she'd calmed down again I offered her a cigarette.

We sat in the kitchen and drank coffee. We sat there without talking as if we'd already told each other everything. I saw that she hadn't smoked for years. She drew on the cigarette and immediately blew out the smoke, held the cigarette up like a pencil, shaking, as if she wanted to write something in the air.

The surfer

This morning I called up the passage in my data file that describes the end of Easter Island culture. What occurred here on a minute scale applies to almost all countries ever discovered by Europeans.

After the discoverers came American whalers, the crews brought brandy of fiendishly high alcohol content, gonorrhea and syphilis, and now and again they shot themselves an islander. Then came Chilean slave dealers. The male islanders who still curious and unsuspecting offered their women and wooden figures as barter were taken and shipped to the islands off Chile, where they were to mine saltpeter. Within a few months most of them died and the few who survived and were returned to the island brought back smallpox. The entire population almost died out. Belgian missionaries came and were driven away with stones. They had built their house out of corrugated iron and night after night their sleep was shattered by the clatter of stones. With highly accurate aim and alternating rhythm the islanders hurled stones from a great distance at the corrugated iron walls. A Frenchman proclaimed himself absolute ruler and established a reign of terror until the islanders murdered him. An English company began breeding sheep. So that the sheep could move freely about the island the islanders were fenced in a pen.

In a few years the culture had been wiped out and the script handed down on the wooden tablets forgotten by the islanders.

It was obviously of the greatest importance to find out whether any written account of this catastrophe, this abduction of people existed. Whether in fact this phase of their ruin had found its way into the script. Were there glyphs that recorded the appearance of the white man? If yes, were they descriptions or transcriptions, by means of which the white man was represented by a glyph, perhaps in the form of a fish bone that one could enjoy sucking clean, but on which one could also choke?

I'd just lit a cigarette and called up the data file when the phone rang. I immediately thought of my mother, saw her sitting in Hamburg, receiver in one hand, cigarette in the other, waiting for me to pick up the phone. That was just what I wasn't going to do. Then the ringing stopped. Britt called, —Dembrowski wants to talk to you.

Dembrowski's clearly articulating voice asked me how I was.

—Fine. I asked him if he'd noticed anything suspicious in the last few days.

—Why?

—Has a greeen Fiat been parking outside your gate?

He'd never seen a Fiat here, he said, besides he'd not left his park yesterday. He'd played boccie with Sann-chen the entire day.

The way Dembrowski says park is extraordinary, not just because he can't understate, but because the way he says it the word so emphatically suggests something cultivated and green, and nothing could remind you more that he once spoke a Saxony dialect that he trained himself to lose after he'd fled to the Federal Republic more than twenty years ago.

Not even the best suit made to measure, the most expensive silk shirt, the handmade shoes of horse leather can hide the Saxonian dialect, which is like the smell of someone's breath. He hated it. A self-hatred that drove him to radically rid himself of the dialect. This required a mad effort. Because as a result of this Saxonian dialect the lower jaw moves forward a few millimeters, and just this anatomically unique feature of the Saxons has to be compensated for by intensive training of the speech muscles. Dembrowski had worked out a training program and at three-hour inter-vals five times every day stood in front of a mirror or, if he thought no one was watching, in front of reflecting windows, and making quick regular movements ener-getically pulled back his lower jaw, which made him look—I watched him once in a hotel cloakroom—like a rabbit vomiting up a piece of carrot. This training to reverse the Saxonian jaw displacement was an essential requirement if he was to go into the stock market, be-cause who'd believe him if, while talking of a net profit of 40%, he reminded you of Party Secretary Ulbricht.

This time Dembrowski didn't quote the latest developments on the Frankfurt Stock Exchange, which had opened an hour ago and whose rates he'd asked for over the phone. This morning he wanted to play a game of tennis.

—I've got to get back to work, I said, I was interrupted.

Dembrowski didn't ask why and how I'd been interrupted. He knows I'm writing about Easter Island, but he never asks what exactly I'm trying to write. I think he considers it a fad writing, of all things, about such a small island in the Pacific. For a time he suspected I was writing about something else, something I wanted to hide from him. Whenever the suspicion flares up in him he asks, studiedly casual to take the edge off the question; —You're not churning out our story, are you?

I used to be able to say no, now I have to lie.

Dembrowski happens to have the somewhat bizarre idea that you can easily make money with books. (While I know, if only at secondhand, that my uncle's financial career is exceedingly modest.)

What always calms Dembrowski down again when he visits us are the books lying around, the travel reports about Easter Island, all the photocopies of the characters of the script, the meaning of the statues, the pollen analyses. Probably he thinks this is how I cover up having nothing to do.

He's incredibly energetic, absolutely bursting with work, (it's a completely mistaken notion that con-men are lazy, on the contrary, as they have to work with reality and appearance at one and the same time they have to work twice as hard). Not only has he begun to learn Russian, he reads the business section of three of four daily papers, enters the stock market trends into his computer, compares, calculates, works out averages.

Unlike me he talks about his work. Unasked he develops a theory about a flattening out of zero-bond profits, statistics pour out of him, parameters, and limiting values.

He's a man of theory. I'm a man of practice. He's a qualified economist. I—here too—self-taught.

▼

Dembrowski studied economics in East Germany, in the GDR a study that, as he himself says, went counter to any effective economy, so more exactly an anti-study, being directed not at the maximization of profit but only at management.

On finishing his studies he became an industrial economist with a mechanical engineering firm where he supervised shortages, but in his free time, and he had plenty, he busied himself with the stock market which didn't, of course, exist under Real Socialism. For which reason he followed stock market trends in the ethereal crackle of broadcasts from the West. He speculated on paper without actually being able to buy or sell a single share. He speculated with zero bonds, preference shares, bull markets, and slumps, speculated in commodity futures trading, with his ear to the radio followed the markets in Chicago, Frankfurt, London, and Zurich, by means of a forbidden and extremely efficient retractable aerial at night turned in to the noise of the Dow Jones.

An informer in a neighboring house reported the aerial and he came under suspicion of spying for the CIA.

Three times the Stasi searched his apartment, his dacha, even dug up his garden lot, but found nothing except market quotations over the last years for IBM, Siemens, Phillips, Mercedes, and Dow Chemical which he, Dembrowski, maintained in the face of the frowning official was material for the study of the decay of the capitalist system. And he could prove this. He could prove that with the enormous growth of capital there was overcapitalization that in fact should already have led to collapse years ago. But with his initial investment of 50,000 (East German) marks Dembrowski would actually have become a quadruple millionaire after exactly eleven years. One of his best holdings was a small IBM portfolio of shares of 20,000 marks, bought in the sixties, that in the meantime had climbed to 1,200,000 (East German) marks.

He fled the GDR, this was in 1974, in an extremely unusual way. All the newspapers reported his flight at the time. And I'd also read about Dembrowski long before I got to know him at the dermatologists' conference. He'd been carried on a surfboard across the Baltic to Sweden. I'm not sure if the surfboard can still be seen in the Flight Museum at Checkpoint Charlie, at any rate I gazed at it in amazement there together with Britt and Lolo only a few years ago. He'd made it himself, probably the first surfboard in the GDR, so heavy it had to be carried into the water by two men: the rear was riveted aluminum reinforced with steel ribs, loaded with small styrofoam balls which Dembrowski had got from the plastics factory in Karl-Marx-Stadt where he worked as a management expert. The board looked more like a torpedo that had been a bit flattened on top. The mast was of wood, also the shaft, but reinforced with steel clamps. The structure reminded an American CBS television reporter of the war joke: Send a German into the woods with a tin can and a pocket knife and he'll come back with a one-man U-Boat.

Dembrowski wanted to flee from the island of Usedom across the Baltic to Sweden.

He sent the surfboard parcel post from Karl-Marx-Stadt to Usedom and on the day it arrived had two fishermen carry it into the water, rigged it up and got on it as he only had two weeks' holiday in which to learn surfing and then still had to wait for favorable winds. Dembrowski fell off his surf torpedo as he tried to pull the sail out of the water, climbed back on again, carefully and with shaking knees stood up, tried to pull up the sail, fell, knocked his shins blue on the aluminum. On the second day—holidaymakers on the beach watched his attempts to climb onto this container fitted with a sail—he slipped, crashed into the mast, hit his testicles and for a moment lost consciousness. On the beach the spectators dispersed, they thought he was sunning himself on his tin contraption. That night with wet towels he cooled his testicles, swollen almost to the size of tennis balls. But he didn't give up and in a week he'd learned not only how to remain upright and to hold the shaft with the sail, but also how to maneuver. Until then the fisherman had always had to tow him back to land in the evening. In the second week he perfected his technique and on the last night of his holiday he put on a wetsuit and set sail in a light west wind.

For days this man sails alone through a watery wilderness, said Dembrowski's defense counsel Dr. Amelung during Dembrowski's cross-examination with a sweep of his arm and the sleeve of his gown fluttering, always in fear of being detected and seized by a GDR patrol boat, of losing his way, of going round in a circle as naturally he doesn't know the compass's magnetic variation. Dembrowski stands in the blazing sun, at night lies tied to the narrow aluminum box so the waves won't wash him overboard. The drinking water he'd taken with him in a plastic bottle has run out. His provisions have become salty from the sea water. He's already delirious when on the sixth day in the grey blue light of the evening he sees land, sails towards it, by now only able to kneel, doesn't know, is this the shore of Real Socialism or of freedom. Had he perhaps surfed in a circle? Then he hears the people on the shore, they're calling to him in Danish. He'd reached Bornholm. The surf torpedo dug crunching into the sand of the shore. (Dr. Amelung really did make the stone stonier.) Dembrowski waded to land. Fell on his knees. He was free. (The court room listened breathless, there was even a murmur of applause from the back benches where a few pensioners were sitting.)

At the time the papers wrote: *Saxon Surfs to Freedom*. For a week Dembrowski was in intensive care. Because of hypothermia. His Polish wetsuit had come apart in the salt water.

The magazines fought for his story of his flight.

He became the general representative of a surfboard company that brought out a board called *La Paloma*. I've seen the ads. Dembrowski on a board, and below: *La Paloma, if you love Freedom.*

And when nobody could see any connection any longer between freedom and Dembrowski, and that was already the case five weeks after his flight, the company cancelled the contract.

Dembrowski had another go at being an inspired inventor.

He developed an anti-slide cream. It was meant to prevent the surfer slipping on a board smeared with suntan oil. It was a paste Dembrowski himself made in a garage in two large laundry tubs. He boiled down washing soap with sand and thyme to a thick liquid, which he put in tubes. The paste was spread on the surfboard, really did remove the film of suntan oil, and you stood more securely on the sand. But this anti-slide cream had one disadvantage: if the surfer moved his feet a lot on the board, which was after all necessary when sailing against the wind, he soon had a wake of foam behind him. Environmental awareness was not so far advanced in 1975 and surfers not so numerous for soap foam in bathing areas to cause any excitement, but then word got round that this anti-slide cream encouraged the growth of foot fungus. Dembrowski couldn't market the new paste that now contained other ingredients. Nobody wanted a *fungicidal antiseptic anti-slide cream*. Two antis in the name of one product was too much, it smacked overly of the makeshift economy of the GDR.

The boards were increasingly fitted with layers of a synthetic material that prevented slipping. This was also when the first non-slip rubber boots appeared in the sports shops.

For a time like me he sold subscriptions, as a GDR refugee he was predestined for this. But going up and down stairs and having to listen to the stories people told tired him. Dembrowski's no listener, he's a self-centered talker. He tried business in various corners of the market in quick succession, opened an agency for GDR photos, then formed a company for a Rumanian hair tonic. An extract allegedly prepared from mistletoe. It was supposed to encourage blood circulation in the scalp, but caused burns and additional hair loss and resulted in a charge of assault.

Then he started a wholesale business for spare parts for old cars. A profitable business that incidentally neither he nor his defense counsel mentioned at the trial. The mechanics, who worked on a voluntary basis and were paid according to results by Dembrowski, swarmed into the GDR, Poland, Hungary, and Czechoslovakia where there were still many old Daimlers, Adlers, Maibachs on the road or standing in barns. The mechanics gutted them. The old parts were reconditioned and then sold at six to seven times their price. The enterprise in which sometimes twenty mechanics were involved caused a stir when some overzealous workers turned up at vintage-car rallies and removed carburetors, distributors, turn signals, windshield wipers, and wheels from unguarded cars.

At first it was thought to be the work of car fanatics supplying themselves with spare parts for their cars, then two of Dembrowski's mechanics were discovered under a jacked-up Adler. The back axle had already been removed. Heinz Dembrowski succeeded in convincing people he knew nothing about his freelance colleagues' excessive eagerness to procure parts. But he acquired such a bad reputation that he had to sell the business. He started a business selling fur-lined officers' coats from Russia, long coats fitted at the waist; they were a hit with the trendies in the winter of '76. (The left wasn't yet quite out of fashion.)

Nobody knew how Dembrowski acquired these coats, the export of which was strictly forbidden.

He got them dirt-cheap and sold them as if they were sable. He conned the stupid cows in the Hamburg boutiques. He had a sixth sense for business. You have to watch out with him. (He'd say the same about me.) I'm sure if he could write our story, which the press took up, he'd do it. He'd instantly sell our story to a magazine. But to do it he'd have to divulge his hiding place.

Today when I read in the *Herald Tribune* that yet another minister in the Soviet Union has been condemned to death for black-marketeering in caviar, or when entire party cadres are brought to trial because of bribery or embezzlement, I think perhaps among them there's Dembrowski's source. Every Christmas he got ten one-kilo tins of caviar. When we were held in remand over Christmas, he waited in vain for his Beluga present. He'd already invited the jailers to a caviar feast. After this they considered him a braggart, in the new year they weren't so pleasant and helpful any more.

Still, Dembrowski invested in the eastern market. While in custody he bought a pretentious villa built in tsarist times in his girl friend's name (to his life's end— like me—he's not allowed to earn money under his own name, unless we pay the victims back the millions). More of a castle than a villa, with thirty-three rooms built in 1903 by the supplier of cocoa to the court. Dembrowski applied for a license for a casino. A few more years and the Soviet Union will have reached the stage where it opens casinos again. Millions of passionate, forcibly restrained gamblers are waiting there for just this. Then, according to him, Russian literature will become interesting again, and you'll make more dough than you ever could before.

Dembrowski suggested a game of tennis in the evening when it got cooler at seven.

Torpedo boats, go for the enemy!

We don't meet often, now and then as I said we play tennis, sometimes, even less often, bridge. Britt doesn't like Sannchen, Dembrowski's girl friend. A graphic artist, who always shows her long suntanned legs as if they were the center of attention, freely displayed or crossed, one knee always raised so you can see the inside of her thigh. At the same time every conversation comes to a standstill around Sannchen. She sits there and says nothing. At first I always felt a certain shyness talking in her presence, everything I said suddenly seemed banal, for which I tried to compensate by an increased flood of words that only made the conversation more banal. But eventually I noticed it wasn't out of thoughtfulness, out of scrupulous caution that she said nothing, but that she really had nothing to say. But even worse is that she can't listen either. You ask her, how are you, and she says: Fine. That's all. She never asks what I'm doing, never asks what Britt's doing, even when at cards Britt's hands are covered in scratches. She simply doesn't ask the obvious question:

What have you done? Britt could then have replied that she'd been cutting roses again without putting on gloves.

Britt wants to cultivate a new rose here for which she's already got a name: Friesian Seraphim. Britt herself doesn't know how she came by this strange name. She's never read Canetti. The rose, such is her horticulturalist's ambition, should be white with a luxuriant bloom. Sannchen never asks how Lolo is, if she likes the local German school, what subjects she particularly likes, what she eventually wants to study. I think perhaps she doesn't even know what Dembrowski did before. Possibly she's never asked him.

All you can do is look at Sannchen. That's what Dembrowski does, especially at her carefully suntanned thighs. No, I want to be fair, Sannchen likes to work, she likes to draw, she's a good, a very good and a successful graphic artist. Her work has a nice coolness and no flourishes. Then this woman, whom I don't like precisely because she behaves as if she were presenting herself on a silver tray and nothing else interests her, when you see her work she becomes desirable—yes—because she's suddenly unreachable and totally undemanding and lost in her own thoughts. She sits at her white drawing board on which there's nothing but a stack of white paper and some pencils sharpened with a penknife. She looks at the white sheet as if she could see something on it, something sketched there, and then suddenly with a calm movement she draws a line and then another line and then a third—when I see her like that, and only then, I understand why Dembrowski left his wife and three children for Sannchen. Slowly from the lines a design for a poster emerges, a poster for an exhibition about the history of the pencil or an exhibition of photographs.

I can still clearly see a poster for a Japanese high tech exhibition. Nippon, nothing else, in large black letters, but the way she'd drawn the O in red and like the rising sun, naturally without any fancy rays, had deservedly won her a prize.

That's just what amazes Britt and me, that someone who shows no interest in anyone else can do such outstanding posters. The posters certainly have a remarkable, and therefore striking coolness in the colors, the forms, and also the script. As Sannchen has nothing to say about her work and Britt isn't that keen on looking at it when the four of us get together we play cards.

I don't like playing cards, which neither Sannchen nor Dembrowski can understand. I hate playing cards, I hate waiting for the coincidence that you have to then exploit.

Nor is being with Dembrowski as friendly, as warm as it used to be. The quarrel we had shortly before our arrest still has an effect. It was nothing dramatic, the cause wasn't as my defense counsel hoped (and Dembrowski's no doubt too) that I'd objected to the fleecing of investors by Dembrowski. It was something quite trivial.

Shortly before the firm went up in smoke Dembrowski had taken himself off here, to Spain, allegedly to come up with a new advertising concept for our brokerage firm. He simply stayed away two, three, then four weeks. I was left in Hamburg to battle with the increasing list of our brokerage firm, left to talk on the phone to incensed investors who wanted to know what had happened to their lovely money. It was foreseeable that sooner or later the ship would capsize. And I said it to him when he made one of his calls from Spain. —So? Who gives a shit, Dembrowski drawled into the phone. Yes, on that occasion he drawled, this man who'd gone to various language and speech schools had lost the nice clear pronunciation that always won me over, in Spain he'd acquired a totally sloppy way of speaking reminiscent of the Hamburg red-light district.

—That's the young woman, Britt said. He's overdoing it, and a foreign language on top of that.

—No, I said, it's because he's living from day to day, it's the dozing by the swimming pool, the games of boccie with Sannchen.

I think I was right because during the trial he reverted to the old way of speaking. But when I phoned him the last time before our arrest, when I told him about all the people who were threatening to bring in the public prosecutor, he said, in that red-light district way, —Man, make some phone calls and get more dough, they're going bankrupt anyway.

I still remember clearly what enraged me, it was the way he called me "man," in other words counted me among those he took for stupid.

At the same time he'd directly and crassly referred to our business secret, about which until now we'd kept silent. It's one thing to do something and another to name it. What he was saying was simply: Us crooks, we know. Me, who'd stayed overnight in the office, who'd swallowed three captagons, who'd drunk three cups of overstrong coffee and had a sour taste in my mouth, I blew a fuse, —You lazy bastard, shut your trap!

At his end the phone stayed silent. I hung up. It was the only time we'd both said what we were thinking.

Dembrowski then made the mistake of immediately getting on a plane in Malaga and flying to Hamburg. He probably wanted to talk things over, or perhaps determine his position, I don't know, we never discussed it. In any case the police were already waiting for him when he stepped into his Hamburg apartment.

We saw each other again in the prison yard when we were in custody, he looked hard at the ground and past me. He showed me he wasn't reconciled because every time he approached me—we were walking in a circle— and I wanted to nod to him he stared past me at the prison wall. After that I never saw him again on the yard walk. He did without it and did his isometric exercises against the cell door.

▼

The night before the start of the trial I hardly slept despite the valium I'd asked the prison doctor to give me.

I was already awake when the bell rang. I went to the cell window and opened it. It was still dark outside and the cold streamed in through the gap. It smelled of fresh snow. I pressed my forehead against the cool pane. In the distance I could hear the noise of cars starting, there must have been thick snow on the streets.

I washed and put on one of my blue suits, hesitated over the choice of tie, then took the dull red with the dark blue pattern and the matching pocket handkerchief.

I sat on the bench and smoked until the sergeant fetched me from the cell. He was an old man who lightly dragged a leg, I felt just a moment's pressure on the handcuff, at every second step he pulled on it a little, or rather he let himself be pulled. If we'd walked any further the iron would have rubbed my wrist open. We went through the corridors past the guards and prisoners to the courtroom. I asked if it had snowed overnight. Yes. He mumbled something about trains being delayed. About streets not being cleared. Then he fell silent. His uniform smelled of cold pipe smoke.

The courtroom was crowded. I immediately spotted Britt and Lolo. They waved, they laughed. The sergeant unlocked the handcuff and I was able to embrace Britt, touching her with the length of my body: her knees, thighs, the softness of her stomach, her breasts. The sergeant turned away for a moment, then he made a quick head movement and we had to separate. Dembrowski sat down next to me, he looked hard into the courtroom at where Sannchen was sitting, a little away from Britt and Lolo. At the back in the last row sat his wife, Renate. I saw how she tried to make herself small, her head pulled down, presumably she didn't want Dembrowski to see her.

Press photographers had come, there wasn't exactly a crush, but still there were four or five.

Dr. Blank in his robe was telling me something, but only for the sake of talking. That's also a part of a lawyer's duties, bridging the embarrassment of merely sitting around. There was a school class in the courtroom taking their social studies course, probably on fraudulent manipulation of trade and tax laws. Many people had come out of curiosity, relatives of the victims I assumed, who were waiting outside on the witnesses' benches to make their appearance. But also people who must have read about it in the papers. Children laughed, chewed, giggled, a girl waved to me, a boy held up his thumb, meaning presumably it'll be o.k. There was nothing embarrassing about the situation and besides, working as a magazine salesman I'd totally lost the feeling of embarrassment, which hadn't—unlike with my uncle—been much developed in me at home.

The court appeared, the judge, the associate judge, the two jurors all stood up, a festive moment. The trial opened.

Proceedings began. Heinz Dembrowski sat next to me like someone taking an exam, his back straight (he's quite small—always suffered because of this), he'd placed his hands on the table in front of him, narrow hands with long shiny fingernails, very credit-worthy they looked, in fact he looked like a Prussian prince, something not completely out of the question as his mother was a maid on an estate often visited by the Prussian crown prince.

Peter Walter, charged with fraud and misappropriation, no previous convictions, primary school, high school, didn't finish, junior high, apprenticed as carpenter, didn't finish, trained as a decorator, didn't finish, various occupations among them car deliverer and cleaning contractor (Britt crossed her legs, her kneecaps gleamed under the black silk), four years as salesman of magazine subscriptions, then eight years as salesman of life insurance.

Dr. Blank had called witnesses for the cross-examination. Berthold came and told the court how hardworking and honest I'd been, selling subscriptions for four years. An important occupation, Berthold said, quite comparable to that of priest and doctor because

117

magazine salesmen are responsive, if they take their time they're counseling and spreading education.

The judge interrupted Berthold, —That will do. The next witness was called: Wesendonk.

As always he wore a navy blue suit, white shirt, dark blue tie with small embroidered pennants. Naturally nobody in the court knew the significance of these flags: Attack the enemy! In the battle of Skagerak this flag signalled an order to the German torpedo boats— hussars of the sea, hurrah!—to attack the English destroyers at the Crossing the T (or was it the night attack that failed?).

At any rate it was Wesendonk signaling to me. He didn't need to look at me, to blink, to smile furtively, he'd simply run up the signal: Attack the enemy!

Wesendonk was in charge of training for an insurance company that I'm not able to name here. After four years of selling subscriptions, four years of climbing up and down stairs, four years of people's living rooms crammed with their memories, after four years —every drop in the bucket counts—I'd applied for a job with the company because I'd have a share in every contract signed, for years you continue to receive your percentage of what people have spent on their old age or leave their heirs in case of premature decease.

The training lasted two months: law relating to insurance and pensions, the various ways of underwriting capital—pensions—and life insurance. The best insurance for a particular age, a particular income etc. Wesendonk was in charge of training salesmen. Motivation for insurance. Positive sales calculations. Reciprocal expectations. Analysis of requirements.

Wesendonk asked on the first day of training what

jobs we'd had. I said four years canvassing magazines.

—Ahha. And what did you do before that, I mean
what did you study?

—Decorating, I said.

—Very good, he said, you'll be a fisher of artistic
souls.

—The best thing, said Wesendonk, after a psycholo-
gist with a diploma had given a talk on the psychology
of selling, the best thing is to forget all this theoretical
junk and concentrate on life. The most interesting stories are always the ones life itself tells. If you want to
sell someone life insurance, then first of all study his
life. Try to find out if the person in question has children. Children are always the best motivation for insurance in case of death. Look for self-employed people
with children. Follow pregnant women, the ones that
aren't running around in designer rags, women pushing
strollers, fathers in parks flying kites with their children
on Saturday afternoon. The crocodile on a polo shirt
could be an indication that this man is a potential client
because rising independent lawyers, doctors, architects, engineers draw attention to themselves, in other
words to their income, with these labels. Aim for spon-
taneous conversations, on a train perhaps, naturally
you always travel first class, go to the theater, go to an
athletic club, to play tennis for instance, ride, sail, not
to wrestle or box.

Wesendonk set up the persuasion game.

In the persuasion game two participants on the
course have to convince each other of the need for life
insurance. I had to play against Schult, a former textile
rep and fast talker.

To simulate an actual sales situation we were paired with two women on the course.

Wesendonk decided the relationship according to the reality. —Married, he asked me. —Yes.

—Good, Wesendonk summoned a woman by the name of Helga. This is your wife. Children? —Yes, one.

Then he asked Schult, who always wore a scarf and a jacket in houndstooth check (the crowing cock on our course). —Married?

—No, said Schult, and that already gave him an advantage over me because naturally that meant he had no children, or so he said. Why should someone like Schult take out life insurance?

—Girl friend, Wesendonk asked. Of course. Schult nodded, a grinning nod that indicated he had several. A show-off, here was a weak spot.

Good, said Wesendonk and handed him over to our course beauty.

We had to react standing. Body language is important, nobody lets himself be talked into paying out four hundred marks a month for his death when he's being urged by a clumsy hand movement, a pinched mouth.

—Mr. Schult, said Wesendonk, you begin. Convince Peter Walter and his wife that they need to take out life insurance.

—Go. Wesendonk started the time on his stopwatch.

Schult said: —Good morning, and then as I'd expected, ah, what a nice child, beautiful, just like her mother.

Naturally this was a glaring embellishment, just like the silk scarf he wore with his outfit. A tactical mistake. My housewife Helga wasn't stupid after all, she wore fairly strong glasses and in her childhood someone had overlooked getting her teeth fixed.

Schult quickly got to the point. Life insurance, wife, child, a secure future, the uncertain times we live in, and so on. I let him talk, let him dig out charts, asked about premiums and pension payments that could be expected in the year 2000, let him secrete his slime like an eel in salt: responsibility towards the sweet child, the beautiful wife, the enormous increase in fatal traffic accidents (yes, truly, the conditions prevailing on the streets could be compared to a civil war), provision for a quiet happy old age, traveling down the Danube, trips to Florence, no worries. He talked at great length about his aunt. She'd not taken out any life insurance, now she depended on social security, she sat miserable in her tiny apartment and stared at the shabby wallpaper. He took the order form and asked what sum I had in mind. But I said I'd first have to talk this over quietly with my wife. She was the one that earned the money.

—Oh, said Schult to that.

—Yes, said my appointed wife sharply, that's how it is, and now please leave us your card. We'll call you.

—Stop, said Wesendonk, now Mr. Walter.

I referred to the furnishings, praised the pictures on the walls, always called Schult's wife Mrs. Schult, until Schult, he had to stick to the conditions, corrected me and said: —My friend. Then I said perhaps the situation would change one day. He forced a grin, after all he couldn't contradict me in front of his girl friend, even if she was it only for a night.

That's exactly when life insurance is important, I said, when you then have children. But we don't want any, Schult said quickly and looked at the woman at his side. She nodded, she let her artificially curled reddish-blonde locks bob up and down, but there was something slow and very thoughtful about the ways those locks bobbed.

—That can change very quickly, I said, a cousin of mine (relatives—no one knows this better than my uncle—always provide the most suitable examples), quite a rogue, lots of girl friends, changed the girl friends monthly until one day he found the right one. (I looked at the course beauty. She smiled pensively.) An Irish student with reddish-blonde hair and freckles who'd come with her rucksack to Hamburg, who asked him the way on the Jungfernsteig. Two months later she was pregnant. (We were in the third month of training. The course beauty's face turned a fine red and Schult who'd stayed derisively silent until now grew serious.) He was a playboy, but naturally he married her. (Schult's partner seemed to draw breath.) But then the Irish student, who was now visibly pregnant, moved to Hamburg. My cousin found a three-room apartment. He moved out of his bachelor apartment. To save on the expense of moving he rented a small truck, was driving his things to the new apartment, to Garstedt, and not being used to driving a truck at a curve came off the road, plunged down an embankment, only three meters, but enough to break his neck.

—His neck, asked Schult's wife.

—Yes. And he's dead. He left a pregnant, beautiful twenty-two-year-old widow—uninsured.

Schult looked at me, his puckered mouth showed signs of helplessness. He looked at the course beauty and she looked at me, anxiously curious. (Did I, she must have been asking herself at that moment, perhaps know?)

—May I offer you an exceptionally good life insurance policy? I'm sure you must be interested. She nodded, hesitant and lost in her thoughts, but it was clearly a nod.

—Stop, said Wesendonk. Very good. Is the story about your cousin true?

—Well, I said, it's a story such as life tells.

That made Wesendonk laugh. —Excellent. It's not a matter of stories being true, but they have to be right, to fit. To be necessary, as it were.

—And now we'll comment on the maneuver. The attack always has to be made in such a way that it can be broken off if conditions become unfavorable. For example, when Admiral Scheer was heading for the British fleet which was moving in battle formation a situation arose of which all admirals since Nelson have dreamed, the so-called Crossing the T. The entire fire power of the British fleet, which could fire broadside, was concentrated on the German battleships moving one after the other into the firing line. These were only able to fire from the front gun turrets. Now, in this inflammatory situation, Scheer ordered a turn that at that time only the German fleet could carry out, an extraordinary feat, a fantastic nautical accomplishment, hundreds of thousands of tons of steel swung round, one ship after another, a hundred and eighty degrees. You have to be able to imagine this, in the battle these steel mountains swung round a hundred and eighty degrees without colliding and withdrew in battle formation, and so escaped the destructive power of the British artillery. And that is exactly what you, dear Mr. Schult, should have done when Mr. Walter suddenly moved his wife forward, when he told you she was the breadwinner, you should have swung round a hundred and eighty degrees and then made your attack on the woman, but instead you ran into the Crossing the T and were sunk by full broadsides.

—Mr. Walter with his attack immediately gained a tactical advantage by aiming for you via your friend, who then hindered each of your attempts to withdraw. You would have needed to win back the initiative. By, for example, sending your girl friend from the room under some pretext: Make us a coffee, something like that. Then you should have explained: I'm against permanent relationships, can't have children, had a vasectomy. Then Mr. Walter would have had to find a way of again bringing your girl friend into the conversation, or find a story—I'm not saying invent one—that would illustrate why many men undergo an expensive operation to make them fertile again, precisely because it's a sign of deep, yes, the deepest affection, which then in turn requires life insurance, etcetera, etcetera.

—Think of battles at sea, here every advance by a unit or a naval formation brings about reactions that need to be taken into consideration. When Wesendonk talked, as always when he was in full flight, white foam gathered in the corners of his mouth.

Wesendonk, to my disappointment, hadn't served in the navy but with the sappers. He wasn't accepted for the navy for which he volunteered because, he said, of a weakness with green. He could see all colors, as he repeatedly assured us, red, yellow, blue, but of all things not green. This he saw, depending on how bright it was, as grey or brown. This caused him deep, irremediable distress. So as a corporal he'd been a driver driving overland, the sea always before him, under way from position to position by double bearing, navigating by dead reckoning and observed position, Seedorf and Hodenhagen. On starboard bow, short flashing light. Bear 234 degrees. Meanwhile dropped anchor, got pissed (also during the Cuban Missile Crisis), checked the tidal range—is there enough water under the keel?

Yes, this star salesman of life insurance, this fisher of souls who'd become an instructor so he could pass on his experience had a natural pedagogic talent that as he spoke revealed an unquenchable yearning for the sea. If he heard the sound of water anywhere his eyes grew damp.

Wesendonk sailed in his free time, without himself being able to take charge of the boat as this depended decisively on being able to distinguish red from green, port side and starboard, because under sail the starboard bow has right of way. Possibly he also took up sailing in his spare time because yachtsmen tell the most stories, the verbal yarn gets spun that Wesendonk could then ravel and unravel professionally.

—May I, he asked the judge during the trial, tell you a true story about how easily a person can become grounded in the shallows and come to grief?

The judge, a patient man, nodded.

—I had a close acquaintance, a lawyer, he worked in an insurance company, the previous winter he'd divorced his wife and married a woman twenty years younger, a speech therapist—her profession is important for the story. While his former, one could say old wife was a good sailor, the speech therapist had never set foot on a yacht. It was spring and he was going for

125

the first time with his young wife on a cruise on his sail-boat, nothing fantastic, a trip to Helgoland. But in the Elbe estuary by Scharhörn sailing downwind he ran onto a sandbar, something that had never happened to him before, and as the tide was ebbing and he wanted to be in Helgoland in the evening where they'd arranged to meet other friends, not wanting to wait for the next tide he tried everything to get the boat afloat again. He turned on the motor. The boat sat tight. He turned the motor off and to demonstrate to his young wife that he's a fit fifty without further ado jumps into the water, which only reaches to his hips, gives the boat a push and gets it to float, helped by a breeze that carries the boat into deeper water. The boat picks up speed with the woman on board who knows nothing about sailing, just sits there looking back at her husband threshing through the water to get to the boat. But it's being driven forward by a fresh breeze, the mainsheet is jammed. The boat's not sailing smoothly, it takes the wind, then slackens again. The man, who sees he isn't going to be able to reach the boat, calls to her: —Let the sail go!

—What?

—The line, he calls, the thick rope hanging from the boom.

—Which boom?

—The one with the sail. Now he has to shout because the boat is getting further and further away. She fumbles with all kinds of ropes—and there are a lot on board a yacht. He shouts, standing in the water to his chest: —Turn the tiller to starboard, to the right. Right! The stick at the back that's on the rudder.

No, riiiight! (She always confused right and left.) Sail down!

—What? (She calls this through the megaphone): what?

—Mast! Sail! Let it go! The groove!

—What grave?

—Groove! Slit! Mast! Slit! Slit!

She thought he'd lost his mind out of fear. She couldn't make out anymore what he was calling. She saw him, and it was the last time she'd see him, standing (or was he swimming?) up to his neck in the water and waving in the slowly gathering darkness.

She was found the next morning. A fisherman noticed the yacht swaying from side to side as if drunk. The fisherman assumed that here was another Sunday sailor, but then went alongside and discovered the woman lying in the cockpit, covered in vomit, whimpering quietly and unconscious.

The man was found two days later on the shore of Scharhörn, dead, his eyes picked out by gulls.

In the courtroom everyone had listened in suspense, even the pensioners in the last row who during the cross-examination had unpacked their stollen, unscrewed their thermos flask—I could even smell the coffee, sat there forgetting the stollen they were holding, from which they'd already taken a bite.

They were all waiting in suspense for some explanation from Wesendonk. But he wiped the white clumps of foam from the corners of his mouth with a handkerchief and was silent.

—And what does this tell us, the judge asked.

—Firstly, said Wesendonk and put the handkerchief

back into his pocket: the man wasn't insured. No life insurance for the young woman, and this despite the fact that he was an insurance lawyer. Wesendonk looked at the judge questioningly for a moment. But the actual problem lies in the difficulty of naming things in colloquial speech for which there are specialist terms. The groove, that's clear to any sailor, what's meant is: the groove in the mast in which the sail is hoisted. But if you say slit, at any rate from a distance, then everybody, especially a speech therapist, has to first find the slit, and in the meantime the boat's already out of audible range, beyond the reach of helpful explanations and descriptions. I imagine the situation's quite similar with stockbroking. That a great deal rests on a misunderstanding between the stock market specialist and the investor. By the time something's been explained to the investor the situation's changed again. And before one can really react to a certain extent one's already out of audible range. This, I imagine, isn't out of evil intent, but has to do with just this temporal-spatial gap.

Wesendonk had made enquiries, had informed himself, wanted to send out a relief convoy so I could make a 180-degree turn and escape Crossing the T. (Torpedo boats! Go for the enemy!)

The judge seemed unimpressed, all he wanted to know was how good I was at the job at the time.

—Quite excellent, said Wesendonk, conscientious, very successful. Mr. Walter specialized in dealing with artists.

That was it. Wesendonk sat down on the bench and pointedly tugged at his tie.

The uvular R

In the afternoon the phone rang. My mother, the thought flashed through my head. But it was Dembrowski. He wanted to postpone the game of tennis to the next day, he'd been invited for dinner by an English real-estate agent.

How sonorously he pronounced it.

I'd got to know Dembrowski at a dermatologists conference that was held at Hamburg University. I'd opened a small stand there next to all the medical publishers and specialist journals. The name of the insurance company and then a sign in a lovely large roman script: Life insurance at its most beautiful. Consult Peter Walter. Two models sat at the stand, a blonde and a brunette. I'd gotten them through a model agency (700 marks per day—a huge investment considering my circumstances).

When one of the dermatologists had signed a life insurance policy I'd take a photo of him if he wanted—and they all did—with an instamatic camera: the newly insured and a model, blonde or brunette as desired—or with both—drinking a toast to good health with champagne.

When they got home the doctors all wanted to show their good, or not so good friends, what a great conference it had been, it had been worth going to (not just because of the tax write-off), and what smart guys they were, two women at once, like out of a fashion magazine the way they laughed when they drank a toast, the way their eyes sparkled, real class. These were photos you could also leave lying around at home for the wives to find who after twenty years of marriage lay mute and heavy during sex like seals on a sandbank.

Dembrowski had also opened an advisory stand, advice on investment: Let your money work for you. A respectable small stand, all too respectable, hardly anything happened there while at mine at five in the afternoon the few remaining doctors who had once long ago studied Latin were singing *Gaudeamus igitur* and both models had ladders in their black stockings.

That evening as I was standing tiredly among the empty champagne bottles Dembrowski, his work finished, came over with that quiet springy step, that small erect figure, and in his beautiful melodic standard German that sounded as if he'd been on the stage for years congratulated me on my business success.

No, he said, but he'd taken speech lessons. *Round the rugged rock the ragged rascal ran.* Dembrowski literally licked the words clean, he was in love with the sounds, labially lascivious, a phonetic-fetishist. Was this the consequence or the precondition of his Herculean effort to move the Saxonian jaw displacement back a few millimeters?

He could work himself up into gushing enthusiasm over the sound of certain words: what a difference between the English Standby-Credit and the German *Beistand-Kredit,* a transposition of only two syllables, and yet *Beistand,* contained the tonal power of endurance, therefore spoke of help, constancy, while the stand of standby already threatened a standstill, the bailiffs. Or take bed. It conveys nothing of the idea of lying on it and making love, but take the old German word *Liegelang,* it's all there, you can feel the whole process of stretching out in the mouth, the tongue. *Lie-gelang*.

The ethnologist Alfred Métraux has given an example of word cannibalism in his book *L'Île de Pâques* (yes, I know, the self-taught always display their education, to educated people we're exhibitionists). It's a story about the early crazy wars the islanders still told when Métraux came to the island. The Miru warriors had defeated their opponents from the Tupahotu clan. The survivors had fled to the small island of Marotiri. Everyday the Miru canoes set out for Marotiri and brought back fresh human flesh.

> *A Miru warrior by the name of Oho-take-tore came from his village to the bay of Ana-Havea where every day the sharing-out of the corpses took place. When he came to the shore the canoes returned from Marotiri were just unloading the enemies killed during the day. Among the dead Oho-take-tore recognized a Tupa-hotu warrior by the name of Hanga-maihi-tokerau. He turned to a group of Miru warriors and said to them: "Companions, give me the body of the warrior with the beautiful name! I want to devour him because his name is so sweet to my ear!" Poie, who commanded the crew of one of the canoes, said to him: "Oho-take-tore, you will not get the body of the warrior with the beautiful name! Why did you only come at sunset?" Without saying a word Oho-take-tore took off his feather headpiece, put it back the wrong way round and left. The people said: "Oho-take-tore is surely angry! What will he do now?"*

131

There was war, you could say war over some roast meat with a mellifluous name.

Language still devours things, as well as people, no one knows this better than my uncle. Nor is he scared off by his own family.

Heinz Dembrowski drove me home from the dermatologists' conference. He asked me if I felt like working in an investment advisory capacity. But even before I could say yes we were interrupted, his car phone buzzed. He lifted the receiver: —Hello, he said, yes, good, fine, very good, I'll be home in twenty minutes. The way he said byeee, it could only have been his wife from whom he was now separated. But he phones her constantly, and now secretly because Sannchen forbids it. Renate, his wife, a head taller than he, also six years older, is bringing up his three sons in a beautiful farmhouse near Hamburg. I've observed Dembrowski on the phone a few times in the last two months, down at the beach restaurant, when he's talking to Renate or to his children. On one occasion, I was on the toilet, I heard him crying. I had to wait a long time in the washroom until he'd ended the phone conversation and was back outside sitting and laughing by Sannchen's deck chair. But he was wearing dark, nonreflective sunglasses.

That time he didn't say more about the investment business, but told me how important a good speech technique was for investment counseling. I took it as Dembrowski undoubtedly meant it, as a criticism of my pronunciation.

At that time, when for example I said gaaden, you could still detect the Hamburg harbor district. My uncle on the other hand always said: garrden, that suggested greenery, birds, solitary weeping willows, and a fence. Whereas gaaden sounds like a district in which there are no gardens.

Dembrowski took me to Ramlerstrasse (with only one m, the educated classes know why), stopped his red Jaguar outside house number 14, new building type 65, with those terraces like pulled-out concrete drawers. Dembrowski said he'd phone me in the course of the next few days, which he then didn't do.

We exchanged cards and he gave me the address of his elocution teacher, Mrs. Bellmann, who taught you more than just to speak clearly and melodiously, by the time she'd finished with you you were somebody else.

After making an appointment over the phone I called on Mrs. Bellmann, a former opera singer whose voice had gone flat at sixty, for which reason she gave elocution lessons. —A clear, ringing pronunciation, she said, is like a promise that what you say is true.

—You have to speak far to the front, separate the teeth, move the tongue, use the sounding-board in the forehead. *Where the west wind swells the water's waves.* Rest on the vowels, make pauses, stress according to meaning and heartbeat. The heartbeat is rhythm, that's all meter is, breath clusters, change of stress, changes in raising and lowering, insistent and restrained, loud and moderate, that already makes everything sound convincing. She reached for the day's paper: *Internationalism and financial liberalism in the marketplace attest to the genuinely European stature of Luxembourg.*

—Please, she said, say just once: genuinely European stature. No, she cut me short, the way you say genuinely European stature plays havoc with the intended meaning, if you're trying to convince someone to buy gold in Luxembourg.

—What do you actually sell, she said, why do you need the pronunciation?

—Life insurance, I deal in life insurance.

—Good, she said, but couldn't hide her disappointment that I wasn't taking a language course to sell the golden real estate of the Costa del Sol or three-meter-long turbine shovels out of titanium hardened steel, or shares in Siemens, or Shell, but only life insurance.

—But, she said, the way you say insurance, that's not insurance, that's no R, it sounds Arabic, a rasping in the throat, it makes one think of Qaddafi, and the "ance" at the end, frankly, it forecasts doom, it sounds like a fatal accident. Nobody'll want to take out insurance with you. There's something repressed, squashed in that immobile R in your pronunciation. Compare it to the uvular R, listen: Insurrrrance, that resounds, that convinces, that impresses. We know two ways of pronouncing R, which is the hardest to say of all the consonants. The rolled R and the uvular R. The rolled R is in the front, here on the teeth, try giving your tongue free rein, let it go over hill and dale: rrrrrrr. Then try pulling the R back along the gums with the tongue, she got up and accompanied the R on its journey into the throat with a graceful movement of her hand: rrrr . . . there it was, past the uvula, vanished in the throat.

—Please, she said and sat down, but it would be better for you to stand.

I tried the rolled R and the uvular R, and both were muffled and just as flat as my tongue was immobile and wooden: grgrgr. A croak.

Once, I'd just turned six, my uncle, the little wise fart

who was ten at the time, slapped my face, a loud, painful slap. Why? Because I'd confused me and I. Grandmother Hilde came and took me in her arms, wiped away my tears and snot with her apron and said: —It's all right, and to him: No need to hit him, he'll learn without being hit.

Not my uncle, they knocked everything into him: books under his arms during meals, don't fidget, sit straight, hold your fork straight, he had to sit there until his plate was empty.

As a child he'd been given a wooden truck, as he told my mother reproachfully on more than one occasion. His father had had it made by a carpenter who made models—it was wartime and you couldn't get anything. A beautiful small truck out of wood with which my uncle, he must have been four at the time, immediately began to play, only suddenly he wasn't playing but sitting on the floor tapping a corner of the loading platform. Clip, it went, clip. —What is it, his father asked, what's the matter?

—The truck wobbles. My little uncle's father lifted the truck onto the festive Christmas table, placed it between the branches of fir and the homemade gingerbread and tapped the loading platform. Yes, the truck wobbled. One of the wheels had been put on too high. It wobbled like a table with one leg too short.

—Well, said my little uncle's father, it's not too bad, be a good boy and go on playing. But my little uncle sat on the floor, tapped the loading platform, clip, it went, clip.

His father threatened to smack his fingers if he didn't stop fiddling. He should be grateful. Reproachfully my uncle tapped the loading area and made the truck tilt.

His father yelled. His mother tried to intervene. The lovely Christmas mood was shattered. After the holidays the toy truck was returned to the carpenter with a request to repair it. He moved the wheel a little. Now the truck tilted to the other side, though not quite as much. His father had to return to the front.

My little uncle stopped playing with the truck. When his mother said: —Give the car away, he gave the car away.

—Wouldn't have bothered you, my grandmother said to me.

—Exactly, said my mother.

That was considered typical of my little uncle, and when my mother said so there was always amazement in her voice, in my grandmother's too when she said to me: —It's good you're not like that.

On the other hand, my uncle wrote fervent essays, eighteen pages long and with more than forty mistakes. Yet he announced that he wanted to be a writer.

On a flight to Frankfurt to which the most successful life insurance salesmen had been invited to a weekend seminar, with cider and *Woman without a Shadow*, I found myself sitting between two men that looked as if they should be called Fatso and Thickhead (the thickhead was really thick and Fatso was gigantic). They were editors, evidently of the feature pages, literature department, from the way they talked about books and evaluating books. Unfortunately I couldn't find out from which paper they came. They were talking about something that was very radical, outrageously radical, something on the stage, something spoken—cannibalism. Above all it was radical.

At some point my uncle's name came into the conversation. I considered suggesting life insurance, perhaps one of them, perhaps neither of them was already insured. I could have said, excuse me, I overheard your conversation, that's my uncle you've just been talking about, as a child he used to tell stories about the Easter Islanders who devoted themselves with relish to cannibalism, something most ethnologists with their bad eurocentric conscience don't even want to mention. And yet its understandable, as man was the only large mammal on the island. Otherwise there were only rats. Fingers and toes were considered the really tasty bits, probably because they were so good to chew clean.

But then I realized it wasn't my uncle who'd written this cannibalism play. What they were saying about him—his ears should have been burning. To mention his name now, to identify myself as his nephew, would have been damaging to business. Nobody would have allowed themselves to be talked into life insurance by the nephew of an uncle who wrote like that, unless I'd said: —I know the person you're talking about, that's what my uncle's really like, though he's four years older, as a child I always had to correct his homework, he was so pedantic and obsessed in other respects but strangely enough not in spelling. Perhaps he was dyslexic. In which case, typical of him not to have taken out life insurance, not to have made any provision for his old age, which according to what I'm hearing you say would seem to be urgently needed. Incidentally according to some instructive statistics most dyslexics are uninsured. Allow me to ask if you have life insurance.

But suddenly the fat one said: Yeahthissonnofa . . . And the thick one said that someone had scratched his Porsche again. Then it was too late to come in about my uncle, and the sign to fasten seat belts had lit up. We were already landing in Frankfurt.

Stiletto heels

I can't leave it alone. I put the plastic bag back on my desk, untied it and picked out one of the larger pieces of wood. I thought the glyph of the eating singer might still be intact. But the glyph has been destroyed, only the hand of the eating singer is still recognizable on a somewhat larger fragment, naturally only to those who'd once seen the line drawing as a whole. For anyone else it's only three fine lines.

Britt left for Malaga early in the morning. She wants to do some shopping, curtain material, towels. But I suspect she wants to look for a wood restorer.

First thing early in the morning I went straight to my desk, turned on the laptop, and read what I'd written. In the next room our Moroccan cleaning woman cleaned, making the usual noise. She brought me a coffee, strong and almost unbelievably oversweetened. Everytime I ask myself how so little fluid can absorb so much sugar. A kind of coffee syrup. For three, four weeks I simply tipped the syrup out of the window until one day my room was overrun by tiny ants, in columns the creatures marched across the tiled floor, climbed the walls, one column crawled across the desk, another up the bookcase, probably they were looking for the source of the coffee syrup. Since then I pour the coffee down the toilet. But the ants have nested in the house. We've sprayed all kinds of insecticides, rubbed down surfaces with vinegar, and the Moroccan woman has wiped the floor with a vile smelling liquid chemical.

The creatures disappear for a day, then reappear, first one at a time, then more and more, coming as I can see now from tiny cracks between the tiles.

I'll have to wait until the noise of cleaning recedes, then I'll pour the coffee in the toilet. At first when the woman brought me the coffee I always thanked her enthusiastically, until one day she poured me a second cup, and then a third. Now I only indicate a restrained thank you by a slight, absent-minded nod. The Moroccan woman is missing the top half of her ears. Perhaps the result of ritual incision, like cutting the clitoris and penis. (I'd say it was to make gender unambiguous.)

But perhaps it was an accident. But I can't imagine any situation in which the halves of both ears could be torn off at the same time. Unless as a child she stuck her head in a tube or, like me, through an iron railing and then got pulled out backwards.

I pushed the remains of the bird man together, swept them with my hand over the edge of the desk into the plastic bag and put him back on the bookshelf with the reports of journeys to Easter Island.

I'd begun reading about Easter Island when we moved out of the basement apartment in Ramlerstrasse. An apartment in a new building, dry, no urine mold on the walls, but the rooms right-angular like boxes, the ceiling oppressively low.

I read then out of self-defense, and that's how it is to this day.

Britt at that time had a well-paid job as the second secretary in a wholesale florist's. There was hardly anything to do there. Now and then she had to take dictation. A dream job, Britt said, if you could read in peace and quiet during the day. But everytime the boss, a small sensitive Dutchman came into the room and saw her reading he said: —You must have a lot of time. Then he found some work for her: checking the files again, numbering the bills that had already been numbered with a different pay-code. So she had to read *Stern* or a book inside a boxfile she could quickly snap shut. Or in the mornings she'd chat with the boss' secretary. In the afternoon the secretary was always at the bank.

Otherwise Britt sat there looking out of the window onto the street, fortunately a lively shopping area. Time was measured by the sound in the stairwell of the elevator arriving and leaving, sometimes the slamming of the elevator door.

Still, on Saturdays Britt slept as if she were dead, as if all week she'd sawed logs, laid tiles, rolled cable drums, she said she was physically exhausted just from sitting around. If at least she could have left like the boss' secretary who had to go to the bank and spent entire afternoons there. Whenever Mr. Westerhuis came into the room and asked for her Britt would say, she's gone to the bank, and Mr. Westerhuis who'd already poured a pot of coffee into himself in the morning would say, —Ah good.

But why two secretaries, when there wasn't enough work to keep even one occupied? Britt just shrugged. Only Mr. Westerhuis, if anyone, knew that, but perhaps the Dutch flower-growing cooperative simply paid for two secretaries and these two posts were a part of Mr. Westerhuis's contract.

Britt only woke when it was almost midday, to then

rush out at the last minute and shop in a somnambulist state. And what she then bought and subsequently unpacked: several bags of sugar, but no rice, tins of tuna fish with onion rings instead of the cinnamon that had been promised Lolo to put on her rice pudding. While Britt wandered through the supermarket I cleaned the kitchen and bathroom.

At about two there was fish from the freezer, á la Bordelaise. In the afternoon just after four, immediately after doing the dishes, the ceiling that was low already slowly sank even lower, squeezed us, pressed us together, left us as if congealed in a compromised silence where everything got stuck, time in the clocks, dust in the air, thoughts in the head, and all I could do was carefully, very carefully draw deep breaths, or the silence would have torn me apart.

Outside the house in a small playground with a small dirty sandbox children went wild, having been put out by parents copulating, getting drunk, quarreling, or just glued to the T.V. in their concrete boxes. From below came the shrieks of the kicked, scratched, hit, battered, all those who twisted each others' arms, tore out hair, threw sand into the eyes, crushed fingers, the shriek of those rejected on a Saturday afternoon. *Divina Commedia, Canto VI.* (Yes, naturally I'm showing off!) To begin with I always rushed to the window if any one voice shrieked louder, more desperately, because I thought the voice shrieking so pitifully, so unconsolably was Lolo's, but gradually I learned to distinguish the shrieks, although shrieks are far harder to distinguish than laughter. I think the species recovers by shrieking, the individual by laughter.

I learned to ignore the shrieks, even the shrill, single,

desperate ones and decided only to go to the window when the ambulance siren began to wail down below.

Now and then when the sun shone we drove in our Opel Kadett (I can understand why no one wants to drive this box except the few brave proletarians that are left who don't give a shit for esthetics) to Schulau on the Elbe, to the docks. National anthems distorted by the wind, dipping of the flag to voices screeching over loudspeakers, gross registered tonnage and destinations: Amsterdam, Recife, Hong Kong.

Sometimes I'd then give a passing thought to the Swede who'd fathered me and disappeared, whom I'd only seen once, and I'd wonder where he could be. Was he still alive?

If it rained, and it often rains in Hamburg, we sat in our slots on our blue ribbed sofa, on the ribbed blue chairs, in the midst of huge sprays of flowers, tulips, narcissi, begonias, roses, huge, small, yellow, red, white, also carnations, that stood in the room in vases, bottling jars, milk bottles, water jugs. Every Friday afternoon Britt brought bunches of them from the office, cut flowers from Dutch greenhouses, mostly tulips, parrot tulips, red, white, salmon colored garden tulips, the leaves firm and vivid as if made of plastic, but strangely already by Saturday afternoon the firm stems had become limp, the blossoms drooped, the blue and red, the red and white striped, the yellow and blue turned pale at the edges, turned into a light brown with rosy spots and by the next morning, on Sunday, they hung dull and heavy in their pots, vases, glasses, jugs as if they were waiting until they could finally drop all their petals, triangular capsules, filaments. But they couldn't. Britt claimed they were fresh flowers, but they hung so limply and tiredly, and still didn't drop a petal. Possibly they'd been sprayed with some secret substance, perhaps they were only a special Dutch hothouse variety, flowers that simply didn't drop their petals, that stayed in a half-wilted state forever. Neither Britt nor I wanted to throw away these flowers that only looked sick, but never dead.

Britt talked about her colleague, the boss' secretary, who had a relationship with a liquor producer. At weekends he came to Hamburg from a small town in Lower Saxony, went with her for a meal to the "Four Seasons," then he drove her to the attic apartment paid for by him, threw her onto the bed, tore at, ripped off her tights, but then, having torn open the artificial silk gusset, he'd suddenly cry: —I can't, I can't, and she'd have to throttle him first, and then with the lack of oxygen contrary to all medical logic his penis rose, slowly, with an effort, just a little. These weekends were exhausting, as exhausting as the whole past week had been and the week to come would be. Sometimes on Mondays she'd show Britt the marks on her legs, not deep dramatic scratches, just red tender stripes. And that was it again.

—Hold me tight!

We'd lie beside each other, Britt's head on my chest, and I'd tell her about the studios I'd seen during the week. Because, following the advice of Wesendonk, I'd become a fisher of artistic souls. I looked up the addresses in *Who's Who*. I've seen many—it's a peculiarity of artists to want people to visit them in their studios. I'd seen how they work with felt and fat, glass and granite, plastic and aluminum, how they mold steel, polish wood, break up granite blocks with jack hammers, artists who wanted to put up golden needles in front of the Reichstag in Berlin, millimeters thin and 360 meters high, who wanted to wrap up, tear down, blow up buildings, artists who drew under a magnifying glass, welded in asbestos suits, worked with jack hammers, who on canvas roasted infants dipped in mother's milk in electric cookers, who painted with marten-hair brushes, artists who stood at the easel in a suit wearing a collar and tie without ever getting a speck of paint on the lapels, others on the other hand stood in their studios in gym shoes and jeans like oily stalagmites. While I exchanged my briefcase made of some synthetic material, deciding it looked so bourgeois, for a well-worn casual briefcase from the twenties in crocodile skin, they continued to paint, to model, and those who lived dangerously next to their tanks of compressed air or chiselled under stones that weighed tons were less anxious than the minimalists (the most anxious, let it be said here, were the informalists). Those who earned the most were also anxious. The ones who painted a picture in two weeks for which they got 200,000 or 300,000 marks. The baldy with a house in Santa Cruz de Tenerifa, a small 300-square-meter apartment in Madrid, studio in New York, Gramercy Park, a small studio in Prague. What to do with the dough? I offered life insurance and I thought, you have to help these people invest their money, you simply have to take it off them. You have to become a concept artist on the stock exchange, someone who can pole-vault over cycles, who accelerates capital, a master of chaos. These were people who had investment problems, who thought about how to reduce their taxes. Children came in here, the legitimate and the illegitimate, even those that didn't exist yet, already allowed for in tax declarations like a foetus still swimming peacefully and contented in the amniotic fluid of a student. Clearly it's going to cost money. But an apartment one owned could be signed over. Life insurance had to be taken out for the mother and child.

The constructivist suddenly got a very busy look about the mouth. A woman in a bright red leather suit had come into the studio. —My wife, said the master. A black-haired woman with night-blue mascara and the congealed smile of a television watcher. The man addressed me in English: —That is my wife looking for a new network-art. You understand? He introduced me to his wife as a Danish gallery owner, just arrived from Copenhagen. —Which gallery, the wife asked. I didn't have a Danish name ready, so I said: —Kierkegaard. —Ahhh, she says and goes through the studio in her captivating open dress, an angel with a rather full whiskey glass in her hand, about thirty I decided, perhaps forty when you got closer, the jacket to the suit was cut so deep that you saw her breasts, amazingly firm, but the hands were wrinkled and had yellow-brown spots, she was probably around fifty.

Shortly before my arrest I was in Cologne at an opening. A young wild one to whom I'd sold a life insurance policy six years ago. Then he was just beginning to do business, since then he sends me invitations to his exhibitions from every part of the world. I climbed the grey-blue granite steps to a gallery and coming from below slowly saw, on the granite floor in the exhibition space, all the men's shoes in elk and horse leather, the trousers of suits, next to them the first thing that hit me in the eye (yes, hit), all the black-stockinged legs on high heels, above them the signal-like red, the lime green, the metallic blue of silk dresses, in them (covering them would be absolutely the wrong description) the stunningly beautiful, the expensive, the unaffordable wives who collected art for their extremely busy husbands, they stood there fragile on long slim legs jacked up on narrow heels, carefully balancing, knees straightened. The Truffaut films ought to be analyzed from the point of view of the depiction of women's legs so one can learn something about the sexual structure of our society—because high-heeled shoes don't just make the legs seem longer, which draws out the relish of anticipating the place where they meet, they also make the walk more upright and graceful, no shuffling like in unfortunate frog-like health shoes, but a walking paradox. Because what should approach quietly on tiptoe actually arrives with a sharp pecking, look, says this pecking, look, says every step, while the high heels make clear—the more emphatically the higher they are—that a woman on them can't run away, a highly elaborate surrender comparable to the small bound feet of the Chinese that not only turns Mecklenburg cloddishness (which naturally also exists in China, the so-called little Cantonese foot) into something delicate, but also indicates a quiet, constant, enduring readiness, if involuntary, and from childhood the legs are already destined for this, they incorporate pure submission, and high heels signal two things: passive endurance but also active resistance, the peak of pleasure, torment, a kick with the terrible stiletto heel.

The artists too wore double-breasted, well-tailored executive suits, from the dress code you knew the

Deutsche and the Dresden Banks had also gone into the art business.

A sculptor who knocks the cores out of massive granite blocks said to me, —Of course a granite wall can fall on your head. Then it's goodnight, Irene.

That's the professional risk. Still, he didn't want to take out life insurance. You don't look at a cored granite block and think: I must change.

Only the value of the cored granite block changes, according to demand, and as everyone knows that can be stimulated.

Books under the arms!

—We have to get out of here, I said to Britt on the bed in our council apartment, I'd rather be in a basement with urine mold than in this concrete box. Her dream: a house, a garden, going barefoot on the lawn in the morning, growing roses. Britt always wanted to grow a special rose of her own (which she's now doing). Her mother had tried to do this in a small front garden full of dogshit, but had failed. Next door our neighbor was belching again. And in the apartment above Mr. and Mrs. Bäumler, he a technical draftsman, she a saleswoman, were moaning again. Dull pathetic moans, not like next door when Mattes, a telephone technician who sat on his balcony in a t-shirt at weekends, went to the toilet, his thundering farts sounded thoroughly joyful in our bleak house in this district full of concrete, deserted by the briefcase carriers in the morning and only repopulated again late in the afternoon.

Sometimes I ran through the streets in the late afternoon after the evening meal, after the day's work during which I'd poked into all those lives, evening after evening I had to really jog all that talk out of my system. In the meantime I'd called on and insured almost all the artists, at any rate those who were in a position to pay for life insurance. A clientele rich in variety, quite in contrast to most of the independent management consultants and lawyers I later called on to sell life insurance.

Not the commonplace worries and joys here, as with magazine subscribers, the trapped sciatic nerve, the husband who'd begun drinking again, the installment that couldn't be paid, the baby that screamed all night—the life insurance salesman has to listen to his client's views on life. Insurance, dealing as it does with the possibility of death, is therefore about life. Suddenly you have to think about yourself, about the success or failure of your life's plan. What had you once wanted? What had you wanted to be? What had you become? To blame for the failure (in the following order) were: circumstances, the wife, the children, the parents, the school. You hadn't turned out to be the person you wanted to be—and this was the one you now should insure for a lot of money.

On completing the life insurance contract an inventory would be made, and behold, even when as a notary or a doctor or a management consultant you took home 20,000 monthly, life seemed to be the graveyard of your desires. Desires are unfortunately not always as concrete as the socialism-damaged Dembrowski would have them—good eating, compact disc unit, Sannchen, fast car, nice house, holidays on Virgin Gorda or in Surabaya—because mostly there's an implacable desire to be someone other than the person you are, though who that other person is you don't know. But someone different, different, different!

And naturally immortal.

I jogged, as almost every evening, through the new housing district to the district with villas that bordered it, past the lit windows. The desire to walk, to slowly come to my senses, to become physically aware of myself as I walked, the smell of damp earth, a bird startled from a bush, a jarring growl, the barking of a dog, hoarse and dark, a voice on one of the gloomy balconies overgrown with geraniums, laughter in the distance, the metallic clank of trains at the freight depot, to linger over one's thoughts, that means to hold them fast, to let them sink in.

On one occasion I put into practice what I often imagined on these nighttime walks. I got onto a train at the main station, without looking, without listening where it was going, simply to get away, never mind where. For a moment, for a good ten minutes a journey without a goal, until the conductor came and I had to pay for a ticket. Where's the train going? To Basel. All right, one to Basel. And there it was in someone else's face, the amazement you'd hoped to feel yourself. The journey after that was as routine as I might have supposed. Snow was falling outside, fine lines in the light flitting by. In Basel in the evening I phoned Britt. A crazy impulse, a whim. An expensive whim as all the hotels were full because of a conference and I could only find a room at the most expensive hotel there. Britt said, —Give yourself time, as if I had to solve some extremely complicated problem in Basel. But it was quite simple, I wanted to get back as quickly as possible.

—Tomorrow, I said, I'm coming back on the first train.

In the evening I jogged through Basel Old Town, and it was hardly different from running through the streets of Hamburg suburbs.

What is boredom?

You wait, but don't know what it is you're waiting for.

Perhaps I was striving to get nearer to whatever it was. Striving, until striving became the natural thing to do, there was no longer any struggle and thoughts roamed lightly wherever they pleased—but after two hours I was back in the apartment from which I'd fled.

Naturally it didn't have to do with the apartment, as I'd imagined at the time. It also didn't have to do with Lolo, who at that time was loud and rebellious, shrieked, cried, rolled on the floor, it wasn't even the inflated stories I had to hear as an insurance salesman, it was hard to define, an oppressive listlessness that drove me from the house and on these nightly walks, a listlessness, more precisely, an aversion to the idea that you wait, and don't know for what. An aversion that let up—so I see it today—once I began reading every available travel book about the Pacific. Instead of running about in the suburbs I sat at home and read.

My uncle had read to me from Thor Heyerdahl's book, I must have been six at the time. He was rehearsing. I was his audience. I had to sit on a chair. He put another chair on the living room table, got up on the table, sat himself down on the chair under the living room tasseled lampshade, and sitting there like the pope read the bit where a wave washes the parrot overboard.

Heyerdahl's journey was meant to prove the theory that Polynesia, all the small islands and atolls that lie like oases in a desert of water, was settled from America. I can still hear my uncle talking about the Pacific desert. He told everyone about it at the time, my grandmother, my mother, Mrs. Eisenhart, Mrs. Brücker: how hundreds of years ago people had set out on rafts they'd built themselves, woven and made without iron.

I've seen Heyerdahl's raft. It's why I flew to Oslo three years ago. It's in a dimly-lit room and gives the impression, though only bound and woven, of being completely stable and safe. But the tree trunks, as I'd already heard in amazement from my uncle, soaked up so much water during the month's long voyage that a shaving cut from them to Heyerdahl's horror slowly sank into the ocean.

Heyerdahl's theory—I've since become convinced— is wrong. Even without taking into consideration the linguistic similarities between the Polynesian and the Indian languages, countless cultivated plants on the Polynesian islands are of Asiatic origin, therefore don't come from the American mainland. The plants, on the basis of Heyerdahl's theory, would have to have been brought there from Asia only after all the islands had been settled, but which, according to Heyerdahl's premise, wouldn't have been possible because the winds and the ocean's currents were in the opposite direction.

I ask myself if my uncle, that louse, took any further

151

interest in Easter Island. Did he read the latest research?

His mother, my great-aunt, once told me on a visit to our apartment with its weekend wilting tulips—she hummed like a spinning top with pride in her son—that he was in Paris studying ethnology and going to lectures by Lévi-Strauss. Then the name meant nothing to me. Today I ask myself whether my uncle or even Lévi-Strauss (I'm quite conceited) would know why Lolo is called Lolo.

I think my little uncle couldn't do anything except dream his way out of the frozen stillness of his parents' living room to a warmer mental climate. Because at his place you sat at the heavy oak table with its damask tablecloth, napkins, knives, forks, spoons laid out, plates on plates. Everyone in gloomy silence, my uncle with two books under his arms. —Sit up straight, said his father, don't fidget! Who wouldn't want to go to countries where you dance, go wild and have fun?

What interested my little uncle, and about which he pestered the adults, was: Where did the giant statues on Easter Island come from? These giants carved out of tufa? My uncle believed they were the remains of a powerful kingdom that had sunk into the sea.

A childish thought. But the discrepancy between the powerful stone figures, the wonderful wood-carvings, the development of an individual script and the smallness of this island with a population of at most 9,000 really is astonishing. One always thinks territory and population need to be a certain size to achieve such things, and that there would have to be cultural stimulus from outside. Easter Island proves the opposite. Another discrepancy is that between this evidence and the cultural level of the islanders when the Europeans came. The Europeans destroyed a great deal, but some catastrophic event had already destroyed the high culture before the appearance of the Europeans. The island's inhabitants were fairly pathetic creatures who themselves didn't know how they'd come by these stone colossi. All-powerful gods or ancestors must have planted them.

They were, according to the missionaries' descriptions, thoroughly peculiar little people with a remarkable fondness for head coverings. There was almost nothing they didn't try to put on their heads. Missionary Eyraud tells of the half-pumpkins they wore on their heads, and the bird skeletons. One man had put two jugs on his head, one rammed into the other. Another had pulled an old lace-up boot over his head. It was also for this that they stole in such an unrestrained, addicted way from the Europeans, they were mad for their hats, the tricornes, the lacquered sailors' hats, the floppy hats, and the ship's caps, to say nothing of the little caps of the missionaries. The missionaries wrote their reports without asking themselves how this hat mania had come about. My theory: here was the first sign of luxury consumerism. And luxury consumerism exists in every culture, even within the norms of prohibition, of asceticism it still has a shadow existence. The huge ruffs, the baggy breeches, the laced frilled shirts of the baroque were the extraordinary head decoration on Easter Island.

My theory again: the same needs that lay at the basis of this head covering also drove the islanders to create the monumental stone figures that also wore a kind of stone top hat, the *pukao*. Why?

The figures stand—or once stood, because most had fallen as if in a hideous massacre. Colossal legless cripples. They stood with their back to the sea, staring at the slope of Rano-raraku from which they'd been chiselled. One has to imagine the effort, the incredible work involved in hacking these colossi out of the tufa with obsidian axes, then transporting them over hundreds of meters to set them up at the place intended for them. One figure called Paro is 7.80 meters high and weighs 80 tons. Crowned as if by a top hat 1.80 meters high and 2.40 meters wide. Another still unfinished figure measures 21 meters. How were these figures moved? How were they stood upright? There was almost no wood on the island.

On the island no essential challenging activity mobilized energy over a longer period, no area needed to be watered, no bogs drained, no roads built and no fortifications, as there was no external enemy. So the only way left to work off superfluous energy was by waging cannibalistic wars and setting up stone colossi in the landscape. At the same time as the tribes fought amongst themselves and slaughtered each other the attempt was made to overcome death—since stone colossi represent the dead—with mad hubris setting up stone monuments against the transitory. A means, I suspect, of conquering death and triumphing over silence, the expression of a gargantuan feeling for life and at the same time a monumental dialogue with death. To understand the meaning of these figures in the death cult one would need to correctly interpret their arrangement. Which research hasn't been able to do. Research says they stand there like people, by chance, in sheer disorder.

But perhaps order consists of just this disorder, chance, chaos.

I've a plan in front of me of all the stone figures on the island (and of course I'd like to see them one day), where they still stand, where they were left while being transported, also those that were just carved out of the tufa that lie half-finished in their caves and crypts, like the dead, half-chiseled as if they were lifting themselves out of the rock. In one cave there must be a half-finished figure an incredible 15 meters long, the stone hammers still at its feet as if they'd been put down during a break, to have a rest. Other figures have been left lying in mid-transport. Why? What strange inexplicable event halted the work on the figures as if in some fairy tale?

I lay next to Britt in that concrete cell and heard her breathing. Through the Venetian blinds fell fine strips of light from the street lamp outside that made it necessary to pull down the blinds even in summer. So we lay in a sticky heat. If I'd said I can't sleep I'm sure Britt would have replied wide-awake. —Nor can I. Then I would have had to explain why I couldn't get to sleep, and I wouldn't have been able to lie. But how explain, how describe what defies description, the anxiety for which there seems to be no reason? You look into yourself and see no reason.

I'd have had to tell her about the stone figures (which left her and leave her cold) which she knew from illustrations, the black colossal heads with the arrogant, even contemptuous expression about the mouth, the arrogant melancholy. Anyone who can look into himself like that without flinching, without quickly turning away or escaping into some activity, is strengthened and can look on everything with composure.

Strawberry flavor

In the evening I drove to the tennis club. I wanted to take Lolo, who played squash by the tennis courts, with me in the car. But she didn't want to, she preferred to go on the moped. She hates my car which, to be honest, is a dream of my youth: a Jaguar. The last time I visited her my mother also refused to get into the car, I already drove the same model in Hamburg, but in cream. The car was impounded and sold long ago, the proceeds shared among the victims, at any rate among those that came forward, because not all the victims did come forward.

After my escape I bought myself a new one, the same model. In six months Lolo has only twice come with me in this dark blue Jaguar. Once when I had to take her to the hospital in Marabella because of a septic tooth, and once when her bike had a flat tire. Otherwise she refuses to get into the car. She goes with Britt in her VW Golf now and then when it's raining, but she won't get into my car. She'd rather go on foot. She'd rather get soaked in the rain. When I want to take her with me, she says: —Don't worry, dad, nothing's nicer than being in the rain. It's a blow each time she says no, I see how she tries to hide her low opinion, her contempt for the car, how she makes up excuses not to have to get into it. Excuses in order not to hurt my feelings. She treats me, as far as this car's concerned, as if I were sick.

Naturally she knows how much I like it; what childish pleasure it gives me to sit at the steering wheel made of polished and varnished mahogany, to feel the rose-wood-covered dashboard, the soft red upholstered leather on which it's cool to sit even on the hottest days. But now that I've seen the revulsion, the contempt she has for this car, which incidentally she already showed in Hamburg, I can no longer take such uninhibited pleasure in this dark blue Jaguar.

For whom did I do all this, I think to myself, if not for Lolo? And she, of all people, refuses what's offered. She wears second-hand rags, the cheapest jeans, the most hideous shoes imported from East Germany or Poland, lead grey, ghastly to look at. Britt also talks to Lolo about it, considering it altogether too scruffy, at any rate when she wears her threadbare, washed-out, dishcloth of a Breton fisherman's shirt day after day. In the evening she puts the shirt in the washing machine, then hangs it up, and thanks to the dry warm climate can wear it again the next day. In Hamburg as a school-girl she was active in a Greenpeace group. Stock Exchange: God, no! Shares—all she does is shake her head, she smiles, she says: —Too much! She says: I'd like to go to the Antarctic, marine biology. I've not the slightest doubt that she'll achieve what she wants. In a few years she'll be sitting in some research station a good two meters under the ice, and spend the winter there. That's how she is.

She drove ahead of me on the bike. Anybody watching us must have thought here was a man in the best lascivious Jaguar-years of his life chasing a young girl. The two squash rackets were on the carrier at the back. She doesn't play tennis though she learned when she was eight, presumably because I play it and Dembrowski plays it. Not because or since we were charged, on the contrary she thought that was fantastic, she bragged about it at school, no, she didn't like the types with whom I used to play, the trendy yuppies, the bankers, the business people. So instead she plays squash with wild enthusiasm.

Driving from the garden I'd kept watch for the green Fiat. No car anywhere in sight. I wasn't surprised.

Dembrowski was already on the court, he'd taken out his racket, the spare, and the balls. Sannchen was sitting on the bench in brief, wide-cut shorts. She didn't play tennis. She'd crossed her long suntanned legs, her feet stretched out like in a fifties photo ad.

I asked Dembrowski if he'd noticed anything.

—What?

—Anyone outside the garden? A car?

—No, nothing, he said. The public prosecutor's got better things to do than chase us.

—Listen, I said, my uncle wants to write about us.

—So, he said. But then, as he held the racket to his ear to test the tension, he began to look thoughtful, even suspicious.

—Why would he want to do that?

—No idea, but I know it from my mother. He's paid her a visit and asked questions.

—Just like that, out of the blue? Did you talk to him?

I might have guessed it. Dembrowski assumed I'd told my uncle something, he probably thought we'd made a deal, I'd tell our story and my uncle would write it down and then we'd share the fat proceeds fifty-fifty and there he'd be, Dembrowski, depicted as the money-grubber, the unscrupulous fleecer, the man with the criminal energy.

Dembrowski industriously reads academic works on monetary theory, he reads specialist books about management, motivation, successful managers. All books in huge editions. For which reason he has a false impression of what literature can earn.

We warmed up. I hit the balls to him with a flat drawn-out backhand and he returned them with a strained backhand holding the racket with both hands.

He can play a hard game. But today quite a few of his balls went into the net. It was quite clear he was playing without concentrating and gradually getting into a rage because of it. He was already red in the face. He stared at his racket as if it was giving him a bad day. He tried to concentrate on the ball but he was standing there much too tense and the balls kept going into the net.

Dembrowski is a good tennis player. We're almost equal, only he wins more often in tournaments. He's got an almost fanatical drive, which I lack, that reaches into the racket, into the ground. He runs and returns the most unbelievable balls, literally ploughs up the place so that afterwards the clay courts need to be freshly rolled. The groundsman at the Hamburg tennis club once said when he saw the churned-up court, — God almighty, you must be playing with spikes on your shoes.

Dembrowski had wanted to play golf and during the period when he sold Russian officers' coats to Hamburg society women he'd applied for membership in the club on the Falkensteiner Ufer, but was turned down despite being sponsored by two golf club members whose wives went round in Red Army coats.

Dembrowski always returned to the subject of this rejection and explained it to himself like this: the top thousand in Hamburg had a fine ear for the working or peasant class. In him they'd immediately detected an East German cousin. The best made-to-measure suit, the most expensive silk shirt, the best handmade shoes couldn't hide the odor of the Saxonian dialect, which he hated and combated like bad breath.

Also during the trial when he was explaining how he'd stepped into stockbroking (he literally said: stepped into) Dembrowski got onto the subject of this rejection by the golf club. That's how he'd got to know a few other gentlemen active in stockbroking, among them some who also hadn't been accepted into the Falkenstein Golf Club. Dembrowski got lost in the details of the rejection, every time he scratched at the subject his memories burst open like a wound, he talked about prejudice, about cliques, even about sectarianism (a word from some GDR youth course in the far distant past). The judge, a truly patient man, began to flick through the files, the pensioners whispered, the public prosecutor rolled his ball-point pen backwards and forwards with his finger. Dembrowski had lapsed into dialect as he talked about how hard it had been finding land for a new golf club of his own, how much time it had taken to persuade farmers, to convince mayors (the word bribe rings in my ears), here Dr. Amelung tapped lightly on the table with his ball-point pen. Dembrowski checked himself, talked about a speculator, a broker who was a member of the newly-founded Association of Hamburg Friends of Golf and who'd offered him a job as investment counselor for the brokerage firm of Osborn & Partner, with branches in Hamburg,

New York, London. At last Dembrowski could talk economics, his favorite topic, comparing the socialist planned economy with the capitalist economy. Because the stock exchange, which only exists in the latter, is the motor of the economy and capital the fuel, whereas if you seek a comparison under socialism you have to think of a donkey, an obstinate skinny donkey that you need to beat to get it to move, or else tie a bundle of hay in front of its nose.

In contrast the stock exchange and speculation accommodate three basic drives, gambling, adventure, and because the accumulation of property is a part of this, a third basic drive, the striving for profit—which amounts to a unique anthropological combination of drives. This investment of money, its doubling or halving, the tension bound up with change combined with the willingness to take risks is the stuff of in-di-vid-u-al initiative, competition, that's the impetus that drives everything forward, a competitive race. Whereas socialism only advances people with foot problems, a system for pensioners, old and young, badly paid, and under Real Socialism even the wheelchairs are uncomfortable and you have to struggle to push them by hand.

Dembrowski wasn't speaking just as an informed economist, a practicing businessman who'd taken a look at aspects of the market as well as the stock exchange, he was speaking—and this gave him his persuasive power—as an experienced citizen of Karl-Marx-Stadt. —Communism can't work, he said. In a quite fundamental way it can't work. And why not? You only need look at people on the stock exchange, everyone with a phone at his ear: Tokyo, Chicago,

London. Are rates rising or falling, is the dollar rising or falling, an order from the Spanish postal service—laying cables, a modern telephone network—to be placed with Siemens, inside information, then get rid of ITT especially if Siemens makes a bid in Buenos Aires for a contract to extend the telephone network, the German managers are better educated, speak Spanish, have read Cortázar unlike the Americans who still expect their clients to speak English to them. And the next day Siemens shares do in fact rise, 60 points right away, we're away, that's movement, that's action! (said Dembrowski, his Saxonian pronunciation showing through his English).

—Compare this to a session at the Ministry for Foreign Trade, permission to export new drills, but on long-term credit. The drills aren't bad because the manufacturers, east and west, are the best anywhere, but the bureaucrats at the Ministry for Foreign Trade sit at their tables, in front of them plates of ham and sausage, coffee, real coffee, brandy, and cigarettes, Caro, black tobacco, Stalin's revenge, and then more brandy, there they are in those shirts, those nylon skins with the buttonholes bursting open that cut into their paunches, their hips rolls of fat, waistbands under their bellies, great calving heaps of lard only held together by belts made of synthetic material, mmm . . . yes, comrades, they say and then again mmm . . . yes, credit, we'll have to check, have to ask someone higher up, and that someone higher up has to ask someone higher up than him, and then there's someone higher up still, and then right at the top there's someone, only he doesn't know if the drills can be delivered or not, and so the one at the top passes it back to the one just below, and from there to the subordinates and they pass it to those that are subordinate to them, and then three weeks later they're all back together in the same room, the same calving bellies, the same sandwiches, the same glasses with the same vodka that's really good, sixty proof, and the shirts stuffed with bellies again say mmm . . . yes, we'll have to see, mmm . . . yes, we'll have to ask, but you've asked already, mmm . . . yes, but this is something new, can we allow credit, we'll have to ask higher up, and so up it goes up again and then back down until the contracts have long been given to a Swedish, a West German, or a Japanese firm.

—Communism can't work, says Dembrowski, and the court listens patiently whereas I've already heard it all many times, and that's a reason why one finally can't bear people one's known for a long time who often repeat themselves. I could have done it in his voice: Communism can't work because in fact everyone has quite specific desires and pursues these desires with the obstinacy of a beaver that gnaws down even the thickest alders, he'll work himself into the ground for these desires, work until he has a heart attack, one person wants to go to the Bermudas, another wants a Porsche, another a beautiful blonde with long legs, another a mulatto woman, one wants children, the other doesn't, or wants a Ferrari, a trip round the world, wants to go to Rome, South Africa, Iceland, or just wants to make money and will work himself to death getting it. And then the bureaucrat planners come and divide the goods, toothpaste in two flavors, peppermint and sweet woodruff. But I don't like peppermint, don't like sweet woodruff either, when I clean my teeth I am totally perverse and insist on an intense strawberry flavor. As a child I loved strawberries with a passion, with milk and sugar, or freshly picked, well, we all want the flavors that remind us of childhood, that's why communism can't work, it doesn't adapt to demand, it doesn't take into consideration the minuscule and yet colossal difference between the taste of wild woodruff and the taste of strawberries, you're told what to eat, with what to clean your teeth, to wipe your ass, no freedom of choice, no freedom to decide what you want to do or don't want to do, therefore also what you want to produce, a bureaucrat sits on his ass and decides what you should smell, taste, read, what you drink, what you eat. But at the same time this asshole bureaucrat shops in a shop that has goods from the West and cultivates his own tastes. So you get a crippling couldn't-care-less attitude, cars that are anti-style, two-cylinder—that says it all—with gears that drop out when you turn a bend, doctors who apathetically cut out your appendix and leave scars as if you'd been struck with a sword, here (every time he then pulls up his silk shirt and pulls down his waistband), broilers grilled as dry as the Gobi Desert, beer that tastes of dregs, bread like foam rubber. That's how you get a society of apathetic people.

Compare that to the free play of the market economy.

I'd easily won the first set 6 to 2 against Dembrowski. Sannchen only picked the balls up for Dembrowski when he scored. When she bent over I could see those two half moons in her wide-cut shorts. I don't know for whom she was showing them, she should have known they left me cold, and Dembrowski couldn't see them the way she was bending. Then she'd sit down again and arrange her legs. As she was wearing non-reflective glasses you couldn't tell whether she was following the game, which was a good one, or not. I don't think she was. She showed very little participation. Or rather, none. To begin with the game was excellent, at any rate my playing. My returns came hard, neatly placed, I'd won the first game of the second set when I saw the man standing behind the fence. A man with reddish-blonde hair who for a moment made you think of Boris Becker. But then the thought shot through me that this was the man who'd been sitting in the car, who for one morning had watched our house from it. Or was I mistaken? After all I'd only seen the man through binoculars. The man sat there and paid attention to the game. I clearly saw how, unlike Sannchen, he followed the balls, slightly turning his head from side to side. I made one mistake after another, I simply lost my rhythm while Dembrowski was totally successful, a ball from the left sideline where I'd driven Dembrowski came back as a craftily-aimed return that I shoveled into the net. Then the man even applauded. The sweat was burning my eyes. When Dembrowski had won the set and we were standing at the net and I was wiping away the sweat, I asked him if he'd ever seen the man over there. I was just cautiously saying: —He's watching us, when Dembrowski looked over at him from beneath his bright white fleecy towel with which he was drying off, and said: —No.

—I think he was the man in the car parked outside our house.

—What do you mean, I think?

—I only saw him through binoculars.

165

—Rubbish, he's a tennis freak or he wouldn't have applauded my shots.

During the third set Sannchen picked up almost all Dembrowski's balls, while I had to pick mine up myself.

I quickly and totally lost the set. I sent the ball flying in the most unbelievable way, and always in the direction where the man was sitting. Once like a beginner I even sent a ball over the high fence. Sannchen laughed out loud. The man picked up the ball and threw it back to me over the wire fence.

—Gracias, I said, but he only nodded.

—Tomorrow, said Dembrowski, tomorrow evening we'll have another game, I'll give you a chance to have your revenge, but please play properly and with your eye on the ball.

When we said goodbye Sannchen blew me a kiss.

What disturbs me about my car, almost more even than Lolo's refusal, is that Dembrowski also drives a Jaguar. That his is burgundy red doesn't make it any easier.

In the evening Britt came back from Malaga. She had in fact found someone who could repair the wood figure. A man who specialized in repairing picture frames, especially the repair of Picasso frames.

—And he can live off that?

—Yes. What's more, the man knew Picasso. Used to repair his frames.

But I didn't want this figure to be restored. The broken pieces could only have been replaced by a synthetic material, and some were missing because our Moroccan cleaning woman had thrown them away. The figure would have become something different even if it had been possible to preserve an outward resemblance, it would have been smaller, more bent. It just wouldn't be the branch that had found its way from Alaska through the Pacific and been cast up on Easter Island.

I could see Britt's disappointment. She'd made the trip for nothing, because naturally she hadn't found the curtain material, at any rate not the one she was looking for. That she'd only find in a decorator's shop in Paris.

—I think, I said, I've seen the man again.

—What man?

—The one in the car outside the house.

—Where?

—He watched us playing tennis.

No one can get as many shades of meaning out of Oh God as Britt. She can say it lightly or very sharply or, like now, with a hint of laughter that has nothing forced about it but expresses her speechlessness at my suspicion.

—Didn't you recognize him?

—No, at any rate not for sure. I only saw him through binoculars. But he had reddish blonde hair.

—Yes, she said, one of the many Swedish tennis coaches here.

—Perhaps.

Even Dr. Stein came here in winter for tennis coaching. It was with Stein I won my tennis laurels.

Taking Wesendonk's advice, as a life insurance salesman I'd promptly joined a tennis club and although many, especially women, had to wait a year, Stein had taken me on immediately.

Stein, with a degree in philosophy (*Nietzsche, Thought without Beginning or End*), was a lecturer who, these being the days when chairs everywhere were still held by Marxism-preaching professors of the '68 reforms, had to earn a living coaching tennis. Go to the net, yes, nearer, no, don't pull the racket, push it forward, the harder and faster your opponent hits, the harder and faster the balls come back. Do the illogical thing, the unexpected. Tennis is constructive-destructive. You're trying to make your game by destroying the other's game. There are rules but the variations are endless, ultimately it's an endless game. Look carefully at the ball and then at your opponent's reaction, observe how he runs, how he handles the racket, does he slam the ball at your feet or does he hit it to make you run, then work out your position and stroke, then eyes back to the ball, and nowhere else. There's hardly a sport in which you're so alone, in which you're so at the mercy of your strengths and weaknesses. Your ability, your self-confidence, your hesitation, the condition you're in that day. No wind you can blame, no horse that's having a bad day, nothing's more ridiculous after a bad shot than to look at your racket, nothing more stupid than turning to look at a ball that was inside the line, or arguing with a referee about a ball.

—Björn Borg, yes, he said, McEnroe, painful, as for Nastase, don't even talk about it.

Later I was able to tell Stein about Nastase's game which, as a result of getting a bonus from the company as the year's best life insurance salesman, I'd seen at Wimbledon.

Nastase played against Patterson, a well-behaved, dry New Zealander who played perfectly. After losing two sets Nastase was also hopelessly behind in the third set. The outcome was actually already clear. Patterson wanted to make his serve the match point, then suddenly Nastase interrupts the game. He points to the green tarpaulin bordering the court, a few spectators are lying under it looking out. He feels his game is being disturbed. He protests to the referee. Stewards are called. The spectators squatting behind the tarpaulin are removed. Ball boys tug the tarpaulin back in place. The game continues.

Nastase's disappeared.

Suddenly Patterson's alone on the court. He's got the racket in one hand, the ball in the other, wants to serve, but Nastase's gone. They look, they call. Nothing. Then the tarpaulin moves, and Nastase's face appears from beneath. He's grinning.

While everyone was staring at the tarpaulin on the opposite side Nastase hid under the tarpaulin on his side.

Patterson stands there, he bounces the ball, he waits while the spectators laugh. The referee calls Nastase back to the game, but Nastase again disappears beneath the tarpaulin. The senior referee is called, a delegation of tournament officials appears, they debate what to do. There's been nothing like it in the history of Wimbledon. The senior referee, the referees, the tournament officials put their heads together. What to do? Then there's another burst of laughter from the stadium because Nastase's standing at the base line and waiting for Patterson's serve with feigned impatience.

Patterson misplayed the simplest shots. He served like a Sunday player and he lost the game he'd already almost won.

Nastase left the court a victor to cheering while Patterson was whistled off. He hadn't congratulated Nastase after the match ball, hadn't even wanted to shake hands.

Later as an investment counselor I often told this story to those clients who played tennis. (It was too chaotic to win over candidates for life insurance because anyone who takes out life insurance doesn't want to venture anything, he wants certainty.) It can be given a good interpretation, namely the need to get out of the game, out of the general trend of the stock market, at the right moment, and do something completely unexpected, the one thing no one's counting on, investing money even if nobody thinks the investment has any prospect of success. (Naturally there has to be some indication that things will get better again. There has to be economic substance, like Nastase has to play well. Or at least faith in its existence.)

Stein never played in a tournament. Perhaps he was afraid of being a sacrificial victim of laughter as he stood there in his strenuous Zarathustra earnestness, just like Patterson, the laughter of those who didn't take victory, didn't take the match, and therefore didn't take him so seriously. Stein had a cast-iron lack of humor. And that's how he played, sometimes with the best players in the association, all of whom he could beat. Perfect, wonderful tennis, light-footed, almost effortless, the rhythm of the strokes and the movements all harmonized, thrifty and exact. It was like a dance.

Crowds of people wanted to be taught by him, a year's wait was nothing unusual. In 1973 it wasn't just a question of tennis, but of an attitude. A new style had come about and I had the luck to be a part of this more or less from the beginning. A new life style was looking for its own sport. In the fifties, even still in the early sixties footballers with wonderful names like Spundflasche had been the idols, and from that period come former players now working as trainers and listening to what people like Otto Rehhagel have to say. Dribbling, poaching a goal, fiddling, putting it in—set that against killer volley, passing shot, topspin, service court. People, the young on whom it depends, are drawn to the lone fighter, the wily professional who knows the ropes, not to teams who shake hands on the field and promise to fight to the last breath for victory, that's the painful aftermath of the defeat at Stalingrad.

—There's also greatness in losing, said Stein, if you've given everything. Those are great images, the loser returning to his place. To experience oneself in defeat. Did I really exhaust my ability, he asks himself. Were my tactics right? Did I take advantage of my opponent's weaknesses? Was I able to bring my own strengths into play?

He's down, he'll get up, that's your loser.

At the club they said he celebrated tennis as a transposition of his philosophy. So I went, eager and self-taught, to the lecture he gave once a week on Friday at 6. Fourteen female students and two male students sat there. He read out about a man by the name of Derrida, about Anti-Oedipus. I had to listen to his lectures to the end of the term because, though he never referred to it, Stein had his eye fixed on me out of his sixteen listeners. Since then I know what deconstruction is, an experience in hearing and seeing: *Tricholoma equestre,* shipment of clouds, white wind.

The murderer in the ruins

The next day over breakfast Britt said: —You know what I think? You're just waiting to be found here. You can't stand it here. You're on edge, you're pacing like a tiger. Long before you heard about that uncle of yours. And your writing doesn't help you either. Your uncle, I think, feels at ease when he's sitting in his room at home. Not you.

—I do, I said, I enjoy it. But why should I do time? For nothing, absolutely nothing?

In the past we only rarely talked about my work. And if we did, then only about certain cases, about individual clients, for example about Fishy Fritz who squandered his money.

That's the way it seemed to Britt, and she wasn't wrong: they were people who wanted to come by money quickly, who already had too much money, who gambled because they were bored but wanted still more money, because commodity futures trading was like roulette, black or white, prices went up or down. People placed their bets and hoped to win.

They'd only themselves to blame if they lost.

In our anger, in our fury at my arrest, the charge, and finally the verdict, we agreed on this. It was the mutually-held premise of every discussion. She wasn't interested in business matters, any more than Lolo. Only Lolo stressed that she wasn't interested in business matters, whereas Britt would never have said so.

It was really not the case that Dembrowski and I founded our brokerage firm Sekuritas with the inten-

172

tion of fleecing people, as the public prosecutor maintained. A firm founded with the intention to deceive and set on swindling.

That's not how it was.

For four months we ran our commodity futures trading cleanly, traded, made losses, now and then also profits, a perfectly normal business venture. Dembrowski and I phoned people we still knew from the old firm and to the best of our knowledge and in good faith—at any rate, I—invested in cotton or copper or silver, transmitting the investments to the New York or London brokers.

One day the 50,000 marks invested by a jeweller Dembrowski had brought in melted down to 7,000 marks because of a drop in oil.

The man, an expert in the financial field, who followed the rates at home on the screen, phoned and said snappishly, —This is exasperating, put down another 50,000 immediately, on wheat this time, it's been falling for days, it'll have to go up again. I warned him. But he insisted, he was one of those investor clients who always knew everything better.

When I wanted to delete the old margin of 50,000 from the account it turned out that we hadn't drawn up a contract for this amount. An oversight, made in haste. The sum wasn't on the screen, but it was still in the account. Should we invest the money again?

I considered whether to say we still had the money, his instructions had seemed so wrong to me at the time that I hadn't actually placed his order. Naturally that was the most embarrassing of all. The investor would think we ran a chaotic business. You can lose money, but you couldn't just forget about it.

It's better, I thought, to talk about it first to Dembrowski, whose client he was.

Dembrowski didn't say: —Keep the money, he's lost it anyway. He also didn't say: —We can't say anything, we'd make ourselves ridiculous, we get money to invest and leave it lying in the account. He also didn't say: —Obviously we pay it back. All he did was make a small gesture. He stopped me. Nothing more. A short movement of the right hand, and with it our new business began, our criminal energy blossomed. It was a wordless impulse. And that's how it would remain until Dembrowski's phone call, shortly before we went up in smoke.

We already transferred the next investor's money to the account of a company newly founded by us, from which we then transferred the money to the account of another newly founded company, and from there to Luxembourg. And confirmation of the contracts, the deals, can be had for a reasonable price in London. The criminal police were able to follow the money this far. Then it disappeared from the bank computers. How? Unfortunately that must remain a professional secret, even now, not only because of possible consequences, but because Fishy Fritz is having just this route traced. He wants to know where the money's gone. I know he's hired private investigators to find out. I read it in a Hamburg paper that you can buy here the next day. He wanted to make us hand back the loot, he said in a newspaper interview my mother read out to me over the phone some three months ago.

He could have saved the money he spent on the detective agency, he only had to phone my mother. She would have told him where I am, I'm sure. She

174

wouldn't have phoned him of her own accord, her per-
nickety sense of honor prevented that, that would have
been denunciation, but if the man were to ask her she
wouldn't lie, she wouldn't say: —I don't know, she'd
give him my phone number. But nobody thinks a
mother would be so willing to hand her son over to
justice. So no one asks her, which secretly annoys her.
Fishy Fritz simply won't accept that his money's disappeared down a black hole like the house of my great-
uncle.

He said in the interview that when our swindle was
exposed it dawned on him that I'd already told him his
fate at our first meeting. A story about a house and all it
contained disappearing down a hole in the earth. A
coincidence? Or a subtle prophecy dressed up as a
story? Or had this story, as if compelled, fulfilled itself?

My writing uncle would of course be interested, but
for a different reason than the public prosecutor, to
know if and how my conscience reacted at this second
transaction, which was after all deliberate. And I can
only say to the inquisitive louse: —Not at all, no bad
dreams at night, no inner moral voice said: Stop, you're
a swine if you do this, and even the voice of my dear
mother that apparently one is supposed to hear at such
decisive moments, the voice of my piously righteous,
persnickety mother only said to me: —Leave me alone,
will you. Because when I was small I often clung to my
mother, pressed myself to her. —Leave me alone, will
you, she said every time and pushed my arms away.

I hope my uncle won't reach for a slick psychological explanation such as that I compensated for my
mother's lack of devotion by looking for happiness in
making money, no matter how or from whom I took it.

Many do this, as we know, and the word irregularity is exactly the eye of the needle through which no camel passes. But where is the irregularity? It's shadowy territory. If you know someone is going to lose his money anyway, why not take considered measures to protect it? In any case I already informed the next client (investor sounds frivolous, at any rate to my ears) that his money wouldn't be circulated in the big banks, we'd keep it out, it would go into a special account, our deposit account.

▼

Still, it was 75,000. I'd invested it in silver for a real-estate agent. He was the cutthroat who years ago had found us the basement with urine mold, a vulture. He'd taken 500 marks, two months' rent off us as a deposit, a trivial sum today, but at the time much more than we could spare. The swine was called Glaser. Drove up in his Opel Admiral (the name already indicates an attitude), came down the steps, took a look at the empty apartment, the walls we'd carefully wiped down, the waxed linoleum floors, the kitchen polished to a shine with Ata, then headed for the toilet and said: —What's this, you've whitewashed over something here? He scratched at the wall and there it was, blueish, the urine mold.

And that's why we moved out, because of that urine mold that stank of saltpeter. The stink reached into the bedroom. To say nothing of the silverfish you had to shake from your trousers and sweater in the morning, they crawled into your shoes, darted across the kitchen table. And no insecticide could get rid of them for long.

If you crushed them the shimmering silver turned into a little dull grey lump.

But Mr. Glaser only said, —Don't be funny. You only get silverfish where there's dirt, where people don't sweep, don't wipe up, where food goes bad. And this mold, that's because you didn't heat the place. It has to be fixed up.

I said this rathole was always damp, no, it was actually wet, it didn't matter how much you heated it.

—You scrimped on the heating, said Mr. Glaser.

He didn't want to hand back the money, he kept the deposit. Britt and I went back to his agency, threatening to take him to court unless he immediately etc. etc. He rose up out of his office chair, went to the door, flung it open, said, —Get out, immediately, or I'm calling the police.

—I'm going to wrap a writ around your neck, I said.

—Sue, but get out.

Naturally we didn't sue. How could we have sued this cutthroat who knew every trick in the book?

No, I did decide to be honest. My uncle might perhaps have described a real-estate agent in that way. Glaser in reality was called Becker, and though I found him profoundly repellent he behaved decently. He'd rented the basement flat to us and we were glad to get it for a rent of 250 marks, and he also promptly paid us back the deposit.

I'd chosen him for another reason. The professional group I'd taken on at the time with the aim of persuading them to invest were real-estate agents. In recruiting investors we proceeded according to professions. Dembrowski phoned all the jewellers.

I remembered Becker (naturally he didn't remember

me) especially because he collected shells and snails. I'd asked him if he'd collected all the snails and shells himself. Some, yes. The rest he'd bought in Hamburg. His dream (at that time there was no need yet for him to play the successful real-estate agent for my benefit) was to travel to the South Seas and on a beach find a cowrie.

Gerda made the appointment. In the office that only now struck me as pathetically shabby sat an old man in a dirty suit. He smelled of piss. Probably he hadn't changed his underpants for days. On the shelves, on the desk, on the window sill, on the filing cabinet, everywhere there were shells, small, large, gigantic, curved like snail shells, symmetrical, asymmetrical, red, blueish yellow, green. That was the wonderful thing about this otherwise so dreary office.

I gave Becker my card, said we were looking for a new office in Ferdinandstrasse, but a larger office (yes, we were expanding), preferably with a view of the Alster. The office we were looking for wasn't just one size, it was two sizes too big for Mr. Becker. That was obvious. He called his secretary, she should look through the card index for something suitable.

While she cleared away a few shells and flicked through a well-worn card index he asked about the investment business, he wanted something safe, he said, safe.

—What percentage do you offer?

—It depends, I said.

He'd invested his money, a safe investment, but only at 5%. But then, safe.

—Mm . . . yes.

He waited. He wanted to hear what percentage this mm . . . yes referred to.

—15%, perhaps 20%.

I saw immediately that he was going to free some money. The greed, only just controlled, in the face.

—Definitely?

—Only death is definite.

—Ha, ha.

He was the anxious type. An anxiety conditioned by his profession, crammed with small and great disasters, an anxiety that now was part of the anxiety of living in anticipation of the really great disaster.

I didn't like Mr. Becker, not because he was a real-estate agent, that's a profession like any other, I just didn't like that grey face, those fine burst veins on the bridge of his nose, those red inflamed eyelids, those dull dark brown eyes, that mistrustful old man's look, that smell of piss, the way when he was thinking he sniffed his finger, his thin yellowing hair. All things he can't help, Britt would say, who doesn't understand why I reject certain people simply on their appearance, or rather, why I find them off-putting, that's to say repellent, yes, they repel me, something I think most people don't want to admit, aren't permitted to admit.

It wasn't hard for me to convince Becker you shouldn't begin with 10,000, don't dribble, put down a heap.

I don't have to please anybody, not any longer, I don't have to appear likeable to anyone, don't have to take the public into consideration, therefore I didn't have the slightest bad conscience. Only when I was going down in the elevator I felt sorry for a moment for his shell collection because I thought he'd probably have to sell it.

Becker had told me his most beautiful pieces were at

179

home. The house was out of the way, a small house built in the fifties, just a cottage really, he said, to indicate what these 75,000 marks represented for him, all he had in cash, he said. He had an alarm system in his house that was situated near a gravel pit, as he said, out of the way. But what use was an alarm system there when the red alarm signal began rotating on the roof, the siren wailing? The house of the nearest neighbor was so far away that he wouldn't see or hear a thing. And probably didn't want to see or hear. A dog? Yes, but they know they can soon put a dog out of action with tear gas. He asked me what I thought of the financial situation. Could there be a big crash on the stock market?

—Yes, I said, that can happen at any time. If not quite as dramatically as Martin sees it happening.

—Who's that?

—A commentator, writes in the papers. The man predicts the collapse of the world economic system.

A big bang that's coming soon, the stock market collapse in 1988 was only a prelude, then, with market values in free fall, not only will the small banks close their counters, but also the Deutsche Bank, the Bank of America. Then, when there are mass layoffs at Ford and Mercedes, no Hermes credit, no more pensions paid, when Munich Reinsurance can no longer reinsure, then the unemployed will band together, class-conscious bankers jump out of windows, the homeless come out of their underground tunnels, force their way into the mirrored banking cathedrals, warm themselves at fires of mahogany tables and contemporary paintings hacked to pieces, sleep on the pigskin chairs, on the light grey wall-to-wall carpeting, while the vermin come crawling out of the drainage pipes that for years were strenuously driven back by every conceivable means, rats, cockroaches, mice, they'll come up out of cellars, pipes, drains. Filling stations will be robbed, supermarkets plundered, gangs roam the streets with sawn-off shotguns, police with no hope of a pension will loot delicatessen stores with service revolvers drawn, while gangs of judges armed with truncheons organize flour and milk from the producers, that's the farmers, who defend themselves with scythes and pistols. Fortunate those who have an iron stove at home, who can burn the trees in the street and parquet floors, punks and finks roaming the countryside disguised as postmen. Big villas plundered, beautiful wives raped.

For years now there have been models for survival strategies with a corresponding training program for the rich and the richest, strategies everyone should study who is self-employed, independent in a threatened profession: that's anyone who's a real-estate agent, banker, corporate lawyer, or a pollster.

—Really, said Becker.

—Yes. Martin's advice to the rich is that they should stop making themselves conspicuous, not get into any gossip columns (in other words, try to achieve exactly the opposite of the smart trendies, who display themselves, who want to be seen and admired), for the simple reason that envy has a good memory. The best thing, says Martin, is to buy a yacht so that if economic chaos breaks out you can take to the high seas. In my view, not good advice. Because Martin forgets: yachts need crews, they could mutiny and then every trawler becomes a pirate ship, each against the other, each against all, even on the high seas. What good then are

Zero Bonds, Strips, Early Bird, Receipts, Floaters, Cats, Tigers, Mismatches, the nations are bankrupt (the USA already is anyway).

—Yes, Becker said and sniffing drew his finger under his nose, what should one do?

Perhaps my uncle's called on him in the meantime. Sat like me in that office filled with cheap office furniture. On the right next to the desk with its wooden roll top one of those depressing African hemp plants (depressing because with their slender stems and excessively full leaves they look like overgrown front-garden shrubs).

What will he have told my uncle? Probably how trusting he'd been, how gullible, how easily persuaded. He'll say I promised him everything, easy money, 20% profit, he'll have talked about the Leverage Effect. And my uncle will have looked it up: *Leverage Effect. The investor has to deposit a substantially smaller sum with the broker than the commodity in question is worth, as a result greater swings in price appear. With gold the margin a broker demands from the client is, for example, 5,000 US dollars. For this the client can acquire a 100-ounce gold contract, which at an assumed rate of 400 dollars an ounce represents a value of 40,000 US dollars. If now the price of gold goes up by 5% to 420 dollars an ounce, then on a sale at this price the client makes a profit of 2,000 US dollars, which in relation to the investment is 40%.*

Good god, my uncle will have thought, so you really can make big money like this from one day to the next. And that's what Becker also thought, like all the other investors.

Becker will have painted me larger than life to my

uncle, if only to avoid making himself appear small. How trustworthy I seemed to him, so well dressed. Above all he was persuaded by my calm, composed manner. (Mr. Walter is good with words, Becker elaborated on this as a witness in court.) He didn't have the impression he was being talked into something. I'd answered his questions in a businesslike manner, not zealously but in detail, also pointed out to him the risk of loss. The conversation had really come about by chance. What I'd actually come for was a larger office, in the best location, which unfortunately he hadn't been able to offer. But then, then I'd told a story. A story? Yes. What kind of story? A story about the murderer in the ruins.

That'll surprise my uncle. Will he say: —Oh really? Will he say I once told that same story to my nephew? No. No, I'm pretty sure my uncle won't even say he's my uncle. And he won't claim the story as his own.

It's a story my little uncle didn't hear at home in our kitchen. So it's not in fact my story. He picked it up somewhere else.

In the meantime I know there really was a murderer in the ruins. I made enquiries. He was never caught.

Did my uncle let Mr. Becker tell him the story over again? Simply to hear how in the meantime it had altered, how I'd changed it, enriched it, cut it? Or will Becker not even mention this story? He never referred to it in court. Perhaps it embarrassed him. Perhaps he repressed the story, perhaps he didn't really understand the story's significance for his decision to invest all his savings, his ill-gotten gains, and all at once—after I'd told him the story this mistrustful man actually said:

—Good, invest 75,000 marks for me.

He paid dearly for the story, but I think it's worth the price.

It was just after capitulation, after the collapse, in '45, zero hour, a time of anarchy, the black market, lives lived from day to day, hand-to-mouth, improvisation, tobacco grown on balconies, wooden sandals with leather straps, floor polish made of old lubricating oil. The time of the murderer in the ruins—and then the wire noose murderer. The wire noose murderer? Yes. Hadn't he ever heard of him? No, said Becker, he only came from Halle to Hamburg in '59. It was that very cold winter of '47, they kept finding bodies in the ruins, men as well as women, naked, and each one they found had a wire noose round the neck. The murderer was never caught, by the way. Nobody knew anything about him. But one woman met him, a young teacher who'd come from Mölln to Hamburg to hear one of the first symphony concerts after the war.

She lived with her aunt in Eppendorf in the Tornquisstrasse and had to walk to the concert because there wasn't yet any tram, any bus to Karl-Muck Square.

It was January and a light snow was falling. She walked past the mountains of rubble in the Fruchtallee, went down Eimsbüttler Chaussee, which here was a narrow footpath leading over the walls that had caved into the street, went in the direction of Schulterblatt past the burned-out ruins of houses, here was a bath still hanging from a tiled wall, there over an abyss on what remained of a floor stood a scorched metal bed, went from the Schulterblatt to the Neue Pferdmarkt, to Feldstrasse past the Hochbunker with its four anti-aircraft platforms on the roof destroyed by a direct hit, a twisted iron bristle jutted out of the concrete, in the ventilation shafts pigeons cooed, Sievekingplatz, the High Court and Court of Appeal, Wilhelm-Zwo in brick, on to Karl-Muck Square, the Laeiszhalle, the Musikhalle, built with money from the slave trade.

She sat in the unheated concert hall in her aunt's worn calfskin coat, they were playing the Italian Symphony and gradually she forgot the cold, forgot the ruins until the last movement, the presto in rondo form, the saltarello, the little hop that Mendelssohn had transcribed, a quick Neapolitan dance, then she remembered the way back through the ruins that would take her home and she thought about the murderer who in the last weeks had left his victims naked in the ruins with a wire noose round their throat. Suddenly as the violins played her skin began to itch, she twisted backwards and forwards in the seat wanting to scratch her breast, her back, her head. Her artificial silk dress rustled every time she crossed her legs. A woman in front of her turned round, a short angry look out of the corner of her eye. Next to her on the right sat a young man in a suit that was much too big, he carefully moved his arm from the armrest.

In the intermission he asked her what was the matter. And she told him for a moment she'd been frightened at the thought of having to go through the dark landscape of ruins after the concert. Where did she have to go? To Eimsbüttel, Heussweg. She was in luck, he could accompany her as he actually had to go as far as Loksted.

What a long way, she said.

Yes, but he really liked Mendelssohn, Schumann even more, and best of all the Spring Symphony. That came after the intermission.

After the concert, after a last glance at the slowly emptying concert hall in which a few people were still standing and clapping, they left. Only a few street lamps were lit, Sievekoingplatz was already dark. They joined others who'd been at the concert, who had formed a group. But already after Sievekingplatz the group turned off to the right in the direction of Rotherbaum with its undestroyed villas.

The young man spoke about the trumpet entry, it was so fantastic, so wonderful he could listen to it over and over, Schumann had written that it should sound like a call to awaken. It always made him think of a certain day in spring.

Yes, she said, that's how she felt about the Italian Symphony which always reminded her of her brother, he'd been like that, happy, fresh. Had been? Yes, he was a lieutenant and had gone down in the Atlantic on a U-boat. That's bad, said the young man, it's a terrible thing to think about, drowning, that means: breathing water. He'd reported to the infantry in '44, volunteered, at least there he'd have a chance to crawl behind a tree, a rampart. Naturally that hadn't helped, he'd been through it, seen his comrades torn to shreds by a direct hit from a tank. Still, you could decide to fling yourself down somewhere or other when the grenades fell. But in a tank or a U-boat there was no way out. You'd had it. They were steel coffins.

They walked past the mounds of rubble from the collapsed houses. Somewhere, deep in the landscape of ruins a fire was burning, the weak glow flickered over a few façades, a fine snow blew through the cavernous windows.

Incidentally there are still two U-boats in the harbor

under that bunker. The roof was six meters thick. He'd even heard the explosion in Stellingen. The window panes rattled in the blast. Hadn't he said he lived in Loksted?

—Yes, on the border of Stellingen.

—Were there still soldiers on the U-boats?

—No. Of course not.

For a moment she stopped and hesitated. Ahead of them now lay the darkest part of the way, a footpath that led through the landscape of ruins. But then she went on walking and began to tell the story of the three soldiers who had been trapped. In Danzig—or was it Gotenhafen—on their retreat the Germans had blown up a bunker in which hundreds of tons of supplies were stored. But hiding in this bunker were three German soldiers, deserters. When the last warning came over the bunker loudspeaker to immediately leave the bunker they couldn't get out. They would have been instantly shot, in any case. So they bolted the steel doors of a shaft and of one of the bunker rooms, sat down, put their fingers in their ears and prayed. Then the walls quaked, the gigantic bunker swayed like a ship, the first steel door burst open, but the second held. They'd survived. But then they discovered they were shut in. Both entrances had been blocked by huge concrete fragments. But the ventilation still worked. They also had enough to eat and drink to last decades. Only one thing was missing: light. They found no flashlights, no candles, no flares. They only had two boxes of matches with them. Now and then they struck a match, after long hesitation, like someone cast away at sea takes a swallow from the only cannister of fresh water when thirst becomes unbearable. They struck one to get an idea of the various branching corridors, to see where which supplies were, and now and then they struck one to look each other in the face, into each other's eyes. But finally the last match was struck and then there they were in the dark.

Only at a few switches in the corridors the circuits painted with phosphorous paint gave out a faint blueish glow. They stood by these to at least see each other's outlines in this faint glow that was getting fainter all the time. Until these also lost their slight capacity to give light. Now they lived in abysmal darkness. The fear of getting lost in this darkness, of disappearing into it. All they could do was talk. They could touch, therefore feel, and they could reassure each other by telling stories.

—Yes, said the man, what could they have talked about?

About whatever had made an impression on them: experiences, terrible and painful, but also the happy ones. They'll have told each other their desires, what they'd do if they were free. One wanted to travel to the South Seas to run along a beach there and feel the sand under his feet, to see the blue sky, another wanted to go to a concert and hear the Spring Symphony.

—What must they have felt, said the young man and took the woman's arm. She started. I'm sorry, he said, I didn't mean to frighten you.

—That's all right.

—How were the men found?

—A month ago the Poles began removing the concrete rubble, they wanted to get to the supplies and stores of arms. They used small detonations and jack hammers, then, suddenly three figures appeared in the dust. The workmen fled. Three snow-white beings, long white beards, long white hair, the skin white. The three stood in the sun and shrieked, they staggered around and yelled. Dazzled by the sun, they were blinded.

During the story they'd covered the darkest part of the Eimsbüttler Chaussee. In the distance a few lights could be seen in the windows of houses that had remained standing.

They were walking along the narrow cleared path in the middle of the street. There was a smell of wet old mortar, and fine splinters of glass and stone crackled under their feet. A thin blanket of snow covered the mounds of rubble from which here and there a chimney or a wall jutted.

—There's something soothing, said the man, in the indifference with which nature covers everything. Broom and wild lupin are already growing on the mounds of rubble. You'll see them in the spring, then the rubble will blossom, he said and pulled her to him.

She screamed. She saw his eyes. She tore herself free, ran, still screaming, ran until she came to the lights, the inhabited houses, she rang but no one opened, she went on running until she saw the blue police sign. She rushed into the guard room breathless, three officials sat there by a small iron stove and for a moment looked at her in horror. Then they leaped up, shouting:

—Where is he, where is he?

—What's the matter, she said, she'd regained her self-control. She was still panting, but she'd calmed down.

—Where is he, the policemen shouted, and a guard shook her.

—No, she said. I'm sorry. It's nothing. I just got frightened. He only wanted to put his arms round me. He wanted to kiss me. But I got terribly frightened. That's all.

The old police sergeant carefully took her by the arm, led her to the washroom, and pushed her in front of the mirror.

She saw herself, her face red from the cold and from running, her hair wild, she saw her throat—round her neck hung a wire noose.

The flashlight

We'd just got into our stride, Dembrowski had served, I'd returned the ball neatly out of Dembrowski's range, when I saw the man standing at the wire mesh. He stood there like a gnome in a forest, reddish blonde hair, light blue polo shirt. The same who'd watched us play yesterday and I'm now sure, the same who'd watched the house from the car. He was standing behind the wire mesh holding a camera with a medium-sized telephoto lens. He waited until Dembrowski was looking at my court concentrating where to place the ball before serving, and that was the moment when the man pressed the release. I could hear the sound clearly.

We played, and to begin with I again misplayed the simplest balls, until the man showed up on the side opposite me and photographed me from the front. I no sooner felt the telephoto lens directed at me than for some strange reason I was able to concentrate on my play and the ball. It was as if I saw the ball and its trajectory in slow motion.

Sannchen, who was again displaying her naked brown legs, didn't pick up a single ball for Dembrowski, he had to bend down himself every time. He only got in three of his serves. In under an hour I won the match.

Dembrowski was probably thinking of Renate who was in Hamburg, who one fine day no longer wanted to see him or talk to him after having tolerated the relationship with Sannchen for two years. Weekdays with Sannchen in Hamburg, weekends with his saintly wife in the country house. The day came when Renate simply shut the door in his face and had the lock changed (like Mrs. Brücker). Sannchen sat behind her nonreflective glasses and drew one leg out from under the other, then put it, a faint light pressure mark on the suntanned thigh, over the other.

Dembrowski even had to ask her, after he'd gone sweating and breathless to the bench, to get up off his towel.

The man had disappeared during the game. I hadn't seen him leave. Suddenly he was gone.

—Did you see that character?

—Yes, said Dembrowski, he photographed us.

—You were terrific, Sannchen said to me. Your serves were little grenades. They really were. Demmi looked rather old. For several weeks now she's been calling Dembrowski Demmi, which sounds a little like dummy. Dembrowski really didn't deserve it.

—And the man?

Dembrowski only shrugged.

—What are you going to do, Sannchen said, if they find you here?

—What can we do? Nothing, Dembrowski said, emphatically nonchalant.

—And you, Sannchen asked me, what are you going to do?

—Live fast, die young, I said and hit a ball hard in the direction of the fence where the man had been standing. The ball stuck in the wire mesh. I put away the racket.

—Are we playing tomorrow? Dembrowski asked.

—Let's phone.

—Play, Sannchen said, it's the only exciting thing in this sunny shithole, during the day at any rate.

Sannchen had a fixed image of herself: first cool, then fiery.

▼

Britt went pale when I told her about the man. Yes, she was always composed, but for a moment she lost her composure. —He photographed you?

—Yes.

—Strange.

—You said yourself all kinds of tennis freaks live here.

—Yes, but to photograph you.

—We weren't bad today, putting it modestly, we were extremely good.

—Good, Britt said, and then she laughed and said: You're hot stuff, you should play in the association. She left with that small slanting line on her forehead that she always has when she's really worried.

I went to my room and got my leather shoulder bag. It's light and comfortable to carry by hand or— on longer journeys—over your shoulder. I put in a sufficient supply of dollars, a shaving brush, a razor, a toothbrush, toothpaste, soap, two undershirts, sports shirts, two pairs of socks and my light raincoat (you need so little when you're on the run!), and naturally my nice new Danish passport. Andersen. My namesake Christian Andersen not only traveled with several suitcases, but also with a big hatbox. In the box a coil of rope with which to escape, should fire break out in his hotel. Such are the fears of the tellers of fairy tales.

I only need this bag. In the next few days I'll be putting on my Queens tennis shoes (light, durable, and elegant), wearing my jeans (don't get dirty), a sweatshirt (in a respectable grey blue) of the best quality, that way you can hitchhike, but also go into any five-star hotel. The light raincoat is important. You can't come out of the rain into a hotel in a soaking shirt and ask for a room if you're not carrying anything other than a small bag.

For a moment I hesitated, should I take the pieces of the bird man. The small plastic bag would easily fit into the shoulder bag. But then I imagined my uncle writing, he'd have me put the plastic bag in the shoulder bag. So I left the pieces of the bird man where they were, on the bookshelf.

Britt came into the room, sat down in the chair without saying anything and watched me going through the document folder. I put my international driving license, which also went under the name of Andersen, in my pocket. If I could choose a nationality I'd happily be a Dane.

—Don't forget your inoculation certificate, Britt said, and then after a short pause: You know, I sometimes wonder if it wouldn't be better for Lolo to take her college entrance exam in Hamburg. It would all be over in a year. Then you could, she hesitated, move freely. By the way, your mother phoned again. She said she read the cards for you, which she's never done before, she wanted to tell you, to give you some information. She's going to phone again later.

—Take the phone off, I said, and take care Lolo doesn't put it back on.

I wonder from where my mother got this superstitious streak.

After we had opened our brokerage firm Sekuritas I went to the Grosse Trampgang. The district had been bought up and renovated by a newspaper. None of the old shops were left, not the stationers run by Brunkhorst who'd been inside for ten years for stabbing his wife to death with a breadknife, nor the *Scharfe Eck,* a saloon with two cast-iron columns where after the late shift the wharf grandees drank endless amounts of cheap wine. Now it was called *Bella Roma,* the columns, the walls gleaming white, the tables narrow and with shining white covers, you had to reserve a table at least a week in advance.

The new buildings behind the Steinweg, a few public-assistance apartments, then the municipal apartments. This had once, after the rubble had been removed, been a wide open space. Here we kicked a ball. Marked the goals with a few bricks. When it was time to eat Grandmother Hilde leaned out of the window and blew a whistle into the Grosse Tramp-gang.

My uncle sat at the table, his elbows glued to his sides. I first had to wipe away my snot, wash my hands, tuck my shirt in my trousers. My mother was again at a suburban hairdresser's on a month's trial. My uncle ate, but he was digging with his questions into Grandmother's memories. —You used to work in a munitions factory. —Yes? —What? You made grenades.
—Ten hours a day. Home front. There was a woman who always ripped out the priming wires. —Why? —Well, then it just goes plop when it's been fired, it doesn't explode. Saved some more lives, she'd say. —Did you do it too? —Well you see, it was forbidden, it was sabotage. They sent you to prison or a concentration camp. —And in the evening? (I had a feeling there was something else he wanted to know, he already knew the story about the grenades, I'd already heard it too.) —In the evening we'd be sitting here with Mrs. Becker, she was also at the munitions factory. And Mrs. Eisenhart would come up too. Black paper stuck over the window panes: black-out. —And then? —And then the air raid sirens went. Then it started, doors slamming, people calling, tramping on the stairs. Everybody down! Into the air-raid shelter.

Everybody, only not Grandmother Hilde, she only went when the cat slunk out of the house. Grandmother Hilde sat there knitting socks for Step-grandfather Heinz who at the time was on guard duty for the Greater German Reich somewhere near Minsk, my own grandmother knitted, one row plain, one row purl—without light—and waited, knitting in the dark kitchen until it grew quiet in the house, until Eisenhart,

195

the air-raid warden, helmet hanging off the back of his head yelled up the stairwell: —Everybody out? Until Eisenhart had bolted the steel door to the air-raid shelter from the inside and it was still in the house, then she put her knitting aside, quietly went to the apartment door and went up the stairs, feeling her way, past the apartment in which later the Claussen family would live, climbed the stairs up to Mrs. Brücker's, then the narrow wooden ladder to the attic, felt her way past old bed frames, frayed armchairs, splintered picture frames, to the skylight, opened the attic window and looked out at the night sky, looked out across the roofs at the city that lay in darkness, and waited, still, holding her breath. Searchlights scanned the grey dark, scanned the sky, the darkness, there, from the south, far away, a dark rumbling there where Harburg is, then the first dry shots of the 8.8 ack-ack gun on the Veddel, the bark of the 2.2 ack-ack on the Brückenbogen across the Elbe. The city lay there. The city waited, the city had carefully stepped to one side in the dark. The Alster was no longer where it usually was, the river had shifted itself a good kilometer to the west. The Alster was half nailed shut, covered in pontoons. Nor was the railway station in its usual place, the bombs that were meant to hit it would fall into the waters of the Alster. The rumbling was drawing closer and closer, got louder, a roaring that filled the entire sky. Below, hiding in the dark, lay the city. Two, three houses away there it was again, the light signal that Hilde had already seen twice. A small, intense beam of light from a strong flashlight. Two long, three short. Suddenly over the harbor hung Christmas trees and angel's hair rippled down from the sky. A little later the detonations of the overheavy high-explosive bombs. A red glow in a southerly direction, there lay the wharfs, there the U-boats were built, Howalds wharf, Stülken wharf, Blohm and Voss, the fuel tanks. She saw an airplane in the cluster of rays from two searchlights, suddenly it tipped out of sight, tiny, glittering, resurfaced again in a lower beam of a searchlight, a parachute and then another, we'll hang out the washing on the Siegfried Line.

The Brüderstrasse, the Grosse Trampgang remained standing, while a few hundred meters further away entire rows of houses were flattened by extensive bombing. The house remained standing with its kitchen, with Grandmother and Mrs. Brücker, Mrs. Eisenhart and air-raid warden Eisenhart who looked out darkly from under his helmet when the ground shook, when houses swayed, the lights went out, children screamed, when shelves with jars of gherkins fell down. But the house remained standing.

Grandmother saw a connection here with the secret light signals.

My uncle with his blossoming fantasy maintained it was Grandmother Hilde, who'd given the light signals. And each time as proof he showed me the outsize flashlight that lay, already rusted, in a corner of the small room at the bottom of the house.

The thread game

This morning I overslept. Britt had already gotten up. She was sitting with Lolo in the kitchen. Lolo was spooning out her organic muesli. She grumbled that the receiver had been lying next to the phone all night.

—Who should phone anyway? I asked. This was unfair of course, because I was saying I didn't think her friend, the wimp, was capable of finding out our phone number. Lolo said nothing, only pushed the muesli aside and got up.

—Don't get up, Lolo said to me, I'm going alone.

But I wanted to take her to the gate like every other day because this was how the day began for me, with this short walk to the gate. At some point, probably in the next few days already, she'll tell me I should stay in the house because it's embarrassing to always have her father wave as the bus leaves, because after all her school friends are on it. I said the gate gets stuck. —I can manage, says she. I'll take care to shut the gate.

—I'll do it, I said, I enjoy it. After that she couldn't say anything, at any rate not today.

There was no car in sight on the street. But I wouldn't have been surprised if I'd found the man with the red hair outside.

For three days now Lolo has been giving me a hurried kiss on the cheek. Before then we used to have a quick nose rub like Eskimos. We did this for about four years. Then sometimes she'd call for me at midday at the office where I worked earning my first spurs as a broker. We'd go to have an ice cream and Lolo would practice her English. She'd lead me as if I were Japanese through Hamburg's inner city: Here was the first settlement, the famous Hammerburg, in 800. Last year they found a lot of kitchen utensils: spoons, knives, crockery, and also remains of meals, for example, cattle and chicken bones.

In the Hamburg History Museum I'd shown her the finds, the pottery fragments and bone remains. Then our ancestors, 1100 years ago, had a steak between their teeth, now we slurp egg soup. Strangely Lolo wasn't interested in what had driven my uncle—and therefore me—to the museum, the pierced skulls in Room 2 of the pirates, the Vitalien brothers, Störtebekers men, executed on the Grossen Grasbrook. There gazing straight ahead stood Störtebeker, collar removed, hands in chains. There in a row one next to the other stood his men. To the priest with the cross: Strike! The executioner lifts the execution sword. And whack, off he runs without his head, it's lying in the grass gazing up into the sky, straight into the clouds. The headless body runs past the men standing there, runs past three, four, begins stumbling, one more step and then one more, stumbles past the seventh and falls.

Those past whom Störtebeker's corpse had run had their lives spared.

—Is that possible, Grannie Hilde asks.

My little uncle says: —Of course. Then he always came up with the story of the cock that an old woman in Trittau grabbed by the feet, flung down on the wood block, and struck off its head. Then the bird flew off without a head, flapped really high into the air before it crashed to the ground. It lay in the green grass that was turning red and still flapped its wings.

The one who stood next to Störtebeker was his favorite, how dear he held the others you could tell literally from how near they stood to him, to the last man who stood there lost and out of reach in the deepest darkness.

My uncle, you should know, as a child looked for

Störtebeker's treasure and he found a gold coin on the Schweinesand. He showed it to everyone.

—Oh, said Lolo, he probably bought it.

—I don't think so, it would have been much too expensive.

—Look at that pigeon, it's limping.

Lolo wasn't interested in my uncle, nor was she ever interested in hunting for treasure, or in islands.

▼

I picked up the bag, it's really light, you can run a good distance with it and thanks to Dembrowski's drive I'm in good condition. The laptop is a little heavier than the bag, but it's also comfortable to hold or to carry on a strap over your shoulder. Still, for a sudden journey with an uncertain destination it's a little cumbersome.

I'd be interested to know how my uncle writes. Does he write by hand or use a typewriter, or does he sit like me in front of this small contraption that electronically projects onto the screen what's taking shape in the brain, making it far closer to thought processes than the typewriter which because of its mechanics is only an extension of the hand and the fingers? Has my uncle already got a data modem? He'd be amazed then if parts of a text were to disappear, others shifted or rearranged, if my instructions were to show up on his screen.

I was introduced to computers by Manfred, one of our phone consultants, and by Gerda.

Gerda was cross-examined as a witness in court. Gerda, the faithful. Without Gerda we'd have crashed a lot earlier, but with her everything ran perfectly smoothly and almost without a hitch to the end, at any rate as far as office work was concerned. No bungled deadlines. No unanswered phone calls. No letters put to one side. Gerda has a phenomenal memory for voices. The mastiffs on the line she always immediately in the friendliest manner called by name, even when they only yelped the name of their investment counselor into the receiver. You always got the impression there were at least 30 people here working under pressure to increase the investors' money. Investors who had lost their money were immediately called back. (You have to tell the patient immediately on waking from the anesthetic which limb had been amputated. If he discovers its absence himself he can go into sustained shock.)

Gerda said in court how hard, how conscientiously I'd worked. To the public prosecutor's question, who gave the decisive instructions, the accused Dembrowski or Walter, she replied: —Mr. Walter. My heart almost stopped with fright.

In the morning, she went on, Mr. Walter was always the first to arrive, in the evenings, often with me, the last to leave. Often it was midnight. That was because the stock exchange in New York shut at 4 o'clock, with six hours time difference that meant 10 o'clock, then the trades still had to be noted down.

Had she noticed anything, any indication that the money wasn't being placed?

No. Not in the least, never, what she'd been able to oversee was all very correct—in Mr. Walter's case, after all she'd been his secretary.

The public prosecutor drew her attention to the fact that she was giving evidence under oath.

—Yes, naturally, yes.

Had she not noticed the victims were increasingly protesting?

Yes, of course. She'd rather assumed that the trades had been badly placed, in other words bad luck, perhaps ignorance, the stock exchange, the market was so unpredictable.

—Did you never notice any sign, shall we say, that would allow one to conclude that money was being taken from people?

She hestitated. I observed Dembrowski from the side, not furtively, but tense and for all in the court to see. Dembrowski looked over at Gerda with studied indifference.

She was thinking, then finally she said, —Actually no, not in Mr. Walter's case.

—And the accused Dembrowski?

—Recently he was mostly in the south of France. He phoned now and then. Now and then he'd let fall some remark that had made her suspicious.

—And what did he say?

—Well, on one occasion he said: Get on with it, man, make some phone calls and raise some dough, people are going bankrupt anyway.

Had the accused Dembrowski said that to her?

—No, to Mr. Walter. But she'd been able to hear because the phone was turned on full.

—How did the accused Walter react?

—Outraged. Yes, he slammed down the phone.

—Did anything in particular strike you about Mr. Walter?

—Strike me? (A quick look at me). Lately, that's to say before his arrest, he seemed overworked.

—How did this show?

—Sometimes he stood at the window and pressed his forehead against the glass.

—His forehead?

—Yes, I think he did it to cool his forehead. He was trying to concentrate. And one day when I spoke to him because a client had asked for him on the phone, he said (she again looked at me): The bird man carried the egg tied to his forehead.

—What?

—Yes. It was very weird. He was totally overworked. You could say he was a nervous wreck, though he was always quiet, always polite, never shouted. But I think it cost him a great effort. He went on taking all phone calls. People were mostly very angry. They'd lost a lot of money. Some phoned several times a day. Mastiffs we called them, after the Roman fighting dog. Just the day before Mr. Walter's arrest a very angry investor phoned. Mr. Eichhorst had taken the call and spoken to the man.

Eichhorst, an early riser like me, usually came to the office after me, at about seven. After Salin, Eichhorst was our most successful investment counselor. He could perhaps have pushed Salin out of first place, but Eichhorst had scruples. He had, for example, no pensioners among his clients because he was of the opinion that only those who had spare money should speculate. Eichhorst jogged to the office in the morning, summer and winter he ran from Uhlenhorst along the Aussenalster to the inner city. In the office he took off his sodden track suit, showered (he was the only one to shower at the office), put on his blue-grey trousers and light sweatshirt and sat down at his computer with his special muesli which he'd soaked the evening before in the office kitchen. The news from Tokyo and London appeared on his screen. —What a shitty mess, the Japs are making mincemeat out of the bare asses. Short-sighted zigzagging idiots. He spooned up his muesli:

—Shit on it, the living hogs.

Eichhorst takes his profession seriously (he's still working as an investment counselor). I sometimes had the impression he was the only one in the office who was seriously concerned about increasing people's money. All the others knew what the game was, I think. Naturally no one put it into words. You saw it in that they were only interested in the rates when they fell, then they could tell people the money was gone and talk them into having another go. Eichhorst could get extremely angry over losses and profits sincerely pleased him. We let him have his way so there'd be profits, as in the case of the secondary-school teacher who wanted to cash in his profit, and with that pulled out the small, seemingly insignificant stone that brought down the entire structure. He was one of Eichhorst's clients.

—Great curling heaps of shit, everybody and his dog has taken short odds on lead, the shit has really hit the fan. Eichhorst had brought this taste for rich fecal language back with him from New York where he'd worked in one of the most respected brokerage firms.

Eichhorst has a good heart. He could say in court in good conscience that he'd tried everything to increase his clients' money. No, he'd never realized that money hadn't even been placed. Apart from which, he'd always taken care that no client speculated with the money he'd put aside for an emergency.

Eichhorst really does have a good and a big heart, he takes part in all the marathon races that he can somehow or other get to, flies to San Francisco, to Nepal, to Tokyo (monthly he earns a net 20,000), wherever there's a city marathon, sometimes only for a weekend. Then he'd come back the next day looking transfigured, he'd run through a cloud over the Golden Gate Bridge, or through Moscow, next to a writer from the Allgäu, took off with him on Red Square, something accelerated in the left side of the brain because, he said, —Suddenly we were floating on air.

Shortly before eight the first phones began to ring in the still empty office. The ones who phoned this early were afraid for their money, they were the ones who laid on the pressure, who the evening before had asked for a statement of their account and not slept all night, who asked themselves how it could have come about that their hundred thousand had melted down to five thousand, who wanted to know exactly how it could have happened. They'd read nothing in any paper anywhere about a crash on the market, on the contrary, they'd talked of a *friendly market*. The tearful ones called, the ones who said with trembling voice that all their savings were gone, the security for their old age, gone, the money they'd saved for an emergency, gone, their money for traveling, gone, they pleaded, try everything, everything to get at the money, they'd already be satisfied if they got back even only half the money. Then the ones who really wept, who were ready to scrape together all the money they had to have another shot with 20,000, then the businesslike ones who weren't going to have another go, who'd written the money off, they were the most pleasant, the ones who gave up, and then finally the most unpleasant, the mastiffs, those who threatened the public prosecutor, the police, the Department for the Fraudulent Manipulation of Trade and Tax Laws, many of them hot-tempered, some got the rage out of their system over the phone, then put down more dough, others phoned daily, got into a fresh rage every time, wanted to see their accounts up again and no delay, gave deadlines—which they then allowed to lapse—by which certain figures had to be reached, —Otherwise, they said, and I hope you get my meaning, you're in deep trouble.

These were the mastiffs.

They all required very careful psychological handling when the losses increased. Eichhorst patiently explained the latest developments on the stock exchanges in Tokyo and New York. I went into my office which was separate from the large main office. I saw Eichhorst talking into the receiver, which he held clamped between his head and shoulder. We were the first in, Eichhorst and I, we had to prop up the despairing in the morning. For this Eichhorst received 20,000 marks in cash, monthly.

From my window I could see a narrow strip, restricted by house fronts, of the Binnenalster, but I had to press my face to the window. Now and then a rainbow would light up, always when the spray from the fountains that were hidden by the row of houses was blown to the side by a strong west wind. An Alster steamer crossed the view, a few swans, shortly before winter set in they had to be caught so they wouldn't freeze in the ice.

A swan once got frozen in the ice on the Isebek Canal. A fish dealer, Mr. Green, tried to free it. Mr. Green put a ladder on the ice and crawled on his stomach to the bird which snapped at him in blind fear, with a desperate, wild but determined beating of its wings and with jabbing bites, until the ice under Mr. Green's weight slowly turned dark grey from the water running over from the bank. Mr. Green crawled, or rather, climbed on all fours on the ladder back to the bank where people stood watching, the bird had quickly calmed down and was cleaning its feathers with its beak.

Eichhorst waved to me, took the second phone, put his hand over the other receiver, said to me: —A mastiff. You'll have to take over, the man can't be calmed down.

I first saw the man to whom I spoke then during the trial, a dainty little man with a bark like a terrier's that I can still hear. He looked over at me, looked over at Dembrowski, in his face something like rage, or rather hate, a triumphant hate. He said he'd spoken to me on that occasion after Mr. Eichhorst had first talked to him to calm him down. He'd tried to show why the money had disappeared by citing rates. But you can't just stubbornly keep putting money on something that keeps sinking. Why did you do it? He'd asked for a plausible explanation for the loss. After that he'd asked to be put through to one of the two directors, he pointed his finger at me, looked at me and fell silent.

—Yes, and? asked the judge.

—First I let him talk without interrupting. He told me, and he'll want to repeat it here, that people have outrageous ideas regarding a doctor's earnings, he in-

207

vited me to accompany him, to join him for a day at his office, on his house calls, the endoscopies, the effort it took to keep going until late in the evening. He asked for an explanation for the loss of his money. He said nothing, again he looked at me.

—And? asked the judge.

—I told him the code, the investing code by which in fact the first 30,000 he'd invested, as it were on a trial run, had been doubled in two weeks, this secret code had been cracked, then everything had disappeared, even the additional money, and then I told him the story about the hacker, a paraplegic hacker in Hannover, a genius, known in international hacker circles, feared by banks and defense ministries, he was the one who'd cracked the code, who'd (and I told him this at the time under the seal of secrecy because the criminal police were still investigating), and who'd—and then I fell silent for a moment on the phone—transferred the money, what's more to an account held in the name of Robin Hood. In the courtroom people laughed. The pensioners in the back rows laughed. Somebody dozing in the last row woke with a startled snore.

—Exactly, said the doctor, exactly, people laugh. It was my fault even to have listened to this story. I said, rubbish, and hung up. Another mistake, of course. There are stories one shouldn't listen to in the first place. If you listen you've already fallen into the trap. They're the clever stories. Naturally I didn't believe this hacker story. I talked to my wife. Go straight to the police? Start legal proceedings? Impossible. Don't you see? Even the policeman taking down the statement would be secretly laughing behind his hand. It's not happening to somebody poor, he'd be thinking. He'd

208

enjoy it, obviously. You make yourself out to be a fool as you're telling the story. You can't repeat the story because you're involved yourself. Don't you see? I refrained from taking legal proceedings. And I considered for a long time whether to appear here as a witness. The shame. That's the word. It needs to be said.

▼

At night I couldn't get to sleep, roamed the house, went into the garden, sat down in the tepid night air and smoked. Then went back to my study, took the bag, looked through the documents again, took the plastic bag from the shelf and picked out the largest piece of wood which had once been the back and on which the rest of the carved glyph of the eating singer was still visible. How light this fragment was. I put it— my uncle can write whatever he likes—in my traveling bag.

On Easter Island the thread game was a favorite. It's a game you find everywhere, among the Eskimos, the Aborigines, we played it in the Brüderstrasse. A game that made the otherwise so monotonous life on Easter Island more bearable, the only variety apart from dancing, riding the waves, carving figures. A thread would be knotted and thrown onto the ground, then from the pattern—and the patterns can be infinite although the area of the thread is finite (oh beautiful chaos), about half a meter—a story is told, one that can be inspired by real events or freely invented but that always creates a different situation, a new event as coincidental as the pattern, and yet there's order in it, the order of permanent disorder, a story at one and the same time both finite and infinite. A story both unique and belonging to all.

The man with red hair

From a balcony shaded by an awning the view over the bay, over the harbor, over the old city is fantastic. I'd deliberately rented an apartment on the twenty-first floor. I soon found the house. Immediately after landing here in Salvador da Bahia, while still at the airport I made enquiries about a furnished apartment. It's criminally expensive, but luxuriously furnished. The apartments to which one goes up in a mirrored elevator have, this was important to me, a second entrance (or exit), via a tradesman's elevator.

I gave the porter who sits in a little hut in front of the apartment building a generous tip, in case anyone asks for me he's to phone me while the visitor is on his way up. The tip was so big that he'll phone me anyway, even if my visitor gives him money. He'll—obviously—also pocket this sum and warn me. (I hope.) The police here don't take the private elevator. They're too badly paid for that, and the pension is low.

I've been living here for ten days and have only just unpacked my laptop and put it on the balcony table. Until now I've simply not had the urge to write. I read every German, English, and French newspaper I could lay hands on and in the first days roamed the city, especially the old city.

You get a good view of the cathedral towers from here, at night they're lit up and look like two little

Christmas trees. Right on the second day I went to look at the cathedral, which is considered the first sight to see in Brazil. An overextravagant grandiose baroque façade, its stucco work hidden for centuries under a layer of clay. Some years ago a piece of the smooth plasterwork broke off and revealed the splendor underneath. The inhabitants had plastered the façade three hundred years ago when Dutch pirates showed up off the coast, Calvinist bookkeepers who were known to dislike all Catholic decoration and not only took the gold and silver from churches but with their little hammers, like true cultural revolutionaries, smashed everything into little pieces, though more systematically than the Red Guard as they only shattered the porcelain covering on the walls of a temple in the Summer Palace in Beijing as high as their arms could reach. (The person who told me this, a German steel manager, added that standing tall he could have cleared up a good meter higher.)

Every time I see the two lit towers in the distance I have to think of Christmas Eve (probably the stylized Christmas trees on the Alsterhaus), and this though it's so hot here the sweat is running down me as I write. Somebody, Nietzsche, Graham Greene, or Abraham-a-Santa-Clara once said the tropical climate was unsuited to mental effort, but not on the other hand—but surely Nietzsche and Abraham-a-Santa-Clara won't have said this—to making love. You can hear it every night through the open windows and from the surrounding balconies: moaning, panting, shrieking, laughter, voices, music. (Connoisseurs, I read in a men's magazine, do it to music. But you'd have to avoid thrusting to the beat. Or you'd suddenly find yourself thinking of that disturbing word goose-step). So anyone who isn't on his mattress is out on his balcony where people eat and drink and laugh. A clumsy moth flutters around the light of a lamp, but isn't drawn to the blue light of the screen. Insects are rare up here and there are no mosquitoes at this height.

When I rented this apartment I took care, as I've said already, that there should be two exits. One leads via the lobby to the private elevator, a second is in the kitchen, through it you can get to the freight and tradesman's elevator.

They say in this country there are no racial barriers. To get a true picture you need to use both elevators. In the private elevator you meet almost exclusively whites, in the tradesman's elevator you meet almost exclusively blacks and browns, all the cleaning women, cooks, and children's nannies. People behave in a friendly way towards each other.

Yesterday when I met my cleaning woman (an elderly woman!) outside the building I said a few words to her in that soft lascivious language (Dembrowski would have enjoyed it); she laughed, replied with a few words slowly and as if talking to a child, then we parted. She went to the back to the tradesman's elevator, I went up in the private elevator, saw myself endlessly refracted in the mirrored walls, pulled back my shoulders and drove my fingers through my hair.

Outside in the harbor the white lights of the anchoring ships.

I had actually wanted to go on writing on the first day, I could even have written in the waiting rooms at the airports, an advantage of this contraption.

What I imagined: my uncle imagining me breathlessly, feverishly describing what happened that morning after the tennis match: how someone rang at the garden gate, how Britt asked through the intercom who it was, how when I heard the voice say my name, ask if I was there, I grabbed the binoculars and ran up the stairs, ran to the bedroom and looked over to the gate, there clearly visible behind the railing stood the man with red hair. Britt asked what he wanted. His name, he said in that Hamburg inflection so familiar to me, was Bender, he was a private detective. He had an arrest warrant for me.

—If you continue disturbing us, said Britt, I shall call the police.

—No need, said the voice of the man with the red hair, I've already brought them with me. And there they were, the two local policemen whom we knew and with whom we exchanged greetings. I could clearly see them tugging at their leather belts in embarrassment.

Britt said: —Just a moment, I'm coming to unlock the gate.

I ran downstairs, a fleeting kiss: —You too. I grabbed the packed bag and the laptop. I saw Britt slowly walking over the graveled path to the gate. I ran behind the house, got on the moped and drove down the narrow path that led to the door in the wall at the back, unlocked it, pushed the moped out, and drove to the town. I parked the moped at the supermarket, took a taxi to Malaga airport. That was it.

The Danish passport is perfect, you could call it the real thing. No problems getting past the border police at the airport, only the woman at security control said: Ola, and showed her white teeth. Presumably she'd never seen so many dollar bills before. But you're allowed to take out cash. I sat in the departure hall in front of the panoramic window, I'd bought cigarettes in the duty free shop, sat and smoked, outside a plane being signaled in, reflected in a pane of glass, a tanker drives past. My uncle, I suspect, would have given something to know how I felt. Some predictable stereotypical response: agitated, anxious, nervously smoking?

No, I could have shouted for joy. I sat there but I wanted to jump up, not out of a restless fear that at the last moment there'd be an announcement: Mr. Andersen, please come to the information desk, no, it was the desire to move on. When the tents are taken down the horizon is endless again, say the Tauregs.

I boarded the plane, fastened the seat belt, the engines started. The flight was to Salvador da Bahia. Not that I'd chosen Brazil in advance as my destination, I could also have flown to Uruguay or Mexico or entered the United States and simply gone underground. Begun a new life, married another woman, had children, a life as a media consultant in Los Angeles, as a hotel owner or simply someone of private means in a house in Beverly Hills. But I've gotten to know myself (an advantage when you've reached your forties), I would have gone to pieces with such a carefree attitude that nothing mattered. I would have become ill with homesickness, how else explain that on the Costa del Sol of all places I kept thinking of Hamburg. The Grosse Trampgang. The perpetrator returns to the scene of the crime. I didn't take the next flight to the USA, but a plane to Brazil, to Salvador da Bahia. Brazil has complicated extradition arrangements, as we know since one of the English train robbers has shown himself lazing there on Copacabana beach.

▼

The telephone rang and I started violently because I thought it was my mother, but as usual it was Britt. Only she knows this number, I phoned her three days ago after moving into the apartment.

Britt had already told me when she first called how she'd gone to the gate, how it turned out that the detective with the red hair and the Hamburg dialect spoke no Spanish, how she'd spoken to the policemen, how she'd said the way the man was behaving was all very strange, he's looking for someone, she said translating, but the description of the person he was looking for seemed more to fit himself, how the two policemen suddenly changed their behavior, no longer fiddling with their belts in embarrassment but fairly brusquely requesting Mr. Bender to come with them to the police station, how she apparently translated this for him and said they wanted to go with him to look for her husband on the beach where, as she'd told the two, he'd gone, how the man then raced off, the police now after him because they thought he was trying to run away, how they stopped him, grabbed his arm, twisted his arm when he tried to pull free, how they pushed the stunned private detective into the car, then drove off, but then phoned, three hours later. There was a telegram, an exact description, confirmation from Interpol, unfortunately, they said in Spanish, your husband is the wanted man.

Dembrowski was quickly arrested. He came to the garden gate carrying a packed suitcase. So he'd packed too, though unlike me only packed warm clothes as summer in Hamburg was coming to an end. And Fuhlsbüttel apparently wasn't as overheated as it used to be and prisoners ran around in undershirts even in winter.

—Give up, Britt said, let's go to Hamburg.

—No, I said to Britt, I don't want to, not yet.

—Your mother phoned again. She read about the failed attempt to arrest you. She said she'd seen it in the cards. She wanted your phone number. I said I didn't know it. Of course she didn't believe me. She talked about your uncle again. What he wants to know is how you went into finance and what your intentions were.

That was exactly what the court wanted to know. The leap from selling life insurance to investments. Was it planned with the aim of later making myself independent in order to cash in huge sums of money, as it were a long-term, planned deception?

To counter this suspicion my defense counsel called Rob as a witness. Rob had been a headhunter and then later started an agency to promote promising tennis talent.

Rob was summoned on the second day of the trial. An important witness for the defense, said Dr. Blank, to establish it was no conspiracy dreamed up well in advance. Britt again sat with Lolo in the first row, next to her Sannchen, and in the last row among the whispering pensioners, perhaps they were already discussing the verdict, there sat Renate, Dembrowski's wife, tall and slim, ash-blonde, with dark eyes set far apart. She stared across at Dembrowski, but whenever he looked in her direction she ducked a little behind the man sitting in front of her. She'd once said to Britt: —I love him, though I often ask myself why I do.

Sannchen had taken off her mink coat, sat in the really very overheated courtroom in a short silk dress, dark blue—it almost looked as if she'd come from a funeral. But for a funeral the dress was unbuttoned too low at the front so that when she leaned over to her handbag, which was on the floor, you could see her breasts. She reminded me of those English women who'd shown their men (naturally only the lower, the non-commissioned ranks), the sailors on Her Majesty's ships their bare breasts as they sailed from South-ampton to the Falklands: if you come back, sweetheart, here they are, cushions of pleasure. Britt wore a discreet dark grey turtleneck sweater, without jewelry. That had been seized. Sometimes when the witnesses talked about the loss of their money she'd twist a strand of hair round her finger, the only sign of her nervousness. She'd painted her nails red, but a discreet red. Lolo sat next to her and was bored when the talk was about Dembrowski, picked at her fingernails, gazed round the courtroom. A slight vibration of her hair, she was obvi-ously shaking a leg under the bench, probably her right, the way she does or did at home because here, or rather, in Spain, she suddenly stopped doing it and would sit completely still and lost in her thoughts. When they talked about me she listened with concen-tration. Now and then she gave me a furtive wave. The judge also noticed, but was nice enough not to say anything.

Robert, known as Rob

Rob stepped into the witness box. Profession? Head-hunter, now agent for tennis talent.

Robert, called Rob, had begun a banking apprentice-ship and wanted to become a tennis pro. He broke off the apprenticeship and for two years played in German and American provincial tournaments. Then, after a series of defeats, he gave up his tennis career and com-pleted his banking apprenticeship. Robert went to America and after four years came back as Rob, the headhunter. He'd met a man in New York who dealt with managers and that way earned more than a top tennis player.

As headhunter Rob entered the New World of the Federal Republic, where he immediately made the serious mistake of putting headhunter into German and introducing himself as *Kopfjäger*. This word inev-itably suggests small, black Indian heads dried in the sand, with their overlong hair and lashes. In my view thoroughly esthetic objects that in their shriveled state illustrate the essence of the living head, its thought-filled heaviness, and therefore its strength.

In Germany Rob met not only with sneaky prejudice, but with open hostility, and was introduced at a party as a dealer in human beings and seller of souls. Rela-tions were still draped in the old Franconian style. Ei-ther people were sought through announcements in newspapers, and then all kinds of possible and impossi-ble candidates showed up, or you were after a particu-lar individual: company X wanted the manager from company Y. If you weren't able to meet the man at the golf club or at the Lions, this only worked by arranging complicated invitations so you could get to know him and make him an offer. A complicated social code of behavior was set in motion, as if Spanish grandees were marriage-brokering. Rob had come to make this more simple.

Everything can be bought, he said, that's obvious, and almost everything can be sold. There only has to be a demand: kidneys, ice cream, children, women (á la carte from Indonesia, Ghana, Colombia etc.), academic honors, turbines, and even stories. To lament this fact like my uncle does (who by the way does nothing except sell lamentable stories), is touching and passé.

Whatever you want to buy or sell you can buy or sell if you can make clear to the other side what advantages the deal brings. It's how you do it. A question of representation.

Rob began to work as a headhunter and his fees were high.

While still in Los Angeles he'd heard that an American engineering firm wanted to buy a small factory in Bavaria that produced mechanical saws and screws. The first thing that had to be done was to shake up the management. The firm wasn't exactly bankrupt, but hadn't expanded for years, which was almost like being bankrupt. The man who ran the firm, a friendly Bavarian, member of the citizens' association, at weekends put in an appearance as a yodler in a hat with a tuft of chamois hair, in a band dressed in folk costume in which seven men from the firm played brass. This in effect made it impossible to fire the seven, and that was how they behaved, rehearsed during working hours, were absent in the mornings after a hefty drinking bout. The American management sacked the yodeling director. He, who'd made mountains tremble with his jubilation, consequently fell into a depression (after all, he was already 56), at home went down to the boiler room where he sat all day, then later also all night in a chair, first without speaking, then without moving—only when the burner flared a quiet shudder ran through him.

Two managers were to replace him. An internal communicator and an external communicator. Modern American management, as Rob explained to me. The internal communicator oversees the finances, the firm's structure, keeps an eye on the balance sheet, especially when it's been so doctored as to become noticeable, he's somewhat stiff, sparing of words, the ideal type wears suits with sleeves worn to a shine, a desk man, someone who holds things together, who makes merciless cuts where a saving can be made, who takes unpopular decisions, fires people or sends them into early retirement, even those that have been with the firm for a long time, he's someone who doesn't permit himself any sentimentality, a genius at organization inclined if anything to pessimism who can smell out decay, disorganization, disaster, who in other words guarantees the optimal functioning of the firm, who oils the firm's internal machine, ruthlessly changes parts, energetically tightens screws.

The internal communicator can look like Quasimodo, be short-sighted, have a speech defect; the external communicator has to have an attractive appearance, cut a good figure, play sports (if only because of the contacts), preferably have a pleasant voice, speak clearly and be married to a woman who knows how to listen and dress. The external communicator, said Rob, should be able to approach anyone, if he were to compare himself to a tree then the quebracho tree, totally bouyant, above all he must show the determination of Luther as when he appeared before the Augsburg Diet: Here I am, I cannot do otherwise. Unlike Luther however he mustn't be pigheaded. The external communicator, Rob explained in his relaxed but all the more convincing manner, has to be able to sell ice cream just as well as high-pressure turbines, envelopes, or mechanical saws. Mechanical saws for example even when the potential buyer has no garden. Because mechanical saws prevent colds.

—What? How?

—Quite simple. The air dries out from central heating. But not if you heat with an oven. Central heating is mechanically fueled heating, lifeless, you hear a sound in the pipes now and then, perhaps a gurgle, or a monotonous distant thumping. Nobody has yet examined the link between central heating and depression. Compare central heating to a Danish cast-iron stove. The blaze and crackle of logs, the smells from the different kinds of wood.

—But why, I asked, I thought the man was selling mechanical saws.

—Yes of course, said Rob, but wait—amazingly this healthy form of heating also gives you a relaxing activity because you can saw wood in the cellar, it's really enjoyable sawing environmentally-friendly and cheap firewood into small logs with the small handy mechanical saw, *Homeworker* model, it's useful, wonderfully restorative work after an irritating eight-hour day in the office, something you can do in the yard, in the garage, in the cellar, even in your living room because the saw has reduced sound, and it has a shavings ejector that you can direct where you want so the wood shavings can be easily swept up.

The external communicator has to be able to do all this, he has to know the small, workaday desires of people, has to find convincing motives for buying his product, motives that then go back into the product, that remodel it in such a way that people buying it are satisfied.

The external communicator whom Rob had placed in the Bavarian firm did in fact have a small mechanical saw for domestic use made, with reduced sound and a powerful adjustable shavings ejector. The saw became a sales hit.

Rob had quickly found this external communicator.

The internal communicator was far harder to find. This applied not only to this one case, but was a basic problem. Whereas what distinguishes the external communicator is that his appearance strikes you, therefore he gets known, the mark of a good internal communicator is that his outward appearance attracts no attention. He works in silence, he prefers the office, his favorite place is the desk.

To find the right internal communicator Rob had developed a method of his own. He acquired the phone numbers of managers who were responsible for the internal organization of companies. He then phoned them on a Saturday morning. Those that didn't answer he immediately crossed off his list. Three answered. He said he had a lucrative job offer: An American firm had taken over a medium-sized company and was looking for an internal communicator. What? The numbers man, you could say.

One was about to be pensioned off. Another had just bought himself into the firm. The third Rob met for a meal in town. How would they recognize each other? He'd wear a red handkerchief in his breast pocket.

It was Rob's trademark, this red handkerchief. Tie and handkerchief in discreet red silk. How else could he have described himself, it would have sounded like a frivolous exaggeration: 6 foot 3 inches tall, hair lightly parted, falling loose, with white blonde streaks in the summer, calm movements, slim, thoroughly fit, good posture, light blue eyes. Himself the perfect external communicator.

He didn't have the missionary zeal of Heinz Dembrowski who deeply believed in stock market speculation, who saw it as a guarantee of affluence and liberty. Rob had the relaxed friendliness of all those who can undress in brightly lit rooms without having to think of disturbing details (my legs from the knees down are too short). A happy nature if there hadn't been that slight anxiety that could quickly escalate into a flapping, nervous, hectic rush when something didn't immediately go his way. That's why he'd given up professional tennis. If he did a shaky serve, then another that was out, his technically brilliant playing immediately collapsed, he'd get more and more timid, anxious, weak, and misplay the simplest balls, so that even I beat him now and then.

(And in bed he was—actually I'd made up my mind not to tell any bedroom stories, the following is only an explanatory detail—he was like a man who'd been swimming for a long time in an icy stream. I know this from one of Rob's former girl friends who hawked her bedroom stories. With him, she told Britt and me one evening, it was a long unsuccessful wrestling match that you had to start over and over, until at last, she said, he was up and then he was off.)

Just as he could anticipate his opponent's play, so he had a finely tuned feeling for moods and followed changes of opinion at a very early stage so he could then represent the anticipated opinions cleverly and with conviction—and that way helped to give them validity. For him to be in a minority was like being excluded, like having to stand in the corner, not being allowed to join in the game. That was how his testimony was in court. It became evident that he severely condemned our business practices. I believe, had it been expected of him, he'd have allowed himself to be driven into saying that when he introduced me to the world of finance he'd had the uneasy feeling that I might perhaps not have the character to resist the temptation to make crooked deals. But Dr. Blank questioned him skillfully and also let him talk about himself, and the judge was patient and let him talk. Because later Rob had got us most of our investors and had earned richly along with us in our fraudulent dealings.

It made me think of what Dembrowski, schooled by the Free German Youth, had called Rob: an opportunist by conviction.

It was just this ability to quickly and surely recognize the strengths and weaknesses of others through his own weaknesses that would have made him not only Germany's first, but undoubtedly also greatest headhunter, had it not been for two catastrophic misplacements that then ruined Rob's reputation and consequently his business.

Banknotes, washproof

I like going through the old town quarter. The narrow cobbled streets remind me of the Grosse Trampgang even though the houses here are painted in the brightest colors: white, red, and blue.

On a slightly sloping square stands a cast-iron column, a plaque explains to the stranger: Here a hundred years ago slaves were publicly whipped, here an iron bit was put in their mouths when they had cursed their masters.

Then screams of pain filled the square, today a Brazilian tourist guide is explaining to a group of German tourists how the iron bit was fastened to the lips; doing this she sticks her finger with its silver painted nail in her mouth.

On the square there's a luxury hotel famous for its view over the bay and harbor. The bar's miserable, lousy drinks. No comparison to Nelson's Bar down on the beach.

Up here are the tourists from North America, mostly retirees in Hawaiian shirts, women with piled-up hairdos (as if my mother had been at work), in the brightest colors: metallic grey, blue, blonde. A group of young Swedes, Polar Circle pallid, is being tipped out of an airport bus.

Two streets further along is the tropical gangland, tangle of plastic strips at the open doors, a few women in long chaste white dresses that emphasize their dark skins even more, on their heads skillfully twisted turbans of red and blue cloth. A few children in the act of shooting each other with plastic pistols.

A classic building, the old Anatomical Institute, a ruin. The stone Hippocrates sitting at the entrance has ferns growing from his lap, his hands and feet are leprously eaten away. Next to it a neglected garden, the only one in this district, monuments under the palms, medical men in cutaway and stand-up collar, some apparently presidential candidates who had died by pistol shot and poison. A square lined with tall tattered palms: stands, eating-houses, the throb of drums breaks against the façades of the buildings, seven men are beating empty oil barrels, a girl with a penny-whistle accompanies the rhythm, brings the drummers in, waves her arms, everyone's moving, listeners, onlookers pushing, shoving, swaying, over there someone leaps up and already the others are leaping, the drumming hits you right in the chest, they're dancing a dance in which every limb dances itself to exhaustion. Turn the corner, in the alley the drumming, the whistle blasts are already in the distance, turn another corner, silence. Cats. From an open balcony door moans of pleasure of two voices, one higher, one lower, beyond the open balcony door in the dark of the room a wild ride, naked to the waist, a red turban, that's how she rides in a wild gallop through the hot afternoon.

I was warned in advance not to go alone in this district. Tourists apparently are always mugged here. Two months ago an Englishman, clinging too hard to his camera, was stabbed. So the district isn't very different from certain parts of Berlin, Rome, or New York. I'm not afraid, but I'm not carrying a briefcase, not wearing a wristwatch, a ring, only a few *cruzados* in my trouser pocket so as not to—in case it happens—further provoke some embittered street robber by not having anything, and then he'd feel he'd been taken for a ride.

Thinking about my uncle who's taking up more and more space, here too. So I asked myself, walking along these streets, if he, who travels a lot as I know from my mother, knows this city. Did he walk these streets with the same timidity and hesitation that he used to go down the Silbersackstrasse (the poetry of those street names!), past all the tarts, pimps, and drunks?

Then, although he was quite a bit taller than me, he always looked really small, it was me that had to watch out for him. You could sense that he didn't come from the district. He didn't have that smell of dust and sweat that had dried in the fresh air. He smelled of laundry detergent. On several occasions he was beaten up by other children, apparently for no reason. But I knew the reason. Even when intimidated he still had his arrogant look. He simply looked differently at the future, you could say. And naturally you could see that he couldn't hit back. He hadn't been taught that at home, that if somebody goes for you you immediately hit back with all the strength you can muster. He'd hit back as an experiment. At the last moment he'd brake the blow, hesitate, falter for a second (you mustn't hit!), a slowing down of movement before the blow in the face instead of increased acceleration. You should not, as every brawler in the port district of Hamburg knows, aim for the surface, the skin, the thought of it bursting is irritating, you aim for some point beneath, somewhere where you can direct the hatred you feel for this other person inside that skin, like a stone inside a fruit.

So he'd come from his respectable Eppendorf district where there was always something that had to be fin-

227

ished, finish eating, finish drawing, finish doing your sums, finish your writing (and then you were finished), come to us in the port district, sit at Grannie Hilde's table not timid anymore but like a little prince, eat without digging your elbows into your neighbor, hold yourself straight, his father'd say, don't mumble, chin on your collar, don't fidget, posture, get on with it, do it, boy, do it. That's why, as his behavior shows, he's still fighting his father to whom he still sometimes has to prove things—does he know this? And so he comes to him in his dreams, the revenant, the nightmare, the weight on his chest, whereas the advantage of many fathers, as I've already said, is that I was left in peace once they disappeared. Only my mother, she's still here. She'd say, every time my uncle came to us: —The stories that boy tells.

He told stories and that was how he made you forget his big nose, as I saw once later at the Orchid Cafe. I was working as a magazine salesman, he was studying. He was sitting with some young people, all obviously friends, at a table by a pool covered in water lilies. Next to him sat a girl, eighteen, perhaps only seventeen, holding his right hand with both of hers, or rather, reverently pressing it into her lap. Next to them the parents, hers, clearly well-to-do. A girl all social climbers rave about, I say this with specific knowledge of the up-and-coming middle class: the little girl-woman. Because later I saw this woman frequently at the side of investment-hungry businessmen. A decorative type, if that's what you like, in fact there are copies of her in display windows, as a doll: an unobtrusive nose, but strikingly large eyes shaded by lashes, a slight pout, a silky gleam to her hair which falls softly onto her face or gets shaken. Slender limbs, delicate wrists and ankles. The girl at my uncle's side had blue marks on her shins, which betrayed the hockey player.

My uncle told his story and I stood in the shade of a potted palm and watched them laughing, yes, they all laughed and laughed, the young people and the older couple, the girl's parents. Perhaps they're laughing about me, I thought, perhaps he's just now told how I, I was five at the time, once locked myself in the bathroom in a cafe. I'd been invited by my uncle's parents for coffee and cake to the Alster Pavilion. And I'd run off to the bathroom with my uncle because it looked quite different from the lavatory at home. Here everything worked, was light, covered in chrome, in mirrors. But I couldn't turn the door handle and when I tried to crawl under the toilet door I got stuck, lay there with my head on the pissy tiles, my chest wedged tight, couldn't move forwards or back and shrieked, and everybody who came rushing into this pisshole laughed. Then it turned out the door couldn't be opened from the outside without crushing my ribs. A fireman came and I had to be sawn out of the door.

Then my uncle showed me how you opened the door from the inside. The doorknob had a little button that you had to press to turn the handle.

I'd never seen a handle like that in the port district, probably it was the very first doorknob with a button in Hamburg. At the table they were laughing, six young people and the parents: a man who first hangs his new Burberry in the garden for a month before wearing it, a woman in a discreet Rodier dress. They laughed, the nice parents, the nice young people. He wanted to get to the top, my uncle, climb the heavenly ladder, head

229

west in the direction of the setting sun, the Elbchaussee where the money is. So did I.

I had lunch in a simple restaurant in the port, a charcoal grilled fish, you pick the flesh with your fingers, no fork, no knife, just squeeze a lemon and a few drops, a jet of juice squirts out.

Something I usually enjoy, paying, dipping into my pocket, pulling out a bundle of notes, counting them and adding a good tip, disturbs me here, in fact, I feel aversion every time, more than that, revulsion when out of my pocket I pull these limp, yellow-brown notes that absorb the humidity. You have to carry them in thick bundles in your trouser pocket, and it struck me how fashion adapts to lifestyles, because in the frugal days of hitchhiking tight jeans seemed the appropriate pants, a comb and twenty marks in the back pocket, while for comfortable journeys to the beach hotels of the south baggy trousers seem right, where the valueless currency of the beautiful Third World can find a place in the deep folds of trouser pockets.

These notes are so disgracefully soiled that you touch them with revulsion and think you can feel the grease and sweat of all the hands through which they've passed. That the notes are for big sums doesn't stop them getting soiled. Often the original figures have been stamped over and reduced, 100,000 turned by a small stamp into 10, occasionally though the numbers of zeros were significantly raised by a stamp. Printed on the notes are touching scenes from the Republic's period of rapid industrial expansion, and right now the times are similar: bearded men make lively speeches to a reverentially attentive and bearded audience. Certain major artists are portrayed on some of the notes: sculptors, a studio in the background, painters, composers. A poet unknown to me, a man with glasses, sits at a desk. On the reverse side of the note a poem is printed. The note had been stuck together three times with tape, but a part of the poet's desk is still missing.

Compare it to our banknotes back at home, that stay banknotes even when they've been twice in the wash. Here after one wash, if you leave them in your trousers, they dissolve into a fibrous paper lump. You can feel the stability of a currency—at any rate, I can. The pleasure of handling the money. It's not by chance that in Switzerland, if you shop in Zurich, which I've always liked doing, you get the impression that you're always getting freshly-printed money for change. The size of the institution that withdraws and destroys old money in a country also informs you about its creditworthiness. And the ant depicted on the thousand-franc note reveals every bit as much about the mentality and economy of Switzerland as the notes of printed poetry about Brazil. And how smooth, but firm the Swiss franc notes feel to the touch, a firm tenderness, not be be compared to the plastic cards with which you pay in the USA. Perhaps there's a connection between the loss of what can be sensually touched, namely the silver coins, the beautiful dollar notes designed according to the golden section, uniform in size, of which there are now fewer in circulation, and the increasing work, and perhaps even sexual neuroses.

This afternoon I was in the local library to see what books they had about Easter Island. But they don't have any academic books in English, French, or German, and even in Portuguese (which I don't understand) there are only four titles, all popular science

231

picture books. A climate hostile to books. In the humid salty air books draw in water like sponges, swell, get moldy. In the library it smells like on hot days on the Holstein moor, of decay, wood, grass, but here nothing gets preserved, the Graubolle bog man would be unthinkable.

I saw him when I was a child, he sleeps in a glass case on his turf bed in Aarhus, brown and flat as a Peking duck, his throat slit, not because as the proud bearded professors of Teutonic Studies imagined he'd had illicit sexual relations with a girl, but because he'd been sacrificed. Apart from the remains of a healthy vegetarian diet, sustenance for the journey into the beyond, also found in his stomach and preserved best of all were roundworms. The fingernails are dark brown, almost black, but in such good condition that you can see the fine grooves in the horn.

The external communicator

I don't think my uncle will meet Rob, however inquisitive and tough-minded he is tracking down my story. If he wanted to meet Rob he'd have to fly to Los Angeles. Rob moved there a year before we and the firm went up in smoke. He'd stopped being a headhunter and in Los Angeles started a Financial Agency of Hopeful Tennisplayers, FAHT for short. I acquired two shares at 10,000. One in a then 12-year-old Chinese boy from New York, whom Rob had seen practicing in a back yard on Spring Street. The boy was practicing serves standing in a tar barrel so he'd hit with as great a stretch as possible, calmly and from above. The other share was in the son of an eye doctor. Rob described him as tennis-autistic, he did nothing except play on the family's own court, sometimes at night he'd wake his private coach to try out a new serve about which he'd been dreaming. The boy was assymetrical, right and left looked like the halves of different people. The right arm, the right shoulder, even the right half of the neck were those of a weightlifter, but on the left side you could see the gangling fourteen-year-old still in the process of growing.

Since then I've followed the tennis reports from all parts of the world. But neither of the tennis hopefuls ever appeared in any of them, not even in the preliminary rounds. Something went wrong—that's how you'd have to put it. I'd like to have known what. Destinies left dangling like cut threads.

I'd like to have asked Rob myself, but this clearly wasn't possible while he was being questioned as a witness—he'd just flown to Germany for some indoor junior championship.

But even if he'd been easy to reach for my uncle, Rob could only tell him what he'd already said in court: he'd got to know me as the right hand of an external communicator, whom he himself had previously placed in a paper factory.

This external communicator was my teacher. I admired him. I could laugh at him and still be amazed by him. I think he could—if one had the choice—have been the father I'd have wished for myself. I never had to take him quite seriously and he was the total opposite of all my other fathers. While he, destined to plunge, was convinced that in me he'd found his business foster-son. It was he who always said: —You have to write about your work as a life insurance salesman. Naturally he also quietly hoped I'd write about him, I'd be his biographer. I want to do it here so that my uncle, the vampire, doesn't get hold of him. Perhaps he's already called on him and questioned him and if you question him everything pours out of Christian Godemann, external communicator: he'd tell how I came to him when I was still a life insurance salesman, how I carefully prepared myself, read up in *Who's Who,* a few dates there, quite clever of me, hobbies and so on, how I informed myself about his wife who wrote poetry, how I showed up at his office, having been given an appointment by his secretary, how I brought the conversation round to the town of Aschaffenberg where his wife was born, and then to Heinse, how I quoted from an old literature lexicon and told him a story: Heinse, librarian to the Elector of Mainz, after months of work had laid down an educational path through the books by putting red strips of paper between all the pages of world literature where erotic or sexual scenes were described, as it were tempting snacks along this educational path of pleasure. An enormous, knowledgeable, loving task undertaken by Heinse to please the life-loving Archbishop, because it was a literary educational path through the history of the life and customs of the last two thousand years. After the Elector's death—Heinse also died very young—a really narrow-minded bishop became Elector. One day he went to the library and began to read the pages with the red markers on the assumption that a path of healing through literature had been marked, pious pages that elevated the soul, but suddenly found himself on quite a different path and ordered all the markers to be instantly removed. An assistant librarian counted 2,436.

Godemann will tell my uncle that with this story I got onto the early death of Heinse and with Heinse onto the increasing number of deaths today in traffic accidents, and then finally I asked him what life insurance he actually had—and then he'd said he was totally insured but he needed an assistant, a right hand as it were. He'd just advertised the post. Someone, he'd tell my uncle, who could keep him, Godemann, from his work for almost an hour with a story knew a thing or two about the secret desires of people, he was sure to be a good sales adviser. That's what he'd tell my uncle, that's what he told the court.

I'd got myself an appointment with Godemann. His secretary opened the door, five minutes, she said, and he pointed to a leather chair in front of his desk: teak, teak, teak, a hundred-year-old giant of the rain forest had been sawed to pieces and joined anew at right angles. The desk—a wastepaper basket.

Godemann knew of my uncle, it was one of the few occasions I was able to bring my uncle into a business conversation. Yes, he'd read something by him. He got up to pull a book out of the bookcase, and then I saw it and got a shock. Something was hanging out of his trousers. What was it? A pale blue penis? A handkerchief? Godemann put my uncle's book down on the table. He'd read this one. I saw he'd caught the end of his shirt in the zipper.

I pulled myself together and said: —Your trousers are undone.

—Oh, he said, stuffed the shirt in his trousers, pulled

up the zipper, took off his Cartier glasses which made him look as if he were working in a kitchen deep frying, stuck the side-piece in his mouth, looked at me with his short-sighted eyes. And then he said it: —Would you like to be my assistant? I'm looking for a right hand, as it were. The pay is good, I should add. Your job: Brainstorming, something we'd do together, gathering material for speeches etc., above all, new ideas. I think you understand.

—Yes, I said.

At a first glance the external communicator didn't necessarily look like an external communicator, with his permanently smeared glasses, his splattered shirts, jackets, trousers, from which you could read the day's menu. But when he talked you understood why Godemann was the external communicator, he could talk himself and his listeners into a state of enthusiasm that resembled religious mania. He was a sales genius, a genius at discovering new products, a genius of merchandising.

In the first weeks already I witnessed how he sold a Catholic monsignor by the name of Bär a huge amount of typing paper. I was going to write "talked into buying," but that wouldn't fit, and would falsify the work of persuasion that went into it.

Dr. Bär, a church lawyer in a black suit, white collar outside black pullover, lilac socks, had until then regularly ordered the 10,000 sheets of typing paper used yearly by the episcopal diocese from a Bavarian paper factory. But now he wanted to cut down on other estimated costs because prices, as he himself said, were altogether too shameless and not at all Catholic. He'd said this right at the beginning of the conversation, and naturally with the tactical intention of putting pressure on the external communicator, by making it clear that he would need it to be a really favorable offer. Everybody thinks, he said, that the church can pay anything. Even some of the new negotiating parties had put estimates before him that were far too high. He drank the coffee the secretary had put on the table, he turned down the cognac Godemann offered him.

When I phoned Dr. Bär to arrange an appointment with the external communicator I'd imagined the deep voice, which spoke in a cultured Bavarian dialect, belonged to a popular, sociable man fond of sensual pleasures. Then this gawky rack with black-framed glasses showed up.

—I could have saved myself the time, said the rack, and the journey, I should have asked for samples to be sent.

—Yes, said Godemann, if I could be granted a wish it would be for a day of 25 hours, just a modest wish for 25 hours, one extra hour, only one, to think about all I don't have time for during the rest of the day.

—The less time you have, said Dr. Bär and nibbled one of the vanilla cream wafers he'd been offered, the quicker it goes.

Godemann took off his glasses, for a moment put the side-piece in his mouth as if he were sucking it. —Yes, he said: What is time, asked St. Augustine. Yes, it's hard to measure time. Because there is no past and neither is there a future. But the present is without dimension or duration. Again the side-piece disappeared into his mouth. He sucked the side-piece, not overdoing it, not actually sucking hard, but you could see what he was doing, I saw the side-piece move in his mouth. But how can you call something long, asked St. Augustine, or short, if it doesn't exist. Because the past no longer exists. And the future doesn't yet exist.

Dr. Bär crossed his legs and dug in his earhole with his finger as if he were trying to pull out a plug. Probably he was thinking he needed to answer because Godemann again had the side-piece in his mouth and you noticed the short tongue movements by the frame. Thoughtfully he looked at Dr. Bär who suddenly was sitting there like an examinee, he carefully put the wafer he'd already bitten into back on the plate, but before he could say anything Godemann again took the side-piece out of his mouth. But when was time past long? When it had just passed? Or before, when it was still present? Surely it could only be long if it actually was something that could be long?

Godemann suddenly looked at me, and so I tried to differentiate between what is and was and will be and what was and is and will be. We ought to say time past was long in the sense of time that had once been present, because only as time present had it been long. But the present is without duration and therefore cannot be long.

And again he put the side-piece in his mouth. Dr. Bär could now have said, perhaps wanted to say, I'm a lawyer, I wanted to order paper, I haven't read St. Augustine, but know the bishop wrote a treatise about St. Augustine, at any rate Dr. Bär sat up, the schoolboy astonishment had vanished.

But then Godemann said: —What we live by constantly, obviously mostly without questioning it, structured by our watches, our appointment books, by the watchful eye of my secretary, Mrs. Bittner—is time. What from the outside always appears to us in small segments, in minutes, hours, days, weeks, time counted, easily overseen, leads us, should we ask on what time is founded, to the fathomless. He briefly put the side-piece back in his mouth. Nothing can be taken for granted, if you think about it it's like the flying donkey.

—For God's sake, what flying donkey?

—Yes. The brothers in the Dominican monastery wanted to show Thomas Aquinas the flying donkey.

Dr. Bär sank back in his chair.

—I'm sure you know that Thomas Aquinas was called the dumb ox by his fellow monks. A heavy man of unusual size and with a mighty posterior who silently shoveled food and knowledge into himself. One day after he'd sat at his place in the refectory, taking up two seats—they'd had to saw off the arm of a chair for Thomas so that he could sit—suddenly the brothers called to him: —A donkey's flying past outside. And what did St. Thomas Aquinas do? He ran to the window and looked out. And when the merry monks were splitting their sides with laughter, he said, returning to his food, it seemed likelier to him that a donkey could fly than that monks would lie.

—A nice story, said Monsignor Bär, a story I didn't know.

—Read Umberto Eco, said Godemann. Because there's something behind this story. The story says: everything is possible. The Middle Ages were a time when miracles abounded. They were the reality. Reality was delirium. So why shouldn't a donkey fly past? Not everything was calculable yet, and when it was, then only by feet and cubits, by parts of the body that were always at hand and still highly inexact. Because where was the prototype of the hand? The prototype of the cubit?

What did Monsignor Bär think? You could see it in his face: Good god, what's all this about? What's he driving at? What does he want? What a mystery?

Godemann put on his smeared glasses: —The hand of a southern Italian is smaller than the hand of a Swede. A human chaos, the time of the sectarians. Heretical sects made the streets unsafe, wanted to build wondrous worlds. Sodomy and fantastical utopias, murder and manslaughter, cubits and feet. Then suddenly Thomas begins to put order into the world. No more hallucinations now, instead things can be calculated, therefore become more conceivable, tangible— Thomas praises the desire to swim, understandable with that enormous weight—and so slowly with great mental effort people develop eyes for size, for measurable size. A few hundred years later the Spanish measure Florida. Slaves chained to each other are driven into the swamps, the mango forests, shivering with malaria, bitten by vipers, to measure the land with standardized chains, to lay chain on chain. They die in their thousands from fevers, emaciated, with running sores, and this is how with great effort an attempt is made to create order in the world, to find a uniform verifiable measure for continents, countries, streets, and paths, for all sizes.

Where's he heading, I thought, he's lost the thread. He'd told me before the Monsignor came that the Monsignor's paymaster, the bishop, had done a doctorate on Thomas Aquinas and was a recognized St. Augustine scholar. But Florida? The slaves? The viper's bite.

—This chaotic state of affairs slowly disappears, says the external communicator and again takes off his glasses, puts the side-piece in his mouth, immediately takes it out again: —In 1792 the French Academy of Science decides to lay down a uniform linear measure, the forty-millionth part of the earth's meridian. Because unlike the degrees of latitude—they also refrained from taking the equator—all meridians are of the same length, and as people are uniform so they should take the earth's circumference, which is uniform. And to establish this forty-millionth part means to determine its length, a length not simply arbitrarily cut away, but exactly calculated from the earth's circumference, therefore also ve-ri-fi-able. And so in June 1792, in the year the monarchy is done away with, two mathematicians and astronomers are sent off, members of the Academy of Science: Pierre Méchain and Jean-Baptiste Delambre. Méchain works in the direction of Barcelona, Delambre in the direction of Dunkirk. The meridian is to be measured between these places and the point of intersection, Paris. But what does this mean in a land where revolution reigns, the peasants are in revolt, and there are famine riots?

—The two travel with their theodolites through a country which is drowning in blood and violence, where the opponents of the Revolution are locked in a special ship on the Rhône, where even the stone saints of Nôtre Dame have been symbolically beheaded because it was believed they depicted emperors and kings—Mr. Bär sits up straight in the chair—in this country then, while real or supposed opponents of the Revolution are hunted down, the two with their theodolites climb hills, bastions, church towers, all the prominent places they need to climb for their work of measuring, but precisely because of this come under suspicion—weren't they English spies, staring at the countryside through binoculars and then noting things down in a numerical code? They're driven off with pitchforks, bloodhounds set on them, they're imprisoned, released again after intervention by the central government, they work in the glowing August sun of Spain and the wet cold storms that sweep across from the Bay of Biscay, the king, Monsieur Capet, is beheaded, Robespierre dragged to the guillotine, Napoleon comes, the Directoire is set up, when finally after seven years both scientists are able to end their work in the year 1799.

—The two bring with them the standard meter which before had been merely estimated, as it turned out now, quite accurately. The meter, cast in bronze, is put up at the Palais de Justice in Paris, here anyone can check the measurement whenever he wants, no longer any arbitrariness, any length you want, but—this is the true revolution—a calculated segment of the creation measured by human intellect (Godemann gave the Monsignor a quick nod), the forty-millionth part of the meridian of the globe. And from that time on all other measurements have been calculated from it: volume, area, weight. Unification et simplification. Vive le dix! And this standard meter is also the starting point for the DIN format.

—The DIN format? Mr. Bär moved to the edge of the chair, he sat there as if he was going to pounce.

—Yes, said Godemann and briefly sucked the sidepiece. The German industrial specification, thanks to which the paper fits into the envelope, unlike in Italy,

242

Brazil, in the USA, or even India, where if you buy typing paper you never know whether when folded the page will fit the envelope, where then to get it in you have to make an extra fold which then leaves one of those ugly paper bumps that always comes through the envelope, or else you reach for the scissors, cut off the extra piece, then see that the new edge of the paper is crooked. Nothing for it, you then have to cut off another wedge from the paper, which now makes the edge on the other side crooked, so again you have to cut off a little strip and so it goes on and on, until you see that the edge of the paper has now reached your signature, now there's nothing for it but to write another letter. I'm sure you know those folded, mutilated letters from underdeveloped countries, a result of two uncoordinated sizes. But what does DIN standardization offer? Production of the right size (he tapped on a pile of DIN A4 typing paper which he'd taken care to put on the table), the sweat of the fever-stricken Florida slaves is here, the icy nights of Dunkirk, the flying donkey, the problem of the measurement of time, and as you can see here, our watermark that always when I hold the paper to the light makes me think of Thomas Aquinas swimming, the measurement that man has taken from the creation, not presumptuously, but rationally.

—Is there a discount for quantity? Monsignor Bär asked, intimidated. The firm from which he previously bought paper offered a discount of 2% per. . . .

—Of course, said Godemann. For an order of 200,000 sheets we give a discount of 2%.

You could see the disappointment in Mr. Bär's face. Now Godemann handed over a sheet and Mr. Bär held it to the light coming through the big window. And now slowly a smile came to the Monsignor's face, a very inward, radiant smile. The watermark showed a small stylized fish.

On this paper you could truly be called upon to write.

Mr. Bär ordered 200,000 sheets for the diocese, of course with the watermark, he said, and handed the sheet over the table to Godemann.

The lizard in the bottle

I'm convinced my uncle at some time also wrote on the paper with the fish watermark. The fish, by the way, was Godemann's idea, some years before I became his right-hand man. The technical director told me how it came about.

The management, the external communicator having just been taken on by the board of directors, were at a routine meeting where he was having the production range explained to him, when he held a sheet of typing paper to the light as if from it he could read the turnover for the next three months.

—What's this?

The watermark on the paper showed a rhombus.

—A rhombus, said the technical director. Godemann took off his smeared glasses and put a side-piece in his mouth.

Everyone at the table fell silent: the internal communicator, the personnel manager, the manager for development, the technical director. When Godemann took the side-piece out of his mouth he came out with it:

—We'll have to change the watermark.

But, said the director, the firm has had the rhombus as a watermark for half a century.

—What if it has? Old mistakes are still mistakes. A rhombus is completely abstract, without a story, therefore it's always the same and always empty, without feeling, without memory. What does a rhombus mean to anyone? At most, it reminds you of school. Geometry. Who can identify with it? Anybody? No.

He briefly put the side-piece in his mouth. Everyone was silent. When the side-piece came out of his mouth, so did the new watermark: —A fish.

—A fish?

—Yes, that's exactly the watermark, a stylized fish. It's also a sales motif for the entire fish industry, for all the factories that smoke and can fish, the shipping companies, the manufacturers of nets, ship's propellors, and compasses, they'll write their business letters on it and anglers their love letters.

What he didn't yet have his eye on was the Catholic church, which fishes for souls. That was added to the list by Monsignor Bär. The genius of the external communicator consists precisely in his being able to feel out new sales areas and their mainly subconscious desires, says Rob.

In the same way once during a company meal, I can testify to this, Godemann took the side-piece out of his mouth: —We have to economize.

Everybody at the table fell silent, yes, some quietly put down fork, knife (leg of lamb was on the menu).

—So much gets left over at meals, said the external communicator, so much that in an earlier age what dogs and pigs would have eaten under the table gets thrown into the trash, goes into the garbage. The same with paper. It ends up on a rubbish heap or gets burned—it could have been recycled, yes, that could even be its trademark: previously used, darker in color, no longer an hysterical white but with traces of the past, brown spots, fragments of packing paper, the silver splinters of tinfoil, black shining spots, tiny remains of announcements of bereavement. That would be a new esthetic, no longer the replete crackle of those noisome sheets of paper but a muted grey inclining almost to understatement, no watermarks that anyway belonged to the days when they still made original copies, but recycled products, less is more, functional, nothing fancy, no waste—the term environmentally friendly didn't yet exist, but I'm sure it was at the tip of his tongue when he said: —Paper that protects nature. Man, he said, is the shepherd of life.

A month later the new typing paper came onto the market. It looked like toilet paper. The external communicator only succeeded after much persuasion in getting a few wholesale dealers to take up their offer.

This was at a time when pamphlets against technology were still written on bleached white paper, guaranteed wood-free and resoundingly strong. (It was no coincidence that our competitors were offering paper under the name *Roman Drum*.)

The external communicator was ahead of his time, too far ahead.

The competition, which we know never sleeps, immediately countered and had their representatives for office stationery spread the slogan: Paper from the rubbish bin for the rubbish bin.

Production of recycled paper had to be stopped after one month.

This mistaken decision was not the reason why the firm, which had been doing well, plunged into bankruptcy. It had more to do with Godemann's uncontrollable obsession, common to many external communicators, with sentimentality, insatiable longings, ideals in which the external communicator sees his fulfillment, preferences and revulsions that mostly derive from childhood and carry no weight from a business point of view, though sometimes turn out to be advantageous.

A manager in the steel industry can indulge his passion for ornithology and participate in the activities of the Society for the Conservation of Nature without it interfering with his work, never mind if he's the chairman of a firm that manufactures seamless steel tubing or workbenches. But if he's a sales manager for Porsche or BMW he'd soon run into a problem, even if it's only insomnia.

Rob, the headhunter, had discovered Godemann when he was business manager of a wholesale furriers and placed him in the paper factory. The external communicator had an inexhaustible passion for literature increased twofold by his boundless love for his wife, who wrote poetry and prose. His passion had never had a disturbing effect on his work in the furriers trade. But as a convinced protector of animal rights he would have come into conflict with his previous work. Would have felt pity for the little mink that's really very sweet, but has to vegetate in small hellish cages until he's killed with electric pincers and his cosy fur pulled off over his ears. Tanned and cured the mink's fur then gets made into a coat, a stole, a jacket. As a convinced protector of animal rights he would have stood in his own way at every sales opportunity. He could never have done the aggressive selling when—perhaps for the last time in the history of fur products—he unloaded fur coats wholesale onto the last provincial stores. He was the one who by opening wider sales-outlets for luxury furs (the democratization of fur, as he called it) first created the conditions for keeping animals raised for their fur; he was the one who drew people's attention, because now just everyone was wearing mink or blue fox, to the poor animals in their small hellish cages or to the baby seals clubbed to death in their thousands so that—the irony of history—the greatest expansion of the fur industry led to its ruin. Anyone who wore a fur coat on the street had to count on being pestered or smeared with ketchup, and even my great-aunt's, my uncle's mother's, small and quite insignificant shop was daubed with red paint one night, there it was on her shop window: MURDERER!

The external communicator had invented the slogan: To each his own fur. He had fur coats made in Hong Kong and Singapore as cheap goods, and backed his popularization of furs with quotes from all kinds of great men from Walther von der Vogelweide via Luther and Goethe to Thomas Bernhard, his love of literature helping him find serious or humorous comments: *My fur and the fur cap and the warm English scarf, I said to myself. Twelve degrees below!* (Thomas Bernhard.) Or: *You're a bug in a rug in a fur, you won't freeze, not even your knees.* (Who wrote that? Right: Heisterbach!)

—Knowledge is power, said Godemann, especially

when you're selling, but you mustn't just read St. Augustine, you have to read the gutter press as well, and anyone who can combine the two will find a way to sell any product because he knows how to find new products.

An entire trade was ruined by the inventive richness, the inspired business acumen of the external communicator, while on the firm he ran he bestowed one turnover record after another. He left behind scorched earth. Furriers, the artists of the trade, had to retrain as bakers or car mechanics, close-out sales and bankruptcies mounted, but by then Rob had already brought Godemann into the paper trade.

His downfall was that he allowed himself to be drawn into publishing. He made the mistake of not just exchanging the commodity X for the commodity money, but of being interested in what happened to the commodity paper, what was printed on it, a matter that should be of no concern to the seller because it clouds his economic decisions, economically a non-starter because then the commodity paper became a special commodity involving personal participation, preferences, desires, obsessions.

He bought a washed-up publishing company. I think he wanted to fulfill a dream of his youth that he'd never abandoned. As he didn't write himself, at least he wanted to publish literature (including his wife's). Added to this, there were more and more unpaid paper bills. He kept allowing publishers to postpone payment, it was enough to tell him the book being printed was outstanding, very special, and he canceled bills and gave discounts. Word soon got round in the publishing world. Soon, as he was also polyglot, he was supplying publishers in England, France, the USA, yes, even Japan, until the company went bankrupt, almost needlessly as the debts that had piled up were all covered, only no publisher paid.

The internal communicator was too weak to assert himself against the external communicator and call in the outstanding debts with the mercilessness the situation required (write twice and then shoot). Every time the internal communicator went to Godemann with all the documents, all the lists, tables of rates of exchange, loans and outstanding debts, to make the threatening situation clear, Godemann tapped him on the shoulder (he could be very jovial) and poured the squirming internal communicator a brandy, one that got every faltering business discussion going again. A rice brandy with an alcohol content of 70% from Vietnam and with a corpse swimming in the bottle, a lizard that looked like a small dragon. You could clearly see the scaly skin, the lobular head, the closed lids—the eyes had been removed, being poisonous, the clawed feet, tiny pieces of skin had come off, fine whitish pieces of flesh floated in the alcohol, and not one of the visitors could bring himself to drink but with astonished disgust watched Godemann empty his glass, turn up his eyes, sigh with pleasure and say: —My elixir of life, a drink that mobilizes intellectual and physical powers, it's said that it strengthened the Vietnamese in their fight against the Americans, it's good for gout and kidney failure, stimulates the gonads and strengthens the will. Once he'd emptied the glass, I witnessed this several times, the negotiations took a positive turn in his favor. It was a magic ritual. He'd also offered me the brandy. I'd declined.

The internal communicator, who normally drank no alcohol, was the only person Godemann ever got to empty his glass, and he did it with eyes shut and shuddering with disgust. —Right, Godemann then said: So, let's have it!

The internal communicator began to recite in an agitated voice, he gave figures, pushed the lists of settlement dates of bills of exchange, of loans across the desk. At this Godemann took off his glasses, in any case already cloudy and smeared, and the internal communicator knew that he was now only dimly discernible to the external communicator. But he went on talking, Godemann put the side-piece in his mouth, breathlessly the internal communicator went on talking because after all he had to stop Godemann, at all cost he had to stop him taking the side-piece out of his mouth again, so out bubbled figures, the ever-mounting outstanding debts, figures, shipments of paper for books, figures, books and more books, among them those that a little later would be offered to the paper factory for recycling, figures, figures, figures. Finally he said the word danger, even though it came out forced he said the word, at that moment Godemann took his glasses out of his mouth, looked at the internal communicator and said: —My dear fellow. The internal communicator fell silent. —Do you know, asked the external communicator, how a plane lands?

—Yes of course. Well, no.

—It crashes.

The internal communicator, I'm not exaggerating, sagged.

—Every landing is strictly speaking a crash, as I recently experienced in Seattle. The pilot had slammed the plane down on the runway from a height of a meter and a half, my glasses flew from my nose. With half a meter there's such a bang that most passengers look up anxiously from their newspapers, with 20 centimeters they feel it in their stomachs, with one centimeter they don't notice anything, but it's still a crash, and so is every landing. And so that's what we need: good tires, good nerves, a good landing strip.

—But, said the internal communicator, that's just it, this landing strip, well, the holes, the length . . .

—Exactly, said Godemann, even on the short industrial airport at Finkenwerder a full Boeing once landed. It wasn't until the pilot had brought the plane to a halt at the retaining wall that drops three meters to the water at ebb tide and gazed into the murky water of the Elbe that he realized he'd made a mistake. These things happen. Godemann laughed and so loudly that you had to laugh too, even the internal communicator. We'll just have to negotiate with the banks. I'll do it, Mrs. Bittner will need to make an appointment for me at the bank on Friday afternoon. —Friday afternoon, I said. —Yes, of course. If it's a question of credit, if you want to extend it, then always on Friday afternoon. Bank managers also want to start their weekend. After all, we're not in China where every day is a Friday afternoon. Do you know, by the way, why the Chinese didn't discover America, even though they had the compass?

I shook my head. The internal communicator also shook his head and said no when Godemann wanted to fill up his glass again from the bottle with the pickled corpse, no thank you, no.

Going under

I'm sitting on the spacious balcony, drinking coffee, there's still a cool breeze coming off the sea but soon, at about eleven thirty it'll get so hot that despite the sunshade I'll have to go into the living room, barefoot. Until then I'll write and think about the external communicator, about Godemann who naturally has another name because he's back in business after being banned for a time in business circles and by the Lions. He stopped being invited to all the functions he cared about and was even cut in the street. A well-known Frankfurt publisher refused to shake hands with him. Godemann took all this with genuine magnanimity, after his bankruptcy never took cover but went everywhere he'd normally have gone. He came to the trial, although shortly before it he'd undergone a prostate operation, and testified on my behalf. He praised me effusively, I can't put it any other way. Which, as my defense counsel, that cynic Dr. Blank said, was not without its problems coming from a man who had steered his firm into a notorious bankruptcy, written up in every paper.

Still, Godemann fought his way back to a leading position as an external communicator. He became the business manager for an umbrella firm, and I think I saw strengthened long umbrellas reappear in Hamburg after an advertising campaign that made a connection between umbrella carriers and some major skirt-chasers in history: Goethe, Camus, and James Dean. Yes, it's true—but you need to know—there's a photo of James Dean with an umbrella, naturally a walking umbrella, not a collapsible one.

This external communicator, Christian Godemann, was my teacher and in almost two years I learned a great deal from him, not only from his wide reading (he'd studied law and philosophy), but how to give the impression of being absentminded by spilling food down yourself so you can then with intense concentration get the better of your careless negotiating partner. His ideas were like storms of enthusiasm in which his crew worked roped to lifelines. And he praised the helmsmen and sailors, that's to say engineers and mechanics, for their above-average imagination and drive. The lights on in all the head offices well into the night, positive, fundamentally positive, full of ideas, precise, quick, tough, flexible, a crew that stayed on course, the flying Dutchman couldn't have wished for a better crew—they were comrades-in-arms, warriors of reknown that he'd gathered around himself like King Arthur at the Round Table.

The fame of all these champions of paper in all its forms, sizes, and colors spread through the German lands. Not so very strange then, that after I'd only been employed four months Rob, who'd placed my teacher, should phone. Could we meet? An oyster bar? Identification: the red handkerchief in his breast pocket.

So that's how I set eyes on Rob for the first time: suntanned, not the yellowish brown of the sun lamp but a genuine Bermuda brown that made an effective contrast to his light blue shirt, bright blue eyes, a dark blue suit, a silk tie, the silk handkerchief in his breast pocket, brilliant red and as irritating as the white feather on the head of a Zulu warrior. A double-toothed steel fork in his hand and the oysters in their bed of ice before him, he asked me if I wanted to be the right-hand man to a steel manager. Bochum, the best deal you could have, even if for the moment the entire steel industry is down, for the time being, soon there'll have to be a total purge. At some stage steel is going to make a comeback. That's when the assistants will have the best chance of promotion, that's when they'll sweep out those aged little people that still liked to be addressed as Herr Director. Are you a lawyer or a management expert?

I had to admit what I find so hard to admit, that I've no academic qualifications. This discrepancy between the natural assumption that you're somebody, in fact the person you'd like to be but nevertheless aren't, always makes it so difficult to explain in ever new turns of phrase that you're not the person you're being taken for. —I'm no management expert, I said.

—Doesn't matter, everybody's a management expert today, said Rob (who also isn't one): —If you're nothing and are never going to be anything you become a management expert. Management experts are the non-commissioned officers of the economy, lawyers and economists make up the officer corps, Rob said, and also in demand are overseers with practical experience. Experience in negotiating, the ability to spot weakness, a sixth sense for the subconscious wishes of buyers who often don't even know yet they're buyers, who for that reason buy, only first they have to be kissed back to life out of their cold froglike existence. There she is, the princess we're looking for. Ha ha. Think over the offer, he said.

I turned it down although I wasn't being paid that

well at Godemann's, in fact I was very badly paid. But I took it as a period of being a student and I wanted to learn more. And that's what I said to Rob, whom after that I'd meet now and then for a game of tennis.

Until the paper factory, almost unexpectedly, went bankrupt. The order books were overfull, the external communicator had developed a new range of products adapted to the consumer's requirements. But it was too extensive and buying the publishing company had resulted in undercapitalization, though there were considerable outstanding debts—then a major check bounced.

I lived through the last hours on the bridge before the ship went down. The internal communicator's frantic phone calls to bank directors, wholesalers, directors of publishing houses, the despairing attempt over the phone to raise the three million that was due, basically a ridiculous sum, to short circuit the creditors and debtors, above all to get hold of Godemann, the external communicator who if he'd stayed on the bridge might have succeeded in pulling the rudder round, talking the bank into extending the loan, borrowing from another bank (why else was he a Rotarian and member of the Lions?). But the external communicator was supposed to be giving a talk at a meeting (which he'd already left) of the paper industry, had been invited to Stockholm (where he hadn't arrived yet) for the annual meeting of the Swedish Office Workers Association. His trail—I followed it by phone—led to a mountain in France (today I know the name: Mont Ventoux), from where Petrarch once looked out over the land and where some prize was being given. Godemann couldn't be reached by us or by the internal communicator.

So the bank, which was medium-sized, bounced the check.

The next day I was out on the street, literally. Because when I arrived at the firm in the morning the premises were locked, all the employees stood at the gate, the clerks and secretaries, and inside behind the double glass doors embellished with high-grade steel corners stood the internal communicator. The doors were locked and sealed. Which was why the caretaker with his tools was also standing there idle. From inside the internal communicator was trying to call out something to me, I saw his mouth open. But though we were all quiet I couldn't make out what he was saying. He looked like somebody who'd gone through the ice and got stuck under it like that boy once in the Isbek Canal.

The internal communicator had gone on working at night like the mechanics who after the alarm had gone off, *SOS Struck Iceberg,* went on working in the sinking, slanting *Titanic* and kept the ship lit up as it went under.

When late at night the authorities locked and shut the gates to investigate tax evasion they forgot the internal communicator. (My teacher was a great teacher because the investigators found nothing.)

We stood outside, the internal communicator inside, and finally from the movements of his mouth I thought I could read that he was calling for the external communicator who was somewhere on Mont Ventoux, his gaze sweeping the plain.

I phoned Rob and asked him if he had a job. For a moment there was silence at the other end. Then I heard, that's bad, very bad after a bankruptcy, if you're

the external communicator's right-hand man something always sticks.

—Listen, I said (by now we were on familiar terms),
for twenty-two months I've been doing nothing but
listening to that man, he could only ever develop his
ideas talking and sucking his glasses.

—Exactly, that's exactly the problem, people are
going to say you should have stopped him sucking his
glasses. That's precisely your job as his right-hand
man. Register as unemployed, let some grass grow over
the issue, then I'll find you something.

So I became unemployed. Until then I hadn't taken
one single weary mark from the Federal Republic's social welfare. Now I got unemployment benefits, had
time, could read and improve my tennis.

A proverb of Solomon's

So my uncle really did make contact.

Yesterday at three in the morning Britt called and
told me my uncle had just phoned her (eight in the
morning where she is, so my uncle's still an early riser).
And he asked after me. Where did he get the number?
From my mother, naturally. But he didn't know yet
what had happened, didn't know about my escape on
the moped. He's chasing after the latest developments,
I can call out: Here I am.

Where was I, he wanted to know.

—Not here, Britt had replied, stressing each syllable.

—Ahha. He'd introduced himself awkwardly, we're
related, distantly so to speak, but you won't know me.

The uncle, he said, well, rather a young uncle, that's to say not so young anymore of course now, well, four years older really. We played a lot together when we were children. (Nice way of putting it, played.) He'd heard, he said, all about me, the hyena.

Britt said I was traveling.

—Traveling?

But all she replied was Yes, and then for a moment there was silence. Not a sound on the line. —It was as if your uncle was in the next room, Britt said. So she didn't say anything either. Until he said, —When does Peter get back? She didn't know. Could she give me a message?

No, he said, he'd call again.

I assume in the meantime he's got my mother to inform him about the latest events. That's if he didn't already know. Perhaps, already knowing I was on the run again, he wanted to talk to Britt, wanted to hear what she'd say and above all how, perhaps he was hoping Lolo would come to the phone. The young are gullible. He could have asked her how things were at school, do you miss your friends? Perhaps he knows about that wimp who never got our phone number out of her.

Perhaps he wanted to ask Lolo for my address. I could feel it, lately I've sensed the presence of this vampire uncle of mine really close.

He sucks people's life stories out of them.

You have to keep the hatches down! Books are vampires, they need life, not just the life that's in them, they really only awaken to life when they're read, that's what they're watching and waiting for as they lie around, sometimes still quite fresh and alert, sometimes covered in dust and yellowed, but as soon as they find a victim they grow red, they glow when they drink their readers' lives because in their sham life everything is fading all the time. And those who write books are also vampires sucking the life out of each and all, sitting in their graves in a half-life, writing. Now and then they fly out looking for victims, for nourishment. Like my uncle: always hunting, but always hunted.

Possibly he's read about Dembrowski's arrest, probably though my mother will have phoned him, will have said he's got away again. She'll have read out to him like Britt read out to me: P. W. sentenced to four years in prison for fraud escapes on moped. (P. W., do you know what that means, Dr. Blank asked me one day while I was in custody. Prisoner of War. Yes, really, there's a war on, only most people don't know it.) —The way it sounds, I said to Britt, escaped on a moped, it really puts you down. —Not at all, said Britt, and read on: W. on the run and Interpol is looking for him.

Don't they have anything better to do?

Dembrowski was extradited to Germany on the double, he certainly won't have appealed against the extradition, on the contrary. Now at last he can see his wife and his three sons again, if only in the visiting room at the prison. Only Sannchen will have to visit at some other time.

Of course Dembrowski could have escaped too. Even more easily than I. His house, his small mansion is in a real park, not overlooked from the garden gate. But, said Britt, he was already standing with his suitcase packed and waiting when the man with red hair arrived with the two local policemen. Because after they showed up at our place she'd naturally immediately phoned Dembrowski. Sannchen answered the phone. —Oh the police, Sannchen had said, genuinely relieved. In a month or two she would have gone to Hamburg anyway without Dembrowski.

And naturally the thought goes through my head too. Simply to fly to Hamburg, drive to Dr. Blank and go with him to the nearest police station.

—You know, I can't take Lolo out of school right now.

That was Britt's careful way of telling me she didn't want to come here. —Naturally the best thing would be if Lolo could take her exams in Hamburg, Britt said, what do you think?

That of course would be a reasonable solution, but what's reasonable isn't usually what you want, what you feel like doing, that wild desire that can't be restrained. But people call restraint reasonable. My uncle's entire childhood was reasonable, whereas mine was thoroughly unreasonable.

I'd be happy to have them both here, I said, and Lolo could go to the international school here too.

—But I'll come, Britt said, a year's nothing.

—A year, I said, is a year. And where do you intend to live?

—Well, the house is standing empty.

So now she'd move into the house that she didn't want to move to then, the house on the Süllberg that I bought three years ago for 1,900,000 marks.

—And if you come we'll meet first, spend two days together, and then we'll go to Dr. Blank.

Why does it have to be two days, I ask myself now,

what makes her decide on two days, why not three or four, or a week?

—No, I said, for the time being I'm staying here.

—You'd be able to write in peace, Britt said.

Britt has never given a thought to whether the book gets finished or not. I'm sure it makes no difference to her either way. But she's probably hoping that in the situation I'm in I'm not going to find peace.

—Are you working on your Easter Island book?

—That too, I said, that too.

Three men and a woman came over from the island. They swam through the waves to the ship, climbed on board on ropes and began to dance. They danced a kind of minuet, hopped on one leg keeping astonishing balance, and stamped with the other leg to underline the rhythm of the song, accompanying this with obscene movements.

Obscene movements is a nice way of putting it, but what the professorial ethnologists don't see is that in fact it all belonged together: the singing, the dancing, and the copulation. To be taken out of themselves, that's what they wanted: to take off like birds, leave everything behind, the island, this restricted world, themselves. The singers too, the Rapa Nui sang as they danced, about their ancestors, about the distribution of the tribal land, about the battle of the sexes. The exertion of remembering, the movement of the song—the reason for the dance paddle with which the singers travel through time and space: that's what I shall try and bring out when I finally have the urge again to work on the book.

Today I walked through the streets of the residential area, streets lined with old mango trees. You have to watch out that you're not hit by the ripe fruits that fall now and then. They're as effective as small missiles, as one can see from the dents on the roofs of cars. The sharp kernel shoots out of the pulp, accelerated by the weight of the fruit.

I enjoy walking on my own among all these people who appear so strange to me. How different, how varied the color of their skin is. I walk uninvolved, I don't even understand the language. I don't need to talk. I don't need to plan. I don't need to give answers. It's like the time when I was unemployed.

In the morning—Britt was already at the advertising agency—I'd take Lolo to school, from there drive to the club, play for an hour, sometimes two, with students and other morning tennis enthusiasts (but never with those housewives smelling of deodorants who killed their mornings on the tennis court). Then drive home, tidy the apartment, do the dishes, clean the bathroom and read whatever I could lay my hands on, not just about Easter Island, with a hunger that couldn't be satisfied because at school I hadn't exactly allowed myself to be overfed. At about two I went to the Greek.

The Greek had opened a snack bar in a converted garage. I sat there mostly on my own, only occasionally a pensioner from the district would come in, drink his beer, and like me eat souvlaki, spaghetti bolognese (better than at the Italian's nearby), or a curry sausage. A narrow room, done up with boards stained walnut-brown, the tables separated by bamboo rods to the ceiling entwined with vine leaves and grapes made out of some plastic that even imitated the grey film of spray on the fruit. Above the counter a cuckoo clock. I'd keep looking at it right before twelve just to see the wooden bird shoot out, call cuckoo twelve times, bow at every call, beat its wings, then shoot back in again. Snap, the little door shut. I drank a glass of Schorle and read the paper.

Then I went out onto the street that here turns from a country road to a through road and from here on has a name. Often there were animal transports at the first traffic light, the animals stood dumb, no squeaking, no bellowing, and I wondered whether they'd been fed a sedative before their last journey. Just occasionally they pushed their gentle mouths dribbling saliva through the iron bars, sometimes horns poked through the slats. Other trucks were on their way to the freight depot, at night when there was a wind from the southwest you could hear the whistling of the shunters, the metallic pull of the brakes, and the clank of colliding trailers.

After the street was widened the shops in the multi-storied houses were shut. The display windows were boarded up or plastered with paper from the inside, the glass covered in a grey layer of dirt. Then came the crossing, a small square, the supermarket, a dance hall in a house covered in grey filth that at the turn of the century had been a villa set amidst greenery. In the middle a circular flower bed around which the street made a loop: the bus terminal. A phone kiosk, a shelter, the lawn cut low, bordered by a low iron chain meant to prevent walking on the grass though two well-worn paths crossed each other on it. One led to the covered bus stop. I'd sit there and wait for the bus.

Some afternoons I played doubles, sometimes with Rob. When we played together we were unbeatable at the club. I was really in good form then.

The bus came, did a turn, stopped. An old woman got out, backwards, carefully feeling her way, holding a shopping bag made out of a light-brown synthetic material that was shedding skin as if after a sunburn. Leaning on a crutch she slowly made her way round the circular flower bed. The bus driver got out, went over to the small gents toilet. Out of the grey of the sky came a distant humming that slowly turned into a roar. Some pigeons flew up. A dog ran across the lawn in a strangely crooked way, cowered, peed, ran off. It suddenly seemed to me quite impossible to make those absurd movements, to swing the racket in a loop with your right arm so as to hit the ball just in front of your body, and at the same time really bend the knees. Over on the other side of the square the old woman was lying on the street. A man pulled her up, took her to the supermarket entrance. Carefully she sat down on the entrance step, her bag beside her, the crutch leaning against the wall. The pigeons were running across the lawn again, that mechanical cooing, that nodding of the head. The bus driver came back, got in, looked briefly over at me, then he started the bus, a shuddering, the smell of diesel. The bus went back to town.

And again you could hear the roaring in the grey sky. The wind, only a breeze, went lightly through me.

Lolo came home in the late afternoon. She went to an all-day school, did her homework there. Together we played a game of general knowledge: How many moons has Neptune? Or we played Mikado. Lolo would run excitedly round the table and you'd think she'd never ever be able to pull out even one stick without knocking everything over. But then suddenly all that frantic excitement left her, her movements slowed down, then as if in slow motion she pulled the sticks out with her fingertips, without grabbing, without any of the other sticks moving. I didn't even have to cheat to lose, like with the game of general knowledge. Sometimes if the sun was shining in the morning we drove to the Baltic. (Please excuse her, I'd write, Lieslotte was absent because she felt dizzy.) We rented deck chairs, bathed, and built sand dams against the waves.

—Why does the water rise and fall, why is there ebb and flood? Here it's only a few centimeters. But in France or England there are places where the tide rises six meters, as high as that tree there, Lolo. Spring, mid, and neap tides.

That intrigued Lolo, it was something she could puzzle over and ask questions about on the journey home. The moon draws the water? But how? How can that happen? Brooding puzzlement, and then out it would come again, that's strange, the moon's a ball, why doesn't it fall down?

I could have said because there's a God that rotates it.

I once rented a dinghy and we sailed on the Trave. I didn't learn sailing from one of my stepfathers (though most of them worked in the harbor none of them could sail), but from my uncle. He showed me maneuvers and named things that I first became aware of through him: the word breeze, the water that suddenly roughens to a dark green, the crow's nest, leaning far out and then luffing.

The wind freshened and it was breezier than I'd expected. We were at quite an angle, I was sitting outboard and Lolo was gripping the seat, she looked pale and held on rigidly. Suddenly she began to sing, she sang a song from some book by Astrid Lindgren: the youngest and smallest sailor on board, little Theodor Kalle, his mother oh she cried, oh please don't go, but the sea called to him: Don't be homesick, little boy, now it's the sea, hurrah, the grey grey sea is your home. But then little Theodor Kalle and the ship went down. As Lolo sang to the waves about the death of little Theodor Kalle she forgot her own fear and she sat up straight and looked out at the heaving waves that now had crests of foam and she sang loudly and laughed and I sang with her because the waves were beginning to seem eerie to me as well.

Britt didn't come home from the firm until late in the evening.

She'd gone from the wholesale florist to an advertising agency whose owner I'd once sold life insurance to to benefit his wife and four children. At first Britt was responsible for public relations, that's to say she phoned, received clients, made coffee, and kept the minutes at meetings. After a year she became the boss' production consultant. She'd tell, as I put the overcooked meal onto the table, how advertising photos had been done for a floor polisher. A kitchen floor, freshly laid and not yet stepped on, had to be as clean, as radiant, as sparkling as the product's name: Brilliant (name changed for legal reasons). They polished, cleaned, filmed, but the floor was still a little dull, a fine, almost hardly perceptible trace of mattness and resistance to shining. Finally someone hit on the idea of covering the floor with water, only a centimeter, and that was what at last gave the impression of penetrating clarity, of a shine normally not achievable, a veneer as it were.

—And that's how they want everything, women too, said Britt, immaculately clean, no defects, no dull places, preferably they'd put everything under water.

The comparison, I thought, was somewhat exaggerated, at least the *they*, who did she mean? And wasn't I included here?

My questions provoked an argument that took up the evening. (Nothing about our intimate lives, I'd decided. But we only very rarely quarrel. Someone who works like I do has to have peace on one front at least.)

One day I phoned Rob and arranged to meet him, not in the oyster bar but in a cafe.

I asked if he didn't know of a job, I had to do something. Quite nice to put my feet up on the table for a few months, but enough is enough.

At the moment it looks bad, he said. Two incidents had put him rather out of business. Possibly in investment, he said, that's the trend at the moment. People are speculating. The stock market, futures trading, options. Maybe there was something in it. He knew somebody in the brokerage firm Osborn & Partner, he could ask. But how?

This "how" showed just how much business Rob had lost. Because once all he had to do was phone and arrange to meet at the oyster bar. But people were talking about him.

An internal communicator, placed in an oil company by Rob, had shot himself just three weeks later. I'd read about the case in the papers. *Manager shoots himself: Mama Help!*

—Rubbish, said Rob, that's not correct, before he shot himself the man wrote on his office wall with an aerosol spray specially bought for the purpose: Mama Hunger! The press thought hunger just too surreal, hence the headline: Help.

He'd asked his secretary to get him some tea, put his feet up on his desk, and shot himself through the mouth.

The secretary, on her way to the office with the teapot, hears a dull bang. She comes into the room, looks at the wall: Mama Hunger! and a few red flecks on the ceiling. She hesitates, thinks the internal communicator has indulged in one of those office jokes the external communicator has introduced to improve the atmosphere at work: fake turd sausages on the grey wall-to-wall carpet, phoney squirts of ketchup on company contracts, and similar stupidities. Only when she carefully looks round the door, because in the last three days the internal communicator has sometimes been sitting under his desk, does she see him in his chair, his feet on the desk.

Three days before he'd had the desk moved so that he sat next to the door that opened inwards. He gave as the reason that he was sick of literally colliding with people every time the door opened. Already as a child he'd preferred to stand behind the door to first observe the people coming in. An atavistic trait, he'd said laughing to the secretary, from the good old dim and distant past when the headhunters came.

Rob had begged the secretary under no circumstances to repeat this because it could somehow have been connected with him, which would have been completely unfounded. Naturally something like that would be ruinous for his business.

But the sentence made the rounds. Yes, it even led to a rhyme—proof of the playful creativity of language in the course of a day at the office: There's a headhunter ho ho haunting the place, he shoves you, he shakes you, and shoots you in the face.

It was an external communicator who finally put Rob out of business. Rob had placed him in a firm that sold cotton-jersey underwear. The man ran things in his new position in such a lunatic way that the shareholders were glad to get rid of him with a million-dollar handshake. *Victoria* (the name of the underwear firm) *shouts Victory. Manager leaves!* ran the caption in the business section of the paper. (I like the business section of the paper the best, unlike the features section it's still linguistically creative: *Unfasten the seat belts—Sales plunge.*)

The suspicion arose that Rob and the external communicator were in league.

Perhaps such cases are not as rare as one supposes. I read while I was still in custody about the manager of a publishing house, an external communicator and before that cultural consultant in Munich, who must have devised a publishing program that, according to the report, put the directors of the publishing house into a shocked state of fear and trembling. The man was just celebrating the new program, with his new team when the company's board of directors released the ejector seat. He went, with compensation of at least a million marks. But to this add another 6 (six!) thousand monthly because for twelve years he helped Munich to shine.

These are exactly the jobs, probably placements, that are going to increase in the future: early retirement with an allowance of millions provided by the tax-payer.

A story taken from life, as Wesendonk would say, catch as catch can.

And in court Dembrowski, lover of diction and victim of Real Socialism, replied to the question, why had he gone independent: —Trade and change are the real driving forces whereas a planned economy can only be a flawed economy because it only inadequately allows for demand. Everything's already in the word trade, in German: *Handel,* old High German: *hantalon,* which is handling, touching, taking hold of, working over, in other words something deeply involving our five senses, something that excites, that trains them. In Middle High German *hantalon* becomes *handeln* (English: to trade, to deal) as in the Proverbs of Solomon: He becometh poor that dealeth with a slack hand: but the hand of the diligent maketh rich—here we see the transition from barter as a communal activity to trading in the sense of business, that is business from which those profit who offer something others can't, consequently gaining more than those who only offer what many others offer, for example, physical strength. Skill, agility, dynamism, questioning the usual methods are naturally valued more highly because able to more quickly satisfy the new desires arising out of the old demands, dynamism, for instance, a division of tasks was already clearly in evidence in the production of flint axes, a development sure to accelerate as old moral

271

prejudices are swept away, most especially that all men are equal—which they're not.

Dembrowski portrayed himself in court as an external communicator, which at the same time presented a certain problem for our firm, as Rob also pointed out in his statement.

One external communicator brings creative chaos to a concern, two external communicators amount to destructive chaos for a firm. He'd said that, said Rob, to Mr. Dembrowski and Mr. Walter when they went independent with Sekuritas. Strictly speaking both were external communicators.

▼

Rob in fact had been able to arrange doubles at a very select Hamburg tennis club, which wasn't easy as the man from the brokerage firm gave his time very sparingly. But Rob was sought after as an excellent player, even if he did misplay a few balls at the beginning. —We'll have to be smart about this, said Rob, because the external communicator expressly said: Please, don't try to place him.

I came onto the tennis court and saw the external communicator for the brokerage firm, it was Dembrowski. I immediately recognized him, as he did me.

Dembrowski remembered the dermatologists' conference, my life-insurance stand, the two models, the polaroid camera.

After Dembrowski and his partner had lost and we were sitting down to a light breakfast in the club restaurant, Dembrowski asked: —You're looking for a new field?

—Yes.

—We're looking for investment counselors, intelligent, good men who know how to talk to people.

—What do I need to know?

—You'll go on a training program. One month. The rest you'll soon learn while you're selling.

—It was that easy, asked the judge presiding at the trial.

—Yes, it was that easy.

Britt only laughed when I told her my pay. —Are you trying to sweep me off me feet?

—Yes, I said, it's that easy, picked her up, 80,000 a year, and carried her out of our cheap apartment, down the stairs, good morning, Mrs. Minnemann, we're moving out.

The window handle

In the witness box one of the victims told how his money had disappeared in our firm. This would be repeated, I knew some of the faces, others I'd never seen before.

Outside a day that wouldn't grow bright, the bare wet branches of a tree, in them a strip of torn plastic.

I was woken in the morning by the shrill sound of the bell. Running and walking began outside in the corridors, now and then a shout, laughter, but muted, nothing like what you see in American prison films.

273

What shocked me about the cell at the beginning was how much it was like—there's no other word for it—a dungeon. Heavy doors with peepholes that only opened on the outside, walls plastered white on which, when the light was on—and in winter the light had to be on during the day—shadow landscapes emerged because the walls were so uneven under the thick plaster—definitely more dungeon than cell. Films had given me quite a different impression of prison cells, I imagined them newer, more geometrical, clinical, not producing the effect that they at first did on me here—dungeons. What really frightened me, what trapped me in my isolation, was the peephole in the door. Not that the prison guards looked in much, but simply the fact that I could be observed at any time gave me a feeling of being constantly at their mercy, always uneasy. There was no part of the cell they couldn't have seen where you could have hidden from observation. Unless I lay down below the door. You could even be observed answering the calls of nature.

On the morning of the second day of the trial I got up, briefly put my feet down on the cold floor, put on my leather slippers, my silk dressing gown (I could still enjoy the familiar little luxuries) and peed in the toilet, an old porcelain bowl in which the permanently running water had washed away some of the letters of the brand name.

I flushed and saw the water trickle down, then the pipe belched and the water came in again from below.

I went to the cell window. It was still dark outside. The weather had turned. It was thawing. The wind was blowing through the bare trees that I couldn't see, a damp, almost warm wind that I felt on my face, and I could smell the Elbe nearby. It smelled brackish.

I thought of how sometimes during the previous winter I'd driven in the morning from the house on the Süllberg to the inner city. Gardens still under snow, the villas painted white where the Biesterfelds and the Godefroys lived. The whirling grey green water at Teufelsbrück, the tugs waiting there for the incoming ships, the lit-up oil refinery, the fluttering flame in the rising dawn, the general stores on the Palmaille, then the three skyscrapers, dirty, grey, ugly, they make you feel sick every time, the baroque church, the Reeperbahn, still lit up, but dead, dead as in the evening when the sightseeing buses go down it, higher up the Schaarmarkt, the Brüderstrasse, the Grosse Trampgang.

On the second day of the trial I'd again put on a blue suit. Blue, dark blue, or rather navy blue, my favorite color. Perhaps because if I think of my father I imagine him in the navy-blue jacket in which I saw him, the only time I did. I sat on the bench and smoked a cigarette until the door was unlocked and the guard came in to take me to the courtroom. It wasn't the old guard but a young one. When I got up and put out the cigarette he gave me a look like Mr. Govert who'd tailored the suit six months ago in London. When I tried it on his eyes had run over me from head to foot with the same searching satisfied look.

—O.K.? I asked the guard.

He nodded, said: —Fine. Then off we went hand in hand down the corridors and hallways, he a good head taller. The cloth of his sleeve, a cheap material, scratched my wrist. His face, pale, full of craters and eczema, little greenish lumps under the skin, some on the surface a blueish color, yellowish boils, one had opened and pus was coming out of a little jagged crater.

You get really close on your way to and from the courtroom.

He'd been four years with the penal system, he said, before that he'd been a border guard between East and West Germany. The people? Small fry, mostly. Once I had Kujau—the one who wrote the Hitler diaries—handcuffed; he was a little fellow, bald, eyes like a stone marten.

—Stone marten?

—Yeah, they're the ones that always chew the car cables.

—Car marten?

—Nah, stone marten, I saw him myself in the morning. Get in my car, out comes one of these little animals from under it, with a bushy tail. I'd already seen his tracks in the snow, little claw marks. Stands there peering at me with sort of button eyes. Crafty, I think to myself, only what's he doing under the car? Only then later when I was braking I knew, I stepped on the brake and the car went skating on: he'd chewed the brake cables. They eat the rubber. Anyway, that's what Kujau's eyes were like, like a stone marten's, quite a friendly man.

—But Kujau's bald. And stone martens are covered in thick hair.

—Doesn't matter. It was the eyes. Someone special, not like the rest, fences, muggers, a bank robber occasionally. Nothing to get worked up about, routine. Well, you're an exception.

—You think so?

—Sure. It's not every day someone puts a hand in the till and takes out 26 million.

—Not 26 million, I said, and no one put their hand in the till.

—And the money, where's that then?

—Disappeared down a black hole.

—Ha ha, I don't believe it. Very very crafty. I know what I'd do.

—What?

—Put the money in a numbered account in Switzerland or Luxembourg, then sit it out for two years, then the Caribbean. And take it easy.

—Not bad, I said. Well, if I'm ever in the Caribbean you'll get a crate of white rum.

—Great, he said, my wife really likes egg nog. She'd never had it before. She's from the Philippines. Got to know her through an agency, 6000 marks, for that I could pick her from a catalogue. I just didn't fancy any of the women here. It wasn't easy. Not just because of what I was after, generally, I mean, all the things they want. The demands they make! Being an official is nothing these days, least of all if you're with the penal system, then you're at the bottom of the heap, any robber who comes along, anyone who's raided a bank is big with them. That's when the women make eyes, they're wet in no time. Otherwise you've got to have dough, take them out. That's how it is. Only mine's o.k. . . . Better off here than over there with the Philippinos, that's what she says, already speaks German. We can already talk to each other, she's learned in three months. I was at the airport waiting, there she was, so small, I thought, God, is she tiny, I can pick her up like a child. I do when I get home, pick her up and carry her

277

through the apartment. She likes it, she laughs, she puts her head on my shoulder. But usually she's very serious and hard working and clean, polishes, cooks. Not that I wanted a woman that just cleaned, my heart wanted something too, not just bed, that too of course, why marry except so you can do it whenever you want? But then she's a bit silent. Don't know if she's enjoying herself or not. Probably like that with all of them from Asia. I know a young farmer from the Wilster Marsh, he's got one from Cambodia. Same story all over again. So, he said as we came into the courtroom, your wife's here too, real classy. I'll unlock you, you can give each other a hug. That's what your heart needs.

Yes, I could hug Britt, I could put my arms round Lolo. Until the court was in session. Until the witnesses marched in, until the lamenting began about all the lovely thousands that were invested in goods somewhere and had disappeared. Where had they gone? During this litany I peered out at the grey day that refused to become bright, at the bare branches, the strip of plastic torn to shreds by the wind, and that's when the window handle caught my attention. A handle made of brass, the ends thickened to two small stylized buds.

They were the same window handles we had in our flat in Isestrasse, that's why they'd caught my eye.

If my uncle stays on my tracks he'll get quite a surprise when he sees our apartment in Isestrasse where we moved shortly after I'd spoken to Dembrowski. He knows the street, he knows the houses. My little uncle was always drawn to that street.

His parents used to live in a similar street until they were bombed out in June '43, after that they moved to a basement, then my uncle's father worked his way up again.

Why was my uncle drawn to Isestrasse? The memory of better days? Memories don't always have to take you back to something you experienced yourself. Because my uncle couldn't possibly have remembered the bombed apartment. Memories are handed on from generation to generation, stories told create clearer pictures than photos or drawings can, clearer often than those one's seen oneself—that way desires are passed on: the big rooms, the molding on the ceiling, the pear tree outside the nursery where you could pick the fruit from the window, the shutters on the high windows onto the street. My uncle carried all this in his subconscious, if at all, because when they were bombed out he was a baby. But I think it was a happy time for my little uncle because then he had his mother to himself. His father was in the war.

Perhaps, to speculate this once about the childhood psyche of my uncle, he was looking for a lost time in the apartments and the façades of houses: the imposing mullioned windows, the ornamental stucco garlands that hung over windows and portals, the stylized shells, debauched idiots, unravelling spirals, hypertrophic eggs, bug-eyed goats, rigid angels. My uncle would stand in the street and stare into the lit windows, the uncurtained living rooms that invited the gaze in Eppendorf, everything could be shown, nothing should be hidden, everything in tiptop condition, everything as and where it should be, bookcases like barricades, reading lamps heavy as thoughts hanging over leather chairs, oil paintings opening a view onto distant landscapes.

In winter my uncle would stand outside the houses in the early dusk and look in, he looked into the windows like others look at a film. I went with him a few times, then stopped. I saw people walking up and down in the rooms or talking to each other. You couldn't understand anything, at any rate not in winter when the windows were shut. Were they yelling at each other or only calling, delighted or full of hatred? One would have needed to see the faces more clearly, they were only a puppet show from this distance. But my little uncle would stand there lost to the world and stare in at the windows. My uncle, the social voyeur.

Hardly surprising that I pricked up my ears when Dembrowski said he'd heard about a vacant apartment in Isestrasse, an acquaintance who lived in the same house had told him about it.

Britt and I had already looked at several apartments, and some of the same size had been cheaper, but none were in the Isestrasse: five rooms, a storage room, a dining-room kitchen. Completely renovated. A hefty rent and on top of that a 30,000 marks deposit.

—How can we do it without robbing a bank? Britt asked.

I'd only just begun as an investment counselor for Osborn & Partner. —We'll take out a loan.

—And the trains? asked Britt as we were looking at the apartment.

—Won't bother us, on the contrary. If anything happens we'll get a good view.

—It's like watching a film, said Lolo.

But Britt shook her head, she simply didn't like this viaduct in the middle of the street over which the trains passed back and forth.

—What, I said. This turn-of-the-century iron viaduct that's so fantastically screwed and rivetted together.

—It makes a racket, always rattling.

—I'm sure you'd soon get used to it.

—If at least the apartment was higher up on the third or fourth floor.

—I don't think so, then all you'd see would be the roof of the trains. Here you can see the people sitting inside them.

—You can hardly see a thing, and two crotchety diagonal lines showed on Britt's forehead.

But then as we were going through the empty rooms Britt after all said: fine, and Lolo wanted the room with the view onto the canal that my uncle had crossed as Birdman when it was frozen. In the sixties some crazy city planner wanted to fill up the canal and build a motorway on it. A citizen's initiative was able to prevent it. (At the time, my only political involvement, I distributed leaflets while chasing up and down stairs for magazine subscriptions. I soon got people talking because of the leaflets and got a good commission.)

Room height: four meters at least, woodchip wallpaper, white, garlands on the ceiling, parquet floors, pitch pine, stripped and sealed. Lolo tested it by skating in her socks through the living room.

A new phase of life began, not step by step, hesitant, hardly noticeable, on the contrary very aware.

We bought sofas and chairs, Swedish design, a matt brown, stylized chestnut leaves, a white table, a standard lamp with a light grey shade, the bookcase white, record player white, television white (as a life insurance salesman I'd seen the trendsetters apartments, all those painters, architects, graphic designers, gallery owners), two 300-kilowatt loudspeakers from which Udo Lindenberg drawled, Britt was mad for him. We hung two oil paintings on the walls, one blue, the other green, by a painter whose life I'd insured. He'd promptly had to borrow money on his life insurance and I helped him. Out of gratitude he gave me the two paintings in which Britt looked in vain for nuances of color. They were the last of his monochrome phase, after that he stuck both his hands into colors and became a highly remunerated wild young man.

From my former decorator colleague with whom in '67 I developed the new dynamic realistic style of window display and who in the meantime sent exhibits to international exhibitions, for 20,000 marks I bought (also on credit) an art object: Neolithic. A panel with sand mysteriously fixed in such a way that you could hang the panel on the wall without the sand trickling down. In this vertical dune landscape there was the imprint of six lifesize bare feet (two adults, one child). Next to them lay a stone arrowhead and a white down feather. An object, two meters by two, that both provided people who had just arrived with a talking point and eased the initial stiffness of greetings.

My mother visited us (in those days we still visited each other now and then) and went through the rooms, went to the bathroom, the kitchen, a built-in kitchen full of chromium-plating with integrated sink, refrigerator, cooker, grill, and asked mistrustfully: —Did you win a lottery?

I'd asked Dembrowski earlier whether the firm would vouch for the 50,000, we needed the money to furnish adequately. —No problem, said Dembrowski. Anyway, you can deduct it as advertising expenses.

Besides, how can you convince someone of the miracle of self-multiplying money if they see you in a dormitory town built in social-welfare concrete and filled with Ikea furniture?

Because it's the miracle that makes them believe. You work and get money for it, that's normal. What's miraculous is to have money, do nothing, and get more money simply because you allow money to interact with time, that's a miracle in which everyone wants to share. Has anyone ever seen a five-mark coin work? Can a hundred-mark note breed? —Naturally—and this *naturally* can't be stressed enough—not, said the instructor on the Osborn & Partner training program. Despite this the money multiplies. That's the basis on which everything has to be understood. Only Jesus Christ could multiply bread and wine, but out of 50,000 marks you can make 100,000, in a month or two you can accomplish miracles. This, without one having to do anything extra, is only possible with money, or rather, capital. And the stock exchange is Cana. There's a very sober economic explanation for this, namely supply and demand, but for the average investor it's like a fairy tale, rather as if gold dollars were falling out of the sky. You have to relate to this. Not talk people into anything, but relate to the secret desires that unite all cultures.

—Your contact with clients is always over the phone, said the instructor, therefore your most important aid is your voice. Talk clearly and not too quickly, also not always in the same tone. Modulate, make artificial pauses that help understanding and at the same time arouse expectations. Never allow the initiative in the conversation to slip from you. Build up your sales talk systematically, never lose sight of the goal: the conclusion of the sale . . . Your personal success. Because you get a slice from every transaction you conclude.

The last witness on that day of the trial was Osborn & Partner's managing director. He declared that Dembrowski as executive and I as investment counselor had always dealt very correctly, very effectively, he said. The firm had never had cause for complaint. On the contrary, in the three years I'd been one of their most successful investment counselors. —We regretted the fact, he said, that both gentlemen left our firm.

A brief, very effective appearance.

After the second day of the trial Dr. Blank was satisfied.

In the cell I lay down on the bench. You don't realize how tiring a day of a trial is. I lay on the bench, smelled the disinfectant, and thought of the window handle. Tomorrow, the next day of the trial, I could simply get up. I could take a few steps to the window. I could turn and say to the courtroom: Goodbye now—and jump out of the window.

Fictitious creatures

Early in the morning before the day's heat began I was already on the beach. Two weeks of blue sky, only now and then a few clouds. I only made the discovery here: this colorless grey is a shaded white, full of subtle and subtlest tones where the light meets the dark. Lying on my back I watched this play of light in the few clouds that came in from the Atlantic: the slow casting of shadow, the brightening of the grey. And the more I see of the sun the more I miss the grey westerly wind in the shrubs. And—naturally—Britt. Britt, the way she kicks off her shoes, pulls her skirt round with a little tug, undoes the zip, pulls in her stomach, undoes the hooks, the way she says: —Come on, let's sing.

Yes, she sings, a loud slow urgent song and listening I forget about myself. Desire is our memory, filled with tiny pictures, glimpses of scenes, moments, scented hollows.

Britt, I wish she were here, at last, and Lolo. But of course they've the redhead on their heels. They must be afraid of putting him on my track. Hunters. They're looking for the money. They follow and think we set out with a spade and are digging up the treasure like Blackbeard on the Virgin Islands. Idiots!

How can my uncle bear it, I think to myself when I try to imagine how he sits day in, day out in his room, his hands always over his eyes, no matter whether he's writing by hand, on a typewriter or on a computer like me. How can anyone bear only to experience through writing?

Does he, I wonder, ever want to drop everything, just throw it all in, leave his lovely wife, his lovely children, his lovely home to roam here through the streets of the old town, just travel, not for two or three weeks, but travel without a goal, without a schedule? He could say he was a pensioner, teacher, architect. He could provide himself with a new biography and that way get to know different people in a different way. It's rubbish, all this talk of not being able to get out of your own skin. It's one of those worldwide sayings meant to prevent people from trying. All you have to do is jump over your own shadow and throw yourself into the turmoil, just be brave, do it.

I was in the old town yesterday afternoon to watch the gamblers again. They sit in the marketplace. Exclusively men. The women just watch. I can't make out the rules of this game of chance. The men fold the notes into accordions. The neat little folds give back a certain stability to the limp greasy notes. Then they're neatly arranged and stuck into each other in such a way that strange, unique mythical creatures come into being, beaked dragons, winged sea serpents, pleated lizards.

Now and then one of these fictitious creatures changes owners. Nothing indicates any bet, any decision as to who should pay, it's as if the one who gets the weird butterfly is the one who adds the last missing note in such a way that no one else can stick in another note without destroying the whole thing. But at what stage is it complete? And who decides? I've never once seen a quarrel break out when one of the players gets the thing. I'd like to have joined in the game once just to learn the rules, but the greasiness of the notes stops me.

The astonishing thing about this game is that now and then a note, sometimes the whole mythical shape gets burned. And it's not just paper that gets burned—the greasier it is, the more it's been in use, the more hesitantly the flames take hold, giving out brownish smoke—but the invisible value contained in the note is offered. To whom? I don't know. Sometimes some of the ash gets scattered on the heads of the girls standing there. But there's nothing solemn about it, it's always done with shrieks and laughter. It may just be teasing.

Still, in this game that strikes me as so strange I think

I see a moment in the history of the origin of money that has a sacred background. All the liberal economists, of whom Dembrowski was one and underpinned the theory with a learned expenditure of words, overlook just this. In money they see merely a commodity with which to barter, whose significance is confined to its most conspicuous function, namely to simplify and make generally valid the process of barter (liquidity) in society.

But already in the Latin word *pecunia* (money) we find cattle (*pecus*). Cattle denoted wealth and cattle were sacrificed to make the gods well-disposed, in other words: increase wealth. Then a transference took place. The animal to be sacrificed was put onto the coin which in turn became an offering, whose value therefore wasn't determined only by the metal. The pig, instead of coming under the knife, came onto the coin. And also the virgin, who had originally been an offering in temple prostitution, was now cast in bronze. So from its earliest origins money has retained something erotic, something sexual, and I think I can still feel it in the notes, a sensation which is highly pleasurable and makes me, I can find no other word, randy.

It's not just the motives depicted, the graphic shapes, the quality of the paper, the quality of the printing that are works of art, so is the invisible value that resides in the notes because it's something not necessary, it symbolizes something extra for which a person, if he doesn't believe in the Politburo or in a god, lives—at least I do. And that's inherent in money, literally!

Anyone who has ever held a bundle of thousand-franc notes in his hand, let's say a hundred thousand francs, feels something of—in Mackay's words—the magic of money. You make an offering and become aware of getting what you wanted. Only you need to know how to deal with it, how to properly enjoy it, how to give yourself over—most people who have money can't—to this enjoyable extra something unhindered by any moral scruples.

But I'm sure it's just this that I wouldn't be able to make my uncle understand, and that's why he's a dead loss when it comes to the question of why people have this urge to earn money and of why all moral scruples are so ridiculous, at least almost all.

The central requirement of justice: remorse. But remorse is merely the hypocrisy demanded by society to which it can legally respond with mercy.

That naturally was also what the press was waiting for during the trial. It wanted to hear an admission of guilt, it wanted to report that both the accused regretted having taken doctors, lawyers, the well-heeled for a ride. There was something sensational about the way we'd made money and the way we'd admitted living in luxury. That was the difference, desires that are usually hidden were here brought out into the open, you openly take your cut, you don't just swindle a little like everyone does, like someone with his yearly income tax when he claims for a few extra kilometers, here people fattened for the occasion were being plucked like Christmas turkeys. But we didn't feel remorse, we didn't cough up our hard-earned money.

And there's a fantastic amount of work involved, as Dr. Blank said, and strictly speaking it had provided employment, 30 people had been employed.

The judge didn't allow that to stand, he reprimanded the excellent Dr. Blank. That was going too far.

Robin Hood and his band invest shady money, wrote a small left-wing paper. This was meant for me—which even made Dembrowski jealous—and only because I'd said we'd seen to a certain redistribution, the money would have disappeared one way or another.

But naturally this sentence was taken as an indirect admission of guilt.

That's where the interest lay for the gutter press, otherwise there wasn't much, no violence, no sex. They didn't know about Dembrowski's love triangle, and there wouldn't have been any honey for journalists there either, it was much too ordinary.

—The one only laughs when you've explained to her why you're laughing, the other laughs with you because she knows why you're laughing, Dembrowski said, both let you enjoy the reason for your own laughter, but in quite different ways. With the one you keep thinking you have to restrain yourself, you mustn't pester her, the other invites you to give her a shock, you can shout, you don't have to watch your step, Dembrowski said to me one evening in Marbella after he'd emptied two bottles of wine.

Britt and I had experienced Dembrowski at close quarters with both women. Three years ago we'd been with Dembrowski and Renate and one year ago with Dembrowski and Sannchen in the South Seas, on Boa Boa, in one of those matted luxury bungalows without walls.

It had been my idea. I'd heard so much from Stepgrandfather Heinz about the South Seas that I absolutely had to go there. At this point for once I'd like to be indiscreet: Sannchen shrieked, but shrieked, the first time we heard it we thought Dembrowski must be tor-

289

turing her in the most gruesome fashion. The next morning there she sat in her opaque sunglasses at the breakfast table under the palms, cool and silent, composedly drinking her coffee.

In the previous year all we'd heard from Renate was deep slow breathing that then turned into a quiet eager panting. In the morning she spooned out her half grapefruit in a businesslike way and said: —My god, I sleep like a log here.

—You know, Dembrowski said when we were still talking to each other, that's to say shortly before he moved to Spain with Sannchen, it's really crazy, strictly speaking it's as simple as could be, and yet it's the hardest thing to do.

—What is?

—With Sannchen and Renate. I wish there was open, recognized, socially sanctioned polygamy, quite simply, I'd like to live with them both. To be quite honest and frank, I miss in the one what I find in the other.

Dembrowski, as a victim of socialism, is insatiable, but in fairness I have to add that he didn't make things easy for himself. He really suffered and suffers, to the extent that he can suffer.

—I envy you, he'd often say, you've got your Britt and your money and a bit of Easter Island too. Basically you're an unassuming person.

—No, I'm the least unassuming person in the world, in my opinion.

He sat there, his back straightened, his hair neatly parted, that profile that made you think of a Prussian prince—I could smell his Grey Flannel aftershave and saw that he kept looking over at Renate in the last row, I could see her luxuriant ash-blonde hair. Sometimes when she raised her head Dembrowski pressed his hands together so that his knuckles showed up white.

Britt always liked meeting with Renate, she liked her calm manner, self-confident and unassuming, whereas she couldn't stand Sannchen. But after she'd thrown Dembrowski out of the apartment Renate also withdrew from us. She wanted a clean break, Britt said, it's understandable, she wants to leave everything behind. And yet she came to the trial and sometimes I saw the way she looked at Dembrowski, and then a quick smile came to her face and she nodded to him. Then the knuckles on Dembrowski's hands showed up white again. And in the first row Sannchen crossed her legs, the silk dress rode up and revealed the top of her stockings, lightly pulled up by her garter belt.

Chaos and tripe

No, I hadn't become aware of the window handle after the testimony of one of the victims, but while Manfred Kubin was giving evidence. Kubin was the economic editor of a well-known magazine and lived opposite us on the same floor in Isestrasse with his wife, an editor on church broadcasting.

In the mornings at 10 Kubin and his wife left the house in their raincoats, belts knotted at the back, if they met us they said hello. In the evenings they got back late, so Britt told me. I didn't actually come home until almost midnight. On Saturdays I'd meet them on the stairs as they carried back steaks, legs of lamb, offal of some kind—which Kubin then always triumphantly lifted out of the shopping basket and held high—but also pheasant, catfish, pike and rabbits, celery, leeks, and carrots with their stalks, guaranteed organically grown. They came up the house stairs on the runner of coconut matting that was always slipping and said hello with a friendly nod. Shortly after that the door from the kitchen onto the balcony next door opened, and on a late summer's day Nanna Giannini, whom I was hearing for the first time, sang to the accompaniment of the clatter of pots and pans. And shortly after that a smell wafted over—our apartment faced east—a smell of goose liver fried with slices of boletus mushrooms, which the two of them would be eating off small plates before the meal. They sat themselves down in their aprons on the graceful iron balcony while with a friendly laugh we retired to our kitchen, the indescribable smells wafting over until one day a hello began the visits next door.

The unusual thing about Kubin was that he was an uninhibited critic of our own economic system and still is, privately, but you couldn't tell this from his articles which I later zealously studied, they were really specialized articles on the economic situation in Italy, France, and England, on the tightness of money, the ECU, and the latest interest rates. They were distinguished by a particular gloomy view of the current economic situation.

We became aware of the man's politics because of the postman. The postman came and handed me a certified letter—I had considerable debts—then he let rip: —They should move over. Take *TAZ* and *konkret* with him. I can smell the type through the door. Drives an Alfa Romeo and wants to talk us into socialism. I always spread the papers out in front of the door, let people see what sort lives inside.

I thought Kubin was a communist, which then turned out to be wrong.

Once when we were in conversation over the balcony exchanging information on how to do a leg of lamb, while we were talking about rosemary and olive oil and I was telling him what I did, that I was an investment counselor with a firm of brokers, he said:

—Brilliant, then you're on a drip feed from this shitty system.

That's how we got talking and then invited to an informal meal on a Saturday because on Fridays I had to wait for the stock exchange to close on Wall Street.

I'd like to say right away it was from Kubin I got the negative view you need in the investment business, that qualifies me to discuss the stock market with critics of the system.

That Saturday we went to the apartment opposite and it was quite a surprise. We'd decorated in white and matt in keeping with the new fashion and there we found everything was black, the very latest trend. Above the black lacquered table tiny lamps that gave out a sharp white light, like spotlights but on a minute scale, lamps that hung on threads that evidently were conducting wires, I stared in amazement as if I'd just come from Siberia. She simply couldn't, said Mrs. Kubin (my name's Angela) bear white any longer, they'd lived with white for six years, the place looked, she said, like an old peoples' home, white furniture on which you can see jam handprints or, she said, and suddenly she slipped off her high-heeled pumps, like a hospital. She went on tiptoe to the black cabinet which was covered with a slab of black granite and got four glasses. —Isn't it grotesque, she said, that after a few years you simply grow tired of things and then throw them out, while other people are still paying off wooden shelves (Thank god, I thought, we didn't furnish in natural wood). —It was you that got tired, said Kubin, not me. —Yes, she said, I'm honest, I don't kid myself, I need these little pleasures. Just like you need the latest theory of fractions. —No, said Kubin, please don't let's discuss furniture design today, only the esthetics of the palate. Let's go into the kitchen.

So Britt and I learned what an informal meal is. You don't just eat in the kitchen, you also witness the preparation, yes, the preparation's actually the event, you sit among all the smells of food at the beautifully-laid table and wait.

—Naturally taste becomes more refined, said Kubin, my grandfather, captain of a four-master still drank rum. If he lit a cigarette and then blew out smoke there'd be a tongue of flame. There's table wine. Umbria. *Civitella*. He carefully pulled out the cork, scratched it, sniffed, poured a little into his glass, sniffed again, thought a moment, then poured the wine, —You can taste every year, swallowed, clicked his tongue, this one's very secco. It's a nice little vineyard, that's to say it was. You used to be able to break your journey there on the way to Rome, now all you can do is buy wine and move on. Two years ago a notice suddenly appeared: German spoken. We spent the night as always in a room on a courtyard covered with grapevines. Outside the nightingales sang, and suddenly Hans Albers, do you remember, Angel, a bus showed up with an alternative tourist group, the motto: Wine, pasta, on a bike through beautiful Umbria. Hamburg students invaded. Turned on their cassette players and joined in raucously: could have been the Reeperbahn at one a.m. So in the morning we fled. But the wine, it's in a class of its own. *Salute!* He reached for a knife worn to a smooth sickle-shape: I get the old meat knives from a butcher, wonderful how carefully they've been ground. Kubin quickly whetted it without looking at what he was doing: A human being needs something to bite, something for his incisors, anything else is rubbish, French cooking now, rabbit in orange sauce, well, all very nice now and then, but I thought, we'll have something different today, what I just got from my butcher, fresh, really fresh, and he held out a finely ribbed, waxy, raglike piece of meat: Tripe, clicked his tongue, the sharp sickle-shaped knife cutting always at his finger tips, cut off long strips.

Kubin's keen on home cooking, said Angela Kubin, and she said, right, let's not be formal, everyone calls me Angel. Come on, she said, and threw a small tomato grown on the balcony at him. You see, Kubin stops everywhere, in suburbs, filling stations are a favorite, that's where you get tips about the little restaurants where mothers or grandmothers still do the cooking. Because you should know at my office he's known as the Schliemann of the kitchen, said Angel.

—Those religious broadcasts, those evangelists, apart from Angel of course, you only have to look at them, that ascetic pallor, that dried-out know-it-all look. You're having a good meal and instantly they show up and say, hunger in the Third World. They always associate a good meal with Witzigmann, like my colleague at the office, that man, said Kubin and cut off the strips of tripe a millimeter from his fingertips so that I thought at any moment his fingertips would fly off, that man with his brown moist eyes, that truffle pig, writing his reports on restaurants that cost a small fortune. Completely false standards. No, I'm interested in folk cooking, basic cooking if you like, operatic arias bore me, always did, but the old popular songs, that's life. In Italy you have to go into the suburbs. You have to know the local dialect, or the only word you'll understand is railway station. And never ask at the station. Because then they all think you're about to leave and they send you to restaurants where they'd never go themselves, where after two minutes the spaghetti comes precooked and mushy onto the table, a ladle stuck in it and slopping out onto the table, no, the secret is to still be able to taste what's in the food, not all this turning it into a mousse, straining it, flambéing it, that's totally degenerate French cooking. "We're doing it French style." Well, we know what that means, only this time you'll taste it. Well, so the comparison isn't right, ha ha, now onions cut small, but not too small.

—Still, said Angel, recently at a meeting of the Third World group she'd read statistics about protein in the Sudan zone that had really got to her.

—But you don't want socialism by default, if I understand you correctly, he said and swallowed some wine.

—And you don't want any kind of socialism.

—No, a kitchen democracy, from the bottom up, he drew the knife like a violin bow across the tripe. You have to select, not any old stomach will do, wash well, salt it then wash again, only don't pickle it, don't wash out the smell, it belongs to the taste, here, smell, he stopped cutting and held a piece of the stomach under our noses: smells good, eh? Stomach, but that's not all, it smells of grass, of hay. The size of the strips is the secret, the amount of time you cook it, a few ingredients, and you have to be present to see the cooking process on its way, watching over the dish is a part of it, you can't in between do the laundry or peer into a paper. I mean, a painter can't leave in the middle of painting and read a paper, or a composer cook while he's composing. Cooking is an art. Vegetables, he cut off two small strips from the vegetable, taste it. Well?

I tasted it. —Mm.

Britt: —Fennel?

—Correct. Bravo. But not any old fennel, wild fennel, that goes with it, just a little, garlic of course. And with stomach you always have to be able to tell from the taste what it is, what organ as it were, usually we stew it, actually it's not just a matter of eating meat, the two-legged animal eats to incorporate strength, cannibalism strictly speaking as he's eating a related species, and at the same time a symbolic act, you have to taste every organ, that's what gives strength.

—Vegetarians, Angel said, and here we were thinking: Let's hope they're not vegetarians.

He poured us more wine: —Or anti-alcohol.

The water was boiling, he cut garlic, threw two onions into the boiling water, then the strips of tripe.

—As an investment counselor, he said, what do you think of Silvio Gesell's depreciation theory?

—No, I promptly laid my throat bare, I'm what they call a trainee, I said, I'm still new to the job, learning the ropes of the investment business, all the options, zero bonds, futures trading, what to invest how and where. At the moment I'm only phoning doctors and trying to get their wives on the phone. Short-term investments, speculating in futures trading.

—All the people that don't know what to do with their money, said Angel, repellent.

—No, said Kubin, not at all, just logical. It has nothing to do with morality, anything goes, only in my view it has to be done in an esthetic way. You buy a beautiful painting from Salome, others put their money to work, that determines everything, there's the beautifully clear logic of the system, and what does this logic show: things move, they march on, they blow you away, but so what. *Salute!* This one's a bit, he swallowed, we'll open another bottle, this one's a bit, I don't know, taste, putting it bluntly, too sweet, no? Everybody has to see they get their slice of the cake, that's obvious, doesn't matter how, which all leads to a constant increase in the amount of capital, everyone everywhere living on massive credit that's in no way covered by assets. But what are assets? Social working hours? Yes, this one's better, the color, look at the color, only it doesn't travel well. Did you ever read Marx, how he used a wine barrel to illustrate a point. Time is money, he said. But time exists because of people, otherwise it wouldn't make any difference. So without people, well. So, a barrel of wine, or was it whisky, gets dearer with time, right, ergo it's because of time, of duration that wine gets dearer. No, not time, but working hours, human time. But that's no longer true, hasn't been for a long time.

—Now eat some bread, said Angel, or you'll suddenly be totally fractious.

—No, you see, there's overcapitalization, there's too much capital and it's all rushing to all kinds of weird places, cored blocks of granite, Penck, platinum fountain pen cases, paintings, and to you too, my love, but also to van Goghs, to loans, to futures trading, never mind, it's beautiful chaos, it's creative, you see, until at some stage it all collapses. Third world countries living on credit, on their last legs, banks in America collapse, Wall Street wobbles, London, Frankfurt, smell, it's ready, he lifted the lid, then capital is going to get sucked into these voids as if they were black holes. Naturally a war would do it too. Capital constantly needs black holes. Right, he said, and began frying slices of white bread in the pan smeared with garlic.

—You and your chaos ideology, said Angel.

—Ha, he said, I'm the only one without any ideology, honestly, if you overlook the fact that I collect recipes, but that's no ideology, that's workaday archeology because, well. Enough of theory, we're going to eat, no more discussion, not a word, swallowing is all that's allowed.

The bed in the corridor

My uncle explained the camel's hump to me. We were standing right by the animal. My uncle stroked the shaggy hide. He said the hump wasn't just a water reservoir but a space for memories (what a strange word, I thought in my dream), the camel meanwhile with soft lips cropped a thorny bush, my uncle stroked the animal's neck and told me to do it as well. As I stroked its neck the camel turned its head to me and carefully and gently got hold of the hem of my coat and began eating it, slowly but unstoppably the coat's hem disappeared in the camel's mouth, a regular grinding, the yellowish-brown, crude but finely honed teeth are clearly visible as they come closer and closer to me. I tried unbuttoning the coat to slip out of it. No good, the buttons had no buttonholes, they were only decorative buttons. I could already feel the coat getting tight, cutting me under the armpits, squeezing my breath out.

Then I started and sat up.

The phone was ringing. By the time I picked up the receiver whoever it was had hung up. Under the shower I told myself it could only have been Britt, nobody else had my number. But then I thought it must have been somebody who wanted to talk to the person who'd rented the apartment before me. The phone number will have stayed the same. In Marbella it was now night. Britt, who needs a lot of sleep, would have gone to bed long ago.

I sat on the balcony and corrected what I'd written yesterday.

At noon I phoned home. Lolo's voice: —Hello Daddy, how are you? She asked about the city, the weather, the people. She'd love to come, she really would, she said, then limited it to just to visit. Mummy's not here, she's gone to Marbella. She's still looking for curtain material. I asked if Britt had phoned last night. She didn't know. Take care, she said, she'd got that from Britt and used to also say it to Harald, that wimp, when he went sailing. She'd met him at the sailing club.

Lolo, to Britt's consternation, didn't want to learn riding, she wanted to sail. Perhaps Lolo remembered how I'd sailed with her on the Trave and how by singing about the sailor's death of little Theodor Kalle she'd overcome her fear of the sloping boat and the waves. Because his home was the grey grey sea, hurrah.

During the midday break I went from Osborn & Partner to the Alster, to the landing dock that belonged to a small cafe. The Alster lay flat and leaden grey beneath white fleecy midday clouds. I watched the sailing students practice righting the dinghies after capsizing. It was a summer day, the hottest of the year. There was almost no wind and the children had to hang far leeward to actually make the boat capsize. I'd taken off my jacket and tie and was drinking some mineral water. The dinghy which Lolo was on with another girl capsized. The girls tumbled into the water. Lolo climbed with the other girl onto the centerboard and righted the boat. But it turned and capsized again, the centerboard now stuck up like a gigantic shark's fin. Lolo dived, dived again, time went by—I was on the point of getting up, then she surfaced again holding the sail.

Later she sat at my table in her wet trousers, her wet shirt, drank a lemonade and said what she'd like best would be to go to sea.

▼

Meanwhile I've become familiar with the dance the women and the men dance on the street. They start to move as soon as they see a European coming and then, when they've recognized me (I often come here) the dance turns into a slow swinging movement of the hips. They're waiting for tourists who show up here mostly in the late afternoon. Business, as Nelson the barman tells me, isn't as good as it was a few years ago when Europeans and the Yankees came here to screw or get fucked (fairies and older women came here too). Showing a cunt here doesn't just mean fucking but good luck, and anyone who screws does—or did—it with the easiest conscience in the world. Now fear of AIDS keeps away the fuck jumbo jets from America and Europe.

I sat there and thought how I'd never been mad for these kinds of adventures that Dembrowski was always after, on every business trip he took on the look of a hunter and got on the trail. He's got an unfailing instinct for his victims, who however never think of themselves as victims. I think that's why he was so uneasy, so dissatisfied when suddenly he was with Sannchen day in, day out. Renate was at home. Renate was waiting. Renate gave him a free hand. Whereas Sannchen had her demands, her expectations. He should hold himself straight, which in any case he did, he should wear shoes with lifts that would make him two centimeters taller and almost as tall as Sannchen. She didn't want him to just sit there in the evening, but to talk about what had happened during the day, about business, and in the middle of the night she wanted a glass of champagne in some criminally expensive Hamburg bar, and so after a hard day's investing Dembrowski would shoot off with her in her Porsche from his stylishly renovated classical manor house in Schleswig-Holstein down the autobahn to Hamburg, to drink a glass of Dom Perignon. But most of all Sannchen wanted to work and earn money. She worked freelance for an advertising agency that was in fierce competition with Britt's agency, for which reason neither spoke about any project in front of the other.

I also understand why in the end she raged so against Dembrowski's arrest, and it speaks well for Sannchen that she stuck it out with him for so long on this enforced permanent Spanish holiday. Sannchen wanted to get back to work, Sannchen wanted to get back to her old circle of friends, Sannchen quite simply wanted to get back to the shopping sprees, Sannchen didn't speak Spanish. Britt on the other hand I'm sure enjoyed the time, she was glad to have gotten away from the firm, to have nothing more to do with advertising. Just as she'd worked hard all those years, so she'd enjoyed the time in Marbella, completely concentrating on growing roses. I think in the first six months she didn't often pine for Hamburg. Only now she's alone in the house she'll find time dragging.

After a while you can get heartily sick of that eternally blue sky, my stepfather once said to me when I asked him about his South Sea travels. And I can also understand Dembrowski waiting at the garden fence with his packed suitcase.

In the end dreams you can afford become unbearable because you're waiting even more for something unknown, other than death that is.

Meanwhile I keep watch to the right and the left, tense as can be, peer into every parked car, of which the streets here are full, suddenly look round, but as if I were just curious about something, not agitated as my uncle with his professional inclination to exaggeration probably imagines it, but just tense.

▼

I'd just completed the training program with Osborn & Partner, had done my first deals with clients I'd acquired by phone—here I could go back to many clients to whom I'd sold life insurance. I did these deals with great circumspection and, as was testified to at the trial, extremely successfully. I only slowly realized how easy a lot of people were about money, and above all, how much money there was around. It was still an extravagance for me to invest 50,000 or 100,000 and I still lay awake at night wondering if I'd filled in everything properly, if in my haste I hadn't forgotten something while talking to the investor and the broker at the stock exchange in New York or Chicago. I'd received the first commissions. And I have to say it, for my own benefit as well, in case it's forgotten: The work was fun.

One afternoon my mother phoned and asked if I could go to the Red Cross Hospital, my grandmother had been taken there that morning, Mrs. Brücker had called for an ambulance. —I can't go right now, said my mother, I have to wait for somebody (for what or for whom was she waiting that day?). I'll go in the evening, she said.

For a moment I hesitated, for just one moment about which I still feel ashamed I wondered whether I should go as I had an appointment with a client. This was a client who wanted to invest a large sum and who had been recommended to me by a successful painter. Then I went to Dembrowski and he said, —Sure, but try to be back when the man with the street name comes. I dashed out, it was a sunny but cool spring day, took a taxi to the Red Cross Hospital on the Schlump. A shabby hospital like barracks, dirty red bricks. The porter told me the room number. Dark corridors, a stairwell, the copper treads trodden down to paper-thin sheets, the room: eight beds, all occupied, all older women, but she wasn't in the room, perhaps the porter had got the number wrong. I asked a nurse who was passing, she sent me to the ward doctor. Who had just left for lunch. The assistant doctor couldn't tell me anything either. Then finally the ward sister came and said, —She's lying outside. —Outside? —Yes. In the corridor, they'd taken her out of the ward. She was already unconscious when they brought her in that morning. The sister shook her head. —A stroke. She can't feel anything anymore.

She lay there, the lids hung heavy over her eyes, mouth slightly open, cheeks deeply sunk. They'd taken out her false teeth. Her hands rested on the white blanket, her breathing was shallow and sometimes it seemed as if the next breath wouldn't come, but then she drew in air even more deeply. How thin her grey hair had become. I sat for an hour by the bed in the corridor and held her hand. The dark brown linoleum had been trodden down to a dull grey in the middle of the corridor and outside every door. Higher up on the white walls was a brown line. It was broken where the paint had peeled off. Nurses went by with bedpans and syringes. Visitors came, in coats, flowers in hand. From afar they looked at me with curiosity sitting right up by the bed, then as they came nearer they quickly looked at the corridor wall. I'd forgotten how salty tears taste. At the end of the corridor there was a window that led to a yard. There, against the light a man and a woman stood in an embrace, kissing. They stood there as if it was the most natural thing in the world while I held her hand, which was rough, and yet soft and warm.

When I looked at my watch it was almost four. I had to get back to the office. The ward sister shrugged when I asked her if I could go for an hour or two.

It only occurred to me in the taxi that I could have taken her from the corridor and put her in a private room. While I sat in the corridor and held her hand that had never occurred to me, it was as if she belonged where she lay.

The investor was already waiting in the office, still young, a modest shy man in his twenties who had inherited several million. He wanted to invest some of the money in art, some in secure long-term government bonds and sound shares, and with some, about 500,000, he said, he wanted to speculate just to get a feeling for capital, but also for the sake of doing something, following the rates and comparing.

I asked him to wait a moment and phoned the clinic. The young man leafed through Osborn & Partners' ultra-glossy catalogue in which there were pictures in glowing colors of the stock exchanges of Frankfurt, Hamburg, London, and New York, that's to say where our company had put down branches.

I gave my grandmother's name, would they please immediately put her in a private room. —I'm paying, private. Yes of course, we're related. You can enquire at my bank. The young man shook his head and smiled.

I had to wait because the nurse wanted to put me through to the ward nurse.

—I'm in no hurry, said the young man, please take your time.

It took a while, then the ward nurse came to the phone. —Mr. Walter?

—Yes, I was just at the hospital. I wanted . . .

She interrupted me. —I'm sorry. She died. Shortly after you left.

I hung up.

—Is someone ill, the young man asked.

—Yes, I said, yes.

—I'm sorry. I can come back, tomorrow or the day after. We can talk some other time.

—No, I said, it makes no difference.

▼

The shadow of the restaurant awning had moved to my feet. I'd drunk a rum with ice and then another. My head felt heavy but I didn't want to go back, not to the big, unpleasantly empty apartment flooded with light. Meanwhile the drummers had gone. They'd simply left their barrels standing. The girl with the penny-whistle had stepped into a hole in the street. She was washing herself. Here some time ago a pipe had burst and three weeks ago a ditch had been dug to replace the pipe, which so far hadn't happened. So the burst pipe was used as a public fountain.

The fruit and souvenir sellers were lying in the shade under the trees, they lay there as if dead. Not far away in the sky vultures circled above the meat and fish market.

Slowly the shadow approached my stretched legs. Soon I'd have to draw them in. The waiter was sitting inside the cafe under the ventilator and had fallen asleep, in his hand a dishcloth. The man behind the bar was also asleep, his head resting on his arms. On the walls the flies didn't move.

A quiet shudder passed through the tops of the trees. Light flashed over the dust, over the sleeping orange sellers, then silence covered them again.

The bird man and his price

This morning I breakfasted in shorts and barefoot on my balcony with its view over the Bay of Bahia. It had been a hot sultry night and it was the first time I'd put on the air conditioning. Next to the coffee cup lay the fragment of the bird man. In the sunlight I carefully looked at the piece, the remains of the glyph that had once been the hand of the eating singer.

On the phone yesterday Britt said it would be better if she didn't phone me again because you didn't know if someone was listening in. And Interpol had been called in. I'd never have thought Interpol bothered with such trifles. And the redhead had shown up in front of the house, not hiding himself at all, she said, but as if he wanted to show he was watching us.

—It's that Fishy Fritz who can't forgive us for having relieved him of almost two million.

In the first place, she said, they couldn't leave because she and Lolo would be followed. And apart from that yet another change of school wouldn't be good for Lolo. It was another year and a half to her exams, they'd have to wait until then.

Now she understood, Britt said, why most terrorist couples didn't have children.

—Why are you talking terrorists? I asked her.

—Why not? It had just occurred to her. By the way, she said, I've just taken the figure to the restorer. As you know, he specializes in frames for Picassos.

For a moment I considered whether to tell her that I'd put the largest piece in my pocket, that the poor man wouldn't be able to do anything with the other pieces, that the result would be an entirely different figure. Because not only was this fragment missing, but also the piece of wood that lay on the floor and that the Moroccan woman had swept up and thrown away.

—How can he even know what the figure looked like?

—I gave him a photo of the figure.

I think it must be the photo that was sent to me when the figure was up for sale.

Dembrowski and I had just made ourselves independent when I read the announcement: an old figure from Easter Island (guaranteed genuine by experts) is being sold privately for 230,000 marks. A criminally high price. Still, I bought it without even hesitating for a moment. I took out a loan. The public prosecutor made a connection between this 230,000 that I had to borrow from a bank and which was therefore detectable and the first—I have to say it sooner or later—embezzlement. He said there was a considerable debt, one that led to this misappropriation. The accused, both accused, lived well above their means.

Naturally I didn't say I'd bought the figure with the loan. So no one knows its value. After my flight Britt had been able to collect the figure from prison after the usual formalities. They took it for a piece of driftwood in which you could see the vague form of a strange bird-tailed man.

—My husband collects strange looking driftwood, Britt had said. She took this bird man valued at 230,000 from the hands of the judicial authorities while in our flat the victims had our last prints seized for a ridiculous 200 marks.

I suspect that my uncle, if he were to learn about the chronological sequence of buying this figure and the embezzlement that followed shortly after, would believe that the one had inevitably led to the other. Whereas I'm convinced the connection is more of a coincidence. We'd in any case have kept the money we'd failed to invest. Why should we pay out what had disappeared in the whirlpool of the great flow of capital?

We earned well, Dembrowski and I, we'd been able to totally pay off the additional expenses that had come about, in my case by buying the figure, and with Dembrowski because of the separation from his wife. Put it this way: the money we'd failed to invest came in handy. The mistake in accounting certainly made our decision not to pay it back easier. But here I need to say that this wasn't a decision made after brooding all night over all kinds of scruples, as my mother worrying about her reputation, or my uncle might like to imagine, to take a course—how can I put it, a bridging attempt, temporary, or that everything could be redeemed by a wave of the hand. In those two years the only anxiety that really disturbed my sleep was caused by wondering when we'd be found out, when we'd be arrested, when we'd end up inside. With this anxiety that never left us for a single day we paid (and I still am paying) for those two years, rich in events, but actually also just rich.

Only occasionally I'd wake up, dazed, sit up in bed,

not remembering any dream but full of some unspeakable horror, then I'd feel Britt's hand warm from sleep on my chest, and I'd hear her voice heavy with sleep.

—You've been screaming again.

Last night after Britt's call I battled with myself whether to phone her and tell her she should stop getting the bird man glued together. But then I thought perhaps the old man with his magnifying glass was already sitting bent over his restoring, that he'd already begun fixing the splinters and little pieces of wood into a shape, probably with the help of some artificial substance. The figure that had meant so much to me would never again exist.

I was in a rage with Britt. A rage, as I immediately had to acknowledge, that was thoroughly self-righteous, because behind this rage there was disappointment—and with me disappointment can turn into rage. I was disappointed that Britt didn't want to come here with Lolo. And this rage is still in me though at the same time I have to tell myself that Britt's decision is sensible.

▼

Yesterday evening I roamed the city's lively streets simply to walk off my rage until I was suddenly startled out of my thoughts. In the crowd on the opposite sidewalk, almost at the same level, among all the dark, black people I suddenly saw a man with red hair. I wanted to cross the street but had to wait a while until the way was clear. I ran across the street, pushed my way past people who in this city because of the heat amble rather than hurry, I barged into people, pushed my way through a group of older women, stumbled over a child sitting begging on the ground, ran on. I told myself it was a coincidence, an impossible one, that I should run into the redhead here of all places. How could he have followed me here? I said to myself there are a lot of tourists in this city, there are even blonde natives, but the more explanations I gave myself the uneasier I became, the faster I ran, until I came to a group of Belgians who were strolling through the city and talking loudly in Flemish. Though one of them wasn't exactly a redhead he was blonde with just a hint of red. But I had to admit to myself that the hair of the man I'd seen earlier had been a light red. I ran through the streets keeping a lookout for a head of red-blonde hair, I went several times up and down the main street. The redhead had disappeared. Exhausted I took a taxi back to my apartment, but got out a few houses earlier, walked along the fence, peered into every car.

I asked the porter if anyone had asked for me. —No.

▼

On the third day of the trial the young guard again came for me. That night I'd brooded about whether to escape on that day of the trial or not until the day of the verdict. What I'd most like to have done was ask my lawyer which would be better, to escape in the middle of the trial or only at the end. On the one hand, I told myself, to run off immediately meant not to have any money. I would have had to go on foot. In my suit, perhaps in the rain or falling snow, I would have been spotted immediately by a police patrol. Or I would have had to get money off somebody in the street, because when you've just escaped from prison you don't want to be caught by an inspector on the subway. And then—where would I go? But then on the day of the verdict another guard might have come who'd only let me out into the courtroom at the last minute. Or perhaps just by chance a guard would be standing by the window. At any rate, I decided to wait until the verdict. Then, I thought, the whole trial wouldn't have to be repeated. At some other time I could sit in prison for the year Dr. Blank had predicted: —You know, a year's nothing. Some people would pay a fortune to take a year's break in peace. You get up to 10 marks a day if you work. But you can also work in peace on your book, resocialization as it were.

The young guard led me through the corridors. A young woman came towards us, also in handcuffs. Her fingers were painted red—because of the handcuffs it looked as if her fingernails had just been torn out.

—Stabbed her lover, that one, a lawyer, you'd think they'd know better seeing they know what to expect, only not a bit. Public prosecutors are the exception. Never had one of them in handcuffs, don't know anyone who did. You'd really score there. He talked his way down the corridors and up and down the stairs. I was waiting for the right moment to ask him to quickly unlock me. Just before we got to the courtroom I finally said: —It would be very nice if you could unlock me again today, and tomorrow. Tomorrow after the verdict it's going to be straight inside anyway.

—I'm not inhuman, you know, he said. What do you think you'll get? I'd say four years.

He immediately unlocked me. First I hugged Lolo, then Britt. —Listen. Put a hundred-mark note in your mouth tomorrow. Then kiss me and push it into my mouth.

Britt looked at me as if I'd gone out of my mind, before she could ask anything Dr. Blank came up and greeted her.

—Please do it, I repeated.

Just the thought of putting one of the notes here, one of these filthy rags, in my mouth makes me want to vomit. But in Germany you can put almost any hundred-mark note in your mouth.

Kubin always had his little joke whenever I started enthusing about the esthetics of money. He, who could talk so convincingly about the esthetics of home cooking, found any talk of the esthetics of money hypocritical. The only thing that really convinced him about East Germany, he said, was the deliberate indifference to the esthetics of money, dull colors, bad paper, poorly-designed coins in the cheapest of all possible materials, aluminum, and so light a strong wind could blow them from your hand. Still, he said, if they'd been fundamental democrats instead of socialist bureaucrats they'd have had to develop a different kind of workaday esthetics. They would have had to turn the simplest into the best: Mecklenburg goose giblets, food fit for people, instead of those dried-out broilers, comfortable simple well-cut blouses and shirts to wear at work, in practical dark blue colors that when washed turned into various lighter shades, the go-ahead for all gays, lesbians, polygamy recognized by the state, free speech, obviously, grants to the dying, protection of the environment, a new bill of rights for animals and plants. Instead nothing got beyond just money and that finally disgusted people because they got junk or nothing at all for it.

On the third day of the trial economic editor Kubin gets questioned again. The public prosecutor believed my moving into the apartment next to Kubin's had been planned well in advance. Kubin after all had plenty of inside information. The public prosecutor is well-read as he gives us to understand by a reference to Balzac's speculations on the stock market. And he suspects—*déformation professionelle*—that behind every coincidence is an intention. When in fact the scheming intention only arises out of the coincidence.

To the question of whether we had perhaps sounded him out Kubin simply laughed and said: —Have you ever heard the experts on economic development give their advice and forecasts? They're the wise men with their computers, and they still have to constantly correct their forecasts up or down.

—All theory, said Kubin, is nebulous, for example the great guru of the stock exchange, Kostolany, divides investors into the tremblers and the hard-boiled. The public prosecutor had taken out his ball-point to make notes.

—When the rates on the stock market go up, Kubin continued, the hard-boiled sell their shares and the tremblers buy them, this goes on until the rates stop climbing because so many of the hard-boiled have sold, then they begin to fall, which is when the shakiest of the tremblers sell their shares, which in turn makes the shares fall faster, at which ever more of the tremblers sell their shares ever faster and the rates plunge through the floor.

The public prosecutor looked up from his notes and peered at Kubin, waiting for more.

—At this stage, said Kubin, the hard-boiled again start buying the shares, they buy hard, and after a while the shares begin to rise again, they rise and rise and first those that aren't trembling too much get back in, then the others, they buy shares, force up the rates so high that finally even the shakiest buy, while now again the hard-boiled get out, the rate stagnates and then tips over and the cycle begins again.

—And what does that mean, the public prosecutor wanted to know.

—Well, said Kubin, to generalize: At the height of the boom the hard-boiled have got the money and the tremblers have got the shares and at the low point, the slump, the hard-boiled have got the shares and the tremblers the money. If this were to catch on—every little investor nowadays reads Kostolany—more and more of the tremblers would become hard-boiled, this would result, when the rates rise, in the hardest-boiled in order to stay hard-boiled getting in increasingly faster, that's to say becoming tremblers, and when the rates fall getting back in increasingly faster, at which point—as the rates react with extreme sensitivity—everything has to move faster and faster, which turns the hardest of the hard-boiled into the shakiest and the shakiest into the hardest-boiled. But what this means, now that the tremblers are hard-boiled and the hard-boiled are tremblers, is that the stock market comes to a total standstill, everything caves in.

The public prosecutor, a man who knew his way around the investment business, threw his ball-point down on the table and wanted to know if Kubin had therefore given me money to spec-u-late (the way he said it, totally provocative).

On principle he didn't speculate, Kubin replied. Otherwise he'd have entrusted money to me at any time for speculation.

The little apple man

We'd lived a year in the Isestrasse when our neighbor's apartment began to smell increasingly of something burning. On Friday evening, on Saturday no longer the fragrance of rabbit baked with rosemary, instead the sharp smell of burned meat. What hadn't been dragged up the stairs: radishes guaranteed fertilized by hand, home-grown leeks with extra flavor, veal sweetbreads, chicken with the tricolor round their yellow legs, hare where you still bite into shot. The chicken would be put in a casserole dish, slept in a simple mustard sauce, dreamed it would soon be melting on someone's tongue, but then in the casserole dish it heard the voices of its cook and his wife on the balcony. Not again, but I said, no you didn't, I did, I don't want to, the things you say, it's what I've always said, in that case no, in that case yes. And suddenly there was a smell of burning and the lovely chicken had black legs. We'd smell burning next door, the two would still be arguing, we'd wonder whether to go over, hesitate, and when the smell of burning began to fade we'd finally decided, go, ring and say: —We're about to fry a couple of eggs with bacon, wouldn't you like to join us. —No no, said Kubin, he'd just burned something but he had a really excellent alternative: Porchetta and to go with it some Canaiuolo. He'd brought the porchetta with him yes-

317

terday from the EC-economic summit in Rome. He'd been there to report on it and had used the opportunity to rent a car and drive over to Cervetti on his own to have some porchetta there and bring a good piece back. A pig like a Peking duck, as it were. And are you now finally going to listen to me, Angela would ask. Actually no, it's more the prototype of the sausage. An entire pig has the bones taken out, but without the pig's body loosing its shape, the pig gets spread out, two kilos of salt sprinkled over it, then it's stuffed with garlic, wild fennel and thyme, sewn up and roasted overnight on a spit. Of course porchetta tastes best warm. He cut slices off the large piece. But even cold it's good enough to worship.

And he actually knelt after he'd cut the first slice and stuffed the meat in his mouth. Then Angela Kubin suddenly stood up, reached for her high-heeled shoes with her black-stockinged legs and said: —I'm sick of your gluttony. She put her glass down on the table with such force that it splashed Kubin kneeling in front of it. Then she ran from the kitchen, the door to the apartment slammed, we heard her running down the stairs.

Britt and I looked at each other and then over at Kubin who slowly got up.

His mouth twitched. Was he going to cry? Was he going to instantly go into a rage? Was he going to start apologizing? Offer explanations, say: Come back next Saturday, I want to be alone? Not at all.

He said, —That's because Angel either runs around barefoot or in those high heels. Even now in winter, even when there's snow on the ground, which doesn't happen that often here. She'd even climb Mont Blanc in her high heels. Only those who dare wear a Danish camel's hair slipper are relatively sane, and Kubin lifted his right foot in its light-brown checked slipper. She's going to pieces a little at the moment, she's got a friend, seventeen years younger. He's still green, in a word: twenty. You know what that means? She's got to see it through. A nice boy. I've seen him, studies Sanskrit. The type that eats hamburgers while he's reading. It can't turn out well. She met him at a demonstration for a free Timor or independence for the Saharis, or something, I don't remember. With his Danish camel's hair slipper Kubin opened the garbage can and threw the chicken down its folding maw.

—A pity, I wanted to introduce you to this recipe. An old one from Genoa. Although the Genoese didn't really know how to enjoy themselves, always dressed in black, always somber, their cooking isn't exactly going to bowl you over, but *polos al cane* is the exception. Why *al cane?* The recipe comes from the sedan-chair carriers in Genoa. They always had mustard in the house. They spread it on their heels so the street mongrel wouldn't bite their legs. And mustard chicken probably came from this excessive use of mustard. But the mustard has to be mixed with honey, then a generous measure of pepper, fresh thyme, some basil, a bay leaf chopped small. Yes, he said, this Sanskrit lad doesn't bowl me over. All he does is make me feel paternal. A pity. If at least one could be torn apart by jealousy. One's a little hurt, of course. When did you last read of anyone stabbing his wife to death because he found her in bed with another man? And then why, when she'd explained why she needed this. —A thousand good reasonable reasons, said Kubin, I'm convinced there are no more tragic heights or depths.

Neither in private life, nor in society. The logic of liberalism has triumphed in taxation and in love. Anything goes. But only on a small scale, anything big is out. I mean, look at the pathetic politicians, those shabby little swindles, the chancellor has his private secretary collect 30,000 apples as a party contribution, no receipt, I mean, love too, we all know, everyone's replaceable, oneself included, one's not that unique, only demand determines the value, a matter of price, only there are no heights or depths anymore. All of society is—nauseated Kubin pummeled the air with his hands—is purée.

I thought of the black man in rags I'd seen two weeks earlier lying in the street in New York, frozen in his own vomit, in his rigid fist a smeared paper plate, on it the congealed remains of some purée, quince-yellow, probably cornmeal, still in the form given it by the star-shaped opening of the faucet. Perhaps there was rat poison in the purée, perhaps the man had drunk himself to death, perhaps he'd simply frozen, starved with the remains of the purée he'd picked out of some rubbish bin in his hand.

Next to him stood a cop muffled like a hostage taker, his face but for two slits for the eyes wrapped in wool, in his fist an oversized cudgel. It looked as if the cop had just struck down the man because he'd caught him in the act of stealing the paper plate with the leftover purée. He was guarding the body for which no one was showing any concern. People went by, only looking down briefly from their coat collars.

It was my first day in New York, a training trip for the brokers Osborn & Partner.

—Now please don't go on about the Third World,

said Kubin. Which wouldn't have occurred to Britt and me in any case, but no doubt he was thinking about his wife. All those hospitable Africans, those samba-dancing Latinos, those pro-life Indians, let them, he said, first shovel up the shit they leave behind daily.

He cut us slices of pork and said: —Try it, taste it, it's cultural history on the tongue. If people could learn to taste, smell, touch again they wouldn't need to lay down more roads.

—This Canaiuolo has no additives, nothing, not even enzymes, you're tasting sun, water, earth, all of nature and marvelously all in liquid form.

—What one needs to examine today, said Kubin, is the connection between the apple that Newton watched as it fell and Newton's losses through speculation when the South Sea Company went bankrupt. The little apple man is the symbol of the chaos theory. Because that's our metaphysics. I know where God lives: in Wall Street. And that requires a new morality.

—Yes, I said, the Wall Street Stock Exchange had reminded me of a temple, on the outside. But on the inside of a ventricle. A huge space with a cassette deck from which bunches of computer cables hung down like coronary arteries. Beneath them selling and buying took place and from these coronary vessels rose arteries, the tubes of the former pneumatic post, through which cables now electronically pumped capital to the world.

But Kubin just shook his head, said: —Rubbish, no, that's a false picture, sweetheart, rubbish, do you know what the stock exchange is?

—A cloud.

▼

Three weeks later we heard crashing and shouts from the stairwell. The black leather chairs with the chromed bars, the indoor linden trees in luxuriant growth were being carried out, exotic horsetails, palms taken down the stairs, a piano was carefully maneuvered out of the house.

—There are reverberations, Kubin said, when he came over to us that night, holding not a bottle of Umbrian country wine but a small styrofoam package. He put it on our kitchen table, a McDonald's box and in it a Big Mac, took it out, let himself be given a glass of Burgundy bought in the supermarket, squeezed tomato ketchup out of a little plastic tube onto his hamburger and bit into the cattle of Argentina and Brazil, right down to the eroded primeval forest, the scorched ash-covered red earth, the grazing land that had turned to steppe, and said: —What a day. My colleague on the features section, a zombie, you should see him, his spiritual life all takes place at the end of his nose, said:

—You have to demonstrate the passing of time by coming to a halt.

Kubin listened. You could hear the distant tap tap of high heels from the stairwell. She never came up the stairs on the coconut runner, you see, so her footsteps always said: I'm coming, I'm coming.

The footsteps went along the landing, climbed higher, and were silent.

Kubin studied the tiny remains of a mighty steer on the rim of his wine glass, didn't wipe it off, broke our sympathetic silence with: —Why is it that our feelings, these tender sensations, that urgent wanting, well, our

322

desires, our subversive dreams, this longing of bodies drawn to each other, that aren't just bodies, but demands, impressions, how is it that this attraction slowly, how can I put it, dissolves, no, regulates itself, turning itself into the familiar and therefore loses its enchantment?

—Language, says Hawking, is the mirror of our consciousness, said Kubin, only someone in a wheelchair could say that. If our instincts come into play then all they'll find is a distorting, a dirty, almost blind mirror. No, it's a shaving mirror. You look in and you see yourself turned into a nose, you retreat in shock—the picture disappears, disappears into infinity. Because what's refracted to infinity here and creates a blind spot can be compared to language, which is covered with fine cilia that scans our desires, our feelings, our emotions, if you like. They look distorted and if you want to take a closer look you discover a blind spot. And only occasionally, broken up, astonishing, they're reflected in the fragments of some object. And then here they are—our unknown desires.

Once, Kubin said, going out for a Moroccan meal with a friend, a convinced Marxist and rationalist, he'd seen a belly dance. A restaurant where, apart from themselves, there were only two other men, one elderly and the other considerably younger, who kept stroking the older man's hand. Then, said Kubin, while he was eating couscous a woman, a dancer, appeared, her breasts raised up in two small glittering cups, her shoulders, her stomach bare, the soft seductive flab held in and forced up by the lightly laced belt round the hips, in other words not that frigid boutique scrawniness. And the woman had danced in front of them and only for them—the gay couple had only looked into each other's eyes. The way the woman tossed her hair, rolled her hips, the way every movement revolved around that wonderful navel, that gentle shadowy indentation, the way she suddenly bellied out her stomach and then pulled it in again, how in a rapturous wild movement she placed a saber on her flying hair that was like a black whirlpool and another on her naked shoulders and, balancing both, legs wide apart, dancing with a revolving movement backwards and forwards of her hips she slowly squatted, and then, at that stage the older man had accidentally swallowed a little bone and almost choked without his friend noticing, but the dancer, and he'd had to turn to see her, she'd noticed that he couldn't breathe. In the flashing saber on her shoulders he'd seen himself, his face, his eyes wide open, he could have got up and danced what can't be expressed in words. Not yet.

And Kubin pushed the remains of the Big Mac into his mouth and the limp, brown-edged lettuce leaf and said he'd work on it.

—On what, asked Britt.

—On a language of desire.

He wiped the ketchup and the fat of Brazilian cattle off his fingers.

—Yes, he said, then I noticed that all this sweaty enlightenment—did I say sweaty?—has left us a rather bleak, sterile house where only lifelong partners still sleep with each other, depending on how each happens to be feeling, you need to really savor that word: de-:pen-:-ding. And as the partners are usually exhausted—by struggling for recognition of their own needs, among other things—all that's left is the

324

totally dull solidarity, no, partnership of marriage.

—Oh, he said, beautiful wilderness, and went over, through the high, garlanded entrance to his flat and lay down on his Japanese double bed the size of a tennis court. Ah, I thought to myself, all the forebodings, all the desires, all the dreams, they're all now lying in a corner like a small, knotted sheet.

The house on the Süllberg

In the evening the phone rang. My mother, that was my first thought, because Britt didn't want to phone again. It rang and rang. I went onto the balcony so I wouldn't have to hear it ringing. From open windows and other balconies voices, laughter, music. At last the ringing stopped. But shortly after that it began again, shrill and relentless. I tried to turn the ringing off, but it came through an electric amplifier on the wall. Finally I lifted the receiver. It was Britt. She said she simply had to phone me, right now, she didn't want to wait for my call. The reason being that she'd just had a long discussion with Lolo, and now she wanted to discuss it with me. Lolo wanted to return to Hamburg. For one thing, Lolo could then go back to her old school and there take biology as her main course. Which of course wasn't possible at the school in Marbella. And this course was important if she was going to study marine biology. And then, she'd thought about this a long time, beautiful though Marbella was she was feeling lonely now that I wasn't there and wasn't going to be able to come back either. And so, she hesitated, she'd prefer to be in Hamburg. After all, she said, that's where all our friends and acquaintances are, and anyway.

And anyway, if I think about it now, what was she trying to say? And anyway, what she meant—perhaps quite unconsciously—was that at some stage, probably quite soon, I'd be there, in Fuhlsbüttel in fact, in jail. But as always these things don't occur to you until you've put the receiver down and you continue the discussion half aloud to yourself. What do you mean by anyway, I should have asked. But instead in answer to her question whether I objected all I'd said was no, of course not, no. But in actual fact I hadn't been asked. What would she have said if I'd said: Yes, I object? I could have said, and as loudly as I'm saying it now: Good heavens, you could at least wait another month or two. I'm sitting here in an apartment on the 21st floor with a view over Salvador da Bahia, at my back a carefully worked-out escape route, my suitcase is still packed for departure, the woman who cleans here still keeps looking puzzled in the wardrobe in which there are only hangers, because of her I bought myself two shirts and some trousers, I've memorized all the departure times of international flights from Salvador, I run through the streets watching out for men with red hair, and you, you can't even bear two months in a wonderful Spanish country house with shady cork oaks in the garden and a Moroccan cleaning woman.

—You didn't even grow your new rose, Britt.

—No, I'll grow it in Hamburg.

—Where would you move to, I asked Britt. After all, we'd had to give up the apartment in the Isestrasse.

—To the house.

—What house?

—*The* house, of course. The house on the Süllberg, after all, it's empty.

—Yes.

The house is empty. It's been empty for almost three years. The house that Fishy Fritz always maintained I'd bought with his money. It was exactly the 1.9 million we'd got out of him. True, I did buy the house for 1.9 million at the time I went to Fishy Fritz on the Baltic. But he continued investing money right to the end, until the firm went under, and by then the house had long been paid for. But there was no way of making him understand this. The other victims, 189 altogether, of whom only 69 started legal proceedings, didn't even register with him. The others had speculated off the books, with money they weren't actually supposed to have, and couldn't therefore be victims. Only these 69 had paid tax on their money, for which reason they were bitter, and the bitterest of them all was Fishy Fritz. It was pure coincidence that his loss amounted to exactly the sum I'd paid for the house. Everyone knows that when money changes hands it changes ownership. Not so Fishy Fritz, he considered this house paid for with his banknotes. Only it didn't belong to me. It belonged to my sister-in-law. So he had to take revenge. He wants me in jail, wants every single mark that I earn to the end of my life to be seized and handed over to him. But he can't get at the house, not even if he turns black with anger. In court he said, I've gone grey with anger. And in actual fact when he did appear in court, after the six months that lapsed between my arrest and the trial, he'd gone grey.

327

Now Britt wants to move into the house into which she'd resisted moving in the past.

Some six months after Dembrowski and I had founded the investment firm Sekuritas I heard from a client that an old sea captain's house was up for sale in Blankenese on the Süllberg.

I drove there, went down the stone steps: in a little garden stood a half-timbered house, the mullioned windows painted white, a low thatched roof, upstairs above the portal a semicircular window, a classic sea captain's house built around 1800, a slightly curved front door decorated with small carved amphora. I went through the downstairs rooms, up the wooden stairs, upstairs under the roof the floor levels were slightly uneven and the rooms interconnected, in the two hundred years the heavy oak beams had settled so they no longer creaked, but were uneven as railway sleepers. Up there I looked out of the semicircular window. The little garden shimmered in the hoarfrost and below lay the Elbe, here very wide. A freighter was slowly coming in, the capstan corroded by rust. Gulls over the stern.

I looked at the grey green torrent, the freighter slowly disappeared below the hill, you could hear the siren, two short blasts that meant it was coming into port. And then I knew that I'd buy the house despite the insane price, one point nine million, which I naturally didn't have.

On Christmas Eve there was only an old key under the Christmas tree, a key with a little red bow. —What is it? —Don't ask, you'll see.

At night I drove with Britt to Blankenese, led her to the house on the Süllberg and said: —Unlock the door!

328

Britt went through the house and said: —It's beautiful! Her manner a little exaggerated, a little theatrical, she'd clapped her hands and cried: It's beautiful!

In one of the low rooms under the roof I'd put a bed, in the attic room an armchair, a table, two chairs. Crockery for two people, and six empty rooms. Within a few days, so I'd imagined, at the latest by New Year's Eve we'd be able to spend the night there, with a view over the Elbe and into the New Year.

But Britt resisted, talked about Lolo and then finally Kubin who couldn't just be left on his own in his empty six-room apartment.

We saw the New Year in with Kubin in our apartment. Britt had made a Pomeranian savory potato dish. Kubin ate without appetite. He'd drunk a lot of strong Bordeaux. —The American Empire is going under, he said, not because of overcapitalization, but because all the faucets, gas cocks, all the levers, valves turn to the left, in other words into the fist, and therefore because the thumb can't use its full leverage you get less power. Because in transmitting power the muscles aim outwards, for which reason turning something off to the right with the right hand is more powerful and effective. But turning off is fundamentally more decisive than turning on. To turn on you have to turn a long time before something is on, it is so to speak a necessary, totally functional decision. But turning off is a moral action. To turn something off is a decision of conscience made by the individual. But if there also happens to be a physical barrier, then the ongoing, excessive loss gets programed in, so that in the USA everywhere and endlessly something is getting overboiled, left running, seeping away. It's the entropy of turning the tap to the left, but at the same time the end of a move to the left.

And what about all the left-handed people in the USA, Britt wanted to know.

—Exactly, he said, it's an evolutionary adaptation. Percentage-wise the USA produces more left-handed people than anywhere else in the western world, socialist countries don't come up with comparable figures. But by the time the majority in the USA are left-handed the American Empire will have gone under. Only it doesn't matter, and that's what's good about it.

Shortly before midnight Britt and I went out onto the living room balcony to drink a toast. The first rockets were climbing into the sky, gold rain coming out of the house next door, bells ringing, ships' sirens sounding from the harbor: Happy New Year! At that very moment behind us there was a terrible bang, a detonation, a scream. The thought that Kubin had blown himself up in our kitchen went through my head. Then I heard him shouting in the living room and we saw flames behind the living room window, and him behind them in silhouette. We rushed into the living room where Kubin was reaching into the flames, tearing down the burning curtains and screaming horribly.

I ran into the kitchen to get a bucket of water. Britt, with more presence of mind, got the doormat from outside the living room and with it beat what was left of the burning curtains and the genuine Tibetan carpet that was already smoldering. With hideous screams of pain Kubin had pulled down the burning curtains. When I came in with the bucket of water the fire was out.

But at what a price! Kubin was groaning and whimpering. His hands were burned. I phoned for a doctor. But all the doctors were out on emergency calls, treating all those people who had lit their cannon crackers in their hands, their pockets, and even between their teeth. Kubin moaned that he'd wanted to fire off a rocket in our living room that was meant to fly outside and drive out all the evil spirits in our apartment, the way it was done in the villages of the Basilicata. But the rocket hadn't gone out of the open balcony door into the night, but made a slight curve and gone into the curtains, got caught, exploded, and instantly set the material on fire.

We stood on the balcony and from above saw Kubin finally get into the ambulance.

The next evening he came to us in the kitchen like a boxer in white gloves, no, like a snowman he sat there, a glass of red wine in his white gauze fists.

And that's how he sat there the next evening when the stock exchange had opened again in the New Year and I came home that night. Kubin's two fat gauze fists were on the table. He could hold the glass of red wine with both fists and raise it to his mouth. —Well, he said, the Dow Jones has gone down, often does at this time, it's the shareholders that have to sell shares because of little Jesus.

Britt lit a cigarette. She hadn't smoked for a year. I was just going to say, you've weakened, when she took the cigarette out of her mouth and held it out to Kubin who put his head forward to her hand, she put the cigarette between his lips, he inhaled greedily, then again, repulsively greedy I thought, then Britt took the cigarette from his mouth and put it on the ashtray. It wouldn't have surprised me if she'd gone on smoking the cigarette herself, but she put it on the ashtray. Without looking at me, without any explanation, without saying a word she went on reading the paper.

Kubin stared at the cigarette from which smoke curled up. Britt leafed through the paper, took the cigarette and held it out to Kubin without looking, let him snatch at it with his mouth like a child wanting a pacifier, let him have two or three greedy puffs, put it back down on the ashtray and turned the pages of the paper.

I had to get up, had to leave the room simply because the sight embarrassed me, it was as if I was an unwilling witness to an intimacy not meant for me.

—If you want to butter up the shareholders, invest in the dollar now, it'll go down soon, said Kubin. The Americans are going to announce another budget and trade deficit. Act on the assumption that it's going up. It's going to fall. Then you can say: Bad luck. Ha ha.

Although we never spoke about it, it seemed clear that Kubin knew that we fleeced people. Later Kubin disappeared with heavy tread into his echoing six-room apartment.

—Now look, I said to Britt.

Britt only gave me a quick look and laughed: —No, of course not.

When we were in bed I asked Britt whether we shouldn't now at last move into the house, which was standing empty. —Oh, said Britt, we can't do that to Kubin now. First his wife runs away, then he burns his hands. He can't even do anything for himself.

—Good, I said, we'll wait.

The next day I came home earlier.

Kubin was sitting in the kitchen, he'd brought his Big Mac with him again, it lay unwrapped like a work of art in the open box made of synthetic material. Lolo was eating black bread and butter with celery salt, which is apparently supposed to be very good for the complexion. To her distress she had three pimples on her forehead, she kept touching them, kept looking in the mirrors, of which we had several hanging and standing in the apartment.

Lolo poured herself tea, pouring a great jet over the table cloth.

—Good heavens, pay attention to what you're doing, I said.

At that she leaped up and ran crying out of the kitchen.

—Leave her, said Britt.

—Well, how much did you get out of them? Kubin asked and stretched his head, or rather his chin, in the direction of the hamburger. Britt took the hamburger and held it out to Kubin. Kubin took a bite, took another, chomped in silence, with his two white snowman's fists took the glass of red wine, swallowed, and again Britt held the hamburger out to him.

The sight revolted me. There was something obscene about this lack of any distance between them as Britt fed Kubin and Kubin let himself be fed by Britt. It was as if I'd skipped a whole phase of the relationship, as if something was being kept from me, wet kisses, passionate moans, deep looks, the urge to grab each other, undo the blouse, pull off the shirt, not just take off clothes, but tear them off. What I was seeing was the kind of trust that exists after years of marriage between couples who squeeze each other's pimples.

How did Kubin wash himself? That's right, I thought, he can't even wash himself with those gauze

hands, he can't, it occurred to me, even do up or undo
the zipper on his trousers, button or unbutton his shirt.

—Listen, I said to Britt that evening, how does he
actually get dressed, how does he undress?

—To begin with I undid his shirt and trousers. Well,
he couldn't do it himself. Now he's got a private nurse.

I tried to calm myself by imagining Britt had dressed
and undressed Kubin in the routine professional manner of a nurse. But a picture kept intervening of the way
the two of them had sat in the kitchen and how Britt
had drunk tea, read the paper, and from time to time,
almost without looking, held the hamburger out to
Kubin. What repelled me was that Kubin waited greedily, taking everything for granted. If he'd said, come on,
let me take a bite, then it would all have been only half
as bad, but that speechless, expectant, demanding vacant look, then the way he snatched, chewed, that, I tell
myself today, was outrageous. Today, writing about it,
I think my outrage was probably jealousy, jealousy I
wouldn't admit to myself at the time of the way Britt
was feeding the man, looking after him.

After two weeks Kubin was able to use his hands
again. Britt never mentioned the estate on the Süllberg,
it was as if the house didn't exist. She simply wanted to
push it out of her thoughts. Finally I asked her if she
didn't want to move to the house because she'd miss
Kubin's company.

—Nonsense, she said. You surely don't think . . .

No, what she'd miss would be the subway trains
going past on the iron viaduct outside the window,
because of which she hadn't initially wanted to move
into the apartment. Now she said, —You know, if I
look out of the window I want to see life outside and

not stare at greenery. Green calms you down. No, after a while green makes you melancholy.

—But from the house you look at the Elbe and not just at subway trains passing. All you can see in the cars is whether people are wearing summer clothes or winter coats.

—But that's just what's so nice, it's like a thought rushing past, a sketch, then you have to fill in the rest, have to imagine it. I often see a woman with a red hat, she's on the train in the afternoons at about five. If I come home early, I wait for her to go by. And I think she's also waiting for me, keeping a lookout. Because she always sits on this side, sees our building, our apartment. And sometimes I see a girl, she always sits in the last car and looks out at the back, at the rails. Where's she from? It's already evening. And where's she going?

—From the Süllberg you can see the ships coming and going, barges, tugs, yachts, tankers. At night you see the navigation lights gliding past.

—Yes. But you know, she said, I'm not mad about ships or water.

And Lolo?

Lolo absolutely didn't want to leave the apartment and move into such a swanky house. For Lolo everything imaginable had suddenly become swanky and, as she said, too flashy, everything I did was a size too large for her, stock market, banker, broker, the dark blue suits, pale blue shirts, the color-coordinated ties, just garish, the white antelope-skin chairs, ghastly garish, the cream-colored Jaguar embarrassing, the silver shaving brush garish, and now this house in Blankenese, with all those people running around that took the

335

commuter into town, the men in their Burberrys, the women in their respectable twin sets and pearls, just bilious.

And when a week later I again brought the conversation round to the house, Britt said, —Here I can quickly go out shopping, the cinemas, the subway are near. I can cycle to work. And then her friends lived just round the corner.

And then another week later, without my even mentioning the house, she again said: —No, I'd miss not having a market right outside the house.

—You've got that in Blankenese.

—No, not this market, under a viaduct. You were right then, when you said it was a wonderful construction. When I go shopping I always hear the noise of the tracks overhead. And I think how right you were.

—All right, I said, then we'll wait.

One day in February about five weeks after the curtains had burned I came home in the evening, there was a smell of roasting, of garlic and thyme in the stairwell. In the kitchen stood Kubin, his hands no longer bandaged white, only with Band-Aids. —A light evening meal for the radical broker, he said, for the fighter on the front of fortunes. He'd made a special trip to the abbatoir that morning before going to the office and here's what he'd bought, he pointed to the pan, in it lay coils, tubes. You know what that is? Nooo. They're the intestines of suckling calves, and there'll still be some mother's milk in those intestines. Believe me, a feast for the gods. Actually they should be grilled the way they're done on Testaccio, over a pine-cone fire. We'll do that sometime. I've got a little grill on the balcony. In two weeks I'm flying to Rome, I'll bring back pine cones. Sit down, I brought a Gerghetto, try it.

Kubin never asked what instructions we'd given, only always how much we'd made that day. How much our investors by phone had hauled in. —26,000. Not a good day, he said, even more important you should get something into your stomach.

From that day on Kubin cooked in our kitchen. He came from the office at about seven and cooked the first dish, for Lolo and Britt, and then at about eleven he began supper, as he called it. When I came home at around midnight the table was laid, two plates, two water glasses, and a simple but unbeatable delicacy was put on the table: blood sausage, from a butcher on the Sternschanze, baked herring that he'd marinated according to some Hallig recipe, with it beer from Melldorf. And while Britt who had to be at the advertising agency in the morning for brainstorming was already tired because she couldn't get her essential nine hours sleep, while she sat and drank one last glass of wine with us and then sank into bed, Kubin sat there hearing about the people we'd fleeced. I was still wide awake, I'd drunk a strong coffee at 10 to keep my wits about me.

Occasionally I drove from the office to the house on the Süllberg. In the same way that I once ran through this barren suburb to leave behind all the chatter, now I sat in the house, in a silence where all that could be heard was now and then the creaking of wood. No talk, no voices, no one to disturb me. I looked out of the window at the night's storm, the flickering of lights, navigational lights over in Cranz, from the distance the beat of a freighter's propeller, regular and powerful, I imagined I could feel the vibration in the house. A green light glided quietly by. I gazed into the wonderfully alive silent night. My uncle, who's probably looked at the house (my mother is sure to have told him about it), will have been amazed, because the house was where we'd once picked out our dream houses.

He'll think this house was a further incentive for my criminal energy, but he's wrong. When I bought the house our foreign account was already flooded with money. It was just two months earlier that it all began with the sum we'd inadvertently not invested, it was a coincidence, just as it was that at this time the figure of the bird man was put on sale, unique and irreplaceable.

I've had the fragment lying here next to the laptop, how light it is, how fragile the figure was, with its three carved strokes that once stood for the eating singer.

The surf boat

To be honest, I wasn't indifferent to all the people who testified in court and spoke of their distress. Above all not to the old man I'd already seen sitting outside on the first day of the trial when a late arrival opened the courtroom door. I waited for his appearance in the witness box not just feeling disturbed and uneasy, but with a degree of fear.

Behrens was called on the last day of the trial. Name: Behrens, boat builder, formerly self-employed, age 63. He said one day an investment counselor had phoned him, had explained the opportunities for earning money, had given him examples of how you could quickly make a profit. That all sounded quite plausible, he said, oil prices were rising at the time, Mr. Saldin was saying, you see, that if a month ago you'd bought for 100,000 marks you'd now have 16,000 marks more in your account, he'd shown me the newspapers, the old and the new rates. You like to think you're not stupid, and Mr. Saldin looked as if you could trust him with your wallet. Not that he tried to persuade me, on the contrary, he said, think it over quietly, study the rates. That's what I did. And the rates did in fact continue to rise, and if at that time he'd bought oil for 100,000 marks I'd have made 30,000. Then you think to yourself, why work so hard, why have all these worries, because there's nothing much to be got from boat building anymore, only surf boats. And when Mr. Saldin phoned again I said, all right, and I gave him 30,000. And within four days there was in fact a profit of 5,000. I thought, how nice, coffee's gotten a little more expensive. So I took my savings, and a loan from the bank, 70,000 altogether. And they put that into coffee, and within three weeks half of it had gone. Mr. Saldin said you have to reckon with that, all you can do is put in some more to bring up the profits sharply. So I took out another loan on my business, then half of that went, and then strictly speaking I was bankrupt. It wasn't until then that I got suspicious, I wanted to talk to the manager. He came and explained the loss. Then I made an additional payment of the last loan that I'd got from the bank. Afterwards Mr. Walter paid me a visit.

Behrens told this quietly, looked over at me, not angry, not in a rage, more as if he pitied me.

—I'm ruined, he said, forty years' work, all gone. And it was my mistake. I was credulous and stupid.

▼

The road led through a hilly landscape of terminal moraine, the fields of rape flowed by in wide yellow waves, between them like foam the blossoming whitethorn in the hedgerows, and suddenly gleaming blue—the Schlei. The boatyard was in an old brick house, next to it, under thatch, similar to my empty house on the Süllberg, stood the boat-builder's house. Outside on the Schlei an excursion boat that now in the early afternoon was on its way back to Schleswig.

In the workshop four people, the boat builder, a workman, and two apprentices were working on a large wooden boat. It smelled of glue, varnish, and wood. The screech of the saw. A rib was being bent in steam in a long cylinder.

I thought, how extraordinary, here are people still working by hand, like in the old days or in a museum. I'd thought everybody earned money through money, apart from those who were in law or industrial technology. Others made commercials or like Britt wrote copy, or they were commentators on the money market like Kubin in the financial section, or criticized it like his wife on religious programs, and then there were people who examined these people, x-rayed them, made ECGs, prescribed pills.

I'd like to have been in the workshop just to watch, without Saldin, without the intention, the need to say anything about profit margins, the fall in prices and market trends, above all not to have to lie. Simply to be able to watch the wood shavings curl beneath a plane, the workman's hands pass testing over the planks, to be allowed to watch the way you watch others work when you're a child. A few weeks earlier I'd been in New York and had dealings there with a stockbroker (for the sake of appearances—after all, we had to give the right impression). After that I'd roamed the streets and on Broadway came across a man who was fitting a window pane. I stopped and so did others, people in suits and outfits, briefcases in hand. We all watched as the man slit a section of the pane with his diamond cutter, then separated the glass strip by striking it hard with the edge of his hand, then fitted it with two clamps into the opening in the shop window and fastened it with metal borders. All who'd watched with curiosity, myself included, then went on our way. We'd all been witnesses to a rare, strange activity.

—No, said the boat builder, it's not a lifeboat, it's a surf boat for the Ivory Coast. They don't have a lot of harbors, sandy beaches everywhere, so the natives have to paddle the boats through the breakers. The ships are anchored beyond the breakers. The boats take copra and cocoa to the ships and bring something or other back to the shore. They have to be built stable. There's quite a bit of force behind one of those breakers. They have to float, even if they fill up.

—And you want to give all this up, I asked.

Saldin gave me a threatening look, a signal to keep quiet.

—What can I do, mind you. Hardly anybody wants these surf boats anymore. They're building harbors everywhere with development aid. They cost millions and they're pointless. They can't load that much. Boats are getting cheaper. And there's no shortage of people. It's an art, you see, steering one of these boats through breakers. The Kruger blacks are the best. It's a shame, he said and ran his hand across a rib. I can hardly get oak anymore that's properly matured, at least five years old. It's all sawed into veneer.

We went over to his house, his wife made tea, and Saldin explained the losses to him, said the collapse in cocoa really was unique and couldn't have been foreseen. Mr. Walter can confirm that. I nodded, and when the man looked at me waiting for an explanation I didn't say, your money's gone into our account, Mr. Saldin got 20% commission, he's got an easy conscience, he can afford to have. This was the moment, as I fell silent and couldn't think of anything to say, the moment when I felt as I suppose my uncle imagines it, I thought about myself and I found myself repulsive, I thought of myself with revulsion. And if I'm to describe this revulsion, then what comes to mind are the plates that go under flowerpots on window sills, yes, I didn't think, you're a swine, I see the plates under the flowerpots, white plates with little gilt lion's claws at the sides, the gold worn away in the course of time. Britt wanted underplates like these, we were always looking in antique shops, but never found any. I thought they're sure to sell these plates, I thought for me they'd sell them, they'd do it for me. And suddenly this for-me struck me as repellent: I'm the one, I thought, who makes money out of the misfortune of these people. While Britt, if she were to find these underplates in an antique dealer's, would be able to buy them and be happy.

—Have you sold your business already? I asked.

—Yes, he said, it's already sold. On Mr. Saldin's advice.

—Stop speculating, I said. You've lost too much.

342

A look first of incredulous astonishment, then horror came to his face. —You think the money's lost?

—You just have to go on trying, Saldin interrupted.

—No, I said, it would be better if you didn't speculate anymore.

But in his fear of losing everything Behrens insisted on putting down another 10,000. An attempt to win everything back.

Later in the car on the way to Hamburg, Saldin said, —You can't afford to be sentimental in business.

—No, I said, and accelerated.

—It was important to go to him, said Saldin, and you were right to dissuade him, I think in his despair the man would have run to the police.

—But to fleece him, of all people?

Saldin looked at me. —You can say that about any of them. Then you'd have to lay down ground rules, whom can we approach and whom not, a charitable investment business, as it were. People are free to make their decisions, that's my opinion. All you do is try and encourage them.

Buy a heap

Saldin knew, but he wasn't an accessory because he didn't let on that he knew what happened to the money. Not even on that occasion when he could have replied: What you're saying's hypocritical: Don't take the money off this boat builder whose business would have folded anyway, but take it off some general practitioner who knocks himself out working day and night.

And he didn't give evidence against us in court, only said, of course he wasn't in a position to decide how and where the money would be invested, after all it wasn't his job to check bank statements. No, he said, in reply to a question from the public prosecutor, he was always properly paid. He did his work, he was paid for it, and that sufficed.

Saldin radiated unshakable uprightness. Light blonde hair grey at the temples, like Rob always suntanned, a tan that he got on short holidays in the Caribbean. He was our best man, had the highest turnover, was usually in first place on the board we'd put up in the office and always got a bonus for it. He was a brilliant salesman, better than Eichhorst, Dembrowski, and also—this isn't false modesty—better than me. We all sold by talking, he sold by listening. The way he sold, people believed they'd find their peace of mind through what he was offering. He radiated, I say it without envy, what every headhunter would give his soul to possess: self-contained contentment, cool credibility, a smiling and relaxed manner, and in an age where a show of discreet success itself radiates trustworthiness, in short he had exactly what American salesmen trainers call a totally positive aura. And Rob, who got him for us shortly before going into tennis management, had declared him a unique asset. Saldin drove a violet Saab-Turbo, the color going back to when he was with the Sanyassins. Already then active as an investment counselor and extraordinarily successful, probably no one suspected that anyone so geared to nirvana could be interested in making money. He talked about it, said it was important because it was

344

the only way he could free himself from the group to which he'd belonged for years at university, a revolutionary student group that aimed to bring Albanian conditions to Germany.

Saldin had broken off his English studies and begun studying Albanian. With two comrades he was given the task of translating the works of Hoxha. Saldin (I've changed the name, he's still in the investment business) sometimes talked about it when we celebrated a day of another hundred thousand, and the way he told it we fell off our chairs laughing. And what was funny about it was that as he told it it was hard to believe that someone as easygoing, as relaxed, as cheerful as Saldin could ever have belonged to a political cell of international compulsives (as he called it). It was as if he'd lived some other strange life somewhere among people who were only allowed to see black and white television, who had to hand over all their money excepting a small reserve, who had to use every tea bag twice, whose female members were not allowed to use make-up and had to wear bras. Why? Saldin laughed, revealing the laughter lines in his face. Well, the reasoning went like this—thesis: You can only reach the masses by appearing to them in a familiar, unfrivolous guise. Antithesis: But almost all young working women stopped wearing bras long ago and use a lot of make-up. Synthesis: Correct, but in Albania they wear bras and they don't wear make-up, this shows that German women lack class consciousness. And that's why they can't be reached.

Every Friday morning they sold a militant workers' paper outside a factory, that's to say they paid for the paper out of their own pockets because no worker wanted to buy it, and tried to distribute the paper. But the workers didn't even want it free.

But it was always: Buy a heap! Come in your masses! Fight in your masses!

But the masses were nowhere in sight. —You couldn't overlook that forever, Saldin said, and wasn't there something slushy, sticky, malleable like dough about the word masses? Then came doubt and within three weeks it drove me from the party, accelerated by the holy zeal with which the comrades persecuted me, as if that was the way to suppress their own doubts after I'd expressed the first, minor reservations. Had I always correctly accounted for the newspaper money? But we never sold a paper. That's a filthy lie! The papers were always accounted for, and now suddenly he has papers left over. Probably he took more and didn't account for them all. And now he even claims he paid for them out of his own pocket, as if suddenly the workers didn't want the papers. No! Or didn't he pay for all the copies for which he should have paid? So he could have sold more, he helped himself to some. No!!!!

One day his comrades took him into the hallway, beat him up, searched his room. What were they looking for? Proof that he was working for the Defense of the Constitution—or even better—the CIA.

The next day Saldin flew from Poona to the Bhagwan, there he found peace of mind. From now on he only did what he felt like doing, not more, not less.

—You have to let things happen, simply be ready. The important thing is, he said to me, you mustn't always constantly be wanting something.

346

—Díos míos, Saldin said, when the car careered on a bend and the tires screeched, the way you drive, it's a journey through hell.

—I was under the impression you had to be home by seven.

—Yes, said Saldin, but Sabine can wait.

Another new name. Sometimes I envied Saldin when I saw the women who sometimes came to pick him up from the office. But this feeling, this little jab because I wasn't going around with such beautiful women strangely enough never lasted long. And the others at the office—the staff were mostly men—moaned as if they were dreaming when they saw the women.

—Where did he get to know these women, Eichhorst asked.

—Where do these fantastic women hang out? Where do you meet them? And the big question, how do you get anywhere with them?

Saldin never spoke about his women. You'd see them sometimes and occasionally when you phoned him a woman's voice answered. He lived in an apartment in an old building in the Jungfrauental, and he would have been the perfect investment counselor if he didn't sometimes just disappear for two or three days, simply stayed at home, cut off and shut in, missed all his appointments, and then no one knew what he was doing.

A popcorn rubdown

Walked the streets in the evening and peered into all the parked cars as if the redhead, if he was still in the city, was sure to be sitting in a car.

In front of me a man slid across the street, his shirt torn, his legs tiny and thin, bent upwards, with flipper feet like some mythological creature. The man supported himself on his knuckles, only lightly touched the ground with his buttocks, then reaching far out with his powerful arms swung himself forwards.

He kept shouting. I'd decided not to give him anything because I never give beggars anything. On principle. If no one were to give them anything they'd do something to regain their self-esteem, collect bottles or rob banks. But the man shouted and people began to take notice of him. I quickened my step but he stayed at my heels with his shuffling and his shrill yells. To get away from him I would have had to run, perhaps even then he would have been able to keep up with me and people would have thought I'd hit the man or even robbed him. Finally I threw him the greasiest and limpest note in my pocket. He sat down instantly.

In the niches of the house walls shadowy figures, women, men, and children who were camping there for the night. For a while I wandered the streets aimlessly until, tired and sweaty, I came to the harbor. Women were sitting there, candles burning, shells laid out in a circle. I watched a woman behead a cock, hold the still-struggling bird, massage the body to milk the blood from it into a bowl in which flower petals were floating. Suddenly she pointed at me, said something to me, a dark black face. Under her turban grey frizzy hair. One of the women standing by her translated what the Great Mother wanted from me, an offering, money naturally. I gave her two large notes (after all, she wasn't begging). Then she put her hand on my forehead, a surprisingly cool hand. Then she began to dance, a man beat a small drum, the women around her clapped to the beat. The woman danced with eyes shut, suddenly stopped in front of me and without opening her eyes laid her hand on my forehead again. And it was good, this dry hand. I would have liked to feel it on my forehead for a long time. I smelled the cock and the blood. Then she said something, all I understood was popcorn. The woman who spoke English translated, there was a spirit in me, it was driving me, and that was the reason I was so agitated. To calm down and get rid of the spirit I had to rub myself down with popcorn.

I wanted to give her another note. But she refused. Slowly I walked along the harbor street, then hailed a taxi because I was tired from walking, and drove back to the block of apartments whose lights shone far into the night.

▼

The last weeks at Sekuritas until the two men in leather jackets came were like a bad dream from which I only ever woke for three, at most four hours, when in order to wake from this nightmare I stuffed myself full of valium and dozed off. I woke. The telephone was buzzing far away somewhere, yesterday I'd turned it down low. I lay there bathed in sweat, next to me Britt who still had a good three hours of her nine of sleep ahead of her. Next to the bed stood the computer that showed the quotations from Tokyo. The price of cotton had risen contrary to all reasonable expectations while the price of silver had fallen. At least this way loss and profit were avoided. I'd made the mistake of seriously speculating, unlike Dembrowski who'd retreated on a creative holiday to Spain, I'd begun seriously delivering money to people. Not out of exaggerated honesty, also not because, overwhelmed by my conscience, I wanted to be a benefactor to the investors, but purely and simply out of fear that the whole swindle would be exposed. The phone had stopped ringing. Meanwhile the alarmed investors were also phoning us at home, although I had an unlisted number. But somehow— perhaps by threats, but possibly someone had taken a bribe—they'd been able to get my number from our telephone operators. In the early morning at six they wanted to know, immediately, now, what had happened to their hundred thousands. In the next room the telex—I'd had it installed a few weeks previously—had printed all the rates. Every morning I resolved to simply switch off the machine once and for all. I tore off the strips of paper curling on the floor, a heap, a crazy tangle of figures that I threw into the wastepaper basket. I took two captagons to be in shape for the next nightmare and turned on the espresso machine in the kitchen. And saw my round distorted face in the chrome of the machine. I missed Kubin.

Kubin had moved out a few months ago. He couldn't bear the emptiness of the six rooms any longer. For a time he seriously considered taking in a family seeking asylum from Sri Lanka, just to show his wife who was still living with her Sanskrit boy what real solidarity with the Third World was, but he'd given up the idea because, he said, he'd never relished Indian cooking, and then that smell of curry in the apartment. I missed him, even though lately he'd only rarely come over. But when he then sat in our kitchen at night he was the one who took away my doubts, not by encouraging me to continue taking the money off people—we never spoke that directly about it, but because he sang the praises of entropy, of chaos.

Sometimes we met for a glass of beer. On the last occasion, in the Meisenfrei, he said: —You look totally overworked and shattered by worry. You're losing your way, you're going back to old moral standards we've left behind. That's a shame, I've always been for the new man. And praised you everywhere. What had he meant? I went onto the living-room balcony and looked at the viaduct. It was still dark and cool. I made myself some tea, put on my bathrobe over my dressing gown and sat on the balcony. Now and then a car drove by. Then the first train came. It was lit, there were only four people inside.

I sat there, smoked, drank the espresso, and watched it grow light above the roofs. A whistle, and then another whistle, thin, clumsy like a child's, but then the whistle grew longer and modulated into a melody that fell and rose. The song came from the crests of the lime trees on the street, somewhere thrushes were nesting, blackbirds, chaffinches, a competition began, invaded the air, filled it with song, a warbling, merciless, lovely battle for possession of the air.

The end was foreseeable. At some stage one of the investors would go to the police, one who'd given up any hope of getting his money back. Because presumably this until now had kept back some other investor from bringing in the police: if he did there would then be no chance at all of him getting back even a mark. He could put us in jail, in other words take his revenge, but not get compensation.

So my mistake was that during this period I tried to calm some of the claimants with money, tried to get hold of money, and here abandoned our method of letting plain, pure coincidence prevail, of simply blindly going in and out of exchange rates. (With every deal we got 250 dollars commission, no matter whether the investor made or lost money.) I tried to make money through purposeful transactions.

I began phoning brokers in New York, Chicago, London, and Tokyo (verifiable, because the phone bills in those last three months were enormous and consequently deductible, the tax office can confirm this), meticulously studied the movement on the markets, phoned Kubin and let him give me tips, put the computer by my bed, installed a second telex in the apartment, phoned investors, brokers, moved a few million around instead of leaving them safely in our account. It soon became clear that the tips and arrangements with other brokers were only bringing greater losses, yes, the scale of losses piled up to such an extent that for a time I even put in some of our own hard-earned money. Our spoon was too small to reach into the big pot with the other brokers like Price & McDuff. If I put in an order for three million of cotton on short because the rate was going down, then in New York the people at Price & McDuff put in two million so that cotton suddenly rose, when I'd just heard from them that it had to fall. The boys in New York will have laughed. The more honest I became, the more easily they screwed us. Until now we'd simply drawn most of the money from the circulating capital, diverting it to a numbered account, now the millions wandered off. And the sharks in New York were devouring us. They did business through arrangements and insider deals that were forbidden. These were the big guns like that Boesky whom they got by pure chance because of forbidden deals and who then had to do two years inside.

We were free-riders. We were the small fry. (I'm not saying crooks!) We tried to go along for the ride like those subway surfers who cling to the doors of trains as they leave and ride to the next station. They're not the honorable running-board surfers of former times (when there still were running boards) who wanted to save on fares, but esthetes who strike a bold pose as they hang from open windows and smile at the passengers, with the ever present danger of suddenly being shaved away from behind by a signal post. But when you're doing this you have to smile, you can't look glum like I did then. That was what Kubin had meant.

▼

The day before my arrest we'd met Fishy Fritz. For a year I'd looked after him, had explained the losses to him that were sometimes lessened by small gains, explained and always been able to get him to put in more, and then still more money. Then after a year Saldin took over. That way I shortened a few long Sunday afternoons for Fishy Fritz and his wife. All Saldin could do was listen. Fishy Fritz's wife had had an operation, they'd taken out a tumor. Sometimes we'd have to take

353

turns, Saldin and I, to explain losses that had gone into the hundred thousands, to explain and make putting in more money palatable. The judge who asked Fishy Fritz how it was possible that he, a successful entrepreneur, had repeatedly allowed someone to elicit money from him, got the answer that he couldn't really understand it himself. Naturally he'd taken a look at the office, modern, furnished in the very best taste, in the best location. An open-plan office accommodating about thirty people talking on the phone. Everything of the very best: a gleaming company brass plate, a pale grey fitted carpet, computers, chairs in pigskin, art photographs, abstract prints, friendly discreet secretaries, and then we too, and here his knowledge of people had failed him, had always seemed thoroughly trustworthy. A businesslike answer that accorded with what he'd previously read in the financial sections to each of his questions. It wasn't that I told him lies, rather that in what I said there was a minute, but significant, displacement of the truth. After all, he met with us two days before the firm collapsed, two days before my arrest, and as he'd have to admit wanted to put in more money.

—I'd have paid again, he said, I was totally trusting, although normally I'm a suspicious person. I allowed myself to be deceived, I was naive, one could say stupid, but I'm not so stupid, so naive as to leave the two gentlemen the money that they have somewhere in some numbered account. Even if I have to employ a detective agency to the end of my life to get the money out of these gentlemen.

—At the time, that's to say two days before the police stepped in, I insisted on seeing the managing director, Mr. Walter, who had looked after me at the beginning. Again they explained the losses to me as due to incomprehensible movements on the stock exchange, that it was really a game of roulette. They had the computer print-outs at hand. My mistake was that I didn't ask more searching questions, I merely nodded occasionally so as not to reveal that I hadn't understood certain figures, certain stock market developments. And the trust? Yes, obtained by devious means, by asking after my wife's health, all concern, all friendliness. When my wife was operated on Mr. Walter sent her a huge bouquet of flowers every other day.

We'd met for lunch with Fishy Fritz in the oyster bar. Saldin had booked a table a little apart from the others, our problem table, as we called it. Fishy Fritzy told about his flight. With his little Cesna that he flew himself he'd got into the tailwind of a DC-10. —A mistake from the flight tower, he said, I got shaken up, I was shit scared. He hadn't changed much. His hair had got more grey at the temples. He was carefully shaved, and in his ear there was a little diamond, that was new. I couldn't stop myself looking at the diamond. Until he put his fingers to it. —Yes, was all he said and laughed a little embarrassed, that's my girl friend.

So he's got a girl friend, I thought, that was news to me. Champagne was brought. We toasted. To the breakthrough, I said, that's got to be on the way.

—I hope so, said Fishy Fritz. And you could see him give his face a serious, even an angry, thoughtful expression, he wanted to threaten, he wanted to say, this can't go one, then Saldin asked: —How is your wife?

—Better, he said and began to refold the cloth napkin, pinching it. She's made a recovery. I'm still not allowed to be present when she undresses. But she's no longer at that stage of sitting around in silence. She used to pore over the real-estate pages, took an interest in property, and she had a good nose for it. After the operation she suddenly dropped everything. Now, for about the past three weeks, she sometimes drives to Kiel, goes to the cinema in the afternoon. And she's suddenly started reading again. Strange, she's reading, he paused, champagne glass in hand, she's reading biographies of architects. She never used to be interested in that before.

He squeezed lemon on the oysters that lay there so open, so vulnerable, carefully raised them to his mouth and with a slurp drew them in. —She sends you her regards, he said to me, she likes to remember that first day when you came to us, that story about your uncle and the house that disappeared. She wanted to come with me, but she doesn't feel like flying yet, and I've still got to go on to Amsterdam, a meeting of the fishing industry. She didn't want to come for that, and she didn't want to take a train from here to Kiel.

—Have you told her about Christa yet, Saldin asked.

—No, he said, not yet. Somehow you miss the moment to tell the truth. And then it keeps getting harder, and then suddenly, after the operation, you find you can't do it. I've thought about it over and over, how should I say it: I know a woman. I've met somebody who means a great deal to me. Both are equally impossible.

He squeezed lemon on the next oyster, pried it loose with the fork, and stared at it for a moment as if, before devouring it, he were having a quiet dialogue with it.

—Yes, he said, yes, that's how it is, and it oppresses me.

Saldin listened. A measured, non-intrusive listening that didn't feign exaggerated interest or insist on eye contact so he could nod or shake his head according to requirement. Saldin knew how to sit and be silent, and in his face there was sympathetic curiosity, no, compassionate calm, yes calm, of course the eyes were also a part of this, pale blue, a color as we know from sales psychologists that establishes trust, that hides nothing. Saldin knew how to keep silent even when there were pauses. Strangely, in Saldin's presence silence was never paralyzing. I envied him this ability to simply keep silent. Unlike me, born to talk, but condemned to it as well. That's why people crowded to our apartment, mostly clients, more and more of them came in the evenings or on holidays, they'd invested 30,000, and planted their backsides on our white antelope-skin chairs because they were bored with their wives, their husbands, their girl friends, bored to death. They wanted to be entertained. I worked hard at it. And I let myself be well paid for it.

I thought of the appointments waiting for me in the afternoons. Investors demanding their money back, making angry accusations, there were even men who cried. I thought of what we could expect if we were busted: delight, hatred, crooked smiles. I thought of how frightened I'd been when as a child I was locked in a room, a terrible punishment. I swallowed an oyster, alive, tasted the salt water, the Pleiades on my tongue, in my throat, still alive, swallowed, screaming but mute, thought, hideous mute screams, no one hears them, no one sitting here looks round, men, women

357

talking about shipping lines, about the new Penderecki production, about raised dividends, about preference shares, about a lyric poet having an affair with a politician, they don't hear the screams, they're deaf like Saldin with his so very attentive face like a pointer's, I thought, but his eyes are blue like Fishy Fritz's, like a stuffed animal, I thought, with his little diamond in his ear, that was new, he'd had that clipped into his ear for Christa because she found him so dreadfully serious, he said and looked at me. Suddenly the silky soft protein mass dissolves, gets burned up. —I, I heard myself suddenly say, have got a scream stuck in my throat.

—What, said the rag-doll man, you don't look well.

—Yes, you look ill, said the pointer, you're overworked, totally overworked. You simply have to relax more, that's important. —I, said the soft-toy man, sometimes fly to Christa in Lübeck at the weekend, do nothing, laze around, as the young say. I had to relearn that, on Sundays we lie in bed until twelve, until one. Christa gets up, makes coffee, then back into bed. She's studying, she's training to be a radio technician, she'd like to go to sea. At some stage in the afternoon we get up, go for a walk, buy a cake, go home, and get back into bed. I hadn't done that for thirty years, the last time was with my wife when we first met, then we were both still studying.

Burned up, the pure protein finds its way into the bloodstream, gets into the gonads—life itself consuming life, I swallowed the juice, the taste on my tongue: seashells and algae. —We just have to throw in some more, said the pointer, if we put another 200,000 on corn, and this time concentrate on corn, it has to go down, I've had word from Chicago, if we put it on short we can make good the losses.

—Good, said the soft toy man, then I'll just have to shell out some more. Are you feeling ill?

—Yes, I said, I have to get some fresh air. Excuse me.

The Swede

I left the oyster bar. I took a few steps in the direction of our office and thought, I'll drink two strong coffees and then meet the next mastiff. But then I felt the sun warm on my face, and I went in the direction of the harbor. Should I phone Gerda, ask her to give my apologies to the clients? She could say to them I'd been taken ill. But I just went on walking. I didn't care what she said. I didn't give a shit.

I went up the Steinweg, there at number 52 my great-grandmother had lived. In the meantime the house had been torn down and replaced by a half-modern building. My great-grandmother had raised six children on her own, her husband, a blacksmith, had moved to Glückstadt with a younger woman. I see her in my memory, I must have been six at the time: big, muscular, with a backside like a barrel, across her stomach the imprint of narrow long rods. A corset, as grandmother Hilde explained. My great-grandmother is supposed to have once taken away the truncheon from a Latvian SS man who was laying into a man from a concentration camp who was digging in the ruins. She only got away with it because she still had the steel helmet, black with soot, on her head, her brownish-grey hair burned, her eyebrows singed, even her lashes only little yellow lumps. She was a fire warden and had saved a woman and two children from a burning house.

At the corner a new cafe had just opened. It had been a bar before: The Jolly Seadog. I went in and ordered a double espresso. Round marble tables, black lacquered chairs, a chrome bar, a transparent floor of some synthetic material in which car tires lay as if frozen, used ones but also new. On this artificial ice sat all the young people from the surrounding offices, they sat there, lacquered, coiffed, they said nothing, smoked and saw themselves in duplicate, triplicate, endlessly in the wall mirrors.

Only one man there was my age. He sat opposite a young woman with a blonde pageboy. He was talking to the girl, talking and gesticulating, like me, I thought, or like my uncle, he was moving around as he sat like someone in a fight, a boxer, his footwork fast but not frantic, his shoes treading the plastic ice, the upper part of his body swinging this way and that, his hands making little excursions into the past, into the story of himself, into the destinies of others, forcing them up with a hook from below, driving them forward with a straight right or a left, flooring them with a mighty swing. This man was fighting, he was working off something, unlike the others who just sat there and only said: Look, I'm sitting here, look, the way I'm sitting here, bold upright, but as if I'd been cooled by the floor with its frozen tires. Meanwhile this man was fighting his way, panting inside as he reached into the future so that he could finally, finally, get to the young woman sitting opposite him. She, some twenty years younger, in a neat miniskirt, crossed one shining black silky narrow thigh and delicate kneecap over the other shining black silky narrow thigh and said nothing, listened, waited, assessing but not disapproving (the fight hadn't yet been won or lost), an elegant economy in every movement, the way she smoked, the way she removed the ash, the way she drank from the slightly misted wine glass. The man looked old and wrung out, a hard worker, and by coincidence I saw myself in one of the mirrors in half-profile, didn't look into my eyes, their glance always invites one to come to terms with oneself, I saw myself without eye contact, my face grey, tired, so tired, and I was freezing cold although on that afternoon it was unusually hot.

I paid and left.

I went through the Brüderstrasse to the Grosse Trampgang, climbed the stairs. They were new, no longer the two trodden-down semicircles, the stairwell light accompanied by the hurried ticking of the meter. Bright colors, clean plastered walls painted white, the door on the first floor, a smooth blue-grey standard door, was new. After hesitating a moment I rang, listened, but heard no footsteps inside. A threshold sealed the door. In the old days you could always see a strip of light under the door and that meant she was there, even on sunny days there was a light in the corridor of the apartment, it was that dark. I only had to knock and the door opened.

Remarkably, Grandmother Hilde was always in the apartment. She only went down to shop and even then she left the light on. I can only remember one time when there was no strip of light under the door. I'd come from the hospital. A nurse had given me her handbag, in it two pairs of glasses, an old well-worn leather purse, a handkerchief, a bottle of eau de cologne and a small leather case for photographs, four photos. On one of the photos my little uncle and I are standing holding two sticks of candy, sucked small.

—The dress, the nurse said and looked at me, and the coat? —No, I said.

I stood outside the door looking for the key in her handbag, the meter still ran for a moment, then the stairwell light went out. I stood in the dark.

▼

Grandmother had given us five marks and we'd gone to the Hamburg Cathedral. My little uncle was set on going to a freak show. The king of Albania was on show there. During the afternoon performance the tent was almost empty. We sat there and sucked our striped spiral candy.

A man and a woman came onto the stage, both hairy, monkeyish, the man with a dark, blackish coat of hair, the woman light brown, their faces hairy too, though less than their bodies. Both wore a loincloth, the woman a narrow red cloth over her breasts. They held hands.

A woman in a tailcoat said they both came from a remote valley in the Himalayas. They'd stolen the tea supply of an Italian expedition in the night and been caught eating the tea leaves from their cupped hands. —Two snow people, ladies and gentlemen, also known as midget yetis, they live naked in the snow. Then their fur is thicker than it is now. What you're seeing now is their summer coat. Here in Europe they only have a summer coat, even in winter. The climate's too warm for them. If they find a freezer they put their arms in and rub their hands, the way we rub our hands in winter over a stove. They only really come out of themselves in winter on really frosty days, then they feel really well.

She gave first the man, then the woman a push with a little stick. Both opened their mouths and let out croaks. —Did you hear! That's yeti language, said the woman.

People laughed, shouted: Cheers, and held a bottle of brandy out to the yetis. The two midget yetis clung to each other and the croaks turned into shrill screeches. Clinging to each other they went off behind the curtain.

The woman announced the two unique non-identical lilliputian twins from Canton. The Chinese lilliputian twins cycled in on two small bikes, rode side by side with outstretched arms around each other's shoulders, did graceful pirouettes and lifted the front wheels high, cycled about on the rear wheels, swayed and sang: There once was a king in Thule.

And then the king appeared. An old man in a velvet uniform, with silver and gold braid sewn onto it. He stepped to the edge of the podium of wooden boards.

—I am the rightful king of Albania. I am a helmsman and when I was on shore leave in Albania in 1923 I was declared king. After three days I was deposed by the opposition party of King Zog, who incidentally was just a failed student. The communists drove me out of the country. But I shall return. It is my pleasure to invite you all. Keep your entrance tickets, they will entitle you to greet the beggar you see before you when he is king in the palace of Tirana.

A few people, already quite drunk, leaped up and shouted; —We're coming, we're coming. They raised their Steinhäger bottles and shouted: Cheers.

The king of Albania left the stage.

—Mind you keep your ticket, said my uncle.

I still have the ticket. It's in the photo album, a little blue piece of paper with a red horizontal line printed on it and the number 34 56 21, that I know by heart.

▼

One day my father was supposed to be arriving, my real father, the one who'd accidentally scored the bull's-eye. A Swede, that much I knew, helmsman on a tramp steamer that for years had sailed the Pacific.

The Pacific, an endless stretch of water, not a sound, no wind, no beat of a wave.

And now he was coming, he'd take his revenge against the other fathers who'd locked me out or in, who'd threatened to hit me or did hit me, he'd take his revenge against the teachers who hit and the bigger boys.

It was a Friday evening and everyone had gathered in the kitchen, only my mother had gone to the harbor to collect him. Grandmother was kneading dough for a cake, Step-grandfather Heinz and I were cutting open plums and taking out the stones. —Don't eat so many or you'll get diarrhea!

My little uncle had also come despite being forbidden by his father, the little louse sat in the corner and everyone forgot about him. Grandmother flattened the dough with a rolling pin, laid it on the baking tin, rolled up the edges to make the crust crisp, told the story she always told when she was rolling out dough of the time (the only time) she was in Italy on Lake Garda, on her honeymoon with the post-office official. —We went into a little restaurant, sat down, rested our arms on the table, we wanted something to eat, to drink, it was very hot, the signora came running, crying out and waving her arms in the air, what's the matter with her, we thought. Then she lifts up the tablecloth. Only it wasn't a tablecloth, it was dough for noodles, so thin, rolled so smooth. Only now it had the marks of our arms and elbows on it. She pushed both baking tins into the gas oven. Then suddenly the glasses in the cupboard began to rattle.

—Yes, Mrs. Claussen's coming too when she's through with her customer. Perhaps her husband'll come as well, if he isn't digging up another bomb like the other day, one of those six-tonners, a real bunker cracker, that was. Had to wait until the bomb-disposal expert had defused it. Then had to load the thing onto the truck with the excavator. And again the glasses rattled. Having another go.

My uncle, the little know-it-all, got a nosebleed, as he usually did when the glasses rattled. Put a wet towel on the back of his neck. There he sat, his head resting on the back of the chair. I think he was fourteen then. There was a knock on the door and in came Mrs. Brücker, not bringing her very own skinless curry sausage but baked apples. —Put the plates out, will you! In the oilskin cloth on the table there were already two gaping cuts. (Don't cut on the tablecloth!) No, come on, today we'll use Grandma's tablecloth! Handknitted, thick knobbly red and blue peonies. Who brought that bottle of Danzig Goldwasser? Shake it, then the gold leaf'll float. And again the glasses rattled.

—God save us, said Mrs. Brücker, what are they saving up for now? Their living room furniture's decorated birch. No, they've already paid for that. They've got a garden plot on the Veddel, want to build a little house there.

There was a knock on the door, familiar sound, and everyone fell silent. Is that him already? My mother had phoned the shipping company. The ship was going to arrive earlier, it was coming up the Elbe with the tide, and again there was a knock at the door. In came Mrs. Eisenhart and Mr. Eisenhart. They had goose giblets in their cast-iron pot, done the Mecklenburg way. She'd bought the goose at the fish market, carried it home under her arm, put it in the small dark pantry, nailed its feet tight to a board and force fed it. Bread dough and gruel rolled nicely into balls like little bombs, right into the gullet and massaged down the long neck, right into the stomach. (Sometimes downstairs we heard the screams of the goose.)

And again there was a knock on the door.

—Is that them?

No, Mrs. Claussen. She was still glowing, red cheeks, well, she'd come straight from work, her dress tight and bursting open over her erect breasts. My little uncle's nose started to bleed again. Mrs. Brücker put a bottle on the table, kirsch, homemade, pure, nothing added, made her brew at the garden, plums and cherries. Step-grandfather Heinz rubbed the cork against the bottle, poured himself one. —Brrr, that went down well. What's keeping them?

Grandmother Hilde took off her sweater, under it

the black dress with the white lace collar, really solemn and festive. —Come on, put your jacket on. And Step-grandfather Heinz pulled up his shirt sleeves again, let the sleeve bands snap and put on the jacket, pinstripe, double-breasted. —You should wear it more often, said Hilde. —And you the dress, Sundays at least.

Step-grandfather Heinz had got out the squeeze box, was playing "Rolling Home," there was a discreet knock—my mother's tender knuckles.

There entered—and had to duck his head—a giant, behind him my mother, tiny. In my memory his face is a blank. I remember he put his hand through my hair, then he sat down on the chair that had been drawn up to the table for him.

—Good to see you again, said Grandmother Hilde, breaking the embarrassed silence, and went to the stove, took the roast from the oven, mother carried the roast to the living room as if it were her work, put it on the mat on the laid table in this room that was normally unheated and always cold. Now the cast-iron stove was rumbling. Step-grandfather Heinz took off his jacket, then Eisenhart, but not the Swede, he kept on his blue jacket that looked like the jacket of an old uniform, dark stripes on the sleeves where he'd taken off the golden insignia. And later Step-grandfather Heinz said: —Been really well ironed, that jacket, must have been a Chinese did it. Lot of Chinese on ships as stewards.

The best plates were heaped with slices of roast meat, with red cabbage, with potatoes (*Soltauer Grenaten*). Everyone talked on top of each other, the Schwarzbrand was a merciless 70 proof.

Only the Swede sat drinking in silence. He hadn't yet said a word. Was he mute? Were there mute helmsmen? Didn't they have to give orders, yell when there was a storm? Top the mainsail! Splice the mainbrace! Did he actually speak German? He sat there, ate and drank, not excessively, you couldn't have said he stuffed himself, he poured the drink in. When glasses were raised to drink a toast he drank a toast, friendly, nothing sinister about him, but he was silent.

The table was cleared and freshly laid, the sharply-peppered goose giblets came onto the table. And again the table was cleared and more brought in: baked apples, and again plates were carried out and then again glasses were raised in a toast. And emptied, and Mrs. Brücker sang with Step-grandfather Heinz, both had really beautiful voices, soprano and bass, and then again there was a toast and everybody laughed and drank. But then suddenly the Swede was crying. Nobody noticed at first because he wasn't crying loudly, just quietly to himself. Only then the conversation came to a halt, the laughter stopped, Step-grandfather Heinz put down his squeeze box that gave a last sigh, Eisenhart put down his glass, and all stared at the Swede sitting at the table, head in his hands, sobbing quiet but heaving sobs. The tears ran down his face. Mr. and Mrs. Eisenhart got up and left quietly without saying goodbye, also Mrs. Brücker and Mr. Claussen. Grandmother made some coffee, but by then the Swede who was supposed to be my father had stopped crying. With the back of his hands he wiped the tears from his eyes and all he said was: —Tak. My uncle was sent home and I to bed.

The next morning the Swede had gone and never came back.

Sunk in an asphalt lake

So my uncle saw my father.

Later my mother said somebody else was my father, a man in slippers and braces, someone who'd been in jail, the type that sits with a beer bottle in his hand in front of the television watching somebody sitting with a beer bottle in his hand in front of the television, the type that gives himself a dry shave, the type that smokes Juno (Juno long and round and good in the mouth), the type that washes his Opel Cadel on a Saturday afternoon and then rubs it dry with a sponge.

—Rubbish, said my little uncle, that's not your father, your father's the Swede. He's king of Easter Island. His ship ran aground, he survived, the only one. The islanders chose him to be their king. And they only let him come to Hamburg on condition he doesn't speak.

I was seven or eight then, a happy time when you still believe everything.

Perhaps the telling of every tale begins with naming the procreator, the father. Where are you from, where are you going? A question observation doesn't answer, the one that starts the debate. The mother-to-be, the birth can be seen, many pictures show it (the nursing mother is also the one who gave birth). Here in Salvador da Bahia wood figures sold on the street depict just this: a child slips out between the legs of its mother. But that the penis has anything to do with birth is mere speculation, not something immediately evident. As someone that works hard at informing himself I of course know about the Etruscan votive offerings from the holy springs at Veji, and naturally also the obelisks, Shu and Tefnut, and the statues of Hermes. But do they refer to procreation or to pleasure? They've far less to do with each other than family planners assume. Until the 18th century only women, not men were infertile. A woman became pregnant because of God's grace, because of springs that gave fertility, because of good spirits, because of sitting at night under a walnut tree, because of cooking chervil with frog's spawn and drinking the liquid. Something preceded birth that could only be construed by thought, not by intuition.

I had tried to discover something about how the Easter Islanders imagined the act of procreation, but unfortunately found nothing other than that in the third and fifth months of pregnancy—but never in the fourth or sixth months as even numbers were considered unlucky—the father-in-law of the pregnant woman gave her the contents of an *umu*, an earth oven. On that day a mystic bond linked the food eaten to the unborn child. But what kinds of nourishment signified what? Did certain kinds of food affect whether it would be a girl or a boy? Unfortunately we don't know this and won't unless the script reveals something.

Not long after my father had shown up and then disappeared again I saw my mother crying. She was sitting on a chair, her face in her hands, and sobbing, sobbing so loudly she didn't hear me, I had a key, opened the door and let it fall shut. I wanted to go and put my arm round her shoulders and ask why she was crying. But I was afraid I'd disturb her, that she'd push me away, and so I quietly left the apartment again.

Then my uncle suddenly stopped coming. Why? I would have liked to talk to him about it.

I missed him at the time much more than my fathers who came and went, even though he was only four years older than me.

For a time in the afternoons I'd sit at his mother's waiting for him, but he didn't come, and when he did come he scarcely had time. Then I started playing tennis, I'd earned money for the lessons as a ballboy. I met him once at the tennis court and asked him if he still had the entrance ticket to the king of Albania. As he was leaving he said: —That's all childish nonsense.

After that I never went to his house, but—unlike him who probably forgot me until he read about me in the papers—I followed his life from a distance, not zealously, not with bated breath, but all the same with curiosity and I think I can say with sympathy.

I once saw him, years later. I was in Munich at a conference of the best life insurance salesmen. He must just have finished studying, as I heard from my mother.

The insurance company had installed us in great style at the Bayrischer Hof and I'd driven out to the suburbs, it was a Saturday, to look for the house, council housing, a two-story building similar to the one in Norderstedt where we were living at the time. There was his name by the bell. Judging by its position on the list of names it was the middle apartment. I walked round the house. It was a warm sunny autumn day. The tenants were sitting on their balconies sunning themselves and drinking beer. I looked at the balcony that must have belonged to his apartment. Among the geraniums against the concrete wall two bare feet. His bare feet, that's all I've seen of my uncle since then.

He liked to stress how hard he worked, his work

discipline. But on this one occasion when I saw him he was sunning himself.

There are quite ordinary everyday situations when things speak to us and tell us the truth. We only have to know how to interpret them—these mythical everyday images.

On a trip to a firm of brokers in New York I was at the Trump Tower, on the gilded sales floors. Small silver escalators carried me to the heights, from floor to floor spanning each other and narrowing at the top like a grotto glazed with gold, where water rushed 20 meters down over granite slabs, past floodlit luxuriant greenery and bright red and yellow flowers. (I felt them, although they looked so artificial they really were real.)

The hanging gardens of Semiramis, sparkling, glowing, shimmering. In the boutiques on the different floors directly and indirectly lit were women in silver stilleto heels and skirts slit high, what you'd call sexy. I went along the corridors and only then realized that some of the women were alive and working as sales-girls. This despite the fact that as a former trainee decorator I've a good eye. It wasn't the dolls that had become like humans, but the women that had become like dolls the way they were standing here, their weight on one leg, so rigid, so immobile. Faces set under shadowy lashes. Dresses in silk with massive bows, synthetic women packaged like praline chocolates. To be eaten. Strangely enough there were no customers to be seen. They probably only came towards evening.

I was staying in a first-class hotel that had only opened a year ago. Every nail in the fitted carpet still glistened. I'd just sat down on the white toilet in the large marble-fitted bathroom when I heard something whistling, scratching, and scurrying next to me. I leaped up because I thought a swarm of rats were scurrying behind the shower curtain in the bath. There was nothing. But I could distinctly hear the whistling and scurrying. It came from the hollow space behind the massive built-in bath. The animals were romping inside, on the 27th floor with a view of New York that they wouldn't be able to enjoy. Probably during the building of the hotel they'd been attracted by the food the workmen had left around and been built in. But what did they eat? The insulation on the pipes. I think their own young. After all, the hotel had already been standing a year. Perhaps here in the hollows of this luxury hotel they'd already created an ecologically-stable environment for themselves. The rats multiplied exactly to the extent that they needed nourishment. And when in thirty or forty years the hotel is demolished a swarm of snow-white rats will come rushing out.

▼

This morning I was so restless that I couldn't stand to be in the apartment, I raced through the city constantly looking behind me, raced until my shirt and trousers were soaked in sweat. When I got back and wanted to get past the porter with a quick greeting, he said in his gruesome sounding English: —There was someone who asked for you, Señor Andersen. He shows me a photo. That was you with a beard. And with a laugh he tapped his upper lip.

—And what did you say?

He laughed. —Nothing. I said I don't know this man. And that was the truth.

—O.K., I said, and gave him twenty dollars. It wasn't too little and it wasn't too much. Otherwise it could enter his head that I'm big fry, someone from whom to earn big money. —Phone me, if someone asks for me.

Upstairs I stood on the balcony smoking. A phrase was going through my head: his legs turned to jelly. But I didn't sit down, deliberately not. I wanted to feel the shock and that phrase in my legs. How had this man—and naturally I'm thinking of the redhead—found out my address? How did he know my lovely Danish name? Perhaps our phone really was bugged.

I've packed my bag. Light and handy as before. For a moment I thought about driving to the airport immediately. But there are no more planes today, and I still want to wait a little. And the apartment's been paid a month in advance.

I turned on the television because for a moment I was firmly convinced my picture would be shown on the news. Which, as I instantly told myself, was rubbish. Here nobody's interested in a little swindler. Here they only look for you if you've killed at least two policemen.

A report from Germany. People dancing on the Berlin Wall. The voices in the background drowned by the reporter's Portuguese. Unfortunately I couldn't understand anything. Dembrowski, I thought, lives an amazingly lucky life. He'll be out of jail in eleven months and then finally be able to realize the dream of his youth, opening a brokerage office in Karl-Marx-Stadt. Although like me he's forbidden to practice a profession for four years, that's sure not to count in East Germany, and if there should be unification he'll put the firm in Sannchen's name or in Renate's, if Sannchen's in no mood for Chemnitz.

—Do you know, Dembrowski always said, how hungry people in East Germany are for stock markets and the investment business, if the Iron Curtain comes down then things will really take off.

For a moment I wondered whether to give myself up. But, as I've learned in the meantime from Dr. Blank, that wouldn't change the sentence, I was sentenced in accordance with the law: four years with remission for remand. With good behavior that still leaves a year.

I tried phoning Britt. At the house in Malaga no one answered. Perhaps she's already flown to Hamburg with Lolo. In the house on the Süllberg there isn't a phone. That was wonderful: the large empty house in unbroken silence far from any street. Sometimes when I was exhausted and fighting a nauseating cough I drove from the office to Blankenese with a bottle of red wine and 200 grams of Parma ham that I'd asked Gerda to get for me. I'd sit drinking and eating at the table with a view of the Elbe at night, I'd think of Kubin, my palate forming a dome over grapes, over the earth, the sun. My coughing would stop. I'd be able to breathe properly again. Outside in the dark the various lights that marked the course of the channels.

I'd sleep in the house. Britt then always said when I phoned her at night, —Yes, unwind. Don't turn yourself into a wreck. But I was turning myself into a wreck. Why and for what?

▼

In court I wanted to offer an explanation, as it were the accused's last words, in which I tried to set out my reasons for the way we'd run our business, not an apology and not a confession. Because only someone convinced of his guilt can confess.

I filed the short speech in the laptop under: *The asphalt lake.*

—*The asphalt lake*

In the Natural History Museum in New York there's a group of animal skeletons that were found well-preserved in an asphalt lake. They're set up exactly the way they were found. A scene that makes all the surrounding skeletons of giant saurians seem boring. The dramatic situation has been captured as if in some x-ray of primeval times. From the square mass of asphalt, which consists of natural asphalt, juts the skull of a large prehistoric beast. The jaws are open as if it were drawing a last deep breath before finally sinking into the glutinous black brew. A saber-toothed tiger has just stepped from the firm shore onto the asphalt lake to tear at the almost submerged animal that it would normally never attack. Already one of the foreleg bones has sunk in, only with difficulty is it able to withdraw the other from the glutinous stringy mass. The hindleg bones have already sunk in. Yet with the next step it takes it will reach its victim, seize its head in its jaws. Sinking without any hope of escape into the asphalt while it devours its fill. On the shore, faithfully reproduced with earth and stones, the skeleton of a wolf is already waiting, as if it knew that the far larger and normally dangerous saber-toothed tiger will soon sink. But here paradoxically to carefully slink closer would be fatal, only a leap onto the sinking, defenseless saber-toothed tiger can provide a satisfying meal— and a leap back in time from the body to the rescuing shore. The wolf is still on the shore, his mouth gapes to howl. He still hesitates. Will he step greedily, but cautiously onto the asphalt lake—or will he take a powerful leap onto the saber-toothed tiger?

I read the text to Dr. Blank during visiting time. But he only said: —I don't understand it. Leave it.

And so I never offered an explanation before my escape.

Escape

On the day of the verdict I put on my dark-blue cashmere suit, a suit of the very best quality, one in which you could be out in the pouring rain without it losing its shape.

I sat on the bench, not especially excited, and smoked. After all, this escape attempt wasn't a matter of life and death. Naturally I was extremely tense, tension that was concentrated purely on myself. I thought of what might happen, but my thoughts didn't anticipate what lay ahead, instead I was totally aware of myself, at every moment I was clear, this is me: my fears, my hopes. The exact opposite to those yawning afternoons in our social concrete. It's the secret acceleration of life that people also experience when they throw dice, play roulette, when they skydive, when they fall hopelessly in love on business trips or meet for a quickie in the storeroom, when they shoot down missiles on simulators, when they're expecting some totally unique, extraordinary event that will make them feel they're alive again. An extraordinary heightening of the moment, that's what I felt that morning waiting to be taken out of my cell.

Everything depended on whether Britt would actually have the hundred-mark note in her mouth—no, I would have run for it then even without money. Even more important was that the pimply guard should uncuff me as soon as we entered the courtroom.

Everything else would sort itself out, I only had to get to Luxembourg. There I had an account (I needn't be afraid to say it here, in the meantime it—and with it a ridiculously small sum—has been seized.) From there I could go on to Spain, to our country house. Britt had always wanted to live on the Mediterranean, already when we were living in the basement with its urine mold she'd said to me, —Why do people live of their own free will in this shitty city if they've got enough money?

In those days Britt hated Hamburg. Not me. The thought of spending the twilight years of my life in the house on the Mediterranean was only tolerable provided there was the possibility of always returning— and for longer periods—to Hamburg. That was something Britt and my uncle had in common, both of them could live in any other city provided it had one more day of sunshine than Hamburg.

Britt had found the house in a newspaper advertisement, a unique bargain, and I bought it—after all, we had to invest the money. Britt put in a great deal of time and effort into rebuilding and renovating the house. The old stone covered by a layer of crumbling plaster was again laid bare. The walls of the first floor were freshly painted and tiled white. Britt had selected the furnishings with a great love for detail, everything done sparingly, but that made everything that much more striking: a living room laid with bright, yellowish sandstone, an empire corner cupboard with gilt mountings, also very simple, adorned only by two small gilded sphinxes (my favorite animal-women) bordering the semicircle at the top, an Expressionist painting, a Kirchner, that we'd bought at an auction, *Pines in Baltic Dunes,* chairs in a beautiful, natural brown leather, also the sofa, in front of it a simple glass table, all the walls white, in front of the long wall exactly opposite the terrace door and harmonizing with the garden a large Italian vase, white, brimming with fresh flowers every third day, flowers bought by Britt at a nearby stand where, I think, they lived off us.

That had been her wish in the days when she worked at the flower wholesalers: no Dutch hothouse tulips that never lost their petals, but a huge bunch of fresh flowers every third day.

She had gone into everything down to the smallest detail, where and how the wires for the lights should be laid, in what colors the two bathrooms should be tiled, what plaster should be mixed to fix the mirrors. Britt had taken a fanatical interest in this house that was in crass contrast to her indifference to our house in Blankenese. That was only my house, it was never her house. She liked to say: —Your student den on the Süllberg. And in fact that's what the only room she liked looked like: a mattress, a table, two chairs, an armchair. Still, now and then we drove to the house because we could sleep alone and undisturbed on the mattress.

▼

The cell door was unlocked and—I froze with shock—in came not the young guard who was always so lively and ready to talk, but the old uncommunicative man from the first day of the trial who'd always only ever answered with a grumpy yes or no.

I stood there and must have looked at him with such shock that he said: —Well, this is it. Don't worry, they're not going to be that hard on you. There's time, have another puff.

I drew on my cigarette, then he put the handcuffs on my right wrist and we went through the corridors of the prison over to the courtroom. I wondered whether I should ask him to unlock the cuffs as soon as we were in the courtroom, but I thought he might then deliberately not do it and watch me with greater suspicion.

I asked him when he was going to retire. Two years to go. Was he married? Yes. Had been. Did your wife die? No. No point, I thought, offering this man money, a thousand or two. This man isn't going to risk his pension.

As we entered the courtroom Britt and Lolo came over to me. The guard hesitated, looked at Britt and then Lolo, then he set me free. I wanted to nod to Dembrowski who was fiddling with his tie, but he made a show of looking away. Lolo came and said:

—Good luck, Daddy! Clearly Britt had let her into the secret. And then Britt came and without a word and with a puckered mouth kissed me, kissing with exaggerated, abandoned panting, pushing something hard and smooth into my mouth with her tongue: the hundred-mark note.

The public prosecutor was sorting out his files. Dembrowski put a hand through his blow-dried, freshly-washed hair. Sannchen was standing next to him. Further away stood Renate with the other spectators. She looked over at him with her inquisitive sad gaze.

Dr. Blank said to me, —Probably four years, and a few years more banned from a profession. In the meantime you can deal in property.

—I will, I said, and all the best to you.

I went to the window.

I had no trouble at all turning the window handle, smooth and cold in my hand, a brass handle with nobs like buds. I pushed open the window, stepped onto the window ledge, turned round once more, glanced at the courtroom, a quick impression like a photo—so it's all in detail before my eyes to this day: the guard is just wiping his mouth and nose with the sleeve of his uniform, his tired astonished look; the pensioners in the last row have put their heads together, probably they're casting the vote for the verdict among themselves; the old woman who knitted throughout the trial is comparing arm-lengths of the pullover, light grey with blue stripes; the public prosecutor is hunting in his files, looks up and at me; Dr. Blank has raised his right hand as if he wanted to wave to me, if it weren't for a look of stupid astonishment on his face, even his mouth is slightly open. And then Dembrowski's face, his eyes, his look, incredulous, quick, like a buzzard's. In this picture Britt's face is indistinct, as if blurred, but all the more clear for that Lolo's grin, as if she were about to cheer.

I jumped down and ran in the direction of Karolinenstrasse to the subway. A lawyer came towards me, his black gown over his arm. I laughed, I gave him a cheerful wave, a little surprised he raised his hand, he must have thought here was someone who'd been declared innocent and was racing overjoyed through the streets, in his delight having forgotten his coat in the courtroom, but then I heard someone running after me. So I was being chased. Had the guard jumped out of the window? A civil servant? A voice, breathless, but well-articulated: —For God's sake, wait!

I turned. It really was Dembrowski. The lawyer had stopped and turned to look, two declared innocent. Two men in their best suits running and laughing like stupid schoolboys.

We ran to the Messehallen subway. —You're crazy, Dembrowski gasped. Terrific. As if we'd rung all the bells on some house. After half a year's silence we were talking to each other again, if only by calling out. We stood in the subway and waited for a train to the main station.

—Old Swede, you could have, you should have, at least, said something: Do you want to join me? Dembrowski gasped, as if he hadn't persistently kept silent throughout the entire trial, pointedly turning away when I waved to him in the prison yard. —You could have said something, Dembrowski said, as if there never had been a rift, as if I'd never said: You lazy bastard. —So I jumped up, ran to the window, Dembrowski said in his stage German, still breathless from running. By then they were shouting in the courtroom. Chaos. They were shrieking. I stepped up onto the window sill. The public prosecutor who was standing almost next to me grabbed me. Yes. I could feel his hand, here. And Dembrowski, Dembrowski who'd been so unfit during interrogation, had to hold his aching sides. He bent forward a little like a long-distance runner. Then straightened. And then Dembrowski snorted: —The public prosecutor said: Just a moment, please.

The people around us, well-wrapped in their winter coats, looked at us full of suspicion while we, still a little breathless, laughed and got even more breathless.

—Where are you going? I asked Dembrowski in the subway.

He gave me a look that said, you know that. He didn't say it, not because of the people squeezed together, hanging onto the straps in their coats smelling of cabbage and tobacco, but because he took his goal as self-evident. I got out at the main station.

I said: —Look, I've only got a hundred, I can only get to the border with that, second-class. Without money you're putting us both at risk. Can't you get some money from somewhere first? —Where, Dembrowski asked, from Sannchen, from Renate, they'll already be waiting for me there. The accounts are all closed here, no. There was no way of shaking Dembrowski off.

I bought a ticket to Trier, went to the platform, a train to Cologne was leaving in eight minutes. With determined liveliness Dembrowski stayed close to me, because one thing was clear, he only stood a chance if he had me with a valid ticket at his side. We sat down in the dining car. With the remaining 15 marks I ordered a small pot of coffee, with two cups. We still needed money for bus tickets and suddenly I had to calculate everything twice. We'd have to last four hours with this little pot of coffee. We were sitting at a window in the dining car and riding through a cold, wet winter land-scape, in front of us the remains of the coffee, long gone cold, slopped in the cups. The Yugoslavian waiters slunk around grumpily after we said no when they asked us for the third time, did we want something to drink. The inspector came, I showed him my ticket, second class. Dembrowski pointed in the other direc-tion, where the first-class cars were, and said his brief-case was there with his ticket. Knowing his man, the inspector said: —That's all right. You simply had to believe Dembrowski with his bright princely Prussian gaze, since the trial his pronunciation needle-sharp again, his tailor-made dark grey suit in the best mate-rial, his manicured hands with their blueish oval finger-nails, no one traveling without a ticket looked like that, and it was certainly the first time Dembrowski was traveling without a ticket.

And Dembrowski gave the impression of being cheerful, but then he had to make quite an effort to drive out the dark thoughts that kept springing up in me, because he'd simply attached himself to me and with that put my escape at risk. He broke my gloomy silence by talking of everything that had happened in the meantime, about Sannchen who now insisted on marrying, and that meant he would have to get di-vorced. Sannchen, who yesterday had made a terrible scene in prison of all places because Renate had met her in the visitor's room, with his three sons too, who were all going to the Waldorf School. Sannchen had got upset because he didn't immediately agree to divorce: — Why, we've lived very happily together until now. This "together" had agitated Sannchen, because "together" couldn't just have meant her but also, at least unconsciously, Renate. Sannchen had called him a pasha, and the guard on duty had grinned and, without Sannchen seeing it, given him a V sign. Which had embarrassed Dembrowski, after all, he wasn't from some brothel.

While he was being held for interrogation Dembrowski had wangled a new business—this word wangle was still a relic of his crude vocabulary of the last months—and what's more in Russia. What was going on there since perestroika, simply incredible. As a Dostoevsky reader the thought had instantly come to him, a license to open a casino, imagine it, after eighty years they can play roulette again. That's the business of the future. Through a front man he wanted to buy the huge villa of a former cocoa supplier to the Tsar. Then wait until he got a license for a gambling casino. The developments were simply breathtaking. —The sun, said Dembrowski, is rising in the east.

So we got to Cologne, got out of the dining car to the accompaniment of a Yugoslavian curse, and onto a fast train without a dining car to Trier.

I had to stay in the corridor, keeping watch for the inspector. Dembrowski locked in the toilet, the inspector outside. —Who's in there? —My colleague, I said. —So? —He didn't feel well: heart.

—Shall I ask if there's a doctor on the train?

—No, he's a doctor himself. Just leave him. But thank you, please give me your name. I'll write to the railway manager, one can't always only complain, you have to praise where praise is due!

—Thank you!

By bus from the station to the border. The river, the frontier, customs. We'd never get across without a pass, because the customs officials here were only waiting to check. A few farmers driving their tractors up and down, and then suddenly out of the rain appear two gentlemen in made-to-measure suits who want to cross the street covered in cow dung on foot. Any customs official, no matter how sleepy, would have asked for our passports. —No, Dembrowski said, we can't do it without a passport, and clung to my arm as if in the past weeks we'd been one in heart and soul. But he knew there was damn all left of the hundred marks in my pocket.

No, all I want to do here, and it sounds like material for an early evening television serial, is briefly mention certain things: how we built ourselves a raft out of beams and planks, took off our shoes, rolled up our trousers, lifted the raft into the water, got onto it, pushed ourselves out, capsized, plunged into the icy water, lost our shoes and swam to land—I could hardly breathe, the water was so icy—how we waded to the bank, wet, exhausted, and horribly frozen, how we made our way to an inn—what a picture, two men in their best suits, best shirts, silk ties, but soaked to the skin and barefoot, ask for a room. The housekeeper at the little reception table, the look on her face, first surprised, frightened, then helpless, no, stunned.

Only a totally plausible, or rather implausible story might explain our state to the woman and at the same time persuade her to give us a room even though we had no papers, no money, no credit cards, nothing. The story I told her? I'm not going to tell it yet, I'm going to save it a while, my masterpiece as it were, a story, Dembrowski said later, right out of the Arabian Nights. Perhaps one day I'll offer the story of our escape, along with this story, to television. Otherwise my uncle, who plunders everybody, will set to work. He forces a beginning and an end onto stories such as there isn't in life. What he delivers is life shot down, stuffed with words, that's why he has to keep on looking, he's always hunting, he's a person driven. He wants, I think, to open our eyes to the hellish engine room inside us, but he does it with the indignation and strain with which the man in the cafe was talking to the girl. My uncle is incorrigible because he's not indifferent to things, he wants them to be different, he wants to change the world, obviously he too should rub himself down with popcorn to get rid of his demon. He should just sit back and let things happen. Like this disc that fits into a small envelope and which I'll send him like a good fairy, a present on one fantastic condition: he puts his name to it, but doesn't change anything, not one single word.

We only got a room with a double bed as all the other rooms were taken, but to make up for that the loan of the landlord's shoes. We dried our suits and shirts on the central heating, taking care they didn't shrink. The glasses of grog stood on the hideous white night tables with their wrought-iron lamps, and Dembrowski was picturing to himself all that he'd do in Marbella: tennis, bathing, reading, and then Sannchen. For seven months he'd had to do without her. In the night he fantasized aloud, smacking his lips. I had to move to the edge of the bed.

The next day we put on our dry suits, the shoes, into which Dembrowski had to stuff two handkerchiefs so they didn't slip off his delicate Prussian feet. The housekeeper drove us to a border crossing where we were able to enter Luxembourg without being checked.

What followed was very simple. A trip in a taxi to the bank in the capital. We sent the housekeeper a check that must have made her think she'd given shelter, as in a fairy tale, to two maharajahs. We emptied our accounts except for a small sum.

We came out of the bank with two plastic bags, like tramps, only ours stuffed with millions. Paid the taxi driver, gave him a princely tip.

In Luxembourg we each bought ourselves a Jaguar, unfortunately not in the desired colors, but paid for in cash. We laid the bundles of money out on the table. (In Luxembourg with its liberal banking laws this astonishes no one.) We paid without bargaining over the hefty surcharge for immediate delivery.

Then, so that we could register the cars and travel on without any problems, we acquired two passports. In Luxembourg passports, if of good quality, i.e. genuine, are not cheap. We were able to choose our nationality. Since then I've been a Dane and travel under the name of Andersen.

The island

Like an orange the setting sun hangs over the runway.

I'm sitting here in front of the panoramic window and waiting for the flight to be called for Santiago, Chile. From there I've a connecting flight to Easter Island. I wanted at least once to use my laptop in accordance with its name. I'm sitting in a chair and the thing is on my knees. Beside me my briefcase and my light raincoat.

Today earlier in the morning the house phone rang. It was the porter. In his English, which I could only understand with difficulty, he said: —There are tree misters here and asked for you. God bless you, mister.

He was a practising Methodist. But I'd obviously paid him more generously.

I took my case, the laptop, rang for the service elevator and while they were ringing at my front door went down, downstairs went round the corner to a crossroads, hailed a taxi, and drove to the airport. It was as easy as that. I'd like to have known if the redhead was one of the three men, or whether they'd simply handed over the warrant. Perhaps the professional passport forgers in Luxembourg also work with Interpol, for some small change thrown into the hat of course.

My flight has just been called.

▼

The island from afar: black, bulky, like a huge triangle in the distance. On approaching: the shadows of the

389

mountains, the crater walls, the green of the vegetation, the blue-grey of the water in the crater, bays, cliffs, and before them ribbed and ruched like a ruff, the surf. The plane was filled with an American tour group of senior citizens. My guess on seeing them get on the plane was that most of them were retired academics. And in fact the man who then sat next to me was an emeritus professor of education from the University of Pennsylvania who had wanted to visit the island for twenty years and was now fulfilling his dream. To my astonishment he had a very accurate knowledge of the culture, yes, he even had a theory of his own for deciphering the script on the wood panels. He thought that in it he could see a description of constellations of stars in connection with sacred feast days. He said that on the plane there was an emeritus professor of mathematics who had also worked on the script and she had stored all the signs in a computer. She'd come to some thoroughly astounding conclusions. I told him my reservations, and he asked: —Are you an ethnologist?

—No, a stockbroker. (I nearly said, it was on the tip of my tongue: A prisoner on the run.)

He gave me his card, I wrote down my address for him. —Ah, he said, you're Danish, glad to meet you, Mr. Andersen.

I wasn't as alone as I'd thought in my attempts to decipher the Easter Island script. —Have a look, he said, and pointed to the window: there the crater of Rano Kao, a little lake overgrown with reeds with blue patches of water, behind it the landing strip, gently the plane came down. The little airport building with the Chilean flag. Slowly the propellers ran down.

I didn't have to wait for a suitcase, so went straight

to the exit where several men were pushing their way out, none of them looked Polynesian, they could have been Italians, Yugoslavs, Spaniards. They tugged at my jacket, wanted to take the laptop out of my hand and the bag with all the lovely dollars from my shoulders. The discoverer Roggeveen and Cook and all the others had been robbed as soon as they arrived. I held the bag tight under my arm. The taxi, a rattling VW bus, took me to the one good hotel on the island. It was fully booked. The driver mumbled something and drove me to a little hotel that looked more like a youth hostel. There was something insipidly cheerless, yes, dreary about the whole place, in no way comparable to Salvador da Bahia. And the people in the hotel too displayed a surliness, no, a melancholy, no, an insulted rage. The woman at the wobbling table with the torn cardboard sign "Recepcion" threw down the room key with a contemptuous gesture, and when it slid across the table and fell to the ground made no move to pick it up. I bent, picked it up and went to my room, a small space with a creaking bed, a cupboard whose veneer had splintered off, a tiny table at which I'm sitting and writing. I've put the fragment of the bird man on the table. So at least after a long journey a part of him has come back to the island.

The evening meal: a slice of tuna that curled up at the edges, charred underneath. The waiter pulled my plate away although I still had a piece on my fork, as if expecting him to wait until I'd finished eating was asking too much. Perhaps he took the plate for the sole reason that he was just passing and didn't want to come back.

Though the red wine according to the label was a

Bordeaux, it tasted of fermented apple juice. The American tourists were in the bare dining room, all of them friendly, quiet people who booked educational trips: Culture of Easter Island, Ruins in Guatemala, Florence in the 14th Century.

The woman at the reception desk couldn't or wouldn't tell me exactly who the Europeans were that lived on the island. She was erasing something in the guest book and it took an effort for her to say: Missionaries, a few ethnologists. A few Americans, Belgians, and English. A Swede?

—Maybe, she mumbled and brushed crumbs of eraser and paper onto my shirt.

—Where does the man live? She told me the way.

How do you get such decidedly unfriendly people? Perhaps it has to do with the fact that there are no real trees on the island, therefore not that deep and stirring green. There are many peoples (the majority) that have had similar bad experiences at the hands of whites without developing such aggressive xenophobia. On the other hand here this had happened in a narrowly-confined space, some islanders were already shot in 1722 when the island was discovered, just like that, for no reason in particular. Whalers carried off men and women, sailors brought gonorrhea and syphilis, rape was the order of the day. Sometimes, rarely, an explorer saw the islanders as human beings with an extremely complex and fine culture, like Chamisso who saw Easter Island in 1816, but didn't land. To cite him, a quotation I wrote down while on remand: *I seize this opportunity to solemnly protest the use of the term "savage" in connection with the South Sea islanders.*

Fine. But he was an exception, the rule were the

slavers who came to the island and carried the islanders off to Chile where most of them died, the few that came back brought the pox with them. The missionaries who threatened them with hell and damnation if they didn't give up their faith, their priests, their script. The Frenchman Dutroux-Bornier, lord over life and death, who set up a reign of terror, a Sodom and Gomorrah on the island, an inescapable tyranny until the islanders killed him. And for four decades now the tourists have been coming.

I took the way I'd been told to the man, who lived at the end of the street and rented horses on which you could ride to the statues. It was a prefab with a corrugated iron roof. Naturally this was not where the king of Easter Island lived. Still, I knocked and felt a mounting agitation that took my breath away, though I told myself there was no sensible reason for it excitement made my thoughts dart about, what if the door were to open and there he stood—the Swede. Like the excitement when I sat in the kitchen and waited for my father, and there was a knock on the door and in he came, sat down at the kitchen table and was silent. The king of Easter Island. I knocked again, at the same moment the door opened and an old man appeared, bent, tangled white hair, a pipe in his mouth hanging from a gap as if made for it between his teeth.

I asked him if he was a Swede. No, a Finn. Did I want to go to the statues? He could take me.

—Yes.

Hamburg? He'd been there a few times.

Of course he wasn't my father, but he might just as well have been. He'd sprung from my uncle's adolescent fantasy.

The Finn gave a price for the horses that was totally shameless. I agreed. I told him to come for me tomorrow.

A light rain is falling outside, or rather, a heavy rain, single heavy drops falling from the sky like tears. The wind drives them against the windowpanes and they run down.

I found the Bible on the night table. Once in the USA, I read, three representatives had met and carved out a pious plan: from that day throughout the entire world, down to the last tiny corner, even to here, Bibles of the Gideon Association are placed in hotel rooms.

> *But he then spoke: To whom does the Kingdom of God compare, and to whom shall I compare it? It is like unto a mustard seed which a man took and threw in his garden; and it grew, and became a great tree, and the birds of the sky lived beneath its branches.*

In the morning I drank coffee of a kind I haven't drunk in years. It reminded me of the malt coffee my mother sometimes used to make. The bread felt like foam rubber and tasted like it too.

The retired professor of education sat down next to me, ate a brown crumbly omelette and wanted to know what explanation I had for the decline of the culture, because the social system had already disintegrated long before the arrival of the first Europeans, as one could see from the many statues that were either incomplete or had been abandoned during transport.

For a moment I was tempted to say that was exactly what I wanted to write about. (Wanted, I thought. Did

I still want to, or rather, was there still any need?) As I scooped out a stone-hard boiled egg, I explained my theory: we could assume that a ruling group, the Long Ears, had immortalized themselves in these figures, while a larger group, the Short Ears, had to work at overcoming death, and that finished them off. Herein lies an irreconcilable conflict, not only social, the conflict is also metaphysical.

Another conflict: Every social system collapses with an unchecked increase of numbers in a limited space. We know that from rats. The island's like a prison. There were no tasks, no land to be won from the sea, no irrigation projects to be built, no rivers to divert, no swamps to drain. A favorable climate allowed what was necessary to life to grow. An immense collective boredom sprung up that sought an *ersatz* activity and led to the creation of these colossal statues, which however only led to repetition, in other words monotony, and back to boredom, and this—an unbearable state of mind that can even lead to collective suicide—is most easily dispelled by aggression, by destroying the rules, relishing chaos, war, rape, ritual, and culinary cannibalism, murder and manslaughter, I said and prized the yellow-brown yolk like a stone from its surrounding steel-blue layer. Strangely enough it tasted of malt. An egg from the primeval chickens of Easter Island, I thought, while the friendly old pedagogue talked about social restabilization in the battle for survival. An egg from one of those chickens that many centuries ago had come through the surf sitting on the heads of swimmers and then flown the last hundred meters to land.

When I went into the hotel lobby I recognized him immediately although he was Chilean, the detective.

Wherever you go they're unmistakable, at any rate to anyone on the run. Something deliberately purposeless in the way they wait, in their eyes the effort to go unnoticed. And strangely enough, I felt relief. I knew I'd be flying back, I'd be seeing Lolo and Britt again.

I wondered whether I should try to secretly leave the hotel, because I wanted to see the statues, but then I went to the reception desk. A telex, torn, lay on the table next to the guest book.

I put my room key on the table.

—Señor Walter? the man asked.

I only hesitated a tiny moment, wondering whether I should say my name was Andersen, but then I nodded and explained to him that this morning I wanted to see the statues, I'd saved for years to do it.

He thought about it. But no plane was leaving the island today, and no ship. Finally he nodded.

The island was ruled by people with long, hanging ears. They were very shrewd. It was they who erected all the ahu on the shore. The work was carried out by the short-eared people whom they had enslaved. One day the Long Ears said to the Short Ears: Go and throw all the stones that cover the ground into the sea! But the Short Ears answered: We will not do this because we need the stones to produce our food. They serve us to steam our dishes, and also by causing yams, sugarcane, and taro to suffer. Because when plants suffer they grow and get fatter! The Long Ears were enraged at such disobedience and swore to destroy the Short Ears.

396

The Finn held the stirrup and I got onto an old nag with a sagging back. The Finn got onto a horse that was a little younger. I was amazed at how lightly, even elegantly the old man swung himself onto the animal. We rode at a jog trot through the place, past a dilapidated fence that in the days when the island had been an English possession had penned in the islanders, while the island was given over to the sheep. We rode through a hilly green bare landscape until the first black colossus appeared at the crater, then another and then another, they stood on the slope of the volcano, massive, legless, as if darkly brooding they had slowly sunk into the ground, in their faces a stony indifference as they stared up the slope, their backs turned to the sea, giant cripples, they stood here and gazed into the beyond.

A minibus arrived, the American tourists got out. I saw the professor of education take his admiral's cap off his bald head and wave to me with it. I thought it must feel good to grow old knowing you'd worked and achieved what you wanted, and then to retire and travel the world.

The tourists, hungry for pictures, began to photograph the figures, and they photographed them for each other, stood next to the figures that stared arrogantly past them—a reminder of death, according to the guide, an Englishman, because we have to understand these figures as ancestral portraits of the ruling groups.

At the foot of the peninsula called Poike the Long Ears dug a ditch that stretched from the north coast to the south coast. They filled it with twigs and grass because they intended to roast the Short Ears here. Now in Potu-te-rangi lived a short-eared woman, and she was married to a man of the Long Ears. Her relatives and friends of the clan of the Short Ears didn't know why such a massive ditch had been dug, and they asked themselves what could be the purpose of the wood and grass with which it had been filled. The woman of the Short Ears pressed her husband with so many questions that he told her the ditch was an oven in which the Short Ears would be roasted. That same night the woman went to her relatives to tell them this: You see my house, she said, when the Long Ears have lit the fire in the oven approach them from the back and attack them from behind! Then push them into the fire! And instead of a feast of Short Ears there will be a meal of Long Ears!

Clothes were spread out on the stone slabs, lunches taken out and unpacked. The tourists began eating, napkins on their laps, and it looked as if an old people's home had come on an excursion. Many of the women and men were wearing straw hats, others baseball caps. They thoughtfully chewed tough chicken legs, pulling at dentures with their fingers. You could see that the islanders were taking revenge for all those that had been converted, killed, shot, carried off, raped.

The woman returned to her house and said: Now you must act quickly! She then sat down at the door of her hut and made as if she were weaving. But in reality she wanted to warn her people of danger.

When she saw the Long Ears preparing for the attack she gave a signal. The Short Ears came to her house and threw themselves at the Long Ears who had just lit the wood and grass at the bottom of the ditch. Surprised by the attack they offered not the slightest resistance, but fled. But where could they go? They plunged into the fire where they all—men, women, and children—perished.

The tourist group packed up their lunches. The women and the men carefully picked up the bottle caps and mustard sachets off the ground, then—some of them waved to me—they got on the bus. The bus disappeared with threatening exhaust fumes behind the mountain. The stillness, the screech of gulls, the roar of the breakers.

The Finn had stretched out on a blanket. From here you couldn't tell whether he was sleeping or only gazing into the clouds.

I went over to one of the statues that stood there slightly leaning, a somber brooding stone cripple. I sat down at its feet. Other stone figures had toppled, lay face to the ground, or stared into the sky. A picture of mute grief.

Above me petrels circled, slowly, quietly, effortlessly. I looked out at sea, at the refracted light. The wind had dropped, but from the distance came powerful waves, foaming breakers that shook the ground. Far away in the Pacific storms had raged. This was the picture with which I wanted to live in the coming year, during which I wouldn't be seeing much: there were three small, three tiny islands, no more than splinters of rock, swimmers climbed onto the island rising furthest out in the ocean, Motu Nei, and waited there for the seabirds to come and lay their eggs. The first egg the swimmer found he bound to his forehead and swam through the breakers, through the shoals of shark back to Easter Island. He brought the egg to his master, who now for a year gave him a name he himself had dreamed, a name from another world, and with which he would now have to live chastely for a year, separated from others, a year of self-examination, a holy year—a year that also lay ahead of me.

> *Only two warriors succeeded in overcoming opposition as they made their way over the mounds of corpses. They hastened to Anakena and sought refuge in the cave of Ana-vai. The Short Ears pursued them there and poked at them with sharp sticks to make them come out. The two men ran from one end of the cave to the other, letting out a strange noise as they did so, the sound of which always makes us laugh: Oriorion.*

There was no way out from this island.

I thought of my uncle who was the first to tell me about this island, and wondered whether he himself had ever been here. I thought of the Swede who sat in the kitchen and cried. And I thought of the piece of wood, the fragment of the bird man that was lying on the small wobbly table in the hotel. And with a sudden shock I thought that the cleaner at the hotel might throw it away. Only then I told myself that made no difference either.

I sat there hour after hour, now in the shade of the statue, then again in the sun that was now in the southwest, felt the light wind, let in the play of light, the screeching of the frigate birds, the smell of algae and salt. The clouds are the earth's thoughts. Grey, the color of resurrection, grey that towers and shines white in the sunlight, shading lightly into blue grey in which darkness is already gathering, there round, here in threads, then dissolving, driving forward new shapes.

I started. A little stone had hit me on the shoulder. Laughter. Children were standing here begging, holding out their hands, shouting something I didn't understand. I got up and gave them some dollar bills. After all, I didn't need the money anymore. They laughed, impish light laughter. Laughter that I hadn't heard before. Again they held out their hands. Anyone that has that much money must have still more, they must have thought. They threw small stones at me. A game, an old game as I knew from travelers' accounts. The stranger, but also the one who returned to the island after a long absence, had stones thrown at him. It was a sign both of grief and joy. Grief, because irrecoverable time had passed, joy because he was still alive. Because he who came had returned from another world. A world from which all came, to which all went. From which one didn't know who would return. The stones were meant to cleanse, to show that the one who had come was no ghost. They were meant to establish contact. It was like a rain of meteorites. Playfully I avoided their throws. They laughed louder and threw bigger stones. I had to jump from side to side faster and faster, and in what at first had been aimless jumping I slowly recognized myself to be making quite definite movements, they were forcing me to jump in a certain direction, and from my movements I noticed that I wasn't just jumping, I was voluntarily dancing an involuntary dance that kept getting more violent, faster, and yet more supple. In my extreme concentration to avoid the stones that kept getting bigger I could feel how gracefully I was moving, it was a game similar to one we'd played in the ruins of Hamburg when we threw chunks of stone at each other that kept getting bigger—and I once hit my uncle on the forehead, he still has the scar—so I danced until I felt the blow in my face, on my cheekbone, a piercing hot pain, suddenly blood was running down my cheek. I stopped and tasted my blood.

The children stared at me, not hostile, not timid, a little curious.

I'd arrived, at last.

I went down slowly to the old man. He was talking to a policeman sitting in a jeep. Beside it stood the two horses, grazing.